RISE OF THE VISCEREBUS

THE FIRST CHRONICLE

WORLD OF THE VISCEREBUS
BOOK 3

OZ MARI G.

AUTHOR'S NOTE

This second edition of Rise of the Viscerebus was made because I realised just how amateurish my first effort was. We have included a Glossary of Terms in this edition. I apologise to the readers of the first edition.
I invite you to let me know if you were one of those, and I will send you a FREE digital copy of the Glossary of Terms. Please send me an email at ozmarigranlund@gmail.com

ACKNOWLEDGMENTS

My eternal gratitude to:

My son, Joshua. It's a blessing to have someone as smart as you as my child. You challenge me to be a better writer, a better mother, and the kind of human you would be proud of.

My beta readers, for attacking the material and not me. Your generous and honest feedback helped whip this book into a better shape.

But most especially to you, Johanna W, for the objective opinion and for pointing out plot holes and character flaws.

And to my BFF, Caca J, for the kind words, the constructive criticism, the suggestions and the encouragement, and for being a staunch supporter.

Finally, to my two cats, iO and Laki, for sitting with me during the long hours of the writing process.

CONTENTS

PROLOGUE

Manila, 1996

In a dark alley behind a nondescript building on the poor side of the city, a man waited anxiously under the shadows cast by the awning above the backdoor of a clandestine abortion clinic. He was waiting for two clients. The first would be the *iturrian*, the source, the second was the *ontzian*, the vessel. He was tempted to light a cigarette to help him tolerate the stench of uncollected garbage, animal piss and excrement just a few meters from him. But he also did not want to give his location away. It was difficult to do as he was very nervous.

A taxi pulled up at the entry of the alleyway, and a pregnant woman got off the car. She paused by the entry, nervously looking around. Her neck craned forward as she tried to peer deep into the dark depths of the lane in front of her. He darted from under the awning and the only light source in the alley, and waved frantically, but quietly, to the woman.

Still, the woman did not move; she looked more scared now

1

than earlier. He must have appeared very suspicious, so he relaxed his face into an innocuous smile and approached her.

"Ms Matilda Gomez?" he asked, his tone even. The woman nodded. Relief registered on her face.

"Mr Brion?" she asked and took a tentative step forward.

"Yes. You are late. Was it the traffic?" he asked, took her elbow, and walked her toward the backdoor of the clinic.

"I had a hard time getting a taxi," she replied.

"Okay, let's get you ready," he said. He paused by the backdoor and groped for the hidden doorbell by the side of the panelling. He lifted the protective cover and pressed the button. Seconds later, they heard footsteps coming down the stairs.

A scrub-wearing woman, much like what one would see in a proper hospital, opened the door. She smiled at the pregnant woman and gave him a terse nod. The nurse would take it from here. She ushered Ms Gomez upstairs to prepare her for what could be a harrowing night for the *iturrian*. The door closed once more on him.

With the source in place, he sent a text message to the *ontzian* to inform him they could do the *messis*, the harvest, within ten minutes. He hunkered down with his cigarette. If he was lucky and things go well, his job would be finished in an hour.

———

The room was dimly lit and smelled of antiseptic. Matilda could feel herself relaxing, as she imagined walking out of this place hours later, no longer pregnant, her life back to normal. Her husband, when he returns from his overseas posting, would not know any different. She truly wanted to move on from this mistake and intended to make it up to him, even though he would not understand why.

From the corner of the room, she watched a man putting on the green scrub. The nurse who attended her said he was the doctor. There was something about him that unsettled her. As he came closer to her bed, she had a sudden jolt of premonition. She felt threatened and scared and would have bolted upright if she was not so drowsy.

He did not make any menacing gesture, but—it was his eyes —all black, glittering, and intent, and on his face, a certain maniacal hunger.

"No..." she weakly raised her hand to ward him off, but the drug had taken full effect and she lapsed into unconsciousness. Her own protest faded with her.

The man carefully pushed the hospital gown and revealed Matilda's distended belly. He laid his hand on it, felt the pulse of the foetus growing there. It was strong and healthy, a perfect source. He slowly stuck out his tongue, and it stretched down long and thinned into the size of a straw. The pointed tip speared through Matilda's belly button; it made her belly spasm.

Both nurses turned away. They could never get used to this scene, an *aswang* feeding on amniotic fluid and foetus blood. It was too gruesome.

His tongue penetrated deeper, and the man started sucking the fluid from the sac, his eyes closed in enjoyment. The distress of the foetus was discernible by the violent movement it made. The undulation was visible in the belly of Matilda. Within minutes, the movement quieted. The foetus was dead.

A few minutes later, the man withdrew his bloody tongue

and retracted it into his mouth. He wiped his face with the sleeve of his scrub, and turned away in satisfaction, only to turn back when the vital sign monitor started beeping. They hurried to the patient's side and noted she was dying by the pallor in her skin. She looked almost bloodless. They both frantically tried to revive her for long minutes, to no avail.

"What are we going to do?" the man asked, a worried frown on his face. They shrugged. Humans were fragile creatures, they die easily. While this was an unfortunate event, they had dealt with it a few times in the past. They knew what to do.

"Bury her in the plot of land they advised you to have ready for such a time like this. Help us with the body and let us take her down to your car. Then Mr Brion will assist you," the older nurse instructed him in a calm tone. He nodded and moved to help.

1

THE MEETING

A nother day, a slightly different dollar. Quite a cliched expression, but apt.

Yuana pushed the last button through the hole of her silk blouse and glanced at her reflection with little focus. She picked up her handbag, and her laptop as a reflex action. Just like she did every day for several years.

She sighed. Her schedule was so predictable, so uninspiring.

Although, there was a welcome variation to her routine today - a participation at a tech event later in the day. It was part of her job as their company's Head of Marketing. Maybe it could offer something more stimulating.

She told herself there was nothing to complain about. Her family was wonderful, they did not lack money; her work offered challenges enough that allowed her to exercise her creativity, but everything felt superficial. She was living on the sidelines of her own life. It might be great, but it was handed to her. She did nothing to earn it. She was restless, and deep inside, dissatisfied with herself.

Her introspective mood carried through breakfast. Her mother noticed.

"So, what global issue are we solving today, Yu-Yu? Global hunger or world peace?" her mother asked. She lowered her coffee cup, one eyebrow arched in inquiry.

"None of those, Mama. I was just feeling... low energy, I guess..."

"You mean you're bored," her mother said dryly.

She smiled. "Not precisely. I am just wondering if there is more to my life than being the Head of Marketing of GJDV, your daughter, a De Vida." She shrugged.

Her mother's head tilted to the side as she looked at her closely.

"In your heart of hearts, Yu, if you can have anything in this world, what would it be?"

"I do not know, Mama," she replied honestly.

Maybe it was time to think about what she truly wanted in life.

On the car ride to the event, her mother's question rang in her head repeatedly.

What is it I wanted above all else?

What is missing in my perfect life now?

What is the one thing that called to me, yet I could not seem to find?

Yuana's palms felt clammy, and there was a faint sensation of moisture in her scalp. She was not used to being on stage, but this was part of her function in the company.

I am here to sit as a panellist, and not to make any presentation. I can do this.

When they called her name, she put on a false display of confidence, and pasted a big smile on her face. Loud music and claps accompanied her ascent as she climbed up the low steps, her photo displayed on the three enormous screens onstage. As she took her seat, hundreds of expectant and curious faces stared at her. Her heart pounded in sync with the deafening introduction song as other guests were introduced.

It took ten minutes before her heart settled into a calm enough state for her to enjoy the topic. Being in public eye was something her kind were discouraged from doing for centuries.

The thirty-minute Q and A session for the topic "Sexy Tech for Unsexy Industries" ended well. The questions thrown at her were all about their company's distinct business model - they develop, operate, and maintain a chain of funeral homes and memorial gardens across the globe.

The morbidness of their offerings - memorial plan products, mortuary and forensic pathology services entranced the audience. Most people do not think about mortality until death knocked on their doors and touched their lives.

Her co-panellists were surprised by Grupo Jardin De Vida's keen interest to adopt the latest technology for their operation. It seemed to them incongruent for a company that dealt with something as fundamental as death. Yuana preferred to call it life and afterlife care.

Her pride in their company must have shone through because she received enthusiastic applause from the crowd. She had always believed they provide valuable services not just to their kind, but even to the human communities they lived in.

As she descended the stairs back to her seat, some members of the audience approached her - a mixed combination of startup founders interested in bidding for her business,

members of the organising team who congratulated her and
made introductions to other notable participants, and some
guys who were just interested in getting her number.

Roald watched from a distance as Ms Yuana Orzabal got
surrounded by well-wishers. He saw her picture earlier in the
event app as a panellist for the topic and made it a point to
attend and listen to her. He wanted to know if she had the
brains to match the beauty. And he was not disappointed.

She drew the eyes of every participant in the ballroom. She
was articulate, witty, and beautiful to boot. Her face glowed
with health; her eyes sparkled with life. It was bemusing to hear
her talk about death and sending a body to eternal rest, while
her presence was electrifying. The contrast was fascinating.

He intended to meet and impress her, but queuing up to
get her card with the rest would not cut it.

"Hey bro, are you considering queuing up to meet Yuana?
You've got mad competition," Daniel taunted.

"Yuana? You know her?" He picked up on the familiarity in
Daniel's tone.

Daniel nodded. "Yes, our families have been friends for
decades."

"D, you got to introduce me to her," he cajoled.

"No way, bro. She's a good friend. Plus, she is not interested in romantic relationships," Daniel refused laughingly.

"Hey, we are best friends, and I am a good man... Come on,
bro, I just need an intro," Roald pressed.

"Bro, save your effort for the other girls. There are plenty of
women here who would be easier to win. Yuana will shoot you
down."

"Come on, D. You never had a problem being my wingman

before. Why the reluctance now? Are you and her...?" The thought dismayed him.

Daniel shook his head. "Normally, it would not be a problem. Yuana and I even had a long-running gag of setting each other up with the worst potential blind dates. But you are both my good friends, and I do not want to be in the middle if things go wrong between you."

"D, let me worry about that. Come on, do me a solid favour here, I will give you anything you want, just introduce us. It's that simple," Roald persisted.

Daniel sighed. "All right. Just an intro. But you owe me big time, bro. And if she spurns you, don't come running to me for hugs," he warned.

<hr>

It was a seamless and impressive production, she thought, as she scanned the hall. All the big names of the tech world; Google, Facebook, Amazon, Microsoft, Apple, and Tesla, were there.

The digital presentation, the equipment, and all the technological whiz bangs she expected from the industry did not disappoint.

She was walking the exhibit hallways and examining the products in the booths when she heard someone call her name.

It was Daniel!

A wide smile on his face made her smile as well. She had not seen him for a long time, yet it felt like no time or distance passed between them. It was not surprising since he had been a friend of hers since they were teens.

"Hey, Yu! You looked good on that stage, woman."

His teasing smile was wide as he walked towards her, his arms outstretched, poised to give her a bear hug. It should not have surprised her to see him here since he owned an Internet of Things company that automated household appliances and connected it to the internet.

"Hey, Dan! If I knew you would be here, I would have declined their invitation to sit on the panel."

He gave her a big, warm hug, a buss on the cheek, and a playful peck on the jaw as he made an audible sucking sound. It made her laugh, and she swatted him playfully on the cheek to make him stop.

"Ha-ha! Found anything you like yet?" His eyes twinkled in mischief.

"Still looking. There is a lot of exciting technology here, though," she said. She took his offered arm as they walked on.

"You were looking for something in data analytics, right?" Daniel asked, one eyebrow raised.

"Right. Data science, and anything that can keep track of our clients, their social presence, buying habits—all that lovely digital stalking stuff," she joked.

"Well then, let me introduce you to someone in that field. His company is doing just that." He steered her towards a tall, good looking, and smartly dressed guy standing not so distant from them.

She threw Daniel an accusing look. She sensed a setup, but said nothing, as they were already within earshot of the guy. Daniel had a habit of setting her up on dates with unsuitable guys as part of an ongoing private joke between them. Although he had not done so for the last few months.

"Yu, meet my friend, Roald. He's one of my closest friends in the industry, and I have known him for over five years. We met at the Web Summit in Ireland, and we have hung out regularly since then. Roald, this is Yuana Orzabal. Their company, GJDV, is looking for tech in the data science and analytics field." A hint of laughter touched his voice.

Roald held out his hand in greeting, which she shook briefly. She kept her expression blank and polite. This one had a distinct air about him that was not present in other men Daniel foisted on her in the past. His eyes twinkled, and possessed a pleasant, approachable aura. It was a welcome contradiction to his obvious self-confidence.

She realised he enlisted Daniel's help to wrangle a personal introduction. Clever move, but it was not going to work. She elbowed Daniel's side surreptitiously, his stomach muscles contracted as her elbow hit his funny bone.

It was her way of warning him he would get a talking to from her later.

Roald could tell that she knew he was more interested in her than as a potential client and was already on her guard. This woman was as perceptive as Daniel had warned him about. He would have to up his game.

"It is my pleasure to meet you, Yuana," he said. His deliberate use of her first name was to establish his friendly intention.

Her eyebrows raised infinitesimally.

"Thank you. So, Roald, what exactly do you do in the data science field?" she asked.

It was a pleasant question, but business-like. She immediately labeled him into her friend zone. The question gave him a chance to impress her with his credentials.

"My company, Buy-O-tech, designs algorithms. We track consumer decision-making and buying triggers based on their social behaviour. Then we combine the social media footprints of the consumer and their friends. We measure their actual purchases against the events in their life, etc."

He paused, then added, "Our system analyses all these data and finds commonality. Then we look for any patterns. In short, we try to zero-in on their buying triggers," he said, happy to discuss his technology.

"Isn't everyone's buying trigger based on emotion?" A small frown appeared in her forehead.

"Yes, but which emotions? When and how do these emotions trigger the actual buying? This is what we are trying to find out," he replied.

Yuana's eyebrow quirked and gave him a brief nod in agreement. "Okay, that sounds interesting."

"It would be my pleasure to show you a demo of our system. How about we do it over dinner?" he suggested. He caught Daniel's effort not to snigger.

"Lunch would be preferable," she replied.

She easily sidestepped his intention. Roald inclined his head in concurrence. Daniel's grin was grating. He would have elbowed Daniel in the ribs, too, if he was close enough.

"You have a unique sounding name, how do you spell it?" she asked, changing the topic.

"R-O-A-L-D, from Roald Dahl, the writer. My mom's favourite." He liked her focus on his name. It felt more personal.

"He's my favourite too." Her quick admission was friendly, but still distant.

Her gaze was assessing. He smiled wider in response, in the friendliest and warmest way he could manage.

"I grew up with his books. My favourite among them was Fantastic Mr Fox," he said.

"Really? I would have thought it was The Twits," she quipped.

Her smile was challenging. That made him laugh. She was indeed a fan of the writer.

She's got wittiness in spades, too.
He was utterly captivated.

An hour later, Roald was still grinning. She was as smart, as sharp as he first thought her to be. She was fiery yet cool and collected, had a wicked sense of humour, and her quiet self-confidence intrigued him. He won a minor victory during the chat. He secured another meeting with her. A Friday lunch to talk about her data science needs.

Granted, it was lunch and hardly romantic, but he intended to use it to his advantage.

Daniel enjoyed the banter between the two. He watched Roald's effort to move past the business-only barrier Yuana erected. Roald had turned on the charm, but it bounced off Yuana's well-placed armour.

Maybe Roald needed to be reminded that Yuana was formidable, and unlike the lightweight women he dated in the past, he might just get friend-zoned by her.

No doubt a first for Roald. But if there was a woman who could achieve that, it would be Yuana. For as long as he had known her, all her relationships had been casual and non-committal. And her reason for keeping it so remained compelling, one that not even Roald's charms could break.

Contrary to Roald's expectation, lunch was not the success he envisioned it to be. He used every tool in his arsenal, yet she remained unaffected.

Oh, it was an engaging and stimulating lunch; she bantered with him, laughed at his jokes, came back with witty zingers, but she remained coolly distant, unruffled by his efforts, and seemed determined to keep it at that. She treated him like a friendly acquaintance, and while it was aggravating, he understood her reserve. They just met, after all.

The harder he tried, the more she withdrew. He knew then if he kept doing what he was doing, he was in danger of getting written out of her appointment book. So, he adopted a friend-only demeanour for the rest of the meal.

He ventured to ask something personal during coffee to determine why she preferred casual dating. "So, I am curious, why are you still single?"

She laughed and replied, "I did not realise there is an expiration date on being single. What is the usual shelf life of a single woman?"

"Sorry, that came out wrong. What I meant was you do not lack any admirers; I saw that at the tech event. They flocked to you like bees to blossom, and I am sure that was not an isolated occurrence. Wasn't there anyone interesting enough to qualify as a boyfriend?"

She shook her head.

"Why not?" he asked.

"Because they were all bees, and I am no blossom. And most unfortunately, the bees could not tell the difference." She punctuated the statement with an elegant shrug.

He did not understand what she meant, and it galled him to think he was just one of the bees. However, on the bright side, she had given him a forewarning, and he doubted she afforded all the other bees the privilege. He had a leg up over all the others and must use this to succeed where they failed.

As he leaned back against his office chair, he remembered Daniel's warning and realised he needed to change tack. If she wanted to be friends first, he would give her that. Maybe this friend zone could be his back door, and he could convince her to date him after she had seen his true character.

Yuana came out of the lunch meeting entertained. Once he got the hint that she was not interested in a romantic relationship with him, his flirting efforts turned to a more down-to-earth harmless charm. She found him funny, smart, knowledgeable, and generous with his ideas. He was fascinating in his energy, his passion for his work, and his willingness to share what he knew.

It was surprising to find out his tech ideas came from helping in his mother's home décor shop during his university years. Roald claimed he had wanted to earn his own money so he would not need to ask for extra from his parents to pay for his social activities and hobbies, like video games and sword-making. That impressed her. According to Daniel, Roald came from a well-off family, and did not need to work.

An incident during lunch made an impression on her and revealed something interesting about Roald's personality. They served her salad with an extra unwanted garnishing—a live caterpillar in her lettuce. Just before he called the server over, he gently lifted the creature out with a spoon and moved it to a leaf in a bush growing outside the restaurant. When he came back, she asked him why he did that; he explained they would probably kill the creature in the kitchen, and he wanted to give it a better chance of changing into a butterfly. Roald had an innate kindness in him, and she liked that.

It was a pity he was not one of their kind. It would have been too easy to engage in something more involved with him than just friendship. He was far too charming for her peace of mind, so she decided she would not date him, casually or otherwise.

In the succeeding months, Roald took every opportunity to strengthen his bond of friendship with Yuana. He wanted to get to know her, to learn about her quirks, her preferences, her ideals, her principles. His initial motivation for this friendship was to mask his true intention to woo her, but he realised he wanted to be her friend, almost as much as he wanted to be her boyfriend.

She seemed content to keep their relationship platonic, yet he could tell the attraction between them was mutual. After over six months of friendship, he had yet to convince her to date him. He did not want to push hard for it because, despite the flirtatious banter that had become a staple in their interaction, there was no firm sign from her she was ready or willing to date him. He did not want to make it awkward between them by asking her. She was strong-willed enough to turn him down.

He found her independence unique and alluring. She did not weigh herself down with the masculine energy other women seemed to think was required to achieve their autonomy. Yuana did not see the need to engage in the traditionally male activities other self-proclaimed independent women adopted to show their empowerment.

Instead, her brand of self-sufficiency was a blend of femininity, gentle firmness, open-mindedness, and grit.

Slowly and unwittingly, it became a mission for him to become someone she would need and rely on. He wanted to be someone she could relax with, would allow into her life, into her heart. He wanted to be a presence constant in her day, a permanence in her night.

In the few instances where they met socially, and there were very few as she had little interest in such affairs, he kept a friendly presence. He was protective but not territorial, especially when other men flocked to her side. She had an aura of elegant approachability, but she kept them all at an arm's length with ease. Seeing how she dealt with those guys made him want to cross the friend zone barrier badly. He did not want to be in their number.

Once he tried to rouse her jealousy, but that did not turn out well. Yuana, being herself, gave him a wide berth to entertain his date, who was less than pleased at his inattentiveness. It strained his considerable patience and self-control trying to be present and pleasant to a perfectly great lady who did not interest him, while the object of his affection was being present and pleasant to other guys on the other side of the room. It had been such a trying night he would never repeat the exercise.

He became her technical consultant for the technology she wanted and helped her find the software development company who would design the GJDV app. Being around her work hours would be a constant reminder of him in as many facets of her life as possible.

His campaign started by claiming her lunch hours on weekdays. He would either invite her to lunch or drop by with packed food in tow. She was a foodie, and the strategy allowed him to find out her food preferences and dining habits. And it further cemented his presence in her life.

Daniel teased him he was bordering on stalker territory. He reasoned that his motivation to be close to her was not to control her but to sow the seed of the idea he was worth the risk, that being with him would be easy.

He discovered Yuana had an affinity for nature, trees in particular. His love for outdoor activities melded well with her interests. He indulged her love of nature, of the woods, the pristine lakes, and rivers. Now and then, Daniel got invited to their outings either by himself or by her. They became a trio, or more like a two plus one.

He had a hunch that Daniel always agreed to join them when invited because Dan enjoyed watching him suffer through holding himself in check during those outings.

All this time spent with her had a dual benefit of getting to know her and of showing her who he was. The bonus: her time spent with him was less time spent with another man.

Yuana was brushing her hair absentmindedly as she thought about how much Roald got under her skin with his constant friendly presence in her life. He was attentive and supportive, funny, and creative. He was both eye candy and brain food, which somewhat annoyed her because it became harder to lump him together with all the other guys.

What she needed now was a break from the temptation Roald posed. She could very well fall in love with him if she was not careful, and she would rather not do so. Being a female *viscerebus*, it would be hard for her to form a committed relationship with someone outside of their kind. She did not want to face the same choice her mother had to make with her father decades ago—to leave him and cut him off from their lives abruptly and completely.

If she fell in love with Roald, leaving him would be devastating. She was not confident in her own fortitude to live away and hidden from the man she loves while keeping tabs on him and his life from a distance. She did not have her mother's endurance and self-sacrificing nature.

Thoughts of her mother gave her an idea of how to achieve the distance she needed. Her mother was scheduled to fly to Europe for the GJDV directors' forum. They could meet up with her great-grandparents in Amsterdam, who would attend the annual gathering of the Supreme Viscerebus Tribunal. It would be the perfect opportunity and environment to mix business and family bonding. The trip would give her time to rest her mind and her emotions and perhaps set to right her skewed internal compass.

Maybe the European air would clear the cobwebs out of her confused brain.

Roald gave himself one last cursory glance at the mirror, before rushing to grab his keys. He would meet Yuana at the newly finished medical arts wing of the St. Michael's Hospital. The inauguration tonight required formal attire. The hospital board commissioned his father to design it. He was his father's plus one. Coincidentally, GJDV was the major donor of the new wing; Yuana would represent the company.

He was raring to see Yuana. He had not seen her for ten days because she travelled for business. The time zone difference limited their phone calls, so he had to content himself with text messages which took her hours to reply to. It took every ounce of his willpower not to follow her to wherever she was, but that would have driven her away. No mere friend would drop everything just to follow a friend across the globe.

He arrived ahead of Yuana, so he positioned himself near the entrance so as not to miss her the moment she did. He took deep breaths to slow his heartbeat down, to appear calm and relaxed when she arrived. It would not do to behave like an excited dog when she showed up.

Five minutes later, from his vantage point, he saw Yuana emerge from a sleek, royal blue car, wearing a flowy, bright yellow gown, with a high slit that parted to show her leg when she slid out of the car, her feet encased in dark purple heels. Her dark hair was slicked back to one side and a cascade of curls on the other.

She was breathtaking.

His already elevated heartbeat picked up its pace. And at that moment, seeing her now, he realised with a vengeance the reality he and Yuana could never be "just friends". He had always known he wanted more than friendship from her, he never comprehended until now how much, and how he wanted it unequivocally.

Yuana was looking forward to the event. It is the most strategic project of GJDV this year. The hospital wing would be a valuable addition to their portfolio of investment and influence. A necessary tool to further secure viscerebus' *Veil of Secrecy* in the most efficient way possible.

She was also glad Roald would be here. They had not spoken properly for ten days. She missed his easy-going presence, the jokes over lunch, their stimulating banter. It would be great to catch up. The recent trip afforded her renewed confidence that she could manage her reaction to Roald. Just being with her mother and great grandparents reminded her what she had and what she would endanger if she broke the *Veil of Secrecy* by marrying a human.

Walking into the lobby, she took a glance down her dress to

check for wrinkles. Her stride faltered in mid-step when she saw Roald advance towards her. The intensity of his gaze made the smile on her lips waver. Her breath caught in her throat as it hit her - how much she'd missed him, how vital his presence had become in her life. It shook her to her core, and she panicked. She had an urge to run. Only Roald's warm hands on her upper arms kept her in place.

There was no smile on his face, his jaw tight. She felt a frisson of alarm as she met his gaze. She was trapped and unable to formulate an escape plan.

"Good evening, Yu," Roald said, his voice husky, his dark eyes intent.

"Good evening, Ro," she replied. Her breath caught in her throat.

He didn't respond, merely kept looking at her, like he wanted to say something but did not know how to begin, or if he even wanted to speak at all. She would rather he didn't. The tension broke when someone called Roald's name.

It was a man who had Roald's height and facial features. Architect Magsino, Roald's father.

Roald took a deep breath, a frown on his face. He sighed and took her hand, then led her to where his father beckoned them closer. His father stood with the hospital director and some other people Yuana did not know. Up close, Roald's father had the same smile. The crinkles at the corner of his eyes expressed his delight as they approached. She could imagine how Roald would look like when he aged.

"Ah, finally. I am very pleased to meet you, Yuana." The timbre of his voice was identical to Roald's. His silver-tinged hair had the same texture as his son's. Father and son were so alike, except for the lips. Roald's was fuller.

"The pleasure is mine, sir. Roald told me so much about

you." Roald's father would serve as her barrier for tonight. Until she regained her emotional footing.

Her only believable form of defence was to focus all her attention on Architect Magsino. They were both invited to cut the ribbon for the new wing. Roald's father would test her stock knowledge on design and architecture.

Her sparkling interest in the topic was a mask, as she hid behind the beaming countenance aimed at the father. All the while, she studiously avoided the son's unwavering attention.

Roald stuck by her side the whole evening. He contributed little to the surrounding conversation. He kept a steady focus on her until she became uncomfortable under such concentrated scrutiny.

When the hospital director came over to introduce his son, Jon, and daughter, Melinda, she escaped Roald's attention. Jon offered to get her a drink. She suggested they get it from the bar together.

Roald had no choice but to stay with the director's daughter while Yuana went away with the director's son. He was fuming inside. His already aggravated temper, caused by the stress of holding himself in check the whole evening and trying not to kiss her senseless, was further rubbed raw by her choice to distance herself from him.

He could not proclaim himself as her boyfriend, to call her his, no matter how much he wanted it. No right to stop her from accepting attentions from other men, no right to feel protective. And absolutely no right to show everyone they belonged together.

He took a deep breath and glanced in her direction and saw her still chatting with the director's son, laughing at whatever joke the man told. To an onlooker, she appeared carefree, but he caught the surreptitious glance she threw his way, and that was not lightheartedness in her eyes, it was distress.

What was she afraid of?

The look compelled him to take off the friend-only mantle. He had achieved his goal to get through her armour. He was sure of that. Whether she would allow him to go to the next level was unclear. But this would be the time to press his advantage while she was feeling overwhelmed. Tonight, they would have their reckoning. She might erect a new wall in the morning, and he could not allow that.

He scanned the crowd for his father. Luckily, he was close by. Time to free himself. He escorted the director's daughter to his dad under the pretext of introducing them. And thus accomplished, he turned on his heels and hurried to where Yuana was still using the director's son as a shield against him.

Yuana's mask of cheerfulness slipped when he touched her elbow. Her reply to Jon's question about the projects of the GJDV Foundation faded in mid-sentence. She swallowed like her throat had gone dry.

"Yu, can I speak with you for a moment?" he asked. The polite question was for the benefit of the director's son. For a split second, he thought she would deny him, but she nodded.

He led her to the most secluded corner he could find in the crowded lobby, a small space behind a pillar. Yuana gave him a bright smile that did not reach her eyes. She was pushing him back to the friend zone, and this annoyed him a little more, for he had absolutely no plans of going back there.

"Yu, I value you as a friend, so I want to give you a fair warning. Beginning tomorrow, I shall start wooing you."

"Roald... I..." The direct declaration took her by surprise. "I do not get into romantic relationships..."

Her unconscious use of his full first name was not a good sign.

"Yuana, I cannot hang around you pretending I do not want more than friendship from you. I cannot do it anymore. I want the liberty to show you I care for you." His tone was as firm as his resolve.

"Roald... I..."

Her eyes were enormous pools of uncertainty and panic. A slight sheen of perspiration glistened on her hairline. He had never seen her so flustered and vulnerable; but he could not haul her into his arms; he did not have that right... yet.

"Just let me woo you, Yuana, give me a chance to win your heart," he urged her. "No commitments," he added, giving an inch back so she would say yes. He was desperate himself.

"Okay," she said after a moment. She could not meet his eyes.

He released the breath he had been holding while he waited for her answer, and with the exhalation, his tension eased. He would not kid himself into thinking the coming months would be an easy siege to win her heart. Yuana would make it challenging for him, he was sure of that.

He feared something was preventing her from being free to love and receive love. And whatever it was, he intended to battle it by showing her how dependable he would be, how reliable being loved could be.

———————

Later that night, in the privacy of her bedroom, Yuana replayed the events of the evening and reexamined how she felt about it. If she was honest with herself, there was excitement and fear, and something akin to a release. She tried to recall in all her dating years if she had ever dated anyone that got this close to her. Roald was the first guy who managed to. The prospect of what could come out of it was both welcome and unwelcome. The contradiction was unsettling.

She was not inexperienced in handling men, so her panic could have come from facing something she was unprepared for. She never noticed Roald had breached her emotional barrier. Definitely a first.

Her grandmother's words of wisdom rang in her head: *'worry is just premature suffering'*. Her grandmother was right. She was over-reacting. Who knows, this wooing might even be enjoyable?

She had a natural buffer, a pre-ordained defence against falling in love—being a *viscerebus*. She could not hide what she was if she embarked on a committed relationship. And nothing could induce her to give her heart to anyone, considering the consequences. Not even Roald.

The Tribunal had very strict laws against the casual revelation of their nature and their kind to the humans. The consequences of breaking the *Veil of Secrecy* should she fail to restore it at the prescribed time frame was not worth testing. She would be forced to take fatal action against Roald, and it was not something any viscerebus would be glad to do.

She had to be tactical about this. Her best defence strategy was to learn more about how Roald thinks as a man, so she could marshal her own defences. In this aspect, Daniel would be the best person to ask. She should call him in the morning, as it was too late at night.

But hell, Daniel introduced them, so he was partially responsible for the quandary she was in now. And if this would keep her awake, he would have to suffer with her. She picked up her phone and dialled Daniel's number.

"Hey, Yu, anything wrong?" Daniel's throaty mumble floated through the line. He yawned.

"Not yet, but you will help me keep things right," she informed him dryly.

"Okay... what did I do this time?" Daniel asked, wary.

"You introduced him to me... and he's determined to escape the friend zone," she said. It annoyed and alarmed her in equal measure.

"Who? W-what?" The sound of a rustling bedsheet as Daniel shifted was audible.

"Roald told me directly he will woo me. And I don't like it." Daniel's chuckle annoyed her even more.

"Sorry, Yu... But what is the problem exactly? You never had difficulty keeping them within the friend zone before."

"Well, Roald is not like the others. He refused to be just friends," she said. Daniel's obvious enjoyment of the situation irritated her.

"Okay, so what do you want me to do?... Where and when shall I bring the shovel?" Daniel was trying to soothe her ruffled feathers.

"Oh, be serious, Daniel!" Her sharp rebuke, and the mention of his full name, no doubt sobered him up.

"Okay. Why didn't you just tell him you are not interested? That friendship is the only thing you can offer."

"I did... He... would not accept it," she replied with a heavy sigh.

"So, how can I help, Yuana? What do you want me to do?" he asked.

"What is his usual strategy, his usual wooing moves? I need to be ready."

"I cannot tell you," Daniel replied.

"Why not? A bro code of some sort?"

"No. In the five years that Roald and I have been friends, I have never known him woo any woman. So, I do not have any clue on how he does it."

"Why do you think he wanted to woo me? I was perfectly happy just being friends."

"Well, you were unattainable, a challenge, and most men will find such a challenge nearly impossible to resist," he said.

"Maybe I should just sleep with him one time, to get it over with," she grumbled, half-joking.

"No, don't do that. It will not push him away." Daniel's reaction was quick.

"Oh, don't be daft! I have no plans of sleeping with him just to stop him from wooing me. That's like giving him the trophy before the competition even begun," she snapped.

Her sharp exhale interrupted Daniel's chuckle.

He cleared his throat. "I think Roald is serious about you. Roald is like a male version of you, not a player, but not into serious relationships either. I believe he's angling for a forever-kind of love affair like his parents," he added, his tone laden with forewarning.

"Well, that doesn't help," she said sharply.

"Yuana, just remember the very reason you had no serious relationship. That should help you avoid all the emotional traps Roald will set on your path."

"True..."

"It worked for you before, it would still work this time. Although, I have to admit when Roald sets his mind into doing something, he is a determined fellow. He will not give up that easy, so you have a battle in your hands," he said.

"Oh, damn! This is going to be a problem..."

"Well, there's a possibility he could be bad at wooing; it's his first time after all. He could end up doing something that would make you cringe."

"One can only hope so," she said. That did not seem likely, as Roald had never done anything that induced a cringe from her.

A lengthy silence on the other line made her wonder if they got disconnected.

"Do you want me to talk to him?" Daniel suggested after a while.

"Do you think he would listen and stop?"

"Perhaps... But do you really want him to?" he asked.

A heavy sigh escaped from her. "I do not know..."

"Well, you can always preempt the heartbreak and do what all the other women of your kind do in instances like this. Go and disappear. He can't woo you if you are not here, can he?" he said.

"I will not let him drive me away, that would give him power over me for the rest of my life. And you know how long our kind lives..."

She realised she had been looking at this the wrong way. She saw herself as a helpless victim, a passive recipient of Roald's wooing efforts, which placed her in a weak position. What she should do would be to approach this like a competition. Her wits against his. This idea appealed to her, and even better, it made her feel powerful.

Daniel was wrong. It would be Roald who would have a battle in his hands.

2

THE SIEGE AND THE SACRIFICE

R oald's courtship started the following day.
Yuana arrived at the office, looking forward and expecting her usual coffee, but saw something else instead. On her table lay an enormous box, wrapped in silver and blue. A small silver card attached had a message that read:

Good morning, Yuana.
Let me engage your senses today.
~R.

Intrigued, Yuana opened the box and gasped. There was a layer of fragrant, bright yellow champacas. Her favourite flowers. The familiar heady fragrances of tea, vanilla, hay, and peach assailed her senses. A small blue card with a message accompanied the flowers—

Poetry is not the blossom, but the scent of the blossom.
~R.

Wow! Flowers and poetry. Impressive start!

Enthused, she saw two silver ribbons protruding opposite each other from under the layer of Champacas. She lifted it with care. Underneath was a box of mint chocolates. Again, her favourite. A small silver card accompanying it said:

I taste a liquor never brewed– Emily Dickinson.
~R.

That, too, had the two silver ribbons she could lift out. She did and was delighted to find a book. It was the "Good Omens" by the late Terry Pratchett. The accompanying blue card said:

My sight may have been the first of my senses you captured,
but it was merely directed by my heart.
~R.

She was now beyond impressed - Roald accomplished all this within a few hours. He was proving to be a challenging combatant. And this was just day one.

Should I worry?

Not quite.

She then noticed a small digital recorder in the corner of the box. When she pressed play, Roald's deep voice floated in the air. *"You're welcome... Dinner tonight?"* The last silver card that accompanied it said:

Say yes. The sense of touch depends on it.
R.

That made her laugh. She was more than energised; she felt challenged.

Roald would make a good general, judging from how rigorous the campaign he launched to make her fall in love with him. His strategy was multi-faceted, and his actions were well executed.

The Four-Senses, her name for Roald's signature gift box, came in regular schedule. Its contents were always unexpected and varied. The only constant in those boxes was the digital recording of him asking for a dinner date. She could only marvel at the amount of research he had done to find out the things she liked.

At one point, a box came with a bottle of neroli-based perfume for scent. Another one contained gorgonzola and red wine for taste. One was most touching because it had a beautiful snow globe with a small ceramic figure of a man and a woman with dark hair like hers. The scene portrayed a park in the middle of winter, and the music it played was the most beautiful she had ever heard.

Another box came with a Halloween theme, her favourite holiday. It was the middle of the year. His note said:

Anything you desire that is within my power to give is yours.
R.

Their former activities before he began this formal pursuit of her remained the same. Roald knew when to be professional and platonic. And when she was feeling relaxed, he would turn on the charm. In short, he kept her emotional footing unbalanced by being friendly and companionable one moment, funny and playful in another, and the best and worst of it—intense and seductive.

She had to admit to herself she could lose this war to Roald if she did not take care. And she had no one to blame because she unknowingly provided him an ally — her willingness to enjoy the effects of his actions.

It was time to end it. For both their sakes. Tonight, she would have to tell him to stop. The longer she delayed, the harder it would be.

———

Yuana kept postponing the 'speech' throughout dinner. She justified every delay with flimsy reasons until she ran out of courses, and it left only the dessert. She counted down while she stirred cream in her coffee, then laid her spoon aside.

"Roald, this will be our last date." She adopted a formal tone. Roald must understand she meant business.

"And why is that?" Roald sat back, a small smile on his face.

That confused her. She expected a stronger reaction from him.

"I am tired of this wooing business; I want it to end. I just want us to remain friends." She was as firm, as calm as she could project herself to be.

"You agreed to give me a chance to win your heart, remember? Are you breaking your word?" he asked. His tone was gentle, his expression, deadpan.

"I agreed, and I gave you a chance. But that chance has run out." She tried to keep her façade of calm and decisiveness in the face of Roald's composure.

"I have not won your heart yet. And I promised myself only when I succeed would my wooing end." He said it lightly, but the seriousness of his intent was there in his eyes and the edges of his smile.

"Roald, be reasonable. I told you I do not do romantic relationships. And you promised no commitments. Are you going back on your word now?" Her tone had risen an octave. Her pulse thudded against her wrist.

"Yu, I am not asking you to accept me as your boyfriend, all I am asking from you is to allow me a chance to win your heart. It should be up to me to decide if I won it or not, when to stop and give up."

His reasonable tone was causing her panic to surface. "This is interfering with my life now, Roald. It is becoming more complicated, and I dislike complications." She did not want to be forced to threaten him with the complete severance of their ties.

"You are a strong, independent woman, Yuana. If I cannot win your heart, no amount of effort on my part will accomplish the impossible. Those efforts would not have interfered with your routine or your life," Roald reasoned.

She did not know what to say.

"I think I am getting to you, that my efforts are paying off, that I am making headway. That is why it's complicating your life," he added.

"No, of course not!"

"Well then, my wooing should not be an issue," he shrugged.

She heaved a sigh of frustration. She could not fault his logic. Maybe she would have to try another approach.

———

Roald let out a slow breath of relief. He survived Yuana's first attempt to put him back in the friend zone. He had been expecting something like this from her almost every week. At one point, he worried she was going to threaten him with cutting off their ties if he persisted.

He was glad the threat did not come, because he would

have no choice but to respect her wishes no matter how much he disagreed. That would be excruciating, especially since she had unwittingly admitted how affected she was by his efforts.

———

Yuana could not seem to get past the first page of the digital marketing proposal in her hand. Her thoughts were with Roald and how to cut the strengthening bond between them cleanly before things got any deeper.

If she did not engage in his courtship efforts, there was very little chance of him winning her heart.

Why not stop seeing him altogether?

Easier said than done. The problem was, she did not want to stop seeing him.

Maybe her mother would have some wise counsel for her. After all, she went through the same thing with her father a long time ago.

———

"Come in, Yu. Do you need anything?" Ysobella asked without looking up from the document. Her mother was busy signing some policies.

She walked in and sat down by the small coffee table in the corner of her mother's office. They usually sit there when they discuss non-business issues. Her choice of seat piqued her mother's interest.

Her mother pressed the intercom button and requested coffee for both of them, then sat down on the chair next to her.

"Okay, what is our mother-daughter topic for today?" Her mother's casual demeanour showed she had already guessed what it would be about.

Their family always checked the background of every person any of the family members interacted with for over three occasions. Somewhere in their security department, there would be a dossier on Roald. She was certain her mother had reviewed that file at least once.

"Mama, how did Papa win you?" she asked.

Her mother's surprise was momentary, then her expression turned introspective; a slight smile curved her lips. Her eyes flashed at the beautiful memories triggered by the question.

"Through friendship, intelligent conversations, little acts of affection, and a lot of laughter."

Oh, fuck, I am doomed!

It was the same strategy Roald was using on her, and it touched the same vulnerabilities she had inherited from her mother.

"Was there ever a point you thought of stopping everything before things got serious, before you fell in love with Papa?"

"No. You see, Papa and I were friends. We both did not have any intention of getting into a serious relationship. We had priorities and compelling reasons not to get into one. His was to become an excellent doctor. He was an orphan, and he worked very hard for everything he achieved. I had no interest in dating human men, knowing what happened to your Aunt Ximena, plus I loved my work. So, it caught us both unaware. We did not realise until it was too late, we were already in love," Ysobella recounted.

"You friend-zoned Papa and still fell in love..." she sighed.

"Yes. Your father crept into my heart quietly and steadily, unlike what Roald is doing to you, a full-on assault," her mother said. "Yuana, you are in a better position to control your own path. You know of Roald's intention. You can make preemptive decisions."

She nodded, but she was unconvinced by the strength of her own control.

"Mama, what is the best way to... avoid getting involved?" She could not admit to her mother her emotions were already engaged.

"Stop seeing him and find a distraction to occupy your thoughts," her mother suggested.

That was going to be hard. She would have to wean herself from craving Roald's presence first.

So how would I start the weaning?

First, she would stop going on a date with him. This way, he could not say she did not keep her word to allow him a chance to win her heart. After all, it was not the gifts that affected her so; it was his physical presence.

Ysobella took out the huge grey leather binder from the unlocked bottom drawer of her desk. Her talk with Yuana reopened the dam of memories she thought she had buried deep. She never succeeded. Those memories remained on the surface, covered by the thinnest veneer of normalcy.

This binder contained every scrap of information and photos she had of Galen's life since she left him. There was not much as he was a private person. The last entry was a clipping from the Baltimore Sun newspaper dated over two years ago. It was an announcement of the engagement of Dr Galen Aurelio and Dr Natalie Holtz.

The sight of the clipping generated the familiar ache in her heart, a mixture of regret, jealousy, and yearning.

Is Galen happy now?

Did the marriage enable him to move on from their disastrous past?

Had he finally secured the family he never had and always wanted? A family I denied him.

There was no use torturing herself further. She flipped to the other newspaper clippings of Galen. They were articles about his medical missions and coverage of his speaking engagements in the medical forums. Every mention of his name in the paper she had collected like scraps, like the proverbial crumbs that lead to home.

The hurting in her heart intensified. She flipped unseeing to other pages, trying to control the tears that welled in her eyes. With a measure of control back, she looked down at the page opened on her lap. And lost her tenuous grip.

Her back rigid at the effort to stop herself from sobbing, tears dripped on a cellophane-covered paper. The memories attached to the twenty-six-year-old document came rushing back at her like a runaway train.

May 10, 1993

She had been on her feet for the last thirty-two hours of hospital duty, and it exhausted her. She rested her back against the wall while she waited for Galen to drive around the front. They were to have a quick lunch and then he would drive her home so she could take a nap before their dinner later.

They were going to fly to Italy the following day for a month-long holiday. She was ticking off the list of essentials in her head, trying to remember if there was something she had forgotten to pack when Galen pulled into the driveway of the hospital.

Too tired and preoccupied to pay attention to the sly smile on Galen's face, she slid into the passenger seat. She was asleep by the time her head hit the headrest, but awoke to the gentle touch of Galen's hands on her face half an hour later.

"Where are we?" she asked.

Galen kissed her temple and murmured, "Your apartment."

"Are we not going to lunch?" She had struggled to open her eyes.

"If you are starving, we can have lunch, but you look like you need sleep more," he replied.

"I would rather sleep," she murmured.

"Sleep it is then," he said.

He reached over to release her seat belt.

She roused herself determinedly; she did not want to tempt Galen into carrying her to her apartment, as he was inclined to do now and then. He came round to her side of the car to open her door and assist her with her things.

Galen walked with her to her unit, with all her medical files and books, and deposited them at her dining table. He turned her towards the bedroom, peeled off the lab coat from her shoulders, and hung it on the coat rack just behind the bedroom door. He then unzipped her dress from behind and undressed her with clinical efficiency until she was down to her underclothes. She stepped out of her shoes with a grateful sigh.

With gentle hands, he pushed her down to the bed and pulled the covers over her and tucked her in. He leaned over and nibbled at her lips gently, a habit of his that was more soothing than arousing. He then left her bedroom to let her sleep.

Hours later, she woke up refreshed and hungry to dimly lit and fragrant surroundings. The light and scent of cinnamon and magnolia came from two candles at the corner of the room.

Thirty-five minutes later, she was inspecting herself in the mirror when she heard the key in the front door. Galen had arrived. She picked up a small evening bag from her wardrobe and proceeded to the living room.

She stopped in her tracks as she stepped out. An amazing sight greeted her. The room was dim, illuminated only by white fairy lights strung all over the walls and a dozen candles all over. All the red candles carried the same scent as the ones in her bedroom. The coppery red cloth that covered the dinner table set off the formal looking white china set for two and the centrepiece of dozens of white roses.

She looked up in confusion at Galen. Her heart hammered in a deafening beat. The feeling of dread crawled into and penetrated her armour-clad heart.

Galen took her hand and led her to a chair and sat her down. His smile was almost shy. He was nervous, she realised, and it made her heart sink. Galen sat down across from her and poured them both a glass of champagne. She could see he was waiting for her to speak.

"What is this, Galen? What is the occasion?" she asked, trying to sound flippant. She hoped this was something else and not a proposal.

Galen looked at her, reached inside his suit pocket, and handed her a thick, embossed silver envelope.

She took the envelope. Her heart thudded louder as she slowly opened it. Inside was a beautifully prepared and filled up marriage license. Galen's signature was bold and firm. A blank space awaited her own signature. Her mind in a whirl, her throat too thick for words, her eyes focused on the document.

"Bel, please say something," Galen implored.

She smiled weakly; Galen's uncertainty tugged at her heartstrings. "Sorry, it completely surprised me. I don't know what to say..." she had said.

"I understand, I was too absorbed in the setup and the setting that I didn't stop to think how shocking this would be for you," he said sheepishly.

"It's okay. It was certainly creative... I hope you are not hiding the priest in the closet..." she joked, outwardly calm and cheerful, but she was crumbling into pieces deep inside.

"No... no... not quite. The marriage license is my way of proposing to you, my signature on it signifies my lifelong commitment even now. Your signature meant the acceptance of my proposal. You can take as much time as you need to decide when the actual ceremony will be. For now, I just want your commitment to us, my love," he explained.

Serious plea for acceptance, for confirmation, replaced the ever-present twinkle of mischief in his eyes.

"I can't sign this... I have no pen," she whispered.

The relief on his expression was almost comical as he hastily fished his silver sign pen out from his inner breast pocket and handed it to her.

She uncapped the pen and deliberately, beautifully signed the license. There was a brief pause when they both looked at the signed license, the import of the moment indelible. Galen stood up, drew her into his arms. His lips descended to hers, and his murmur of "My Bel," was as deep, as intense, as sealing as the kiss that followed.

The pain of the recollection, of the regret, longing, and the undying wish in her soul for the outcome she would rather have, but did not come to pass, washed over her again. She allowed herself to grieve once more, to allow the free flow of tears to wash the pain away into a dull, manageable ache. As she regained control of her emotions, her heart felt lighter.

She closed the binder and slid it back in the bottom drawer, locking it away this time.

Yuana went back to her own office with a plan. Roald was familiar with her work schedule and her preference in the lack of social activities, so the first thing she needed to do would be to apply a drastic change to it.

She started by scheduling late afternoon and dinner meetings with clients and their subsidiaries. She also pushed her weekly meeting with Roald and the IT team earlier in the day. Lunch with Roald became shorter as she moved her marketing team sessions to early afternoon.

As to her Friday and Saturday nights, she needed to create a girl squad immediately. She spent her youth travelling the world, so she did not have a group of high school or university friends to bank on. To do that, she had to get in touch with the women she met at the course of her work in the past two years.

By the end of the day, she had two groups of girlfriends and booked all her Fridays and Saturday nights for the next two months.

She had limited her encounters with Roald to twice a week, both for purely business reasons. For every other night, she scheduled team-building time with her sales and marketing team. She had eliminated all other opportunities for date nights.

In the end, she felt the satisfaction of a job well done and a sense of loss. With a sigh, she left for home early. She needed a pick-me-up, and only her family could do that.

Roald's frustration reached a boiling point.

Three weeks, countless invitations and attempts to take Yuana out, to spend time with her, all turned down because she had previous engagements. At first, he thought she made it up. But her secretary gave him a glimpse of Yuana's schedule when he dropped by her office unannounced with some pastries and coffee in tow, hoping to surprise her. Yuana was at their south branch for a meeting.

She still took his calls, but their conversations were rushed because of her tight schedule. He asked her point-blank about if she was avoiding him. She denied it.

What a load of crock!

She found a more effective way to guard herself, and it was exasperating. Seeing her with regularity was his small reward for not being able to hold her or kiss her. Now that had been taken away from him and his frustration had reached a catastrophic level.

He paced in his living room for half an hour, then decided he might as well go out to blow off some steam. A much better option than moping and thinking of her and all the ways she had thwarted his best-laid plans. No one was more resistant to loving than Yuana. But he was already too emotionally invested, so he had no choice but to persevere. He grabbed his keys and got into his car. He would decide on his destination en route.

Ten minutes later, he took the first sip of the craft gin and tonic he ordered. No use telling himself to stop thinking about her tonight; it had the exact opposite effect on him. He hoped she was as distracted and as full of thoughts about him as he was about her. It would serve her right for choosing to have a business meeting over having dinner with him.

He was still grumbling when the object of his obsession walked into the bar with an older gentleman. Yuana didn't notice him as she was busy laughing at what the gentleman was saying. The man was elegant, fit, good looking, and about fifteen years older than him.

He directed Yuana to the chair he pulled for her, his hand on the small of her back. The familiarity in their interaction told Roald Yuana was open to this man. Something he had yet to achieve. His heart tightened, his gut wrenched at the sight, and a corrosive emotion came over him.

This did not look like a meeting, it looked more like a date.

Inside, he seethed. The flavour of acrid jealousy in his throat. The precariousness of his position in Yuana's life became all too stark. His back muscles were rigid with the effort to stop himself from hauling Yuana out of there, far away from this man who seemed to have succeeded where all of them failed.

He should walk out and away, but his body refused to move.

He watched Yuana excuse herself from her date and walk towards the ladies' room. By reflex, he got up and followed her. Possessiveness and the desire to have his suspicion allayed drove him.

He waited by the hallway of the comfort rooms and positioned himself at the corner where Yuana would not see him when she came out. He didn't want her to panic and duck back inside where he couldn't follow.

Yuana was putting her phone inside her purse when she walked past him. Her head snapped back up as something triggered her awareness a split second before his hand closed on her elbow and spun her around.

Surprise, excitement, gladness, and longing flashed in quick succession across her beautiful face.

His wrath vanished upon seeing her open expression. He also saw with clarity what he meant to her. His heart was full to bursting with the same emotions, and he was helpless against the pull of his attraction to Yuana.

Nothing else mattered now except the need to kiss her. He drew her into his arms, one hand cradled the back of her head as he guided her face towards his. He could not take his eyes off her soft, plump lips. Compelled, he brushed her lower lip with his thumb to tamp down the ferocious need that coursed through his veins, to give her time to pull away.

But she did not. Instead, her exhaled breath quivered in anticipation, and this was permission enough for him. He sealed her lips with his, demonstrating the enormity of the passion, the craving, the burning desire to make her feel what was in his heart. And when she kissed him back with equal fervour, he poured all the yearning of his soul into the kiss.

He angled her head to deepen the kiss, to savour her better, to imprint himself into her as deeply as he could, and to absorb her into himself as fully as possible. This woman was his better half. He was as certain of it as his own breathing.

The kiss could have been just a few seconds, and yet it felt like an eternity. An eternity that was insufficient. He could go on kissing her, but she broke the kiss, panting, trying to regain control. His arms tightened around her. His wordless statement to her that the pretence was over, and from that moment on, they belonged to each other.

And this was the end of their cat-and-mouse game.

Yuana laid her cheek on Roald's chest, breathless and feeling entirely boneless. She needed some time to pull herself together. There was no denying the truth. Not to him, not to herself. She had fallen in love with Roald.

At that moment, she received the answer to the question she asked herself many times before — the one thing in life she wanted above all else was in her hands now. Yet she would not be allowed to keep it. Not with him. She made the same mistake her mother made and there would be hell to pay.

"No more games, Yuana, okay?" Roald said over her head.

His chest vibrated beneath her cheek, his arms wrapped

around her, gentle yet unyielding. When she did not respond immediately, he pulled away to look down at her face.

"Okay," she said. Her eyes closed briefly. It was easier to hide her dread if he could not read it in her eyes.

"No more running away. You are home now," he said, his voice reassuring, yet wanting reassurance.

She nodded. She could not voice out the real reason she would never allow herself to find a home in his arms, in his heart. For now, like her mother, she would take advantage of the small sliver of time afforded her by fate. She was hopeful it would be long enough to sustain her for the rest of her very long life.

With a sigh, she pulled out of his arms — Uncle Iñigo was waiting, and Aunt Ximena might be there already.

"Come, join us. My Uncle and Aunt must wonder where I am now," she said.

She glanced at her own reflection in the mirror on the wall. Her face was flushed but acceptable.

Her Uncle... a relative, not a date. And Yuana was going to introduce him to them.

Roald smiled, reassured and joyful. He accompanied Yuana back to the bar with a spring in his step.

Later that evening, for the first time since they met, Yuana allowed him to drive her home. He made huge strides today; he met her relatives, and now he had the right to drive her home.

His own drive home was like the beginning of his life. He went to bed thinking of all the things he could do to show Yuana the benefits of having him as a partner, as an integral part of her life. He vowed to make sure Yuana would not find any cause to regret giving him her heart.

Peace and well-being settled on him. It was like finding something vital he never knew was missing until found. She felt like home, his lifetime goal, and her happiness his achievement. And for the first time in his life, he understood what profound gratitude was like.

———

Roald was unaware that for Yuana, their new status did not bring absolute joy. It was laced with a sense of doom, and a sense of hope.

Was there any way to change their destiny?

Any way that could help Roald accept my nature as an aswang?

If he did, would he be able to get past the fact that for the humans, I would always be an evil creature of the night, a literal man-eater, a monster?

Would he be able to adapt to my way of life and live among my kind?

Would it do me any good if I avoided the same fate that befell my mother?

For Roald, their entire relationship would be a lopsided one. He would be the only one making the sacrifices, while she would reap the benefits of his love. He would have to accept her regular consumption of raw human viscera, her shape-shifting nature that may pose a danger to his life, their children that would all be aswangs like her, and the responsibility to keep everything a secret until the day he dies.

She would outlive him by at least a hundred years. Her natural long life which she used to consider a blessing now felt like a curse. When Roald dies, she would have to live the rest of her lengthy life with just the memory of their life together, bereft of him.

That would be her punishment.

Perhaps there was merit to following her mother's footsteps - to enjoy as much time with Roald as she could, to make every moment memorable for him. And to make enough of them to tide both of them over until their inevitable parting. There was value to what her mother did. She made the sacrifice by keeping him ignorant of the truth: his woman was a fearful creature of lore — an aswang.

Hopefully, it would be enough for Roald, as it seemed to have been for her father.

Roald got up early. He was too elated to stay in bed, his body too full of adrenalin. He was trying not to send an early text message to Yuana. She could still be sleeping, and he did not want to disturb her.

He ended up doing a two-hour gym session, and yet he was still pumped. He was contemplating his boyfriend strategies for the day when Daniel tapped him on the shoulder.

"You look possessed, bro!" Daniel commented, his gaze assessing.

"What do you mean?" Roald asked, his thoughts still on Yuana.

"You have been grinning for the last ten minutes, for no apparent reason. So, what's up?" Daniel's eyes narrowed in suspicion.

His grin grew wide. He was too happy to be bothered about being mocked by Daniel. He did not respond as the recent development in his relationship with Yuana was too new and personal to share.

But Daniel picked up on it. His eyebrows raised in disbelief. His expression was so telling, it made Roald laugh.

Without words, Daniel slapped his back and walked away, leaving him to savour his happiness.

Daniel still couldn't believe Yuana and Roald were now a couple, especially since the cost would be so high for her. And for Roald, although he did not know it yet. They'd reached a point where, no matter which path they chose, there would be sacrifices and heartbreak for both of them.

Yuana risked a lot, and it would only be because she had fallen in love. The one thing Yuana yearned for, a loving relationship, was now at hand but would never culminate to the end she deserved. And he felt responsible because he introduced them.

All kinds of emotions he would rather not have assaulted him. He was pained, concerned, and confused. His former casual existence now no longer possible. He was in the middle of it, and he had no one else to blame as he placed himself there, albeit unintentionally.

He wavered between calling Yuana or waiting for her to call him. Knowing her, she would be torn between living for the moment and preparing for the eventual end. For aswang to human relationships, the Tribunal rules may bend, but it would not change the outcome. To a viscerebus, the *Veil of Secrecy* was paramount. It must be above friends, above family, above all else. And there would be harsh measures if the *Veil* was not maintained, measures that would be literally life and death.

He told himself he may be overreacting. There was still a possibility their relationship could wind down into the natural fading of affection that ends up in friendship. They were casual daters, both of them.

Somehow, though, the scenario rang hollow.

The same scenario played in Yuana's mind. She had been convincing herself the best outcome of her relationship with Roald would be to enjoy it, build wonderful memories together, and then let the intensity wane into friendship. One they would both cherish and count among the most memorable of their lives, and nothing more. She could steer them towards that end, after all, their passion could not burn hot forever. Time would reduce it to a mere ember.

She was deep in thought, staring unseeing at her coffee when she felt her mother's hand on her shoulder.

"A peso for your thoughts?" Ysobella asked, her tone gentle.

She smiled up at her mother. If only she could stir the heat away from her life the way she was doing with her coffee.

"It's worth more than a peso, Mama."

"Okay, so I raise it to ten." Her mother sat down beside her.

"Raise it to a hundred?" She took a fortifying sip of her coffee and welcomed the scalding heat of the beverage on her tongue.

"Oh, that serious, huh?" Her mother's eyebrow rose.

"Yes," she replied with a heavy sigh.

"So, out with it, Yuana. What's bothering you? Matters of the heart?"

"Mama, how would I go about having a relationship with Roald and end it in benign terms, one that would not leave a scar?" Her interest in her coffee dissipated with the swirling steam that rose from her cup.

Her mother looked at her. "Living a life always leaves a scar, Yuana. That's what memories are. You cannot avoid it. Neither can Roald."

"Is there a way not to leave a lasting mark?" *A way where it would not hurt so much?*

"It is not up to you how deep or how lasting the mark will be on Roald. That is on him. But the scar on you, how deep this experience would mark you, how long you will nurse the wound, that is your province."

Yuana's eyes flicked up as she realised her mother was not just talking about Roald. Her mother's own scars were deep and enduring.

"Why do you nurse yours still, Mama? Why not let it go?" If this was the life she would face, she would like to prepare for it.

A sad smile curved her mother's lips. "It's a reminder that once, I fell completely and irrevocably in love. And the pain that came with the reminiscing is the measure of how much capacity I have for love. That is my badge of courage." Her mother sighed. "I would like to think that I did something selfless at one point in my life."

Was there a timeframe for forgetting, for getting over a heartbreak?

"How long do you intend to keep reminiscing, Mama? When will you let go?"

"I let go two years ago, Yuana. But, like any habit, it will take time, and time will make it easier."

Time would, hopefully, make things easier for her and Roald, too.

The ride to the GJDV's office was a quiet one. As always, whenever Galen's name or their history together got discussed, the memories of those times would resurface. The pain that came with the recollection had dulled, but the regret was still as strong as ever.

Ysobella leaned back against the backseat and closed her

eyes, trying to stem the flow of those past moments, but it kept coming just the same.

June 12, 1993

She woke up from a nap, yet she still felt tired. It could be jetlag, since she just returned from a month-long holiday in Italy with Galen. She fiddled with the dazzling aquamarine ring on her finger, the engagement ring Galen gave her a month ago, and thought about the signed marriage license stored in her safe. True to his word, Galen never mentioned the document since, but the implication that it was just a matter of time was as present in both their minds as an unvoiced question.

As she fixed herself a cup of coffee, a mixture that included some dark chocolate and mint syrup, she recalled all the days of the past month. She allowed herself to spend it with Galen, as full of joy as possible. It would be a full compensation, albeit a poor substitute for all the years she would lose later. It was her bribe to herself to buy more time with him. They were glorious, bittersweet days, and it gratified her to have them.

She had instructed the covert Iztari team who trailed them to take as many pictures as possible, for those photos would be her lifeline, her tether to Galen and the life they could never have.

Maybe she could squeeze more time with him, a few more months. She needed to break up with him before they announced a wedding date. It would save Galen the embarrassment of a cancelled nuptial.

As she got up, a wave of nausea assailed her, and she ran to the bathroom. In the middle of the waves of dry heaving, a realisation washed over her. Every spasm wrenched from her gut, a punctuation, a corroboration of her suspicion. She did not need a test to confirm it; she knew all the symptoms.

She was pregnant with Galen's child.

Fate had not favoured her wish for more time with Galen. Her clock had run out. The open suitcase she intended to unpack was now a cruel joke. There was no need to do that now. The growing life in her belly decided for her.

Tomorrow, she would erase all the traces of her life here. She must disappear. Galen would never know about the child.

With a heavy heart, she dialled the GJDV security team head, and informed him the Relocation plan would begin today.

The click of the phone sounded like a death knell, and she gave in to the grief crushing her heart, tainting all the joys she had hoarded in the past month.

Three days later, she found out from the report she received from the covert security team leader who trailed Galen, that Galen spent those three frantic days looking for her.

Visions of Galen's pain and desperation broke her heart anew.

She was a fighter by nature, and people who knew her would never think her a martyr. Yet here she was, willing to relive the pain of those last days again and again, willing to get hurt every time. This was the only way to atone for what she did to Galen.

Her form of self-flagellation.

Yuana agreed to meet with Roald for lunch; their first as a couple. This would be an important one. It would set the parameters and the tempo of their relationship. To steer them to a benign parting, it was crucial that their pace was one she dictated, and not the headlong manner Roald would most likely lead them into.

Five minutes later, her secretary ushered Roald to her office. The warmth in his eyes, the smile on his lips made her heart skip a beat. He looked happy, and there was an answering gladness in her heart. He leaned down to kiss her; she turned and offered her cheek instead, conscious of the people around who were watching them with interest.

Roald chuckled, but did not argue.

"Shall we?" she asked, impatient to talk to him and set her rules. She wanted to establish control as soon as possible.

"And we shall," he replied, beaming.

Arm in arm, they walked to the elevator that took them to the Japanese restaurant on the ground floor of the building. Once ensconced in a private spot, with the view of the vast greens of the Jardin De Vida, she faced Roald.

"Ro, I have a request to make," she began. She did not want to lose her nerve, and that would be inevitable if she waited until later.

He picked up on the seriousness in her expression, and his smile faded. "What is it?" he asked. His back straightened, like he was preparing himself for something unpleasant.

"I am not used to this... Can we take it slow?"

"Is that all?" Roald looked disbelieving at the simplicity of her request.

She nodded.

He reached over, closed his hand over hers. His tight grip on her hand communicated his relief. "We can go as slow as you want, Yuana. You set the pace, and I will follow," Roald said, his gaze and tone warm and understanding. "You can take as long a time as you need until you are comfortable with the idea of us." His eyes softened in sympathy and sincerity.

"Thank you for understanding..." Her relief was shallow. Roald had no idea what she was setting up for them.

"I will always try to understand you, Yuana. I know something is stopping you, a fear that you do not feel comfortable sharing with me yet, and I accept that. So, I will wait until you are ready." His words sounded like a promise, one that he seemed intent to keep.

Those words gave Yuana hope, the kind she had never even contemplated before. But it was only day one of their couple-hood. It was too early to tell how this would progress, and too early to predict the end. As her grandmother used to say, *'worry is just premature suffering'*, and she had suffered enough, so she would give her concern a rest for now.

With a temporary decision reached, her heart lightened, and she couldn't help but give Roald a beaming smile which chased the serious expression from his face. Surprise replaced it. Then his eyes smouldered.

Taking heed of her own request to take it easy, she smiled him an apology, and flipped open the menu, forcing Roald to follow her lead.

Behind the menu, Roald could only shake his head. She heard him mutter, "You might just be the death of me..."

Oh, Roald, I hope not. You do not know how close you are to the truth.

2019

He watched Narcisa, his six-months pregnant girlfriend, dust the furniture around the rented condominium unit. His focus was on the size of her belly and thought of the foetus living and growing in it. The ultrasound results confirmed the foetus was healthy. All its organs fully formed, as expected.

He had already prepared the remote mountain lodge he had rented to harvest what he needed. His heartbeat quickened with the prospect that his cure was at hand. He would, at last, get rid of the Visceral Metastasis that plagued him. A disease that had been passed on to him by his father. Anger suffused him again at the thought of his father who caused all this. Johan Brogen Prowze's execution for that crime was not enough for the misery he bequeathed his sons.

Narcisa interrupted his thoughts to ask what he wanted for dinner. He could not be bothered, so he told her so. His girl-friend's fawning nature irritated him. Her simple provincial mind bored him within a few days of meeting her. There were several times he wanted to show her how annoying she was but stopped himself as it was part of his plan to pretend to be in love with her so she would obey him without question.

She was but a human pawn for his goal, a host for the only cure for his visceral metastasis.

Tomorrow, the messis would begin. Narcisa would go out early to buy some items he instructed her to get. He would leave half an hour later and pick her up at the meeting point he had prearranged. She had no clue he set it up so no one would see them leave their building together. He had already estab-lished his alibi when he advised the front desk to watch an eye out for Narcisa for a few days while he was away.

He engineered the last-minute invitation for her to join him to limit the possibility of her telling anyone she would spend time with him in the next few days. And he also did not tell her their destination as an extra precaution. She didn't bother to ask him, her trust in him complete.

He should feel guilty about what he was about to do to her, and to the foetus in her belly, his own offspring, but he did not. The child conceived to provide the only cure for his disease. He was not heartless, though. He planned to make it as painless for her as possible, so he prepared some natural anaes-thetic to keep her asleep and unconscious the entire time.

With a deep breath of anticipation, he relished the coming of tomorrow. Soon, he would live his life unhampered by this death sentence of a malady. The bitter irony of the disease was not lost on him.

Both the cause and cure stemmed from the consumption of the viscera of his kind.

3

THE FALLING

Roald watched his girlfriend of two weeks come down the stairs wearing leggings, a short, loose cotton shirt and running shoes. She carried a small travel bag. Yuana's long dark hair was set in a high, loose bun. Fresh and relaxed, she gave him a quick kiss good morning, and handed him her bag, then proceeded to the kitchen.

The bag was surprisingly heavier than he expected. Yuana carried it with such ease he thought it contained nothing but light clothes. She must be a lot stronger than her slim frame suggested.

They were going to Caliraya today for a weekend getaway. Their first ever as a couple. He had booked a beautiful lake-side property. He wanted everything to be comfortable, enjoyable and romantic.

Ten minutes later, she came out with two thermal mugs and handed one to him. Her beaming expression went straight to his heart, as it always did. He would have kissed her properly right there and then, but Celia came into the living room with a set of fishing poles and gear. She handed it to him, and he accepted it with a quick glance at Yuana. It seemed his girl had some fishing activities in mind during this trip.

Another half an hour and they were on their way to Caliraya. It would take about two hours to get there, but he was looking forward to a leisurely drive. They would take a scenic route, a perfect start to a romantic getaway.

They had gone out of town and on nature trips before, but this would be the first time he would have Yuana all to himself for a good forty-eight hours. His heartbeat rioted at the idea. He had to remind himself that this could end up being a torturous weekend for his self-control. Yuana's request to take things easy meant she still dictated the pace of their relationship. When they would become intimate rested on her decision.

***

Yuana was hyperaware of Roald during the drive. The beautiful scenery barely registered in her consciousness. Thank Aquila her thermal mug contained ginger tea rather than coffee. Caffeine would have been disastrous to her nerves.

The atmosphere on this trip was dense with anticipation and excitement. They were both trying hard to remain relaxed, to pretend this trip was just like their previous nature trips.

She would have found it funny if the atmosphere between them was not so thick with tension. The air between them so charged, thunder and lightning would not have surprised her.

She half wished Daniel accompanied them on this trip, like their other out-of-town trips in the past. He was a perfect foil, an effective barrier between her and Roald. But she also wanted to spend the time with him, just the two of them, as most normal couples do.

Why am I nervous?

She had been with men before. *What is so different now?*

She glanced at Roald. His profile to her as he concentrated on driving. His fingers on the steering wheel tapped in sync with the music. She did not even realise they had background music.

What does Roald have that impinges on my psyche?

Why can't I keep a distance from him?

Her heart quickened as she looked at him, her lungs needing more air, and she had to restrain herself from reaching out and touching him. Her mind could not seem to explain it away.

Roald sensed her gaze and glanced at her. Her breath caught when her eyes met his, unable to smile back when he did. His eyes blazed at whatever he saw in hers. There was a split-second pause before they both quickly averted their eyes. Their breathing hitched.

She knew now what made it so different this time—her heart was engaged, and that made her vulnerable as she had never been in her life. Emotions akin to panic, relief and wonder combined ruled her. It was a stunning, terrifying, and exhilarating feeling all at once.

Roald gripped the steering wheel a little tighter to steady the tremors in his hand. The look in her eyes, the fire in them, shook him. Her reaction showed him it affected her too. It gave him hope that maybe this trip would induce Yuana to commit more to him than before.

She continued to withhold something crucial from him, and while he wanted it very much, he wanted her to have no reservations when she finally let go.

He stole a glance in her direction; she faced ahead. Her shoulders were tensed. There was a stiffness in her jawline, and her hand gripped her thermal mug. Her inner struggle was visible to him and his heart ached for her.

He reached over and soothed the hand that gripped the mug, loosening her fingers. This was his way of telling her that all would be fine. After a while, she released the mug and turned her hand over until they were palm to palm. Their fingers interlinked; they were in accord.

And his heart purred.

All at once, the tension eased, and the awareness between them changed. It became more fluid, like a river that found its course.

Two hours later, they were being shown the beautifully designed lakeside villa that he rented. It was airy and well-lighted. The grounds were landscaped with pink bougainvillea, low palm trees, ferns, and small flowering bushes. Two huge ylang-ylang trees flanked the driveway. The boughs were thick with the yellow blooms, their heady scent greeting them as they walked around the grounds.

The side of the house that faced the lake was all glass. A wide covered patio led to an infinity pool, a short boardwalk, and a jetty. There was a red speedboat at the end. The first floor featured an open planned living room, kitchen, and dining area. The second floor housed three bedrooms, the middle being the master bedroom. A long verandah connected the three bedrooms. There was also a jacuzzi at the corner with a small bar attached to it.

The caretaker paused by the middle of the main bedroom and asked him where the luggage would go. He advised him to leave it where it was. He wanted Yuana to decide their sleeping arrangement. And he would give her the time and space to decide, without the presence of a stranger.

The caretaker left them to their privacy to buy the items in the grocery list he had provided the man prior to their arrival. An awkward silence pervaded the room. Yuana was standing in the middle, looking at the bags. He could guess what she was struggling with in her mind.

"Yu, I am going downstairs to check if they delivered the items I ordered for the bar. I will let you decide our sleeping arrangements while we are here. You can have this room. You can decide where you want me to sleep. Just put my bag there," he said.

He gave her a peck on the cheek and left before she could reply. The magnificent ornate four-poster bed in the room was giving him ideas, and it was not the right time to have those.

Bemused, alone and standing in the middle of the room, Yuana took a deep breath to steady herself. Roald had left the decision in her hands, and she was not sure if she liked it. Part of her just wanted him to decide for them, but she appreciated the reason he didn't want to pressure her. He had promised to let her set the pace of their relationship.

Do I want this?

She wanted this from the very beginning, perhaps from the first time she met him.

Am I ready?

With this level of soul-deep intimacy, where all of her would be laid bare—there was no way one could ever be ready for such an experience.

But if she was going to squeeze every joy out of them being

together, if she was going to create beautiful memories for Roald, now would be the right time.

With that realisation, she made a firm decision. She picked up his bag. Roald would find it where she intended for him to sleep.

———

Yuana found him by the bar, mixing them a craft gin and tonic. He figured she needed to relax. He didn't want their stay here to be stressful for her. And he could do with something that would loosen his strung-out nerves and muscles.

He handed her a glass, and she accepted it with a smile. They both took a sip, enjoying the refreshing wash of the lemon, cinnamon stick, and juniper berries on their tongues. The icy burn of the drink down their throat released the tension in their bodies. They sighed in unison.

"What do you want to do first?" He held out his hand to her.

Palm to palm, they ventured out to the front patio, which was conveniently opened for them by the caretaker. The guy's hosting experience was obvious. He knew how to set the atmosphere. There were flowers in the vases, nuts, dried fruits, and chips in sealed glass jars on the bar and the coffee table, fresh fruits on the dining table.

"I want to do so many things, but I would like to explore the lake first. This place is so beautiful," she breathed. Her expression was soft and wistful. He nodded, willing to do anything she wanted to do, even if it was just to sit on the couch and watch tv.

"Let us go boating later, to explore, and maybe to fish. The sun is too high, and it is almost lunchtime," he suggested.

"Okay," she said with a slight smile. Her expression serene. She seemed contented and at peace. And this perplexed him.

Had she decided? And more to the point, what did she decide on?

This would drive him to distraction, guessing what was next. And he couldn't ask her without putting pressure on her. If she decided against it, his asking might change her decision, and he did not want that. He wanted her wholehearted participation. If she had chosen in his favour, the asking might make her self-conscious, and he definitely would not want that.

He was right. This woman, more than his match, would be the death of him.

Lunch was scrumptious. Benny, the caretaker, turned out to be an outstanding cook. He served them fresh fish encased in salt and baked to perfection, along with freshwater prawns sautéed in ginger, chilis and pumpkin puree; fresh garden vegetables: grilled eggplant and okra topped it off.

Roald made sure that every item on the menu was her favourite. He wanted her to know that her everyday comfort, her happiness, was central to his life.

After coffee, when the sun had cooled down, they spent the afternoon cruising around in the lake, with Benny pointing out every notable point. They went home at sunset. Benny wanted to have time to prepare dinner. The air had turned crisp and cool.

They walked hand in hand along the boardwalk and sat outdoors by the infinity pool. Their feet dangled in the water as they waited for dinner time. Yuana had a faraway look. Her gaze turned towards the horizon. He wondered what she was thinking, and if it was the same thing that consumed his thoughts.

"Do you like it here, Yu?" He wanted to know what was on her mind.

"Yes, I do. I love it. Thank you for taking me here," she breathed. A slight colour tinged her cheeks.

"And I love making you happy. So, you'd better get used to it," he said.

And he meant it. His first order of business when they got back home would be to check out properties there. This could be the site of their future holiday home.

She smiled at him; her eyes glittered with a message that he dared not interpret. Again, he was tempted to ask her, but stopped himself for the same reason earlier. Just then, Benny approached to tell them dinner was ready, and he served it on the table by the pool.

Roald helped her to her feet and led her to the table. Their dinner was light and simple but finished with a rich chocolate dessert and red wine. Benny left them to enjoy the night in privacy and retired early in the caretaker's flat at the corner of the property.

The mood was as mellow as the wine, the night fragrant with ylang-ylang and lake water. He watched Yuana's relaxed face. But the fire in her eyes burned hot in contrast with her demeanour, and it fuelled the flame in his belly. He had to take several slow, deep breaths to temper his reaction to her. He wanted her to decide, at her own time, to give him a sign. And if a sign was coming, he hoped it would be as blatant as she could make it, because he doubted his ability to pick it up in his current state.

Yuana stood up, interrupting his thoughts as she pulled her shirt off. He was too stunned to react as he stared at the curve of her back, as she dropped her shirt on her chair. She toed her shoes off and threw him a glance over the shoulder.

"I'm going swimming. Are you coming?" she asked. Her eyes twinkled; her smile enticed.

"Are you all right, Yu?" he asked, worried for a moment she was drunk.

"I feel wonderful, and in the mood for swimming." Her smile deepened. "Coming?" She asked again as she peeled her leggings off and jumped into the pool in her underwear. She had swum across the pool before he recovered his composure.

He took his clothes off and joined her. He cut through the water to her end, where she had one arm draped over the edge of the pool, her chin propped on it, her gaze on the glistening water of the lake. The cricket song, accompanied by unfamiliar bird calls, and the repetitive soft lap of the water over the bank accentuated the serenity of the evening. The scent of wet earth and ylang-ylang perfumed the air.

He did not know what had absorbed her concentration from across the lake, but whatever it was, it gave him the opportunity to observe her face undisturbed. Her profile was irresistible to him. The plump curve of her lips, the fine arch of her brow, the slim line of her neck, all communicated delicacy and softness, and yet, she had an inner strength that he could not fathom. A sense of mystery that he could not comprehend.

Yuana shivered when the icy breeze from the lake swept towards them. Unwilling to break the magic of the evening, he moved behind her, her back to his chest, his arms caged her body for a second before he wrapped it around her. His lips rested on the side of her temple as he enveloped her with his warmth.

He did not want to speak, he just wanted to savour the warmth and texture of her body curved into his. She melted into his heat as she huddled closer into him. Her sigh of contentment struck straight to his soul and strengthened the ties that bound him to her. She turned and looped her arms around his neck. He looked down at her, waited for her to make a move—to give him a sign.

She lifted her lips to his and nibbled at his bottom lip, then soothed the light bites with her tongue. She repeated the action a few more times without haste. He held still for a moment, giving her the liberty to do what she wished for as long as she wanted, but his self-control splintered in an instant. His groan of surrender made her giggle. He cut it short when he clamped his lips over hers.

The kiss was languid, deep, and drugging, slow, and intense. Her plump lips cushioned his own, as his tongue explored her mouth. The velvet licks of hers duelled with his and sent shock waves to his gut. His brain became fogged with sensations, with her taste, her scent, her touch, her essence. It was not enough, but he could not assume more than what she was giving him now.

He ended the kiss to rein in his craving, to give her time to decide. He was not sure if alcohol fuelled her actions, and the honourable part of him wanted her sober, her choice made with a clear head and a willing heart.

She smiled at him and said, "It's chilly now. Let's go in."

He nodded and loosened his hold on her. They both swam back to the other side of the pool and got out. The chilled air made her shiver as she collected her clothes and the dessert dishes on the table.

He stopped her. "I will take care of the dishes. Go in and shower."

He took the dishes from her hand. When she hesitated, he gave her a gentle push toward the house. She complied and hurried inside.

As he placed the dishes in the sink, he realised he volunteered for this task not just because he wanted her comfortable, but because he didn't know where he stood. The kiss, while incendiary, was not a clear enough sign for him, and he didn't want to assume.

He stopped outside the door of the master bedroom and listened. His heart pounded as he stared at the doorknob. He would be disappointed if his bag wasn't there. He erred on the side of caution and moved to the room next door. And with bated breath and figurative fingers crossed, he opened the door and looked. His bag was not in this room.

There is another room to check.

He moved to the other room, his breath held, as he opened the door. The sight of the empty room blanked out his mind and weakened his knees at the clarity of her decision. Straightaway, his desire surged at the certainty that Yuana had chosen to spend the night with him.

It took him long moments to process that he did not know how to proceed. He was like an untried boy on his first sexual experience. It unsettled him. With his own heartbeat ringing in his ears, drowning all the other sounds around him, he entered the master bedroom quietly. The sight of his bag on the luggage rack confirmed his conclusion, and his heart thudded against his chest.

The muted sounds of the shower penetrated his hearing. Images of Yuana showering flooded his mind's eye. And his already tightly held breath hitched further. The door to the bathroom was ajar, and he didn't know what to make of it. He wasn't familiar with her habits, so he did not want to assume it was an invitation.

With care, he dropped his shoes and shirt on the luggage rack, while trying to decide what to do. He heard the sounds of Yuana finishing her shower; she turned the water off. The brief silence that followed was an eternity as Yuana emerged from the bathroom.

And his breath stopped altogether.

Barefoot, naked, her long hair sopping wet. The dripping rivulets travelled down along her curves and left moisture beads in their wake. It was all over her shoulders and her face glistened with it. A long, white bath towel clutched in her hands as she patted her face. The rest of it hung between her bent arms, shielding from his gaze, her stomach, and the rest of the sweet valley between.

Her eyes, visible above the towel, were on him. The fire in them blazed hot with a challenge. She looked like a woman on a mission.

For a moment, he felt like a prey.

Yuana's heart hammered so fast, she could not think beyond the desire that pooled in her core. She decided hours ago and had been in a state of anticipation since. But she played it cool as she did not know how to proceed, how to tell Roald without sounding contrived.

She had left the bathroom door open, with what she hoped was an invitation he would pick up on, but it wasn't clear enough for Roald. It seemed he was keeping his promise to follow her pace. She would have to make the first move.

He stood bare-chested by the bed when she came out. His sharp, indrawn breath was an echo of hers. He stood transfixed by the sight of her, just as she stood frozen at the sight of him. She had seen him shirtless before, but tonight was different.

Roald swallowed as his eyes travelled along her body, taking in the sight of her sopping wet and naked. She was immobile, caught in his gaze as it moved back to her face. The raging flame in those eyes reached out to her. His desire was almost palpable, his frame rigid with tension.

He took one step closer, then another, until scant inches separated them. His body heat reached out to her, his breath on her face was warm. She could smell the slight scent of chlorine on his skin.

"Are you sure of this, Yuana?" His voice was quiet, deep, and gruff. His eyes never left hers.

"Yes." Her own voice was gravelly, her throat seizing up.

His lips moved closer, almost touching hers. "Last chance to change your mind... There is no going back after this," he murmured against her lips.

"Do you want me to change my mind?" She crossed the scant inch between them and pressed her lips to his.

And that was the trigger that unleashed Roald. With a groan and a brief expression of relief, he pulled her into him and sealed her mouth with his. One of his hands cradled her nape, and the other rested at the low of her back. Both arms tight bands around her, an unbreakable and welcome prison. Her hands were flattened against his hard chest, the towel trapped between them. As their kiss deepened, his shoulders hunched, his arms tightened to press her closer into him, as if he was trying to absorb her.

They ate at each other's mouths. Her blood thickened in her veins; her heartbeat rampaged in her ears. Roald broke the kiss. His lips travelled across her jaw and neck, the growing bristles on his chin abraded her flesh. His lips settled on her lobe as he lightly nipped it; it sent shivers up her spine. Her core turned liquid, her knees buckled. An involuntary moan escaped her lips.

The tip of his tongue soothed the tortured flesh, and it travelled back to the corner of her mouth. He lifted his head. The thumb of the hand that held her nape moved towards her lips, massaging it softly. His eyes darkened, pupils dilated, as he watched her swollen lips throb in reaction.

He drew in a shaken breath. "Jesus, Yuana..." He groaned as he swooped on her lips again.

The kiss was ravenous, almost violent. But just as abruptly, he broke the kiss and moved to her collarbone, his mouth rubbed, then sucked and licked at the vulnerable line from shoulder to her cleavage. She was melting inside like a hot chocolate, her ability to think liquefied with the sensation Roald was subjecting her to.

Roald's questing hand encountered the trapped towel between them. He loosened his hold on her and whipped it away. He discarded it to the side and left her naked in front of him. His indrawn breath as he appraised her body, locked her own breath in her lungs. With reverence, he stroked his knuckles down from the dip that connected her clavicle to her throat to the valley between her breasts.

In response, her eyes closed as she followed the sensation of his hand as it travelled down her body. Her belly spasmed in anticipation when it rested on her belly button. Her arrested breathing synced with his touch.

When her shoulder blades touched the cool wall, her eyes jolted open; Roald had backed her against it. His mouth was on hers again, and gave her deep lashes of his tongue, as his kiss turned gentle but intense. Her eyes closed again as she drew breaths from serrated lungs. It was like drowning. His own gasps for air fuelled her excitement further.

His weight settled on her, and the button of his jeans pressed against her. She was naked against his half-clothed self. It spurred her on. Her hands fumbled at the buttons at the waistband of his jeans.

A hand stopped her. "Wait, Yuana... I won't be able to control myself..." he groaned; his face pained.

"It's a challenge for you then," she breathed, undeterred. He had no hope of stopping her.

"I want to make it last forever," he said, his eyes closed as he tried to control himself. His hand still on hers, holding it flat against his waistband.

"We can have the forever later, I have no patience for it now." She wrenched the button off his jeans. His surprised look at her ferocity and strength reminded her of her nature and his. She gentled her action. He pressed into her in response, his hardness imprinted on her flesh.

Before she could react, quick as a flash, he turned her to face the wall and pressed against her back. She gasped at the shocking sensation of the cool wall on her sensitive nipples. Behind her, Roald kept his palms flat on the wall, his weight pressing her body against it, his hips undulated into her. The movement aroused her further.

Then his lips landed at her nape and rained small kisses and quick licks down her spine, vertebrae per vertebrae. Goosebumps raised on her flesh, her back arched in response. His lips stopped at the last bone, his hands were gentle as he cupped and caressed the cheeks of her bottom, his thumbs grazed the underside of her feminine folds. He brushed the sensitive seam with light and repeated strokes. Her insides clenched. He paused what he was doing, and she almost whimpered in protest.

He turned her forward, her eyes opened at the swiftness of the move. Roald was on one knee in front of her. He looked up at her. His eyes blazed with passion and hunger. His warm tongue traced the shape of the under-curve of one breast. Her fist clenched. Then he did the same with the other. His gaze never wavered as he watched her reaction, as he learned what would elicit the most ardent response. His tongue continued its foray down to her belly button, and past that. She sucked in her breath. The muscles of her stomach tightened as she waited and hoped for what was coming.

But Roald resisted the temptation her writhing body offered, and his lips and tongue moved to the hollows of her inner thighs. From her hipbone down, his kisses traced a fiery line at the edge of the delta of her desire. It drove her crazy. He repeated it on the other side, and it pulled a whimper from her lips. Her plea for completion came out in a sob.

When he finally gave her what she was asking for, he kissed her feminine core like he would her mouth. Deep, slow, exploring licks and laps, his lips soft and insistent. Her juices flowed, her hands grasped his head in reflex, as she held him in place. She could not stop herself as she pressed him deeper into her, while her hips arched towards him in a blatant offering of herself. It was an encouragement, a plea for what she wanted so badly.

Her inner thigh muscles trembled, her knees weakened, her stomach tightened.

"Ro, please..." she implored.

He lifted his lips from her flesh, and with stunning speed and fluid motion, he scooped her up and deposited her into the middle of the bed. He stripped off his own jeans in record speed, his face dark with passion and determination. Roald loomed over her before he lowered himself between her parted legs, his arms hooked under her knees.

Then the velvety tip of his erection, hard as steel, prodded her feminine lips slick with her own juices. She held her breath as she waited for him to penetrate.

"I'm sorry, Yu, I cannot wait..." he groaned against her neck before he breached her in gradual, relentless degrees.

The slick slide was like an eternity with the slowness of his entry. It made her aware of every silken inch of him. They both exhaled in relief as he pushed in. Her breath held as he stilled when she absorbed his full length. They were groin to groin, and she felt full everywhere. Then his hip flexed, and it made her gasp. Roald groaned and started a slow pull out, a reverse journey within her. Her own inhale of excitement echoed his own as he pulled out almost to the tip.

Again, and again, he repeated the movement. His back muscles were like velvet steel in her hands. His breath caught when her hands touched the hard cheeks of his bottom as she grabbed it for purchase. She responded and met his thrust. Her legs wrapped high up his back as she arched into his down-strokes. His lips captured hers in a kiss so combustible, his tongue mimicked the measured thrust of his hips.

Over and over. He stroked in and out, his face strained with the effort to prolong the moment. The cord of muscles on his back knotted. A slight quiver ran through his entire body, just as the tremors in her abdomen signalled the inevitable peak, their breaths in unison against each other's lips. The slow, deep glide was delicious, her insides turned slicker by each entry and withdrawal. It was both too much and not enough. She wanted more of it.

"Deep and slow, Ro... more..." she heard herself implore him. It was so good; her heart was expanding to bursting point.

Both their breaths quickened, their heartbeats in tune as the blaze raged on. Roald's long strokes shortened, faster and faster, tighter and tighter. And at the last second, he pressed as deep as he could go, his groin pressed so hard into hers she felt fused to him. Her core quaked and waves of sensation burst forth from where they were joined. A floodgate of emotion rushed at her, from her, and carried her away. She could not find purchase, and it left her consumed, her energy sapped.

When her awareness returned, her emotions were so high, she could cry. She felt undone to her very core, raw and exposed, and there would be no recovering from it.

Roald slumped over her body, his weight a heavy but welcome load. Their limbs felt boneless and melted into each other. She was enveloped by him, surrounded by his presence. She relished it. Her arms went around his neck and claimed him. It was glorious and poignant at once. His arms tightened, slow and unwilling to move and withdraw from her. They remained locked in each other's arms until their breathing evened out, and their bodies cooled.

As the air turned chilly, their bodies no longer protected by the heat of their passion, Roald shivered. She rubbed his naked back to warm him. He rolled off and took her with him, then tucked her to his side, and pulled the covers on top of them.

After a moment of silence, he kissed her temple and sighed, "I am sorry, Yu. I lost my head," he whispered.

"No need to apologise. I was not exactly in control of my faculties as well," she murmured.

"Give me a moment to recover, and I promise to do better," he said, a teasing note in his voice.

"Give me that same moment, and I will require you to do better."

He laughed softly, kissed her ear, and levered up on his elbow to smooth the damp hair from her face. There was tender satisfaction on his. He rubbed her lower lip with his thumb for a moment as he scanned her face, then he bent and kissed her with reverence.

"Know this, Yuana..." he said, his voice serious. Propped on his elbow, his eyes fierce, his expression solemn— "You have my heart, irrevocably, completely..."

Her heart reacted in response.

"And you have mine," she replied. It took everything in her to keep the sadness from her voice.

"I am glad to know that..." His arms drew her closer into his body as he laid back down. "After tonight, there is no going back," he said, his tone possessive.

"Yes, there's no going back..." her soft reply.

There would be no going forward either...

And her heart broke anew.

4

THE DE VIDA DILEMMA

Roald was excited about today's lunch. Their second anniversary was coming up. And he needed to fish for some information from Yuana about what she might appreciate as a gift. He also wanted to gauge if she was ready to move their relationship to the next level. At thirty years old, he was ready to marry, and there was no one else in this world for him but her.

Normally, he would pick her up from her office, but since her meeting was in the building next to his, they agreed to meet instead. He could not help but smile at the memories this place evoked. This was the venue of their first dinner as a couple.

After two of the most blissful years of his life, no one could fault him for wanting to level it up now. He wanted to complete his happiness by asking for her hand in marriage. He could give her, perhaps, a year of engagement, and then they would get married.

He was watching the door for Yuana's arrival when Daniel entered with some friends in tow. Daniel waved at him in greeting. He waved back. Dan separated from his two companions and approached his table.

"Hey bro! Long time, no see!" Daniel joked. They were at the regular tech meet up the night before.

"I know, you gained weight since I last saw you." He thumped Daniel on the shoulder.

Daniel laughed and patted his flat stomach, "It's the Guinness last night, they're a killer."

"Here for a meeting?" he asked. The two guys who came with Dan, now seated at a distant table, were looking in their direction.

"Yeah, they're founders of a complementary IoT. We are checking if we have synergy," he replied. Dan looked around and noted Yuana's absence. "Waiting for Yuana?" he asked.

He nodded. "Yes, she's on her way. She's coming from a meeting in the building next door."

"Okay. I shall say hi later when she arrives." Daniel was about to join his own party, when impulse prompted him to stall his friend.

"Dan, I'm planning to ask Yuana to marry me," he said in a suppressed tone despite his excitement.

Daniel looked at him in surprise, his face wiped of all other expressions. He had the impression Daniel was not in favour of it but was too polite to say so.

"Weren't you guys taking it slow?" Daniel's tone was tentative.

"It will be our second anniversary in less than two months, Dan. Surely, two years qualify for slow." He felt defensive about his position.

"That seems like a big jump. Why not live together first?" Daniel asked.

"Yuana is not in favour of that. Believe me, I asked multiple times, both in jest and in earnest." He had asked her more than a dozen times. He thought it was the surest way to convince her he was excellent husband material, but she opposed the idea. Her family, according to her, did not approve of such arrangements.

"Do you think Yuana is ready?" Daniel asked, rational as ever. His comment was spot on, a testament to how well Daniel knew Yuana. And it gave him pause.

"Ah... You got me there... I'm not sure. She seems content with what we have."

"Well then, I suggest you test the water a little, and not ask her outright. That will save you the awkwardness on your second-anniversary dinner," Daniel said, with his usual dry humour.

Yuana's arrival saved him from replying, a sweet smile on her face when she spotted him. They both faced Yuana as she approached. Their body language signalled identical warm welcome.

After an exchange of hugs and some teasing banters, Daniel left them to their privacy to join his party seated at a table across the room.

Daniel spent the first half of his lunch meeting distracted with thoughts of Yuana and Roald. If Roald asked for Yuana's hand in marriage, it would be the beginning of the end of their relationship. He wanted to tell Roald so, but he was in no position to warn him. He was not supposed to know. And he could not speak for Yuana. This was between the two of them.

He witnessed how happy the past two years had been for both of them. It seemed the perfect middle ground for Yuana's situation. Their relationship was something Yuana needed, and Roald's marriage proposal would stop all that.

He hoped Roald would listen to him and be careful about this marriage business. Even if Yuana, for some miraculous reason, married him, Roald had no idea what he would get into. Roald knew nothing about living with an *aswang* or marrying one and having children that would all be *aswangs*. The mental, emotional, and physical toll it would require from Roald would be beyond anything he could imagine. He himself, an *erdia*, a half-blood child of a male aswang, and familiar with living the viscerebus life, refused to get into it.

The more fundamental concern for him, though, was Yuana. Her life was about to turn bitter, the one thing she avoided for so long was now upon her. And the knowledge pained him.

He was not a dessert person, but to soothe his anxiety for his two friends, Daniel ordered Murder by Chocolate and a strong coffee to settle his nerves.

A decision he regretted later; caffeine was not exactly calming.

"Home, miss?" Her driver's question jolted her from her thoughts. He was looking at her from the rear-view mirror.

She nodded. "Yes, please."

He nodded his acknowledgement, and soon, they were on the road.

She settled back against the leather seat. The hum of the running car provided the background noise that cancelled the sound of the busy Manila traffic. Her brain returned to its previous preoccupation as they travelled towards home.

The scene at lunch replayed in her mind on a constant loop since she got back from it. Any normal woman would have been happy to find out her man was thinking about marriage, that he wanted their lives linked forever, and yet, to her, it felt like an indictment.

Roald did not ask for her hand outright; he made a casual comment about it, but the effect of that comment was jarring. She had smiled and replied it was too serious a topic to discuss over lunch. He laughed and dropped the subject altogether. But this did not reassure her. His proposal was imminent, she was sure of it. He may even spring it on their anniversary, less than two months from now.

The timer to their relationship had counted down. The deadline to make the choice - to leave him or to break the *Veil of Secrecy*, was now upon her. A choice she could not make from day one, despite thinking about it from the beginning.

Perhaps her family would have insights, solutions, different options...

Yuana sat down in her usual seat at the distinct square table that sat eight. The rest of her family walked into the dining room led by her grandfather Edrigu, who held a bottle of a good Bordeaux. They would have liver for *sustenance* tonight, judging from the wine her grandfather decanted.

Her mother and grandmother were talking about an upcoming party hosted by a new family who joined their *Gentem*. Her great grandparents were discussing a new Tribunal ordinance proposal that needed more study. They were all waiting for Aunt Ximena to arrive from the hospital.

Their family conversations, as usual, were engaging. Tonight, however, her concern was interfering with her ability to integrate herself into their midst.

By the time the small cooler that contained their *victus*, the daily sustenance arrived, everyone was ready and waiting by the dining area. They passed the raw liver around as they all took their individual portions. That done, they sat down to dinner.

Their routine always followed the same flow: easy banter throughout the meal, all serious topics were not to be discussed until dessert. Her great grandmother insisted on it.

As the leche fritas were served, Yuana tapped her wineglass with her dessert spoon to signal she had a serious business to discuss. All eyes turned to her, expectant and encouraging. It gave her the courage to pose her concern straight on.

"Mama, Roald brought up the subject of marriage over lunch today."

The table became quiet. Her family exchanged glances. They all understood the gravity of the subject.

Abuelo Lorenzo, her great-grandfather, reached over and gave her hand a reassuring squeeze.

"What do I do?" she asked when no one said anything.

"We have measures in place, but it will all depend on the steps you will take when the proposal comes," her Abuelo Lorenzo said.

"I do not know which step to take, 'Elo. Roald may not be like us, but I love him, I trust him, and I think he can handle our truth. That he can accept it..."

Her Abuela Margaita's gaze was gentle. "Yu, we understand how you feel, and you are not the first in the family who had to go through this. We really like Roald, but this is beyond love, beyond trust. We need assurance that he could uphold the *Veil*. But the more crucial question for you — would he adapt to our way of life?"

"I believe he can handle it, 'Ela. He loves me..." She heard her own desperate plea for them to support what was in her heart. Although she had her own doubts, she needed for them to give her the answer she wanted to hear.

"We know, we have seen how he treats you, how he looks at you. But can that love withstand the truth of our nature? And beyond that, will he be able to live in our world?" her grandmother Katelin interjected, her face reflecting worry.

"Yuana, do you realise Roald's life will never be the same the moment you tell him?" Aunt Ximena's expression was grim. Out of everyone, she looked most concerned. It was understandable. Of all the women in their family who had the misfortune of falling in love with a human, she suffered the most.

Everything they said, Yuana already knew in her heart. She was looking for a justification to allow Roald into their lives. But the consequences of doing that, if it did not work out, would be fatal to the De Vidas. And to every single one of her kind.

"So, Yu, is Roald capable of all that?" her grandfather Edrigu asked, his gaze probing, his brow furrowed. She was his baby girl, and knowing she would go through the same painful path her mother did, hurt him.

"I'd like to think he can, but, in all honesty, I am not sure." How could she predict how Roald would react to a truth that could shake the foundation of everything he believed to be true?

"Can you not delay this? Give it more time? Is there a need to rush the marriage?" Her mother's tone was gentle and sympathetic. She, of all people, knew what lay before her.

Yuana sighed. "I guess I can delay it. I suspect he will not propose until our second anniversary, and maybe I can delay it further by having a long engagement..." Her mind wanted to grasp at something that could keep Roald in her life for as long as possible.

"Yuana, no. Don't use the long engagement tack. It will be more painful as he will expect a wedding. It will crush him when you break it off, eventually. I should know..." Aunt Ximena cautioned; her mouth thinned into a bitter line.

"Don't jump the gun, Yu. Sure, you discussed it earlier, but you need not decide tonight. It seems to me he mentioned it to you because he wanted to gauge your eagerness to get married. He hasn't formally proposed yet, right?" her mother asked.

Yuana shook her head. "No, but I dread the time when he does. I cannot say yes, and I do not want to say no... I'm not sure I can say no..."

"Well, *apo*, since he hasn't asked you, you do not need to think about it yet. Let us enjoy the dessert. There is not much we can do for now," Abuela Margaita said. Her ever-practical side on display as she tried to lighten things up.

Everybody nodded. But the leche fritas remained untouched on their plates. The coffee went cold in their cups. And with a deep sigh, her grandfather Edrigu opened another bottle of red wine.

The following day, Ysobella got to work distracted. She was worried for her daughter. Yuana would face the same dilemma she struggled with twenty-eight years ago. She had chosen to keep the *Veil*, to protect their kind, and walked away.

She hurt the man she loves, one who loved her very much. Galen would have been a devoted husband and father to Yuana had their situation been normal.

She still thought about the what-ifs now and then. And it never failed to bring her down. And like before, she pulled herself out of her misery by the reminder that her life was good. She had a wonderful daughter and a loving family.

That should be enough.

As she stepped into her office, her assistant Luisa greeted

her with her cup of coffee, made exactly how she liked it. Luisa set her coffee down on her desk and handed her a white, embossed business card. She sat down without looking at the card.

"Ms Bella, a visitor is waiting for you in Meeting Room One, a certain Dr Galen Aurelio." Luisa pointed to the card in her hand.

Dr Galen Aurelio.

Her brain reeled. It knocked the breath out of her lungs.

How did he find me?

After all these years?

Luisa was still waiting for her answer.

"Okay, I will be right there. Make him some coffee," she instructed, her mind still blank.

Luisa nodded and left.

Her heartbeat was deafening, and it became harder to draw breath. Her mind, no longer blank, was now in churning chaos.

What did he want?

Why is he here?

She found herself in front of the door of Meeting Room One with one dominant thought - to see Galen again.

The narrow pane of glass by the side of the door gave her a partial view of the man who owned her heart. He looked the same, albeit older, his thick hair peppered with silver strands. His jawline, still as cut, his shoulders as wide as she remembered. The ache in her belly intensified.

She watched him pick up the cup and take a sip. The surprise on his face after the first sip made her realise Luisa made him *her* coffee. And it was exactly as he preferred it, how they used to enjoy it in their distant past.

He cast a searching glance towards the door and noticed her. He froze.

She saw both recognition and confusion and knew he was

questioning his own vision. She had received that look from people only a few times in the past, and it had always made her feel defensive.

With a deep breath, she stepped into the room with a smile. Her external mask donned—the façade of Ysobella Orzabal.

"Good morning. I'm Ysobella Orzabal, how can I help you?" she said in a pleasant tone, her hand held out in a handshake.

Galen hesitated a bit, but took her hand, and clasped it longer than necessary as if he was trying to determine who she was just by the touch of her hand.

"Dr Galen Aurelio," his brief reply.

He continued to stare at her. She could tell that he was trying to assess how old she was— thinking that she was too young to be Isabel; she could be Isabel's younger sister or daughter. She looked far too similar to Isabel Gazcon. His former fiancé.

"How can I help you, Dr Aurelio?" she asked, a smile still plastered on her face.

Her stomach still clenched. She knew what Galen wanted to ask from her. The same questions she faced a few times in the past from acquaintances who used to know her in her youth.

"This may seem untoward and strange, but are you related to Isabel Gazcon? You look so much like her." Galen's hands trembled a little.

He released her hand with reluctance. Ysobella was glad he did. She was half afraid that he would be able to feel the racing pulse beating in her wrist.

"Please take a seat," she said, feeling the need to sit down herself.

They both did.

"Why are you looking for Isabel Gazcon, Dr Aurelio?" Her calm tone belied the state of her composure.

"I will be blunt, Ms Orzabal, as I am a desperate man. She and I almost got married at one point, at least until she left without a word. And I have been looking for her for almost three decades." Galen's blunt reply gave her pause.

"What brought you here, to my office?" How he found her was still a big question.

"It was a lucky coincidence. Yesterday, as I waited for my driver to pick me up in front of the hospital, I saw a familiar face across the street. The face of the woman I had been searching for all my life—and it was you. I had my driver follow your car all the way to this building. I sat there for a long time, trying to decide what to do. This morning, I decided to call in cold."

Galen's tone was flat, but the emotions in his eyes flashed with meaning so clear she could read the hope he felt then, his disappointment now, and the resurgence of the hope that he would finally discover where Isabel was.

And at her silence, he continued, "You carry a similar name. Is she your mother?" His gaze fixed on her face.

"She is not here, Dr Aurelio. She retired in solitude in Spain." Her standard response was one that every one of her kind prepared and practised for, designed to evade the question and direct it to another matter.

"I must see her, Ms Orzabal. It is why I came back to the Philippines. It is my sole goal in this life left to me." Galen's voice intensified.

"What do you mean by 'life left to you'?" She frowned.

"I am dying, Ms Orzabal. Prostate cancer. And I want to spend the rest of my life with her if she will be generous enough to allow me."

The revelation took her breath away. Galen was dying. She

did not realise just how vital it was for him to be alive and well in some part of the globe, and how much that knowledge sustained her over the years.

"Tell Isabel I will not ask about the past, why she left me. We do not have to discuss it. I just want to be with her." His plea vibrated with determination. "Is she married, Ms Orzabal? To your father? Is your father still alive? Is this why it is not possible to see her?" His anguish was unmistakable.

That could have been her exit. She could have ended it right there if she had confirmed 'Mr Orzabal' is alive and married to Isabel Gazcon.

All she had to do was nod. But she shook her head instead, unable to speak.

Buying time to compose herself, and on impulse, she took his hand. "Come back tomorrow, Dr Aurelio. Let me ask her first."

Galen's face lit up with hope. He stood up and pulled her in for a hug full of gratitude. Her heart sank. The dilemma has come back to haunt her.

With a vengeance.

Ysobella worked all day in a daze. She had called her Aunt Ximena for advice. They called the family for a teleconference over lunch. Food was delivered at Ysobella's office, while Ximena dialled their group chat window on Ysobella's laptop.

One by one, the family members came online, except Yuana. They left her out of the call on purpose. Ysobella preferred to tell her daughter face to face later.

"Oh, Bella, what is the emergency? Are you okay?" her grandmother Margaita asked. She sat with her grandfather, Lorenzo. They were getting ready for lunch at home.

Her mother and father came online next. Her mother, Katelin, was putting away some papers her father, Edrigu, had signed.

"Oh, Bella, you seem worried, what is the matter, Hija?" Her dad noted her distress.

"Pa, Galen found me."

"What?" Their reaction came in unison. No one was interested in lunch anymore.

"How?" her grandfather asked.

"He came here this morning, 'Elo. He thought I was Isabel Gazcon's daughter, and he begged to see her." She could not hide the plea in her voice.

"What did you say to him?" her grandfather asked.

All eyes were on her.

"I told him Isabel Gazcon is spending her retirement in Spain." She felt like she was standing on a precipice, a temporary holding place before she had to make the jump.

"So, what is the problem?" her father asked, aware that something else was coming.

She did not know what to say, or how to say it—what was in her heart now that she was facing the De Vida dilemma once again. But her family waited with patience for her to speak again.

"You face the choice again..." her mother guessed. A knowing glance reflected in her eyes as Katelin recognised the pain on her daughter's face.

"He is dying, Mama. Prostate cancer. His only wish is to spend the rest of his life with me." She could not suppress the sob of agony in her voice.

"Oh..." Her family's surprised reaction was identical. They exchanged looks between them. Everyone understood the gravity of what was facing her. They had watched her suffer the last time.

"What do you want to do, Bella?" her grandmother asked.

"I love him, 'Ela. I never stopped loving him. And I do not think I have the heart to walk away again. Not this time." Her chest ached with the effort to control her emotions.

"So, what are our options? Maybe you can stay with him for a while? Spend time with him until... the end..." Her father suggested, his pragmatic nature on the surface.

"I do not know how long he's got, and I do not want to hide the real me from him this time, Papa. He needs to meet his daughter. I want him to know about Yuana before he finally leaves me." A hint of defiance coloured her tone, but she could not help it. At this moment, Galen's needs were more important than every other consideration.

No aswang could live with a human for more than a few weeks without revealing their true nature. To live together with a secret that big would be a near-impossibility.

"You know the dangers, Bella, what is at stake. We all advised Yuana last night to take it easy, to take her time until she is sure. So, I pose the same question to you - how sure are you of Galen?" There was a gentle caution in her grandmother's voice.

It calmed the manic thoughts in her head. As usual, her grandmother brought back her ability to think beyond her feelings.

"Ela, my heart tells me I can trust him. But I will not jeopardise us, so I will try to reveal as little about us as possible. Perhaps I will start by talking to Yuana. She deserves to meet her father." That decision, at least, felt right.

"Okay, Bella. We will discuss this later, over dinner," her grandfather said wearily.

And a unanimous nodding of heads closed the family meeting, for now.

That night, the De Vidas lingered over dinner. The dessert was served in time for Yuana's arrival close to midnight. Her daughter came home late from her dinner with Roald.

The De Vidas greeted Roald warmly, almost like a member of the family. He was a solicitous boyfriend to Yuana, and they knew how much love there was between the two. This worried all of them, but they could only brace themselves for the pain the youngest member of their clan would go through when the time to choose came. They could only be there to protect her, help her pick up the pieces and start anew. Just as they had done for generations.

They watched discreetly as Roald tried to prolong the night. The young couple displayed their reluctance to part. It did not matter that Roald would see Yuana in just a few hours, as it had become his habit to pick her up in the morning to drive her to work. They all suspected Roald bought his condominium unit because it was a mere ten minute drive from their compound. With Roald gone, Yuana went to the kitchen with her family. There was time enough to discuss during coffee and dessert.

"Are we discussing Roald?" Yuana asked, as she sensed that something was amiss. She looked around the table. All eyes were on her.

"Not really, Yu-Yu, but it's the same dilemma," Ysobella replied carefully, gauging how to broach the topic to her daughter.

"What do you mean, Mama?" Yuana's brows knitted, her dessert spoon poised over her dish.

"Your father is back, Yu... He found me this morning..."

"What?" Yuana's mouth fell open, her gaze darted to

everyone around her. Her face reflected a gamut of emotions at the news. "How?"

Yuana knew her father's identity, had seen the photographs, read the reports and newspaper clippings of Galen, had heard the stories about him. Her shock must have come from the idea of meeting him. With the action that her mother took decades ago, it was a given that Yuana and her father would never meet.

"He came to my office this morning, looking for Isabel Gazcon. He thought I was the daughter of Isabel Gazcon..." She related everything that transpired in her office to Yuana.

It stunned Yuana. "What did he want? Why did he go looking for you after all these years?" Yuana asked, breathless. The glitter in Yuana's eyes reflected the suppressed joy that bloomed in her heart for the chance to meet her father.

"He said he has been searching for me for years. And he came to the Philippines as he needed to find me." Her own longing and the repressed dread bled into her voice.

"Why? Why did he need to find you?" Yuana's brows furrowed deeper. There was wariness in her daughter's tone.

"Your father is dying, Yuana. He begged me to take him to Isabel Gazcon. And he wants to spend the rest of his life with me." Her throat felt tight as tears pooled in her eyes.

"Oh, Mama! I am so sorry..." Yuana launched herself from her seat and hugged her.

When her daughter drew back to look at her face, understanding dawned in Yuana's eyes. Her daughter read what was in the deepest recesses of her heart. Time and distance changed nothing. She loved Galen with all of her being then, and she still did, perhaps even more so.

As she wiped her tears, she read the thoughts that registered on her daughter's face. The similarity of their situation, the timing, could not have been more obvious.

Yuana looked around and saw the grim faces of her family. They all witnessed how much her mother suffered from that break. And how much this recent encounter with her father broke open the dam of emotions her mother kept bottled up inside ever since.

Her grandfather pressed a white handkerchief into the palm of her mother, who dutifully used it to dry her cheeks. Her grandfather stood behind her mother's chair and stroked her back, imparting comfort and strength.

When her mother calmed down, she sat back down on her chair and asked, "So, Mama, what is your plan? What are you going to do?"

"I want to introduce you to your father, Yuana. If you allow it. I want to make it up to him for all the years I have stolen from both of you."

Her heart leapt at the idea of seeing her father, of finally getting to know him.

"You stole nothing from me, Mama. You did what you thought was the right thing to do. And yes, I want to meet him too." She hugged her mother again, too full of emotion to say anything else.

"So, Bella, what is the plan?" Katelin, her grandmother asked. Her family appeared to be well-apprised of her mother's decision, and they were just waiting for the details.

"I will take it slowly. I will start by introducing Yuana to her father. Hopefully, it will suffice, and I would not need to go further than that," Ysobella replied.

There were collective slow nods all around, except her great grandmother, who was staring at her mother. There was understanding and worry in her gaze.

They waited for her father in the VIP corner of the coffee shop at the GJDV building. Yuana was both excited and scared. What she knew of him and their relationship was from the stories her mother told her, some pictures of them together, old letters, newspaper clippings and articles. He was a top-notch neurosurgeon based in New York, and he was supposed to be married. Now it would seem that the marriage was over since he came looking for her mother on the last days of his life.

An elegant, matured man walked through the front door of the coffee shop. Yuana recognised him because he looked like the photos she had seen over the years. Photos her mother collected to keep tabs of him as he lived his life on the other side of their world. But even without her visual knowledge of her father, she would recognise him by the tension that entered her mother's body when he entered the room.

For a split second, it surprised her to see he was much older than she expected. His hair flecked with silver, his face dignified and lined with experience. Then she remembered her father was human and not a viscerebus. He would age faster than their kind.

The wait staff greeted him, and after a brief exchange, he was led towards the VIP room where she and her mother sat waiting. Galen Aurelio looked as apprehensive and excited as both of them. Her mother was at the edge of her seat.

"Ms Orzabal. Thank you for this." He smiled at her mother and extended his hand. She took the offered hand, and he enveloped it between his.

"Thank you, Mr Aurelio. This is my daughter, Yuana." Her mother gestured towards her. Her smile was tight as she held out her hand. Meeting her father was more nerve-wracking than she thought it would be.

Galen smiled into her eyes and enclosed her hand with both of his. "It is a pleasure to meet you, Yuana. You look as beautiful as your mother."

Her heart tightened in her chest. Her father did not know he was clasping his own daughter's hand.

"Please take a seat, Mr Aurelio." Her mother gestured towards the seat between them. The service staff came in with three steaming coffees and some small sandwiches and set them down on the table. Her mother had ordered them for the occasion.

The staff drew the wooden blinds closed to give them privacy as they left. They sat in tensed silence for a few seconds. The ticking of the clock seemed loud, the coffee and sandwiches ignored.

Her mother broke it, "Can I call you, Galen, Mr Aurelio?" There was a tiny tremor in her voice. She seemed unsure on how to start the discussion, and setting the names straight was the easiest path to it.

"Oh yes, please. It will make me feel young to be on a first name basis with you young ladies," he replied.

Her mother's smile did not reach her eyes.

"So, what did Isabel say? Did she agree to see me?" Galen asked, looking at her mother.

Her mother looked back at him; tears pooled in her eyes. She took a deep breath, closed her eyes, and replied, "She did... She's here."

Galen sat up and glanced at the door, but no one was coming in. He looked back at Ysobella and saw tears streaming down her cheeks and realised the truth. He saw past the close similarities in her features, the acknowledgement and shared memories in her eyes. This was his Isabel, in the guise of Ysobella Orzabal.

He pulled her out of her chair and enclosed her tight in his arms. The feel of her against his chest triggered all the memories of their past. Her scent was the same, and she held him just like before. He had his Isabel back.

His own. Finally.

Awareness pricked at the back of his head as he remembered Yuana and realised why she was here. Yuana was crying too, and he dared not believe what was going through his mind, the conclusion it was forming.

He eased Ysobella out of his arms to gaze into her eyes. "Is Yuana mine?" he asked. Ysobella confirmed with a quick nod, her gaze apologetic and apprehensive.

He smiled at her, dropped a kiss on her lips, and turned towards the daughter he had just met. A gift he did not expect. He held out his arms, and after a slight hesitation, Yuana went to him. He enfolded her in his arms, his heart so full of love and gratitude, it was almost impossible to contain them.

His eyes closed at the glare of the bright sunlight rays that penetrated the slits between the curtains. He felt the heat of the rays against his face. It felt like a miracle was bathing his soul with warmth. His heart was full to bursting.

Sometime later, they sat down and fortified themselves with the cooling coffee. They were all exhausted from the emotional upheaval. There was silence while they nibbled on the sandwiches and processed their own thoughts and feelings.

Ysobella sighed and glanced up from contemplating the bottom of her cup, to him. He looked back in response.

"I know you have questions, so ask away. I promise to answer everything I can—" Ysobella's words were a mere breath.

As he looked at her, all the unanswered questions were

running rampant in his mind, answers he was aching for yet afraid to receive, clarifications that may be painful to hear, so he asked the easier questions first.

"How is it you look as young as when I first met you? You didn't seem to have aged at all."

He thought he saw a slight flicker of panic in her eyes, but her smile was sweet. He must have imagined it.

"Genetics, healthy living, diet, exercise, medical procedures, the whole shebang," she replied. "I will tell you more about the whole shebang when the time is right," she added, a sad-looking smile on her face.

"Okay." He lifted her hand and pressed a kiss on it. He understood she was not ready to open up to him yet. The same reason that made her run away from them years ago remained. And he was determined to know what it was, to eliminate it, because he did not want to die without receiving her heart in full, just as he would make sure she received his.

He turned to his beautiful daughter, who was misty eyed while watching them. He examined her face and wonder expanded his heart. This young woman with very youthful looks, the perfect mix of his features and Ysobella's, this girl that was life's ultimate gift to him.

"This explains why my daughter is stunning. Thank god for the wonderful DNA you obviously shared with her," he said.

Yuana's short and embarrassed laugh escaped her as she dabbed her eyes with an embroidered handkerchief.

"Did you tell her about me?" He turned back to Ysobella and asked with no rancour in his heart.

Ysobella sighed and nodded.

"Yes, I told her as much as I can, although I must admit I did not want to build you up too much in her mind, as I was convinced, I would never see you again. I did not want her to miss the father she would never meet," Ysobella said in a slow, tentative tone, as if she was cognisant of the pain those words might trigger in him.

She was right. A slight measure of resentment rose in him, but he quashed it on purpose, as he had no more time for anger and resentment. He needed to squeeze as much love and sweetness out of the remaining days of his life.

"So, what is next, Bel? I am not sure what your plans are but... be warned I will accept nothing less than us being together." His tone had hardened. He wanted her to know his full intent.

Ysobella smiled and replied, "I intend for us to be together, Galen, you and me, and Yuana. As a family. But I hope you will allow us to ease into it and not jump headlong. We haven't seen each other for twenty-eight years, and you have just met your daughter."

Impatience rose in him. He felt possessive and greedy for the time and presence of his Bel and Yuana in his life. He wanted them with him every hour of the day. Especially since his clock was running out. But he understood the awkwardness created by those years of separation. So, he would be patient, up to a point.

For now, he agreed.

"Would you allow me to schedule activities for us? I want to spend as much time as possible with you and my daughter." He looked at his woman and child, and gladness suffused his heart and spread all over him.

"How about we make breakfast or lunch a family affair, so we see each other every day?" Ysobella suggested.

"Yes, I would love that. But I want dinner to be our special time, Bel."

"Let's start now and spend lunch together as a family. The beginning of the rest of our lives. Now, allow me some time today to cancel all my commitments." Ysobella said in a fervent tone.

That was a reasonable request.

"Fair enough." He smiled back at both of them. He glanced at his watch and saw it was close to lunch. "It is almost lunch. What is our game plan? Where do we eat?"

For him, he'd just started to live. The past decades were on pause, and now that he'd found his Bel, his life could begin ticking on again, joyful, and meaningful.

"Can you tell us about you, Sir? What have you done in all those years? Do I have any brothers and sisters?" his daughter asked. The questions were full of excited curiosity.

He reached out and touched his daughter's hair, felt the silkiness of her tresses. He was still trying to take in the reality of his beautiful daughter sitting in front of him.

"Call me papa, if that is okay with you?"

Yuana nodded, a smile on the plump lips she inherited from her mother.

"I never married, Yuana. I spent my time working and looking for your mother. This year, I retired..." He glanced at Ysobella; he was not sure if she told their daughter about his cancer.

"I know about your cancer, Papa. Is there anything that could be done?" Yuana said.

"I'm afraid I have run out of options. I have checked every conceivable medical cure science can offer, including those not available to mere mortals. Remember, I am a doctor." It was poignant that his remaining time on this earth would be the happiest and the most heartbreaking.

"Did you ever have any other relationship after us?" Ysobella asked. It told him she would not begrudge him if he had, because she was the one who walked away.

He weighed how much of the truth he was going to share

with her. "I tried, Bel. After two years of looking for you with no success, I thought it was time to move on. I even had two long-term girlfriends. They were both doctors too. But work was always in the way, and my heart wasn't in it. We parted ways as friends." And that was the truth.

Ysobella's eyes widened, then a line of pain appeared around her mouth. Her eyes brimmed with emotions that seemed like they might explode but she held on to her self-control.

It moved him.

"I stopped looking for your replacement five years ago, Bel," he added, unable to stop the need to push her over the edge.

"I didn't even look for yours, Galen."

The image her words created made his heart expand in magnitudes he could not fathom. Her pain was as excruciating as his, her wound as fresh. His throat tightened, unable to say anything. Restrained by his daughter's presence, he could not haul her into his arms. He lifted her hand to his lips instead and crushed a kiss at the centre of her palm.

The kiss contained every promise, every apology he could offer, and every restitution he would collect from her for the time they were apart.

———

Yuana watched in silence, aware at this moment she was outside of their thoughts. Her parents were so in love then, but unable to be together. This was what she and Roald would face, their situation so similar. The enormity of the pain she and Roald would go through had unfolded right before her eyes, and she did not know if she could put both of them through that.

That evening, a subdued De Vida family came one by one to the dining room. The setting of the table was extra special. It was a momentous occasion, and they would decide on something important tonight.

There was no bantering over the steak and kidney they were having, the steak barely touched, and all of them nursed a glass of burgundy. Everyone was waiting for Ysobella to speak.

All eyes swivelled to her when she placed her glass down, their gaze solemn.

"I need to spend as much time with him, and it might affect our routine..."

"Do you have a plan? How can we help?" Margaita, her grandmother asked. The realities of their lifestyle, the challenge it posed to them over the centuries, were all too present. And it had to be faced every time. As the matriarch of the De Vida clan, her grandmother always took the lead.

"He wanted to spend as much time as possible with me and Yuana. Practically every hour of the day," she replied. She wanted them to hear her willingness to give Galen what he needed.

"Even dinner time..." Her grandfather Lorenzo's remark was not a question, but an acknowledgment of the fact.

She was sure her grandparents had already discussed this earlier. They always functioned as a team. And they both knew what was in her heart.

She nodded, confirming what they guessed.

"So, what's the plan?" Ximena, her aunt asked.

As usual, her supportive aunt was as willing as the rest of the family to accommodate her request. They just needed to ensure it would be safe. As the one in charge of the logistics of their victus, she would orchestrate all the changes needed to ensure this would work.

"I will take a light load at the office. I will go there only when necessary. Uncle Íñigo can handle my work in the meantime. I will live with Galen, so we can spend breakfast or dinner with him. Lunch will be with Yuana. This way, I can eat here either breakfast or dinner..." Her voice trailed off. She suddenly realised how difficult this would be to orchestrate.

"It is far better for you to stop by here before your dinner with him, during cocktail hour, perhaps. We can adjust our sustenance time, or the manner of how we take it, we just have to be careful. You can dine here now and then so we get to know him, and vice versa," her grandfather suggested.

"You can even bring him here during weekends. For an entire day. It would make this family affair more traditional," Katelin, her mother suggested.

Her parents wanted to assess the man their daughter had given her heart to. One who might be the first-ever non-viscerebus part of the De Vida clan, even if it was only temporary.

Her parents exchanged glances. Her father's expression told her he saw this partial integration of Galen Aurelio into the family leading to more.

Edrigu Orzabal, their *Gentem's Chief Iztari*, was in favour of bringing Galen more closely into their midst but wanted to determine the potential danger it might pose to the family. Her father, notwithstanding his position in the local Tribunal, had their security as his key priority.

"Mama, won't Papa ask why you left?" Yuana voiced the one nagging question in her head as they were discussing the plans. Their family was loving and given that they would welcome and accept Galen, the question of why she left would not be far behind.

"He said he wouldn't..." she replied. But uneasiness crept back in.

"He might not ask, but he will always wonder," Ximena said with forewarning.

"Yes, he will. And I am not sure what to say to him yet, but I will try to delay the truth until the very end. Hopefully, being happy together will be enough." She wanted to reassure everyone, despite knowing she was hoping in vain. Galen was not the type to leave issues unresolved.

And just like that, they found the simple solution to her logistical problem without exposing the family and their daily habit of eating raw human organs. It was a simple plan, one that might work for them.

The limited time available to Galen assured the exposure would be temporary. Maybe they could create a new procedure out of this, one that may even work for Yuana's situation.

She could tell that Yuana felt hopeful for Roald and herself, their relationship, their future, for the first time in a long time.

<hr>

That same night, Yuana helped her mother pack her essentials. There was no need to pack a lot, as her father's hotel was not far. They had decided Yuana would stay at home to allow her father and mother time with each other, but they would meet for lunch without fail, and spend weekends and several activities together.

They worked in silence for a few moments, but Yuana could not stand it. She voiced out what was bothering her, "Mama, how much time do you and Papa have?"

"Not long enough, Yu-Yu. He could live to be a hundred, and it's still not going to be long enough." Her sigh was deep. "I will always be left behind. Our kind always is when we fall in love with people like your father..."

"Is there a way to make Roald, and Dad, like us? Any old folklore or myth, perhaps?" It was a silly question, but she had to ask.

Ysobella shook her head, a small sad smile on her lips. "None that I know of. We are born this way." She shrugged. "And even if there is a way, would they want to? Voluntarily and whole-heartedly?"

They both know maybe Galen and Roald would say yes because of love, and because they would not understand exactly what they were getting into.

"I wouldn't ask Roald, Mama, even if I am sure he would say yes."

"Well then, Yuana, we must endeavour to make their lives with us the happiest ever. This way, our love for them will be worth the pain it will cause them."

Without further words, they finished packing Ysobella's small luggage. Tomorrow, her mother would move in with her father. And the morning would bring something new for the De Vidas. No one in their past had ever come back with such compelling reason for them to even consider exposing what they are.

For Yuana, tomorrow felt both scary and exciting, and it felt inevitable.

The air in the well-lit embalming room was thick with the smell of antiseptic. Two men, both dressed in light blue poly laminated scrubs, goggles, mask, blue wellington boots, and gloves, occupy it together with a newly deceased body of a woman lying on the embalming table.

The atmosphere in the room was light despite its morbid purpose. One man was humming *'Born to be Alive'* as he cleanly took out the liver, kidney and heart from the body brought down to the mortuary not more than half an hour ago. His work took mere minutes, his movement practised and economical, his skill clear as he wielded the scalpel.

Once finished, he separated the organs and placed each into small iceboxes lined with clean, white china trays. The boxes were on a low table beside him. All three were numbered. He placed the heart in the first box, and the kidney and liver in the other two. Once done, he peeled the gloves off, dropped it in a sanitised container, then closed the lid of the iceboxes. He then motioned to the other guy to take over the body.

Then he stepped out, taking the ice boxes with him. His destination would be the embalming room next door. He had harvested *victus* from six bodies already and had six more to do before his day ends. Today's organ harvest would be given to the *Eastern Sustenance Delivery team* in charge of distributing them to their recipient.

With the first man gone, the other man started preparing the embalming fluid with a mixture of formaldehyde and several other chemicals. He picked up on the song the other guy was humming, and he ended up humming it himself. Soon, the sound of the embalming machine filled the room as he worked with the body.

The sight of the fresh liver earlier made him hungry, motivating him to move faster. The liver was his favourite sustenance.

5

THE FAMILY

G alen woke up early and had been pacing the living room of his suite for two hours as he waited for the clock to strike nine. He would meet his wife and daughter for breakfast. In his heart, Bel was his wife, and he would make sure it became a legal reality this time.

It was hard not to regret the lost years, or blame himself for failing to pursue a more exhaustive search in the Philippines. He would have found her earlier.

There were still twenty minutes to go before nine, but he could not stand it anymore. He went down to the private room in the breakfast outlet of the hotel.

Yesterday, he'd spent the afternoon looking for gifts for his two loves, to mark the day they officially became a family. He had wondered if Ysobella was still partial to emeralds and if their daughter took after her. He realised he knew no one he could ask about his wife and daughter.

In the end, he got his girls matching necklaces of platinum and emerald. He wanted it bespoke, but there was no time, so he had offered the top end jeweller a considerable incentive to convert beautiful emerald earrings into pendants. The twin necklace would be ready by noon.

Ten minutes to nine, he saw Ysobella's car pull over to the front of the hotel lobby. He saw his Bel alight, followed by his daughter. They were both wearing light silk dresses, his Bel in blue, and his Yuana in lavender. The two women held hands, as if to fortify each other, and together, walked through the lobby doors, where he was waiting in breathless anticipation.

His daughter was beaming; Ysobella's face was calm, but her eyes blazed with emotion. There was an answering lump in his throat. His eyes never left Ysobella's. He didn't even realise he met them halfway, as he pulled them both into his embrace. They embraced him back as tightly. He kissed their foreheads and marched them towards their reserved breakfast outlet.

He felt like a schoolboy, unable to contain his excitement as he sat them both. "I've ordered the breakfast for us; I hope you do not mind. There will be something for everyone."

The silly grin would not leave his face.

"We do not mind, Papa. Everything will be great, I am sure... How was your evening?" Yuana asked.

She wanted to calm her father down and give her mother a chance to recover from her emotions. Her mother was never speechless until now.

"I didn't sleep a wink, otherwise, a splendid night." Her father's eyes darted between her and her mother.

He could not seem to get enough of staring at them. The intensity of his gaze made her mother blush. The intimacy of that exchange made her feel like an interloper into their world, where only the two of them inhabit.

Mercifully, the food arrived, and it was a veritable feast.

It appeared her father ordered everything on the menu and more. A lady wheeled in a trolley laden with the hot coffee pot and three mugs, a small sauce bowl with melted chocolate, and an even smaller one containing mint syrup.

Startled, she watched her father prepare coffee just like how she and her mother preferred their cup. Her dad served them their cup like he had been doing it all their life.

"Thank you, Galen," her mother said with uncharacteristic shyness.

The smell of the coffee infused the room. She could see this was an old, shared experience between her parents, one that encapsulated all the sweet memories of their relationship, one that sustained her mother over the years. This was how her mother introduced the brew to her. Now, she understood the value of it.

As she cradled her own cup in her hands, the hot bottom of the porcelain warmed her fingers, she thought of all those nights when her mother sat alone. She always had the same coffee in her hands, her face wistful. Her mother must have been reminiscing about their old memories together and dreamed of all that could have been between them.

They were contented for now as they savoured their coffee in silence. Breakfast was a lighthearted affair, an unspoken understanding that the hard questions would come later.

It was surreal to be sitting here with her father again, to have their second chance, arranged by fate in a neat package of a breathtaking beginning and a heartbreaking ending. One her mother accepted with both hands and a very open heart.

The courage it took, the strength it required from her mother, took her breath away.

In the past three hours, she discovered much about the man who stole her mother's heart. Her father exhibited a wicked sense of humour. His anecdotes about life as a surgeon had them laughing. His interests varied from physical pursuits like sports to intellectual ones.

He beamed throughout; his eyes crinkled at the corners when he laughed. His voice was deep and had a natural rasp to it. He was attentive and affectionate. She saw what her father was like when he was younger and why her mother fell in love with him.

Galen Aurelio, apart from being good-looking, was a magnetic man. He also had the natural ability to read through her mother's often enigmatic aura. They were well-matched.

While her father talked about his life and every other subject under the sun, he seemed to avoid any mention of their separation. It seemed a conscious effort on her father's part, which meant that it was at the surface of his mind, and he was just giving them time. Her mother's plan to avoid the truth until the very end had no chance of succeeding. She was sure the reckoning would come much sooner than later.

A text message from Roald reminded her she was to meet him for lunch. He informed her he would be fifteen minutes late. She did not expect their breakfast to roll into lunch, and for a moment, she was tempted to invite him to join them. She decided against it. To introduce him to her father would add roots into their connection and would make a clean break harder to achieve. The thought dampened her happiness.

"Mama, I have to leave you two lovebirds alone. I need to meet with Roald, and I have to pass by the office first... Is it okay, Papa?"

Her father nodded, too happy to be upset. She suspected the prospect of being alone with her mother was more than adequate compensation for losing her company for a few hours.

"No problem, Yuana. But make sure this Roald guy is worth giving up your time with me..." He teased and chucked her under the chin. She kissed him on the cheek, did the same to her mother and picked up her bag.

———

Roald found Yuana gazing out into the vast, well-manicured grounds of the GJDV garden. The mini lake glistened at a distance. A wistful expression on her face. But he was far too excited to share his news with her.

Lost in her thoughts, it startled her out of her reverie when his lips landed on her shoulder. She swivelled; one eyebrow arched. She knew by instinct he had something wonderful to share with her.

"You've got delightful news?"

"Yes, I closed my Series A round! I got Access Capital's confirmation they will invest the final one million US into my company!" He pulled her out of her chair into his arms and swung her around.

"Congratulations! I knew you could do it!" She was as breathless as him.

He set her down on her feet and kissed her. His lips warm and gentle, the kiss brief but intense. His arms still locked around her, he contemplated her flushed cheeks.

"That was why I was late. They asked for a last-minute call..."

"It's okay. I will always wait for you," she replied softly.

She seemed surprised at her own words, like she did not mean to say something dramatic but could not help herself. He frowned, his eyes searched hers. Yuana had always withheld a bit of herself from him. He was aware of this from the beginning, and it was a driving desire to tease it out of her until she was open to him. In the three years they had known each other, he thought he was succeeding, until the other day when he mentioned marriage.

He saw the familiar panic flare in her eyes. It was a kind of fear that resembled desperation, and it scared him. But then she teased him and remained quite relaxed during the meal. He thought he just imagined it and pushed it out of his mind. Now, the same niggling feeling was back. But he would not push, he would be patient.

"You seem bothered today. Did something happen?" He tilted her chin up when she glanced away. "Tell me."

"I met my father yesterday. He found my mother." Her response was almost a whisper, but it shocked him.

"Wow! Really? That's big."

"It is. It has been twenty-eight years since my parents last saw each other." Yuana looked sad and subdued.

"How do you feel about this? Are you okay?"

She nodded. Then a soft smile appeared on her lips and it widened, her eyes, misty. His heart clenched at the sight.

"Yes, it was like a surprise gift. It was unexpected, but it was a wonderful welcome thing." There was wonder in her eyes that glittered with emotions.

"When did you meet him yesterday? Why didn't you mention it to me last night?" He wanted to be the first person she would go to when momentous events in her life happened and was a little disappointed that she did not.

"I'm sorry. It was overwhelming. And I was more concerned about my mother. She had never stopped loving him."

He kissed her forehead in apology. *I am a selfish heel.*

"So, what was he like?" He might need to impress this other significant man in Yuana's life.

"Oh, he's wonderful. He's smart, funny, charming, and very

handsome." She sounded like a girl in her teens, describing a matinee idol.

"So, when are you meeting him again? Is he visiting? Or staying here?" He was very curious now. He needed to find out how to approach the guy who would be his future father-in-law.

"We had breakfast with him this morning. Mama is moving in with him, but I will stay at home because we all agreed they need their time together alone. But he insisted on seeing me and having meals together every day." Her words came out in a rush, her delight was obvious.

"That's understandable, since he hasn't seen both of you in almost three decades. So, how long is he staying here?"

"He's planning to stay here, in our lives, for the rest of his... And I hope it is going to be a long life." The sadness that had touched her eyes earlier returned. "He is dying," she added, and there was a catch in her voice.

"Oh, I'm so sorry, Yu." He wrapped her in his arms once more. His heart ached for her.

He realised he would need to give her time to get to know her father better. And that he could not press for marriage yet, at least not for the next few months.

Yuana needed to be a daughter first, for both her parents, more than be a woman for him. As for himself, he needed to be her man during the coming days.

What's a few months, anyway, when they have a lifetime together?

Within his arms, as her cheek rested on his hard chest and inhaled his scent, Yuana was both comforted and saddened. Her mind kept wandering between her parents and her own situation with Roald, her heart vacillated between hope and despair.

Maybe with the return of her father to her mother, there would be a way for her and Roald to skip the separation part, avoid the pain Roald would be subjected to.

If fate would not be kind to her, then she and Roald would be in for a lot of suffering. But for now, she should not think about it.

Her father's entry into her life should take precedence.

—————

Galen sat in comfort, coffee in hand, on the lush sofa in Ysobella's office. He watched her sign the mountain of documents on her table. Ysobella told him they were memorial plans, and they needed signing so they could issue the policies to the buyers.

He was relieved when he found her, happy for having her and Yuana back into his life. He felt light and happy for the first time in decades. As he contemplated his next steps to convince her to move in with him, the need to find out why she left him in the first place rose in his mind. He tamped it down as he promised her in the beginning that he would not ask about it. And he knew this outcome came about fast because of that promise.

He did not want to break his word, but the need to know had grown stronger. He was sure Ysobella still loved him, maybe as much as he did her. And pushing for the truth this early might make her retreat from him again, so it was more important to secure her promise not to leave him again.

With his strategy fixed, he became certain what his next step would be.

He watched her finish the documents. Her assistant Luisa

came and took the stack that she signed, then left the room. The atmosphere turned electric as they realised they were alone.

Galen unfolded his tall form from the couch and approached her. He could see the slight nervous tension in her body, how she was using the worktable as a shield between them. Galen smiled at her. He had no intention of allowing walls, physical or emotional, to come between this woman and himself ever again.

Time and distance had done that to them for twenty-eight years, but even that did not sever their connection, no matter how hard she tried.

Ysobella's heart rate quickened at the expression on Galen's face. She felt like a cornered prey as Galen walked closer. He leaned on her desk and loomed over her.

"All done for the day?" he asked, looking down at her with a trace of relish.

She nodded and busied herself with putting away her stuff into the drawers as she tried to slow her heartbeat down. Earlier, she went through the motion of signing papers with her mind abuzz with mixed emotions. Excitement, apprehension and dread made her signature less and less graceful as she signed document after document.

Meeting her family tonight was more important. They would try her grandfather's plan - to proceed to their house to introduce Galen to her family, have some cocktails, then dinner. It was stressful to think that her family would meet Galen tonight, but not as nerve-wracking as the idea that Galen was going to meet her clan.

But it was the after-dinner plan that was making her

jumpy. She felt like a teenager anticipating her first kiss. The idea of her moving in with him afterwards stole the breath from her lungs every time she thought about it.

Then add her anxiety over the question she was still unprepared to answer - why she left him. He would ask it, and it would be a lot sooner than she would be ready for. She could see the unvoiced question in his eyes every time and sensed his effort to stop himself from asking.

Galen halted her jerky movements with a touch. He lifted her chin to peer into her eyes. "Are you afraid of me, Bel?" he murmured, his voice low. His breath smelled of coffee and mint.

"No... just nervous, I guess..." It was time to face the music. "Let's go?"

She stood up, moved to collect her bag from the side table beside her work desk, and turned expectantly at Galen.

For a split second, he seemed like he wanted to press her, but let it go.

Margaita was satisfied with the spread in the tapas bar. The Spanish wine selection from their cellar would pair well with them. It would be a casual evening, as formality might just make everyone nervous, and trigger questions that could not be answered satisfactorily, much less truthfully.

Tonight's sustenance would arrive in half an hour, and everyone would be home by then.

Everyone was worried about the outcome of tonight's event. The last time they allowed a human into their clan was two hundred years ago. While this would be a temporary situation, the danger to their clan would be real. As the Matriarch of the *Philippine Gentem*, her decision to allow her granddaughter to bring a human into the family was dangerous, and borderline irresponsible.

But her granddaughter's happiness was at stake. Her support was not even in question.

While the choice was hard, the family agreed they would support Ysobella for this brief grab at happiness. They all witnessed how she suffered when she broke up with Galen years ago. If it was not for Yuana, they were sure Ysobella would have given up.

And in all those years afterwards, Ysobella never moved on from Galen. She stopped dating people outside of their kind, and they harboured hopes she would fall in love with someone else, but it never happened. Her heart remained aloof, disengaged.

And now, it seemed like her great-granddaughter could be on the same path. Maybe the return of Galen into their lives would prepare Yuana for what she would face when the time to choose comes.

Lorenzo came into the dining area as she was checking the decanters for the red wines. Her preoccupation was clear, and her husband understood what was distracting her. He took the wine opener from her hand and took over the decanting of the Rosado and Rioja.

Ximena, their oldest daughter, was on her way and should be home in five minutes. She would have their sustenance at hand, a job that was usually Ysobella's would be Ximena's or Katalin's for the unforeseeable future.

"Are you ready, *Cara?*" Lorenzo asked. Familiar admiration filled his eyes. She smiled back at him, her own gaze appreciative of him and the love they shared despite more than a century of being together.

They heard the front door open, followed by the voice of Yuana. Roald would be with her, as it was his usual habit to drive her home. Hand in hand, they walked out of the dining room to greet their great granddaughter and her boyfriend. Yuana and Roald both turned in their direction as they entered the living room, welcome on their faces.

As they reached the young couple, Roald took her right hand and bent down to touch his forehead to her knuckles. "Mano po," Roald said. He repeated the gesture to Lorenzo. This act of respect was the first thing that endeared Roald to them the first time they met him. And he had been consistent in his respectful manner for two years.

"Good evening, Señor and Señora Ibarra," he said.

"Good evening, Hijo," Lorenzo replied. She nodded her acknowledgement. They said nothing more. They were not sure if Yuana had invited Roald to join them, or if she kept the event within the family.

While Lorenzo engaged Roald in conversation about his tech business, she threw Yuana a questioning look - *did she invite Roald to the family cocktail event?*

At the uncertainty in her great granddaughter's eyes, she decided for her. She was certain Yuana would introduce Galen to Roald at a certain point, anyway. It would be better not to create tension between the two young lovebirds while Yuana was buying time for both of them.

Yuana's turmoil would make the Galen situation harder to deal with as a family, especially for Ysobella and Yuana. It was best to deal with one situation at hand. The fate of Yuana and Roald's relationship could wait.

She turned to Roald, and with an inclination of the head, said, "Hijo, I hope you would join us tonight. We have a special family cocktail, as Yuana's father will finally be introduced to us."

Roald was surprised and threw Yuana a questioning glance.

"She didn't know, Roald. It's a last-minute plan," she said.

Yuana threw her a grateful smile.

"It would be my pleasure, Señora. But allow me to go home for a quick change, I am not dressed for it," Roald said. He appeared thrilled at the opportunity to meet Galen Aurelio.

"You look fine, Hijo. But if you feel you need to, the cocktail is in 20 minutes. Will you have enough time to change?" Lorenzo asked.

Her husband did not think it a good idea to include Roald tonight, but he trusted her wisdom, so he would defer the questions till later.

"I can make it, Señor. I live only a few minutes away," he said with a confident smile. He gave Yuana a quick peck on the lips. "See you in a jiffy, Yu." He hurried out to his car.

Yuana gave her a hug. "Thank you, 'Ela. I am so glad you read my mind."

"You're welcome, Yu-Yu." She touched Yuana's face, to ease the slight frown on her great granddaughter's forehead. "Take your mind off it for now. We need to deal with your father first. There is no rush, so delay as much as you can. And while you are at it, enjoy each other. Squeeze every ounce of joy that you can while it lasts and make him as happy as he can be while you are together. It is the least you can do for him..."

Within the circle of her arms, Yuana stood in silence thinking on her words. She could see that it was the most viable path for Yuana for now. She knew that her great granddaughter would never put them in danger on purpose. A breakup with Roald would devastate her. Her family was vital to Yuana, but Roald had become vital to her life, too.

They turned around towards the sound of an unfamiliar car at the front driveway. Yuana's parents had arrived.

Immediately after, the sound of Ximena's car followed. They could hear them chatting in the entryway as the door opened. At the sound of excited chatter, her youngest daughter,

Katelin, and her husband, Edrigu, both came out from their room and leaned over the railing to confirm that their daughter Ysobella and Galen had arrived.

They rushed down to meet their visitor.

Four generations of De Vidas offered a warm welcome to Galen Aurelio and admitted him into their midst, but not into their inner sanctum, yet.

Galen would have to prove himself to them first.

The living room was awash in excitement. The introductions were brisk. Her father interacted well with her family. Nita, their long-time housekeeper, brought out the drinks, followed by her daughter, Celia, who was carrying the canapes. And in the middle of the merry crowd, her great aunt Ximena slipped into the kitchen with the small cooler of sustenance she carried home daily.

These were the people she would endanger if she broke the veil. Her great grandparents, her grandparents, her aunt, her mom. And everyone who was part of the GJDV company along with their household staff, who had been serving the De Vidas for generations. All part of her extended family.

Tonight was a celebration for her parents, so she would stop her miserable thoughts and enjoy with the rest. With resolve, she pasted a smile on her face as she waited for Roald to return.

One by one, members of her family slipped to the kitchen to take in sustenance. When it was her mother's turn, her father reached out a hand to stop her, a quick gesture of inquiry. Her mother murmured a response that satisfied him. She herself was just waiting for Roald's arrival before she took her turn.

Soon enough, she heard Roald's car pull over. He'd showered by the looks of his damp hair and wore a charcoal grey round-necked shirt, dark grey coat, and distressed jeans. He looked like the successful tech entrepreneur that he was. Roald hesitated at the door. He appeared uneasy and out of place in their family gathering.

She met him as he crossed the doorway, held out her hand to him and pulled him into the living room towards where her father was chatting with her grandfather, Edrigu. They were talking about their shared love of Kali.

"Papa, I would like you to meet someone." She touched her father on the elbow to get his attention. He turned, beaming, then his gaze moved to the tall guy beside her.

"Ah, so this is the famous boyfriend, Roald," he boomed.

Her father seemed happy to meet the man who had taken a significant position in her life. He extended a hand to Roald.

"It is my pleasure to meet you, Sir," Roald replied and grasped the extended hand.

"It is my pleasure as well, young man. My daughter seemed to have chosen well."

On that score, she was confident her father would have no cause for complaints. With Roald's left arm still around her, a possessive hand rested at the low of her spine. He glanced down at her. His eyes told her that no words could convey the depth of his feelings for her.

And a lump of emotion lodged in her throat.

Galen caught their exchange and noted their body language. Her father's knowing look told her it warmed his heart to see his daughter would be in excellent hands.

When her father started engaging Roald in a conversation, she took it as a cue to take her sustenance. Celia had been giving her signals for the last ten minutes. She reached back on Roald's hand resting at the small of her back and squeezed it, then eased out of his arms. He looked down at her in inquiry, and she pointed to the kitchen. He nodded in acknowledgement and let her go.

On her way to the kitchen, she thought... this could work.

Celia was waiting for her and handed her a small bowl containing sustenance, a slice of a human heart.

"Yu-yu, here you go," Celia said, her own bowl set by the sink.

"Thanks, *Manang*! Have you had yours?"

Celia nodded.

Yuana swallowed the slice and took a gulp of red wine to wash the smell from her breath.

Five minutes later, she walked back to the living room, refreshed and strengthened, ready to enjoy the company of her family with Roald.

By the threshold of the kitchen door, Yuana noticed how her family seemed to meld well with her father and Roald. This scene should be enough to make anyone in her position feel happy, but dread hovered ever-present in her consciousness.

Roald was chatting with her mother, who stood beside her dad, her father's arm around her waist as he kept her close. She observed from a distance; she did not make any sound or movement, but Roald seemed to have sensed her presence. He turned towards her; their eyes locked. They were thinking about the same thing.

They both wanted the kind of love her parents have for each other. Timeless and boundless, undimmed by distance and years of silence.

He extended a hand towards her; he wanted her within his reach, as if he missed her. She walked towards Roald, needing the same thing, and they both sighed as their fingers touched.

As the evening progressed, Galen noticed how close Ysobella's family were, how attuned to each other's thoughts and feelings. They were warm and friendly, and their care for each other deep and genuine.

He had met no one whose great-grandparents were still this active, this youthful. Ysobella's grandparents could still be mistaken as her mother.

While they exuded a casual, lighthearted vibe about them, he sensed a brittleness in that façade. There was a mystery lurking in Ysobella's family. He realised this may have something to do with the reason Ysobella left him years ago.

As the night deepened, Ysobella's nervousness increased. It was ridiculous. She was a grown, experienced woman of sixty-five, not a debutante on her first date, or worse, like a virgin on her wedding night. She had not been celibate, so there was no reason to be uncertain.

What made this so difficult?

Because my heart is in it.

That was what made all her sexual encounters in the past casual, why it made no impression on her. It was all a meaningless act. This time, as it had always been with Galen, her heart was more than engaged. Since the beginning, he had owned half of it.

Her mother, Katelin, must have sensed her nerves were as taut as a violin string. The family already knew, and they all supported her decision to spend time with Galen, but having seven pairs of eyes watch her leave with him tonight would be a bit nerve-wracking. Her mother engineered an exit that made her choice very natural, almost commonplace.

Aunt Ximena quit the event first. She announced she had

an early start the next day for a surgery scheduled at nine a.m. That was a signal for everyone to wrap up. The living room started emptying in the next half hour.

Her grandparents followed suit and announced they needed their beauty sleep. There were exchanges of hugs and kisses as the three prepared to leave the living room with the stragglers. Her parents lingered on, finishing their drink to help wind down the evening.

Roald took his cue and finished his drink. "Yu, I need to be going as well." He turned to the rest of the party, said his thanks, and bid them goodnight. Yuana walked him to the front hallway and entry door, as was their habit every night.

With Roald gone, Yuana said goodnight to her grandparents and then to her father. They agreed to meet for breakfast every day at her father's hotel. He had chosen a hotel that was conveniently close to their office and home. Finally, she kissed her mother goodnight and whispered good luck in her ear.

For Ysobella, the breakfast conversation, and the departure of Yuana, made her decision to leave with Galen tonight less awkward. At least until she realised she had not discussed it with Galen at all. Now, it seemed like the wrong time to ask Galen if he was okay if she moved in with him.

What if he said no?

It struck Galen he did not know how tonight would end, as he had not discussed it with Ysobella earlier. He was far too preoccupied with the joy of being with her the whole day he took for granted how it would end. They discussed their daytime activities and interaction but realised now he should have at least clarified with her what the plan was after dinner time.

The night was at an end, and more than a few minutes of

lingering would make things more awkward. So, he winged it, hoping he read Ysobella's intent well enough.

He turned to Ysobella, and with feigned casualness and calm, said, "Shall we say good night to your parents so they can rest?"

His statement was open to her interpretation on purpose, and he hoped she would agree with him. She nodded, uncertainty in her gaze. So, he pressed on and decided for both of them.

"Thank you for the lovely evening, Mr and Mrs Orzabal. It has been a pleasure to have met all of Bel's family." He shook Edrigu's hand firmly.

"It was a pleasure to have met you too, Galen." Ysobella's father's grip was equally firm.

He shook Katelin's hand, and they both thanked and wished each other good evening. With his arm around Ysobella's shoulders, he turned to her, and said, "Shall we?"

He hoped his meaning was as clear as his intention. She nodded.

"Yes, let's go." Her smile made his heart leap.

He expected her to ask for a few moments to pack some personal items, so it surprised him when she moved towards the foyer. He followed, and only then did he notice two elegant suitcases standing by the door. His heart leapt higher at the thought his Bel had decided since last night to move in with him. His Bel was as impatient to resume their long-interrupted life together.

And gladness pervaded his soul.

Edrigu watched Galen all evening.

The man appeared to be decent, intelligent, honest, dignified, and truly in love with his daughter. His background and credential remained as impeccable as before, when he first met Ysobella in the US. Probably even more so now as he had become a world-renowned neurosurgeon.

He had Galen's background rechecked and updated since he resurfaced into his daughter and granddaughter's lives. The Iztari network in the US came up with nothing negative about him so far.

Earlier, Galen was startled when he realised something about the De Vidas. As Galen's eyes scanned everyone's faces, deep speculation on his face, Edrigu thought Galen was getting closer to the tipping point.

The man would ask questions soon. He would give it forty-eight hours at the most before Galen demanded an explanation about the peculiarity of the De Vida clan.

The drive to the hotel was blessedly short, because Ysobella had turned quiet, and it made him uneasy. She seemed to dread the rest of the evening, and the atmosphere between them became filled with tension.

Soon enough, they arrived at the hotel. He introduced her as his wife to the front desk when he asked for a second card key. It came out so naturally. Perhaps because he had always seen her as his spouse, but the reminder of the lost years pained him.

The trip to their room, her hand held in his, was tensed. Inside their suite, as they waited for their luggage, she stood in the middle of the living room. Her body telegraphed unease as she perused her surroundings. Galen stood by the entrance as he weighed what tack to take to ease the tension between them.

Since they left her house, she was on edge. Her body vibrated with unleashed energy held tight.

A knock on the door announced the doorman with Ysobella's luggage. Galen directed him to bring the luggage into his bedroom. The second bedroom in the suite would remain unused, or at least reserved for Yuana when she stayed over. Their life as man and wife would begin as soon as he had sorted whatever was bothering Ysobella.

After the doorman left, he found Ysobella, still standing in the same spot, looking flushed and more uncertain than ever. He walked towards her and pressed her down to sit on the couch. He sat beside her and held both her hands in his, warming them.

"What is the matter, Bel? Why are you so nervous?"

He wanted to know what was bothering her, and how to make it go away. And he could not help unless he found out what was making her so skittish. He leaned close to her until their foreheads were almost touching.

"I am not sure... I just am." Her honest reply made him smile.

He took her face between his hands to ensure she would not avoid his gaze, so she would not misunderstand his intention. "Bel, we will do nothing you are uncomfortable doing. I am willing to wait. Just don't make me wait too long. We have wasted enough time."

She took a deep breath and nodded.

"For now, I just want to have you with me, hold you while you sleep, and fall asleep with you. Is that okay?"

Again, she nodded.

"And know this — nothing you can tell me would make me not want to be with you. Not even if you and your family run a criminal enterprise, or have bodies buried in your backyard, or torture kittens and puppies for a hobby. Nothing. Do you understand?" His eyes never wavered from hers. He needed to make her believe he meant it.

Ysobella's inward sob told him he struck so close to the truth. And she would like to believe he meant the words. Tears blurred her vision. Her jaw was taut as she struggled to stop herself from losing control. Her secret must have been such a burden, too monumental for her to tell him.

Galen saw her inner struggle, and it pained him: he could do nothing about it, except pull her close into his embrace, run his hands up and down her back to soothe her as she sobbed on his chest. It was heart wrenching.

The intensity of her distress convinced him she had suffered as much, if not more, when she left him. And in that instant, her tears washed away every transgression she had committed against him when she left. However, the need to know the reason grew, making the urgency more unbearable.

Nevertheless, he endured, continued to hold her until her tears subsided and her body had gone limp. The outpouring of emotion exhausted her, so he scooped her up in his arms, sat down on the couch with her on his lap, and cradled her like a baby. They stayed like that for a long time, contented for the moment.

Galen could feel the thoughts whirling around in Ysobella's head. He did not want her thinking and stressing herself again, so he jostled her a bit to break her train of unhappy thoughts and focus her attention on him.

"Bel, why did you pretend to be somebody else during our first meeting in your office?"

He kept his tone relaxed. He was curious, and he wanted to start with the simple questions first. She tensed for a moment, but to his relief, she relaxed back into his arms.

"It seemed the most natural thing to do when you didn't seem to recognise me. You surprised me," she admitted.

RISE OF THE VISCEREBUS

He shifted her from his arms so they were face to face.

"I know I promised not to ask, and I won't. Not tonight, but will you consider telling me why you left me, at least before I die?" He asked in all solemnity. He was not beneath emotional blackmail.

She took a deep breath and nodded.

That would do for now. And for tonight, it was enough that she would be in his bed and in his arms, just as she had always been every night in his dreams.

Ysobella sighed, grateful for the brief reprieve. She could never keep her truth from Galen for long. He would wear her down, and she would weaken because he deserved the truth.

Do I really believe Galen's love for me and Yuana will be enough to keep the family secret safe?

Is it worth the risk?

Do I have it in me to do what I must if my trust in Galen turns out to be a mistake?

6

YSOBELLA'S SECRET

Yuana rubbed her dry eyes. The clock on her wall showed it was five a.m. She had been lying awake since she decided to tell Roald the truth about her. She could not subject Roald to a lifetime of questions in his head and inflict a perpetual wound to his soul if she disappeared like her mother did.

It was excruciating to watch the joy, longing, regret, and guilt in her mother's eyes whenever she gazed at her father, and she felt her pain like it was her own. While her mother survived the aftermath all those years ago because of the family's full support, she did not want to walk that same path.

What she saw in her father's eyes as he regarded her mother was another matter. It echoed the same joy and longing, but there remained the questions and the fear her mother might disappear again. The emptiness in her father's eyes when he talked about those lost years was beyond bearing. It sounded like a bitter and joyless existence.

She would not subject Roald to the same torture. When they part ways, she would want him to move on properly, if not completely, from her, from them. Roald must be able to live a full life afterwards. She did not want him to spend decades pining for her, she would do enough of that for both of them.

In her heart, Roald would do nothing to hurt her and her family. He may even try to adapt to their ways in the beginning, but to be bound by the *Veil* would ask for too much.

The question was when and how to tell him.

The other challenge would be how to make him believe. It would be impossible to accept something he did not think existed. As a technical guy, he would need solid and irrefutable proof. To do that, she would have to reveal more than what they could bear. To reveal more meant the danger would be greater. That proof would be harder to deny and dispute later.

The question of when was the other matter. A few months? Years? Her father's situation with her mother might take time, and Roald would never wait that long. Unless she was mistaken, she was sure her mother would tell her father the truth. To divulge their secret to two potential witnesses, both respected individuals with unimpeachable reputations that could corroborate each other's claims against them would be irresponsible and dangerous.

She would need to discuss this with her mother, and then the entire family.

How will I get private time with Mama when Papa was always by her side?

She needed to strategize. She was due at breakfast with her parents in a few hours. Roald would pick her up soon, so there was little time to get herself ready.

Roald was looking forward to this morning. Yuana's father invited him to join them for breakfast. He thought of declining, as he felt this should be between Yuana and her parents. But then, he could make Galen an ally in his quest to ensure the highest probability for Yuana to say yes when he proposed. Galen had limited time on this earth, and could not afford to waste it. Galen needed to see that he was good for his daughter, that he would be there to protect Yuana in his absence, that he was necessary to Yuana's happiness. So, the more activities they shared, the better it would be for his cause.

He pulled up in the driveway of Yuana's house, and it surprised him to see her already waiting for him by the front door. A frown of impatience written on her face. He did not even have the time to get out of his seat to open the door for her; she went straight to the passenger seat, opened it and slid in. He stopped her hand as she reached back for her seat belt.

She turned to him, inquiry in her eyes. He leaned in and kissed her. "Good morning, Yu," he murmured on her lips.

That took her out of her preoccupation. She kissed him back with a smile on her lips.

"Good morning, Ro." The preoccupation had faded from her face.

"So, what seems to be the hurry this morning?" he asked.

She was pale, but the kiss gave her a flush on her cheeks and plumped up her lips. He soothed her lower lip with his thumb.

"Sorry, I was just excited about this breakfast." Yuana's smile was bright. But tension creased her brow.

"Me too. I want to impress your father. And I hope you will put in a good word for me..." His joke earned him a grin.

They shared a conspiratorial smile like two people working on a secret plan together. A twinge of guilt hit him; he had a hidden agenda. This was an opportunity to advance his cause.

Breakfast was in her father's suite. The smell of hot coffee and croissant welcomed them as they entered. Her father's well-appointed suite had a stunning view of the city and boasted two spacious bedrooms and a wide-open living room that connected the dining and the kitchen. There was a faint scent of lemongrass in the air that reminded her of spas.

The food came in the middle of their first cup. There were Spanish omelettes, lots of hot bread, fresh fruits, and crepes. It was a relaxed affair, like they had been doing this as a family for a long time.

As discussed between her and Roald, she took the lull in the conversation as her cue to take her mother aside for the conversation.

"Mama, Papa said I have a bedroom here, can you show it to me?"

A minute inclination of her head was a signal her mother had no problem interpreting. They had exchanged it for years, a part of their silent language between mother and daughter.

Her dad glanced at her and her mother with a smile, oblivious to the conspiratorial nature of the room tour.

Roald picked up the hint and engaged Galen in a conversation about kali. He shared the same interest in the martial arts as the rest of the De Vidas. Both men watched their women stand up and leave the table to walk towards the second bedroom in the suite.

She followed her mother towards the verandah and closed the door behind them. Her mother seemed to read what was on her mind.

"Mama, I know you are planning to tell Papa." Her mom did not contradict her statement. "How will you do it? What is your plan?"

"I do not know, Yu. But I cannot hide it from him when the

time comes. And the time to tell him grows closer every day."
Her mother sat down with a heavy sigh.

"Mama, I am thinking of telling Roald," she blurted out.
She was beyond thought, she had decided. And the "how" was
the reason they were going to have this discussion.

Silence reigned.

They were both aware that they would put their family and
their kind in danger by exposing their nature. But the risk of
that had become the easier option than parting ways with the
men who owned their hearts. They were mother and daughter,
destined to go through the same path at the same time.

"Yu, I thought I would reveal it little by little," her mother
said after a while. She sounded unconvinced by her own
proposition.

"How will you do it, ma? Start by showing him what we
eat? What we look like when we are hungry? What we do
when we hunt?" She could not keep sarcasm and sadness from
her tone. That side of their nature would scare the bravest
of men.

"Those are excellent suggestions..." her mother replied, her
tone unsure.

"Is it wise to tell them both at the same time?" This bothered her most, but it had to be asked.

Ysobella's head jerked up. Her mother almost said no. To
tell her father was dangerous enough, another person knowing
would increase the risk. Both Galen and Roald were prominent
and credible people. Plausible deniability would become
nonexistent when one could corroborate the tale of the other.

"Yuana, it's very dangerous to tell them both... you know
that..."

"I know, Mama. It is also easier for everyone if I just do
what you have done, what the others in our clan have done for

centuries; to just disappear for a few years... but..." Her voice quivered and broke off.

There was sympathy in her mother's gaze. She reached out and smoothed her hair.

"Why would you tell Papa? Are you very sure of him?" She could not help but ask. She wanted to shore up her defences, her reasons on why it was okay to tell Roald this early.

"I want your father to be happy, to take only sweet memories about us with him. But I am sure he will ask for the truth, and he will not rest until he gets it. I'm scared it will traumatise him when he finds out, and I can only cushion the blow, make the pill sweet..." Tears pooled in her mother's eyes. "I trust him, Yu-yu. And he has proven his constancy by finding me after all these years. I am certain he won't harm me or you, that he will keep our secret close to his heart. But that was not the question you wanted to ask, was it?"

Her mother's statement made her heart ache with pride for her father and envy for her mother's unwavering faith in him. But her direct gaze made her flinch inside; she was asking her the same question about Roald.

"I trust Roald, Ma. I do not think he will do anything to hurt me, I also believe he will protect our secret..." She had to defend Roald and their love. She needed her to agree so she could convince herself that a happy ending was possible.

"I do not fault your trust in Roald, Yuana. I agree, we can trust him, he will not hurt you, and can even be relied upon to keep our secret. But telling him, just like telling your father, has a bigger risk to them. Can we risk the damage to their psyche when they find out the truth about us? That the women they love were *viscera-eaters*, that our entire family is?"

The statement hit her with a thud to the chest. That did not even enter her mind, she was so focused on what their laws required if Roald failed. She did not consider the emotional toll it would exact from Roald just for learning the truth.

"What am I going to do, Ma? I want to tell him. I do not know if I can live the rest of my life without him, with just the thoughts of the what-ifs as my companion. Papa's return to our lives made me hopeful and made the option of leaving untenable." Her chest ached now; her throat hurt.

"I understand, Yu-yu." Her mother patted her cheek. "Perhaps we can mitigate the risk? Let me tell your father first, gauge his reaction, and we can decide after that."

It was not a perfect solution, but it was better than nothing.

Without words, they got up to rejoin their men in the dining room where their shared laughter could be heard. The lighthearted mood did not change as they sat with them. Both men, with little thought, draped a protective arm around the shoulders of their ladies.

The two men had come to an understanding and formed a solidarity in a common goal, so they were pleased with themselves. The food was delicious, and company was brilliant. All was right in their world.

Galen watched Ysobella tidy up in the living room while they waited for the housekeeping to come and pick up the remnants of their breakfast. She was deep in thought about something, and it made him uneasy not knowing what it was.

He was still half-convinced she would bolt in the middle of the night and disappear from him again. He reminded himself that this time it would be different because he had met her family. It was not like the first time when his only connection to Bel was Bel. Last time, when she disappeared, there was no way to trace her. He did not know where to start.

Galen decided he would spend the day wooing his Bel, much like what he would have done back in the day. His only goal when he came to the Philippines was to look for her. He didn't have any plans beyond locating her. It was sheer luck he found her a mere week after his arrival. But he was flexible and quick on his feet, so he would improvise.

He gently pulled her away from the task she was doing and enfolded her in a loose embrace. "How would you like to show me Tagaytay today?"

He had heard of the beauty of the scenery, and that it was very romantic. He planned to implant his presence in Bel's every waking and sleeping moment. His Bel had a romantic soul, and a love for nature, so Tagaytay would be perfect.

"I would love to, very much," she replied with a smile, running her fingers along his collar. He remembered she loved volcanoes and had a certain affinity for it. It somewhat represented her, normal, calm and peaceful on the surface, yet it hid explosive secrets underneath. One he was uneasy to find out, but had accepted that he must.

"Then we shall spend the day in Tagaytay, my love." He smiled, pleased that she agreed to his suggestion.

His hands unlocked from behind her and slid up her sleek back. His fingers travelled over her familiar form. He kept his touch light; he did not want to alarm her. His right hand moved upward to cradle her nape as he manoeuvred her for his kiss. The touch of his lips was slow, gentle, and exploring. He wanted her to remember, to appreciate the sensations, and to get used to his kisses again. This was part of his strategy— to keep reminding her so she would never forget, so she craved him again, just as he had never stopped remembering or craving for her all these years.

Hand in hand, they walked out of the room. He kept them palm-to-palm during the drive most of the time. The warmth of her hand in his soothed his soul, reassured his mind, and calmed his heart from the fear of losing her again.

During the drive, he discovered that this compulsion was as vital as a kiss and a hug. He looked back at all the women he had a relationship with, trying to remember if he had ever had this driving need to link his fingers with a woman. He never even wanted to in the past, even avoided doing it because it made him feel uncomfortable.

The revelation astounded him — that the act of holding hands was a more profound expression of intimacy. It was the melding of souls; akin to a surrender; the veritable handing over of his heart into the hands of this woman for her keeping.

He now wanted to make sure he would live longer than was fated for him. Before he found her again, his goal was just to see her before he died, but now, he wanted to live longer for her, for their daughter. The universe owed him this. He would make sure he collected.

It was a scary thought to contemplate the power Bel held over him, a power he gave her himself. And Bel knew it. He could feel it. She would never hurt him on purpose, and that was the operative word—on purpose.

It was clear whatever made her run away the last time would be the only reason that would force her to hurt him again. And only by shining the light on it would the threat be eliminated.

He told her last night nothing could make him stop wanting to be with her, and he meant it. But he started thinking her reason for leaving him must be bigger than any normal social obstacles, criminality including.

He began playing scenarios in his head of what could be worse than being a criminal or being crazy enough to torture small animals. And in each possibility, he asked himself if he could get past it. It was a yes, to all of it.

He was certain about his own heart, but braced himself for whatever horrendous truth it would be. It made him anxious.

———

With Yuana and Roald gone, she was alone with Galen and the resolve to create a strategy for the revelation. All kinds of possibilities and scenarios played in her head.

Nothing came to mind that seemed to be the right way. Her decision earlier to stop obsessing about how and just allow the situation to take its natural course was proving hard to do. Every time she had a moment to think, she could not help but strategize. And it was close to driving her insane. She could not seem to come up with the correct steps to take, and worse, it made her anxious and tainted her moments with Galen with unnecessary preoccupation.

What Yuana half-joked about earlier had merit. It would not make sense to Galen if she told him point-blank: the De Vidas are aswangs, and there were more of them in the world. He would need proof. Irrefutable evidence that could be most shocking to Galen, and most dangerous to their kind.

But for Galen to live in their world, their lifestyle, he must know everything. He had to see what they are, what they are not, and why they are not the monsters legends made them out to be. Hopefully, since Galen was born and raised in America, he did not grow up with the old lore about her kind. Without that fear, she could use logic to reveal and explain the viscerebus nature.

Now, the critical question would be the how. Maybe if she

dropped little clues, it would give her an inkling on how he would behave when handed the big truth.

The car finally arrived in Museo Orlina. Their shared love for arts and museums made this the natural choice. Anticipation flowed in her blood as she got out of the car. The visit was the first for both of them.

For two hours, the various galleries in the museum engrossed them. It featured stunning glass sculptures and various other contemporary art exhibits from local and foreign artists. As they emerged from the lower floor onto the roof deck where the coffee shop was located, a breathtaking view of Taal volcano greeted them.

The mixed scent of fresh lake water, green grass, hot coffee and cakes perfumed the air. Their seat in the corner table closest to the verandah afforded them privacy and the best view on the deck. Galen ordered some coffee, cake, and fruits.

"Do you mind if we have a leisurely merienda here? I would like to savour the moment—the view, the ambience, you..." Galen whispered. His warm breath tickled her palm as he planted a kiss on it.

His gaze glittered with boyish charm and seduction. It made her blush. At her age, she should not blush anymore. Galen, however, looked pleased at the high colour on her cheeks. He reached out and traced the reddening patch with a fingertip.

"No, I don't mind. The weather is pleasant," she said, her voice fading.

Her vain attempt to change the topic and break the heat of the moment made Galen grin. Thankfully, the server arrived with their order, and for a few moments, she busied herself with pouring them coffee and serving Galen some cakes. It gave her some time to gather her composure back.

"So, what is next on our agenda for today? Do you want to

drive around, or are you content with just sitting here and enjoying the view until sunset?" She felt compelled to fill the silence with conversation.

"I am happy to sit here for as long as you want, Bel. I am satisfied for now, but not content yet," he said.

His words carried the forewarning of the things to come, of the things he would demand from her. She nodded because she understood.

"I know, Galen. And perhaps the time has come for me to answer your questions. So, I will try to give you as much of the truth as I can. All I ask is for you to be patient with me if I cannot answer all of them now." Her heart hammered against her chest - the door to the truth was now open, and there would be no going back.

"As long as you tell me all, eventually. I can give you time, Bel, if that is what you need."

He reached for her hands. He needed her touch to reassure her and calm his rampaging pulse. A part of him was afraid the truth might be too much to overcome.

She took a deep breath and squared her shoulders, like she was about to face a firing squad. Galen felt her tension and dread from the one question that mattered the most, the crux of everything that embittered their past. And his heart clenched in response.

"Did you know you were pregnant with Yuana when you left me?" He caressed her knuckles, a gentle, reassuring motion.

Her fingers unclenched. It seemed the question was something she could answer.

"Yes, I found out the day I left you... That made me leave

you that day." The reply came out of her in a half whisper. The rasp in her voice carried remembered pain.

"But why? I asked you to marry me..."

Ysobella's eyes flashed in panic. She looked away. And he understood. Impatience rose in his gut. He wanted to press her, but his earlier promise stopped him.

"So, it wasn't because you did not want to marry me?" All those years, he thought she bolted because she did not want to commit to him, that her love was not as deep as his.

"No, not that. It was never that... It will never be that." Her eyes held a kind of pleading.

"So, will you marry me if I asked again?" He wanted reassurance it would not be like the last time.

"Yes." Determination flashed in her eyes, her tone almost challenging.

His heart expanded at the sight, but the thorn of that mysterious reason remained. And it was still causing pain.

"So, how long are we going to avoid the real reason you left, Bel? How long do you want me to wait before I can ask the question? And before you can give me the truth?" He could give her time, but he needed a timeline. The wait would be easier to bear if there was a date he could mark off on his calendar.

She lifted his knuckles to her lips. It was a request for one last minor delay. "Tonight, I will tell you. In our suite, the truth requires complete privacy."

It was his turn to kiss her knuckles. "Okay." He would grant her the few hours of reprieve she asked for. "What do you think of Roald?" he asked.

The change of subject made Ysobella smile. It was a mixture of relief and gratitude.

"I like him. He loves our daughter, perhaps as much as you once loved me," she replied.

He shook his head in a slow, emphatic movement. "No, I disagree very much. One, I still love you as much, perhaps more now than before. Two, he cannot possibly love her as much as I love you. I have twenty-eight years of proof in my favour." He was only half-joking.

Ysobella laughed. "Enough of the buttering up, Galen, or I would be too slippery for you to hold." She appeared pleased, flattered, warmed by his words. A blush tinged her cheeks.

"Sorry to disappoint you, Bel, but no amount of butter can do that..." He grinned. He missed the banter between them.

"So, what do you think of Roald?"

"Oh, I like him. As a man, I can appreciate the depth of love he has for our daughter. But as a father, I wish he would go away, at least, until I am ready to relinquish her. I mean, I just found her. He had a three-year advantage over me, so it should be my turn now."

Approval crinkled the corners of her eyes, the curved plump lower lip invited thoughts less amusing.

"Tell Yuana that. I am sure she would want to spend time with you too. I think the only reason she hasn't intruded into our daily activities was that she wanted us to have this time together first."

"Really? She does not feel awkward about me as her father, a stranger she just met who now demands to be part of her life?" He was unable to hide his excitement at this revelation.

"Oh yes. I know our daughter very well... And you were not a stranger to her. I told her all about you, and we kept tabs on what you had been doing all those years."

"You kept tabs on me? Since when? For how long?" The barrage of questions and the rush of emotions the statement generated swirled together like a tornado in his mind. It was impossible to grasp, it made his head spin.

"About a year after I left. I had every intention to keep the break clean, like what the others in my family did in their time, but I could not do it. By chance, I saw your picture in the newspaper, when you were part of the group of surgeons who travelled to the medical mission in Tijuana. I clipped that article, told myself it would be a onetime thing..."

Others in her family? Tijuana? She was there?

He turned away to deal with the rush of fury that surged in him. At her; she knew where he was, that she was in the same city, but still stayed away; at himself for the missed opportunity.

He fought against the flood of recalled memories of that mission. It was a break from the frantic search for her, from the frustration of losing her, from the pain of knowing she left him on purpose. He spent a year searching for her in the US, in every hospital and clinic, and then did the same in the Philippines, but he did not find her. It did not help that she'd given him a false name.

The fury raged in him, but he swallowed it back to force it down. She was still bound by the same reason for leaving, and he could not have known then that she was there.

"You were in Tijuana at the same time?" His voice hoarse, his throat had gone dry.

"I was. And I hung around Tijuana until your medical mission ended, hoping to see more newspaper coverage of your group. But there was only one..." Her quiet sentence made him turn to her once again.

He knew she saw the flash of anger in his eyes, noted the hardening of his jaw as he pushed it away. He knew she understood and would have welcomed it had he expressed it. She deserved it. And perhaps, if he had railed at her, both of them would have felt better.

"Was Yuana with you in Tijuana?" He forced himself to ask, even when knowing the details would hurt.

She nodded, unable to put to words her response.

"Where was she born?" Questions about how Yuana was as a baby hovered in his mind.

"She was born here, Galen. We went to Tijuana that summer because I needed to get away and to be closer to where you were without being in the US."

Her admission was a balm to his wounded heart.

"Tell me about your life, Bel, after you left me. I need to fill in the missing details in my head about your life, about Yuana's, what you did, what kept you busy when you were away from me."

Again, she nodded. She understood the emotions that drove him.

"We lived all over the world. I flew to England the day I left you and settled in a minor city in the northeast. I would not allow myself time to think about you, or I tried my best, at least. Work became my solace until the seventh month of pregnancy. I flew back here to give birth to Yuana and stayed for another six months. Before we settled in Bizkaia, on a whim, we flew to Tijuana. For one quick stop... It was to be my last attempt at letting go. Yuana and I lived in Bizkaia until she turned six.

"We moved to Cape Town after and stayed there for another six years. Then it was Oslo and Melbourne. And finally, Yuana and I came back home four years ago." Her voice was flat as she glossed over the hard details.

Her description of the past twenty-eight years was dispassionate and casual, but he saw through the façade she had erected over her own emotions. The effort she exerted to control herself and how exhausting it had been, was visible in the slight tremor in her voice, the line of pain in her mouth. For now, the itinerary of those years would suffice, the rest could follow. He would get it out of her soon enough.

"I have one more question, Bel, and then we can stop our Q and A if you want to. Is that okay?" he asked. He did not want to stress her more than necessary. The revelations today had already been more than what he expected to get from her.

"Ask away." Her back straightened.

"When did you stop collecting all those articles about me?"

This vanity question was something vital to soothe his aching heart. The knowledge that she kept tabs on him, the thought that she held on, had a powerful effect on him. It was stitching close the wounds of his heart.

Ysobella looked at him, a sad smile on her lips. "I stopped five years ago."

"Why? After all those years, why did you stop?" he pressed.

"You got engaged, Galen, and I thought it was only fair to let you live your new life without the spectre of me hovering at a distance. Selfishly, I also thought it was time for me to let go." Ysobella had lowered her eyes to the table napkin she was twiddling with for the last half hour. She seemed reluctant to voice her admission.

He stilled her fidgeting fingers and trapped them in his hands. He waited until the uncomfortable silence grew. Her gaze caught in his as he held her head between his hands, and pulled her over for his kiss. Repressed emotion was released in the kiss that was slow and lingering. It was incongruent with the violence of the feelings he held inside.

Her sigh blew warmth on his lips as they pulled apart.

"She never stood a chance, Bel. She was smart enough to recognise she would never have my heart, and courageous enough not to settle for anything less than she deserved. So, she called the engagement off after two months."

"Are you still friends with her?" Ysobella's voice was soft, unsure.

It seemed she took pity on the unknown woman who became ensnared in their lives and got her heart broken because of it. She was collateral damage to their tangled love affair.

"Yes. We worked together in the hospital; she heads the Pediatrics department. We formed a strong friendship after the breakup," he replied.

He saw a flash of jealousy in her eyes. Perhaps she was jealous of the days and nights he spent with his former fiancé in her stead; those little quiet moments of shared joys and pains, the exchange of ideas, fears and dreams. Those moments that they both valued and cherished when they were together.

"What did you do with those clippings? Do you still have them?"

He could not let go of the thought she kept him in her heart all those years. Just like he did her, despite his desperate efforts to exorcise her from his soul.

"I kept them in my desk drawer. I will show them to you one of these days, I promise."

Galen wanted to ask more questions, but he had promised her just one more question, and he had asked more than one. He kissed her shoulder and pulled her close. This would suffice for now.

Little by little, he had made her open up to him. Tonight, he would know the real reason why she left, why she chose to suffer away from him. The thought of the looming truth made him fearful and hopeful at the same time.

Again, he asked himself what could be bigger than his love for her and their daughter that would be enough to be a deal-breaker, that would cause him to turn away from them? His mind came up empty. This unknown truth that forced his fierce Bel to give him up was worrying.

The worry intensified into fear.

Ysobella sent a message to her family to inform them she and Galen would not be coming to dinner. Normally, this would not cause much alarm to her family, as this happens occasionally when one of them travels out of the country. Their structure so well organised worldwide, the supply of the sustenance anywhere would not be a problem. Her absence would be a concern because she told them she would reveal the truth to Galen tonight. Her decision was a dangerous one.

For them. For Galen.

It was seven p.m. when they reached their hotel. Galen ordered steak, some salad and wine while she took a bath to calm her nerves. She was as taut as a violin string. She was both hungry and without an appetite.

When she moved to the bedroom to get dressed, she noticed flickering lights in the living room. The room was full of red and white candles. Galen had set up the dining and living room with dozens of huge candles — some waist high. Galen had recreated the setting of that fateful night decades ago. She emerged from the bedroom with her heart hammering.

She looked at him, speechless. He grinned at her reaction.

"I had the concierge source for them while we were in Tagaytay... I remembered you liked candles. Do you still like them?" he asked. The crinkles in his eyes smiled, his deep dimples prominent on his cheeks. It made him look boyish.

"Yes." She picked up the nearest red candle and the scent of cherries wafted to her nostrils. Cherry and cinnamon candles. His action warmed her and made her braver for the task ahead.

"Hmm... you smell deliciously fresh. And sweet." Galen's voice was husky as he nuzzled the side of her neck. He tugged the neckline of the bathrobe aside to give him better access. "Are you hungry?" His question suggested that he wished otherwise as he nibbled at her collarbone.

His suggestive question was tempting, and she even considered that her revelation might be more palatable to Galen if they slept together first. But her truth might be repugnant to him, and it could taint the experience into something nauseating. She did not want to give him an additional source of nightmares.

Her stomach protested at the thought of eating. Perhaps the wine would help bolster her courage and dull the senses.

"Wine first? And let me get dressed." She felt vulnerable in her robe, aware that she was naked underneath.

He walked over to where the wine and the glasses were. She rushed back into the bedroom. Her pulse had picked up. When she walked back to the living room minutes later, Galen was waiting for her by the couch with two wine glasses. He handed one to her as she approached him.

She accepted the glass and swirled the red liquid in it watching streaks of the wine run slowly towards the centre of the glass. She took her time sipping and savouring the vintage as she searched for the best way to start the conversation. Galen watched her go through the ritual as he sipped his own glass.

She took the seat across from him. Galen's eyebrow quirked at her action, but he said nothing.

"Galen, what would you consider a deal-breaker?"

"Funny you asked that. I have been asking myself the same question since I found you. And I cannot think of any. As I told you already, you can be an animal-torturing killer, a psychopath, and I will still choose to be with you." Galen's reply was firm, his gaze direct.

She contemplated her options on how to broach the subject further. An idea came to her.

"What if I told you I was born a man, and that I am a transgender? Would you still feel the same about me?"

Her question jolted Galen upright. His expression was

blank for a moment, but she saw alarm, denial, and dismissal flit in split-second succession across his face.

"Bel, I struggle to imagine you being a transgender because of Yuana. Unless you lied, and she is not mine..." His tone was half-joking.

"She is yours. But humour me anyway... Imagine I am a transgender woman and ask yourself if you can accept me, if you can love me as much as you do now," she persisted.

Galen paused for some moments to think about what she asked him to do. The silence dragged, every second, suspenseful. The frown on his face, the flash of his eyes held her transfixed.

She could see his attempt to imagine her being a transgender, but she could not read what he saw in himself as he examined his heart.

"Bel, I cannot see past the love in my heart now. It is hard for me to dig deeper into the what-ifs of this premise because I know you are a woman." His sigh deeply. "Perhaps I would not have fallen in love with you in the first place then because our relationship would not have progressed past friendship. All I know is that I love you and imagining you to be a transgender did not make my love disappear." His voice deepened as his intensity increased.

"Throughout the years, I have gone through every imaginable reason I could come up with on why you left me. I had used those same scenarios to justify my anger at your disappearance, used them to convince that it was good riddance, and yet, here I am, I still searched for you, still wanted you. As far as I know in my heart, nothing you can tell me can change that." Galen's colour was high. His eyes flashed with anger, and maybe, frustration.

She stared at him, indecision and despair fighting for dominance in her mind. The battle infused tension in her jaw and every line of her body. She fought against the desire to cry and break down.

"Just tell me, Bel, trust my love for you. Trust I will not do anything to hurt you with the revelation you will give me today," he pleaded. Galen gripped her fingers tight.

A deep breath for fortification and a last attempt to inject more courage into herself, she nodded. "Okay... Will you promise to keep an open mind, to give me the benefit of the doubt, even if what I tell you seems impossible? For I swear it will be the truth."

"Of course, it is the truth, you would not have left me otherwise," he said bitterly, a grimace on his face.

She inhaled deep and took the mental step across from secrecy to full admission.

"Galen, do you know what *viscerebus* are?"

He shook his head, but a slight recognition crossed his face. The term must have sounded familiar.

"Do you know what *aswangs* are?" He blinked at the term. He recognised it, but he looked perplexed. She added, "I... my entire family... and your daughter... we are *aswangs*."

"*Aswang?* As in the supernatural creatures that eat people?" His eyebrows rose, perplexed.

He stared at Ysobella intently, unable to take in what he just heard. His eyes darted all over her face, searching for signs she was kidding. She seemed sincere in her declaration; it confused him.

Ysobella nodded slowly. Tears pooled in her eyes.

"Yes, Galen, in the olden days, our kind eat people or at least specific organs of people that we need to consume to survive."

Aswang? Abruptly he stood and walked away towards the dining table where he left the wine bottle. He downed the contents of his glass in one gulp, poured himself another, and downed that one, too. His emotions played catch up with his thoughts.

Ysobella's face fell as if her world crashed. There was the pain of rejection and fear in her face. She must have stood up when he did, as she flopped down on the couch as if her knees had gone weak. She fixed her gaze on him, her body tensed with anticipation for his reaction.

Galen could not define what he was feeling, disbelief being forefront. Ysobella would never use such an alibi to justify her disappearance as she knew him very well. He was a man of science, where scientific proof would be a prerequisite before he forms an opinion. That she had to implore for an open mind from him meant she truly believed herself to be an *aswang*. The doctor in him kicked in. His brain began running through similar symptoms and medical information that might explain this.

"All of you? Your entire family?" Galen asked.

He needed a catalogue of behaviours and symptoms before he could make a diagnosis. His rational self demanded it. Science could explain even miracles. Every malady and behavioural anomaly, there would be a corresponding treatment.

"Yes, all of us, including Yuana." Her quiet response sounded like defeat, her sigh, a resignation.

Galen moved from the dining table closer to where she was and sat across from her. Ysobella released a relieved breath.

"Where, how do you get the organs?" He asked, although he dreaded the response.

"We do not kill people if that is what you are asking. No one in my family ever killed anyone. Our kind has not needed to for centuries." Her reply was defensive.

Our kind? She believed that there were more of them outside her family?

Then a thought entered his head. "Your business..., does that have anything to do with your being an aswang?" GJDV dealt with dead bodies. It would be the most logical way to get access to human organs.

"Yes. Through our company, our operation, we harvest the liver, heart and kidney of a deceased human. We only get what we need and only when we need it," she replied. Ysobella fell silent, allowing the information to sink.

"And the family of the deceased never finds out about it..." He understood it, and the simple brilliance of the setup.

"They never do. But we make amends to the family by providing exemplary service, and to society by providing free burial services to people who cannot afford it. It is our way of making restitution," she said, her expression even, like it was all very matter-of-fact.

"How long has your family been *aswangs*?" This could be a congenital malady, or a strange belief system. It may be a form of Clinical Lycanthropy, or Renfield syndrome, or some kind of undiagnosed dysmorphia that ran in her family.

"For as long as my great grandparents can remember, and for generations beyond that."

"Do you know how it happened, how it began?" His medical mind abuzz, he thought of the causes that may have led to this.

"No one knows exactly how it began, but our best guess is mutation. The cause is a specific mitochondrial gene. Our being an aswang is a hereditary trait passed on from mothers to their children," Ysobella replied, a frown on her face.

His reaction baffled her. Then her frown cleared as she realised what he was doing. He was trying to diagnose her.

"It is not a disease or a mental disorder, Galen. I can give you undeniable proof." Her voice rose higher. Her face crumpled with heartbreak at his reaction; tears glistened down her cheeks.

Galen wanted to argue, to reason it away, but he stopped himself as he remembered his promise to have an open mind. For a better diagnosis, it was best to let her speak, and provide all the information that he needed.

"I'm sorry, Bel. The doctor in me kicked in. Please continue..." He leaned forward in his seat, his intention to listen with attentiveness. He wanted her to be comfortable and more open with him.

"What else do you want to know?" she asked. Prudence and frustration coloured her voice.

"You mentioned that heart, liver and kidney are the only human parts you eat. You called it sustenance. Why?" He did not want to offend her, but the key to her ailment seemed centred on those organs.

"We do not know why those organs. For centuries we have tried to find out. We are still trying. Our metabolism is different. We are stronger, faster, and we heal quicker than humans. We also age slower and live longer."

Galen blinked: his mind raced back to the first time he saw her again — her youthful looks. But current plastic surgery techniques could have contributed to it. However, Ysobella seemed certain. The level of her belief in her statement was intriguing.

"Animal organs are very similar to ours, so why humans?" he asked.

"Animal organs can serve as a temporary substitute, but there's a limit to how much we can consume. It makes us sick if we have too much of it. Why human viscera? That is the part we are still trying to find out," she said. "All we know is the effect of human heart, liver and kidney to our body. It energises us. It strengthens us."

"What does it do to you if you do not consume those?" He wanted to know if there were physical effects or if it was just psychological.

"It feels like when a normal human is starving, but worse. We behave like anyone in need of food, one will be desperate for it and will do everything to eat. The difference is that our *vital instinct* takes over, and we cannot help but hunt."

"Hunt? What do you mean? How do you hunt?" He was more than intrigued at the layers of Ysobella's declaration.

"We... shape-shift into an animal, whichever animal suits the environment." Ysobella had averted her eyes. She sounded unsure, unwilling to answer.

"Do you only shape-shift when you're hunting?" This could be the way for her to realise the truth, that this was a psychological problem.

"I can shape-shift when I need it, when I want to. The only time I have no control over it is when I miss my victus past the point of bearing. My *vital hunger* takes over, inducing an *automorphosis*, or *reflexive transformation*." Ysobella's head snapped back up, her eyes focused on his face. Her expression cleared and brightened.

"Do you want to see?" Her question came out in a whisper. Her pupils glittered with purpose.

He almost said no. But this was the perfect opportunity to observe how deep her psychosis lie, and maybe this would shake her out of it.

He took a deep breath and nodded. "Alright."

Ysobella stood up and walked towards the centre of the room, unbuttoning her dress at each step. His mind froze as he saw her undressing. His pulse quickened as the silk dress slithered down her legs and pooled around her feet. With her back to him, she unhooked her bra, peeled it off one creamy shoulder, then another. She dropped the item on the coffee table. The tiny clasp on the strap hit the glass top, and the sound reverberated in his head. When she bent down a bit to slip off her underwear, Galen's heartbeat galloped to a degree that each thud was audible and tangible.

Ysobella turned around and faced him. For a moment, his brain refused to move past the reality that he was looking at the naked version of Ysobella. The colours were high on her cheeks, the rosy tint spread down to her neck and shoulders. She looked self-conscious but she did not turn away from his intense perusal.

When the blood reached his brain, he noted Ysobella's toned body, her breasts still firm and high, her butt still tight. Her body had not aged a day since he last saw it this close twenty-eight years ago. When his eyes caught hers and his gaze travelled back to her face, he was even more transfixed by what he saw in them.

There was apprehension, sorrow, determination, and acceptance. Like she feared his reaction but had prepared herself for what was inevitable.

Ysobella swallowed, then turned sideways. He saw a miniscule tremor at the base of her spine, and it travelled up every vertebra to her nape, and back down. A flush of colour started from her sacral region accompanied by a growing heat and it spread all over her body. Her skin vibrated. The colour and texture changed, from flesh tone to a black, glossy sheen. Her long hair retracted into her scalp; the dark brown shade darkened into the same midnight hue. She dropped to her hands and knees; her spine mutated to conform to a four-footed form.

Galen could not believe what was in front of him. Ysobella's naked human form had changed into a black panther. It happened in a flash, but his mind played the details in slow motion. His first internal reaction was to doubt what he saw, but it was undeniable.

The panther sat there, a few feet away, its yellow cat eyes trained on him. Its sleek body seemed poised to pounce. He could not think, much less speak. He just saw his beloved Bel change into an animal; a powerful predator capable of killing him if she wished. If he had not seen it happen, it would be impossible to believe the animal in front of him was a woman. There was nothing to hint of any human form in the cat sitting across from him.

But those yellow eyes drew back his gaze and held it captive. From its depths he recognised her in the uncertainty and the tears that pooled in its feline eyes. And the once unseen hint of his lovely Bel was now visible to him.

"Bel..." It was the only thing he could say, his voice choked.

Upon hearing her pet name on his lips, Ysobella's panther head bowed. Her chest ached with the pressure of the emotions she held back. Her body returned to its human form. Crouched, she dropped into a fetal position to hide her nakedness. She felt exposed in every way. Tears pricked at the back of her eyes, but she squeezed her lids shut against it. She did not know what would happen next. She had laid her reality bare to him. *Would he walk away?* Misery cloaked and chilled her.

She did not hear him approach, but his warm hands cupped her shoulders and lifted her until she sat on the floor with him. His arms enveloped her, rocked her. Tears of relief, uncertainty and grief burst out of her like a dam. The burden of the decades of separation resurfaced in waves, battering her.

He wiped her tears, hushing her. He murmured everything would be all right. And his words made her cry even more. As he seemed to realise, he could not stem her tears. He cradled her head into the nook between his shoulder and jaw, his warm hands rubbed soothing circles on her back.

"Bel, please do not cry... It is breaking my heart... please..." His plea vibrated in his chest; his voice pained.

Her sobs subsided after a while. She found hope because she was in his arms. His voice was soothing as he reassured her over and over that everything would be all right. Her tears had stopped flowing a while ago, but she did not want to leave his arms. If he was going to walk away after this, she wanted to prolong the moment. This could be the last time he would hold her like this. This was the core of the matter for her, not just his acceptance, but if he would stay after what he discovered.

She felt wrung out like a mop, deflated and limp. She lifted her head from his shoulder, and he pushed away from her to look into her face. He wiped the tears from her cheeks; her lashes damp.

"Are you all right?" he asked. Concern was thick in his voice.

She replied with a single nod. She had no more energy to talk, and it was now in his hands to continue the conversation. He seemed at a loss. Galen stood up and held out his hand to help her up. She had forgotten she was naked until icy air hit her and goosebumps rippled down her body. She shivered. He bent down and picked up her dress and handed it to her.

With a sigh, she pulled her dress up to cover herself. Her body ice-cold to the core, a normal aftermath of every shapeshifting back into her human form. It would take a few minutes for her body temperature to return to normal.

Once dressed, Galen led her back to the sofa where her wine glass sat unfinished. He picked it up and handed it to her. She followed his silent instruction and downed the contents of the glass. Galen had moved to the bar and poured himself a cognac. He took a sip as if he needed the exercise to collect his thoughts.

The emotional release depleted her; she could not move or say anything. She sat huddled in the corner; the armrest cushioned her back. She waited for Galen to speak. The decision was his to make.

"Why a panther? It doesn't seem to be what the environment called for."

The question was not what she expected; it gave her pause.

"I am partial to big cats. And I have shape-shifted into a panther more times than any other feline form." She realised Galen was delving into the issue with a light hand.

"When and why did you ever need to shape-shift?"

"Sometimes as a self-defence, or when I am in an area where being an animal would be better, or if I want to experience a place in a different viewpoint," she said.

He took her response in silence but had to gulp his cognac down. Her transformation had alarmed him. And she could understand that. It had shaken his perception of reality.

Galen stood up and poured more cognac in his glass, his movement abrupt. Some liquid sloshed out and spilled on his fingers. He downed the contents and poured himself another measure. Galen walked back and sat beside her. His body language communicated impatience... and repressed fury.

"Bel, why did you leave me? I need to know why you didn't just tell me about you being an *aswang*. Did you think I would reject you if I found out?" His voice was raw, pained, and furious.

She was taken aback. This was what Galen needed to hear more than anything else.

"It is not a simple answer, Galen. Part of it was the uncertainty of your acceptance. Another was the fear the truth would scar you for life. We all have heard the scary stories about aswangs. Imagine if you find out it was true, and the woman you fell in love with was one. It would be traumatic. I didn't want you hurt that way." Her explanation was insufficient even to her own ears.

Galen's jaw tightened; his eyes flashed with anger.

"I got hurt anyway, Bel. And the experience traumatised me when you left me without a word. So, I cannot say which choice would have been less destructive to my psyche."

The bitterness in his response struck at her heart. The anger spoke of the never-ending longing he felt for her during those years they were apart, his efforts to tamp it down, and his failure to do so.

"I got hurt too, Galen. Perhaps as much, if not more, than you. You had the benefit of anger to cushion the blows, I didn't. I had guilt. It was my constant companion all those years. But I had to break up with you because to tell you would be to endanger my family and our kind. Our laws were all rooted on keeping our existence hidden." She needed for him to understand that her choice was difficult.

"Why did you just disappear like that? I spent the first months in frantic search of you, all the while driven mad by thoughts that something horrific happened to you."

The dark frown and gruffness contained all the remembered pain, the sleepless nights, and the torture that he went through. Each syllable abraded her already-injured heart. Her mind supplied the image of his suffering. Her mangled heart continued to pump in pain.

"I did not have the strength to face you and break up with you. I didn't think you would have let me go. And I would not have been able to resist you and walk away." Her throat constricted, her voice a mere whisper.

"You are right. I would not have let you go..." Galen agreed.

He had straightened up, his back rigid. He was the same

determined, unrelenting Galen that she knew. The old Galen would have put up a fight, and it seemed he had not changed.

"Galen, now that you know what I am, what is next for us?" It was hard to ask him directly, but the wait was unbearable.

"Ysobella, have you not learned anything from all this? I found you after twenty-eight years after you walked out on me without a word. You are the only thing in my bucket list, my last dying wish, and you still doubt me?" His irritation was palpable in the sharp response.

The vehemence in his statement stunned her; it kept her mouth shut. But her heart expanded to bursting, and tears of gladness pooled beneath her lids. She wanted to smile, but emotions squeezed at her heart that made it impossible to do so.

Her expression must have penetrated the cloud of fury surrounding Galen, as the irritation that darkened his face vanished. He yanked her close, cupped her head between his hands, and kissed her with a fierceness that almost hurt. She tasted all his frustration. Her tremulous sigh of relief gentled his mouth, and the kiss turned slow, deep, exploring. He imparted all the vows and promises in his soul, in the pressure of his lips on hers, the way he angled her face to deepen the kiss. He ate at her mouth like a starving man. It had been too long for both of them. And this was the first time there were no more barriers between them.

The ringing of the phone was jarring, ending the kiss before they were ready. Galen cursed out loud, and a shaky laugh escaped her. Galen seldom used colourful terms.

It was the room service, calling to ask if they were ready for their food. Galen glanced at her, as he mouthed *food*.

She nodded briskly. "Yes, please... I'm starving."

Galen sighed and confirmed with the staff on the other side of the line.

She was so happy and light she could float on air. Everything inside her unlocked and all her senses awakened to life. Her smile as she looked at him must have been radiant, for Galen answered with a beaming one. Now, they found all the missing pieces of their soul, his and hers. They were, at long last, one and whole.

There would be adjustments for both of them. Most of it from Galen's side, but the confidence he exuded strengthened hers. Galen was aware of the challenges, but the foundation of their love was strong, so they would prevail. Of that he seemed certain.

And his certainty powered hers.

Iztari Pereiz and his team tracked their target into a remote village, nestled between a river and a mountain. Based on the report, the target was one of their kind who still hunted humans. The *harravir* had taken a child from his bed in the middle of the night. The villagers found the body of the boy in the woods, a kilometre from his home, missing a liver, kidneys, and a heart. They had deduced by the amount of human viscera taken from the body; they were dealing with more than one harravir. Or one who hunted for a family or a small clan.

They scoured the area in stealth and travelled upwind to avoid detection. One of his team members picked up the scent of the target and radioed it to his team members. The team then converged at the site.

And in the cover of darkness, they waited. They saw a man emerge from a clearing; his scent confirmed to them he was an aswang. He had not changed into his hunting form yet, so they followed him, making sure they kept themselves hidden.

After a half an hour of tracking, they followed him into the next village and watched him transform into an enormous dog, as he prowled the edge of the cluster of houses. Their target checked for homes with any open doors, or any humans out and about. It was already seven in the evening, and most people in this remote part would already be indoors as soon as the sun set.

Then, from the other end of the village, two drunk men came tottering into their view.

The big dog kept to the shadows as it crept closer to the men and prepared to pounce. The two drunk guys paused in their tracks, one of them turned to the bushes to throw up.

They assumed their target would grab the one who was throwing up as he was in a more vulnerable position, but their target went for his companion. They all sprang into action, net in hand, to stop the attack. The victim gave a long shriek as the big dog clamped its jaws into his neck. The impact of the attack knocked him down like a log. Two of Iztari Pereiz's teammates threw the net into the dog, while Iztari Pereiz pried his jaw open and loose from the victim's neck.

Captured, the dog thrashed against the net that was holding him down. The victim was barely alive. Blood spurted from the bite on his neck. Iztari Pereiz spit on a white cloth that he pulled from his backpack, then pressed it down into the neck of the victim. He wanted to stem the flow of blood and his viscerebus saliva would help.

His barfing companion was still spewing his guts nearby, unaware of the attack.

The victim's shriek and the noise of the thrashing dog attracted the residents of the nearby houses. One by one, gas lamps flickered on, providing illumination to the three Iztaris. Iztari Pereiz sighed. They would have preferred a quieter operation.

Soon, the village leader, an old gentleman, came out of his home and approached them to ask what was happening. Their prepared speech mollified the entire village since the incident was very easy to explain away—that someone had reported a rabid dog loose in the area, and the government deployed them to catch it to protect the villagers. Their target was smart enough to keep his hunting form. It would have been a monumental problem if he panicked and transfigured back into his human form.

Amidst the barrage of thank you's, there was also a volley of aghast comments about how scary the situation was, how fearsome the big dog was, and how lucky that they were there and saved the life of the village brew master. The Iztaris took the 'rabid' dog, who had turned docile now, away from the village.

The target knew he had been caught by aswangs. He could tell by their scent, but he did not quite know who they were, why they were wearing military garb, and what would become of him.

Meanwhile, the brew master's barfing companion fell asleep by the roadside, unaware of what happened. He would not find out till morning.

7

A TASTE OF THE ASWANG LIFE

Morning dawned early for Yuana. Her mother sent her a text message the night before to inform her breakfast this morning would be for her and her parents. Their discussion would be about Roald and her decision to reveal herself to him. Her father took her mother's revelation very well, and she was optimistic about her chances, but the request to exclude Roald did not bode well.

She had informed Roald today would be a family day for her, and she would miss their lunch together. Roald understood, but still insisted on picking her up and dropping her off at her father's hotel since he would not see her the entire day.

Dinner would be at the De Vida's home. The family had been told about her father's reaction to their secret. There were still some concerns, but they were optimistic and would give her father a chance. They trusted her mother's judgement and supported her in this decision, but they all know there were safeguards in place.

Just in case.

And what would come after when the just-in-case scenario

happened was a greater concern for her mother, and for her. No Viscerebus would ever wish it on their worst enemy.

Yuana's usual bright and sunny disposition were missing that morning. She seemed preoccupied, and in a hurry. Her kiss goodbye to her grandparents was a quick peck on the cheeks and a distracted wave. She gave him just enough time to greet her grandparents good morning before she tugged his hand toward the car.

Roald pulled the car over to the side as he exited the gate of Yuana's house and turned towards her. He did not like that something bothered her.

"Good morning, Yuana." He leaned over and kissed her on the cheek. "Tell me what is wrong and why you look so pensive again today."

Yuana looked startled, leaned over and kissed him briefly on the lips and murmured, "Good morning, Ro." The smile that followed was dazzling.

That confused him. *Did I imagine her earlier mood?*

She moved back toward her seat, but he prevented her by holding her in place. His right hand rested at the back of her head as he continued to kiss her softly, savouring her. Her cinnamon-flavoured lip gloss plumped up her lips and tempted him to nibble on the luscious flesh. He indulged for a few moments before he let her go.

Satisfied, Roald turned the machine back on and resumed their trip to Galen's hotel. That kiss was a splendid way to start the day, and he made a mental note to make it a habit from now on. Then he remembered he was giving up his lunch hour today with her, so that would entitle him to another kiss later.

In his opinion, it was a fair trade.

Her parents both looked at peace. Her mother beamed at her from a distance, her father's pupils twinkled with joy and mischief. The truth freed her mother from the burden she carried for decades. And she was happy for them and filled with hope for her own future.

Will I have the same luck with Roald?

Her father walked toward her with his arms outstretched. He pulled her close when he reached her, and hugged her so tight that it lifted her off her feet. He swung her around twice, his delight infectious. She was laughing like a child when he put her down.

"Good morning, my sweet," he said, his voice a deep rumble in his chest. "How is the fruit of my loins doing this morning?"

She gave him a mock grimace, "Fruit of your loins? Really, Papa, did finding out the truth about us traumatise your vocabulary?"

Her father threw his head back and laughed. "Ah, you are indeed your mother's daughter. You inherited her quick wit." Her father chuckled.

He seated her down on his left, her mother already seated to his right. He behaved like the head of their family, whose heart was full, and soul at peace, unbothered by the spectre of any future difficulties.

Over a basket of hot croissants, freshly made omelettes, and cups of coffee, they opened the conversation about her situation with Roald. Her mother set her cup down, reached over and covered her hand resting on the table. It was time to discuss her revelation strategy.

"So, Yu-yu, what is your plan?" her mother asked without preamble.

Her father turned toward her. She guessed her mother had briefed him about it. And now he would be in on their secret and the reason for it. He looked as apprehensive as her mother with the idea of an exposure to another non-aswang.

"Yuana, putting your lives in jeopardy does not sit well with me..." Her father's frown was more than emphatic.

"I trust him like Mama trusted you, Papa..."

Her father grimaced. "Touché."

"How will you tell Roald?" Her mother's asked gently.

She had not planned for the *hows* yet. She was more anxious about whether it was possible. Her father's reaction was a very good indicator.

"I have no idea, Ma. How did you tell Papa? Perhaps I can do the same?"

"Ah no! Definitely not." Her father's vehement reaction surprised her. Her mother threw him a tilted glance, an elegant eyebrow arched inquiringly.

"It's not the... right strategy..." Her father's vague and flustered response was confusing. "There has got to be other ways to reveal herself... to that boy... I will not permit it." A tone of paternal protectiveness was thick in his voice.

She had no clue what her father was talking about. She and her mother watched a gamut of emotions race across her father's face, from alarm to defensiveness and back. Then her mother burst into laughter. Galen threw her an annoyed glance.

What the hell was going on?

Her mother dabbed at the tears of mirth from her cheeks. "Your father would rather you... reveal yourself in another way, my dear. He's being a protective dad," she said, patting the corner of her lids with a napkin. "He finds my way... too revealing..."

"Oh!" And that made her chuckle. It was a unique experience to be self-conscious about nakedness. But her father was human, and he was not used to it.

"How long have you known this guy, my sweet?" Galen interjected, slight annoyance for being the object of jest between mother and daughter was still in his voice. He wanted them to focus on the subject at hand.

"Three years, papa." She was glad to be discussing this with him, glad to get a human viewpoint from someone in love with an aswang.

"How well do you know him? How much do you trust him?"

Her father's concern was understandable since he had just met Roald.

"Well enough, Papa. As I told you earlier, I trust him. But we are talking earth-shattering revelations here..."

Galen nodded in understanding. "I think he is an upstanding fellow, actually. I like him."

His father's words warmed her. She wanted his support, his honest assessment of Roald's character. She would have a blind spot for Roald because her feelings were engaged.

He and Roald were on the same boat, and if Roald accepted what she was, both of them would go through the same challenges.

"Pa, how did you feel when you found out about us?" she asked.

"It shocked me. I could not believe it. Not because I thought your mother was lying, but my logical brain refused to accept at face value what she told me. I was busy diagnosing her symptoms, because I wanted to find a medical explanation on why she was certain she was an aswang. It comes from being a man of science, a doctor..." His shrug was apologetic. "But never did I consider leaving your mother or you, regardless of what the truth was. Even when I was so convinced it was a psychological problem, my primary motivation was to find the treatment for your mother."

"So, when you saw with your own eyes definitive proof, what was in your heart?" If she could peek through her father's soul, she would. She was desperate for validation.

"Apart from the initial shock of seeing your mother transform her beautiful self into a panther, it was just a matter of convincing myself that what I saw was real. My feelings didn't come into it because I already knew nothing changed in how I feel about her." His response came out slow and contemplative, as if he was reliving the moment, and what he went through.

Yuana's heart lurched and expanded with hope, with a fervent prayer that Roald's feelings and reaction would be like that of her father.

"What do you think, Galen? What you have observed of Roald, is it safe to tell him?" Ysobella asked. Her mother echoed the same question in her mind.

"I do not know enough about him to form a firm opinion, Bel. But to his credit, our daughter trusts him, and I am convinced he loves Yuana very much. It is my love for you that will ensure I will do nothing to harm you, our daughter, and your family. It might be the same motivation for him." Her father's words were thoughtful.

"You think he will take it well, Pa?" She had to ask. She needed every assurance she could get.

"My sweet, he might just take it well. And maybe... he and I can adapt to your way of life together..."

His eyebrows rose high, as if his own suggestion surprised him. And it had merit. He and Roald could go through the experience together. It could make the process easier for both of them. It might even be fun.

Immense gratitude for her father bloomed in her chest, tears pooled in her eyes. She hugged her father tight on impulse. Behind him, her mother's smile was wide, as if she thought the idea was marvelous and would solve many problems.

It also improved the odds of success for Roald. The danger of having two reputable men corroborating each other's claim no longer existed by her father's vow to keep the secret safe. And she knew he would keep the *Veil*.

———

The hug surprised Galen, but he returned it by instinct. He was glad he could do this for his daughter and it made him less guilty for not having been in her life before this. No matter how much he told himself no one would blame him since he was not aware she existed until four days ago, he still felt pained about his absence in her life.

"Okay, it is settled then. You will tell him. How?" he asked after Yuana moved from his embrace.

He still did not like the strategy Ysobella used when she told him. He did not even want to entertain the thought. This was his daughter they were talking about.

"Perhaps we can tell him together..." Yuana said.

It was obvious to him she was going to cajole them to help her. Having her mom to back up her revelation, and her dad to reassure Roald it was okay to be in love with an aswang might help matters a lot. And it might be enough, and there would not be a need for any disrobing and transformation.

"Yes. We can do that. When do you want to do this?" Ysobella asked.

"How about tomorrow, at dinnertime?"

"Perhaps you should tell him during the day, my sweet... With us, not with the family. I am sure he has heard stories about aswangs growing up. It might intimidate him to be surrounded by all of you, especially if you all transformed into predatory animals..." A small shiver ran up his spine at the thought.

"You have a point there, Papa. Okay, I will tell him we will have lunch tomorrow with you and Mama. Shall we do it here?" Yuana's voice had perked up with relief now that they had made a plan.

"Yes, it would be best. We have more privacy here. What are his favourite dishes? We might as well feed him properly."

"You make it sound like he is on death row, Pa." Yuana grimaced and pouted.

"Well, in a manner of speaking, it is the end of something in his life. Plus, some say that one is much more likely to accept an immense shock when one's stomach is full," he added.

"Who said that?" Ysobella asked, laughing.

"I did. Just now."

———

They ditched the plan to do a city tour of Metro Manila in favour of a long and leisurely discussion about being an aswang and the De Vida way of life. Galen seemed eager to know as much as he could. He processed every tidbit of information like a true man of science.

"So, Grupo Jardin De Vida is an international conglomer-ate..." There was amazement in Galen's voice as he took in the information about how the viscerebus thrived in the world where they remained the minority.

Ysobella nodded. "We have investments in other funeral homes and memorial gardens worldwide, just as some of our partners who operate a similar setup in their country are investors in GJDV. We share resources with our kind when they are here, the same way they share theirs when we are abroad. But in some operations, instead of investments, we have partnerships." Pride for their company blossomed in her.

"It is amazing how your kind banded together and adapted current technologies. It seemed so seamless. I can imagine how your kind could live anywhere in the world and keep your existence a secret..."

Galen's low whistle made her grin. Yuana was smiling as well. Her daughter must wonder if Roald would think the same of their kind's achievement.

"It started about five hundred years ago, and we learned through experience how to perfect the system. Our Tribunal's goal was to ensure that we could continue to live and thrive with the humans. Your fear of our kind was well-founded, but it no longer exists. Not in the past two hundred years, and yet that fear remained a powerful driver of violence towards our kind."

Galen's analytical mind needed answers, and she was more than willing to provide it to him. If he would adapt and take to their way of life, then it would be best to equip him with the right information.

"Your *Tribunal*, it sounds like most governments, or an organised religion," Galen mused.

"That is an apt description. Like any innovation, it was borne out of necessity. In our ancient past, it was a violent existence for us aswangs. While we prey on humans for survival, they hunted us to defend their own. And we also had to deal with the predation from *our* own kind."

"Your own kind? What do you mean? *Aswangs* eat other *aswangs*?"

Galen's surprise was not new to her. The humans always assumed that they were the only nemesis of the *Viscerebi*.

"Yes, papa. It is not so different from humans killing other humans. We refer to aswangs that hunt humans as *harravir*.

Here in the Philippines, the local name is *tiktik*. The aswangs that hunt our kind, we call them *harravis*, or as it is known here as *wakwak*," Yuana interjected.

"So, you had to battle hunters from two fronts..." Galen paused as he contemplated that. His eyes darted between her and Yuana.

"Yes, our kind had to. The constant hunting from humans and our own kind decimated our numbers, so our ancestors formed the *Supreme Tribunal* with the sole purpose of ensuring our survival," she said. The system was much more nuanced and complicated to explain in one conversation.

"How does the Tribunal work?"

"It's simple enough. Each *Gentem,* or a country, has a local *Tribunal* composed of twenty-four to thirty-six individuals, headed by a pair of leaders, called a *Matriarch* and a *Patriarch*. They implement the Supreme Laws in their country and make sure that the system works. They are also the representatives to the *Supreme Tribunal,* which is a gathering of all the Local Tribunal heads. The supreme law is centred on keeping the *Veil of Secrecy* intact at all times. The system takes all the aswangs into the fold and takes care of them. This was the only way to make sure we remain a secret. The established enterprises all over the world, like GJDV, ensure we have the resources to do so."

Galen nodded, a focused expression on his face as he thought about what she said. He frowned as a concern surfaced in his mind.

"So, is it part of your rule not to marry humans?"

"There is no rule against us marrying humans, as we need to procreate. Only the women can pass on the genes of an aswang, so the Tribunal encourages that. What the law forbids is the revelation of our existence. Common practice dictates that if we fall pregnant from a union with a human, that we leave the man behind..."

A heavy silence ruled for a moment.

"Bel, you broke the law when you told me..." Galen had begun to understand. "Is there a consequence to this?" His frown deepened.

"If you keep our secret safe, the *Restoration Plan* will not kick in. We have seven days to rectify the leak. If the *Rectification* fails, then it becomes the responsibility of the transgressor to bring the Restoration Plan forward." Dread for the remaining possibility dropped like a lead weight to her stomach. The vigilance over Galen, and soon over Roald, would be lifelong. Both men would never find out.

Galen's eyes narrowed in concentration. She could feel the question forming in his brain, and she wished he would not ask.

"What is the *Restoration Plan?*"

"The transgressor... me... would have to restore the *Veil of Secrecy*. And the most expedient way would be death..." she breathed, "I would have to kill you, Galen."

Galen gasped; his eyes widened. They both stared at him, watched as the full comprehension of the enormity of the risk and the supreme trust they gave him dawned on him. He swallowed as emotion overwhelmed him. He pulled them both into his arms, his breath laboured.

"Do not worry, Bel, I will never put you through that. I swear to you. And if, by mistake, it happened, you would not need to do the act, I will spare you that," he said in a fierce promise, sealed by a kiss on both their foreheads.

Tonight, he would face the family at dinner. Galen understood that this would be a test for her family to see if he could handle the fundamental instinct of a viscerebus. His reaction would determine if her family would trust him to keep the *Veil* intact.

She wished her heart was as confident that he would prevail, but her anxiety persisted.

Margaita sat in her favourite thinking chair with a glass of red wine in hand. Her forehead knitted in contemplation when Lorenzo walked into the room. For a few moments, he observed his wife worry over their granddaughter and great granddaughter. Being Punong Ina, the matriarch made the matter of the revelation so much more complicated because it was rife with political consequences and repercussion.

But as a De Vida, family would always be a priority. There was no question about their acceptance of Galen in their midst as they judge his trustworthiness. In the meantime, for Ysobella and Yuana, they would welcome Galen with warmth. He might well be the first *non-Erdia* human taken into their fold. Perhaps, if this worked, it would set the precedent.

At the sound of Galen's car, his wife stood and joined him. They waited for Galen, Ysobella and Yuana to come in. They entered all three abreast. The joy in the faces of their granddaughter's family lightened the tension-filled mood in the house.

A short time later, Katelin and Edrigu came down to join in the gathering. His son-in-law, Edrigu was more restrained, as he observed Galen's interaction with the family. His daughter, Katelin, was more open and relaxed as she conversed with the man her daughter had chosen and risked the *Veil* for. Katelin had the most optimistic mind-frame in the family.

Ysobella stood and watched while her parents engaged Galen in a probing conversation. There was a line of stress in his granddaughter's smile. The stress of the evening weakened her earlier joy.

"How are you doing, Bella?" he murmured to her as he handed her a glass of Barbaresco.

Ysobella glanced up at him and took the glass with a grateful smile. "Thanks, 'Elo..."

"You look worried..."

She took a sip before she replied with a tiny nod, "A little bit... Is Aunt Ximena here yet?" There was a slight tremor in her hand.

"Ah, you missed sustenance last night... Don't worry, she should be here soon. And she's going to bring liver..." He patted her hand in reassurance.

Ysobella grinned. "We could have testicles tonight and I would not notice it."

"Fortunately, human testicles do nothing for us." He grimaced. "The idea alone makes me want to give up being a Vis."

Ysobella's chuckle was worth the mild discomfort.

True to form, Ximena's car pulled up at the exact time. They all turned towards the front door as Ximena entered with the familiar icebox that carried the victus, a human liver they would have for tonight. Nita rushed towards her and took the icebox to the kitchen.

Ximena joined them, accepting a glass of wine from Edrigu. A quick buss on the cheek of her mother and all the women in the room, a brief exchange with Galen, then she flopped herself on the sofa, and kicked off her high-heeled shoes, unconcerned about etiquette.

His first born looked tired.

"Long day, Cara?"

"Yes, Pa. I just came back from Havensville Antipolo to see how the three families we brought in from Talim Island were faring. The entire clan needs comprehensive training and indoctrination. They were so deep in the old ways. They were desperate and dangerous." Ximena's explanation, while addressed to everyone, her eyes were on Galen. She was testing the man.

Galen stayed silent.

"Havensville is one of the housing communities we put up for our kind, Galen. We provide them with homes, education, and employment. We also provide them their sustenance, so they do not have to resort to hunting humans," Katelin interjected.

Katelin saw the question in Galen's expression and his hesitation to ask, so she volunteered the information. It was predictable of her. His second daughter was the peacemaker of the family.

"You moved them from Talim Island... so how were they living before you brought them in?" Galen's question was of pure curiosity. He seemed keen to understand rather than pass judgement.

"They were hunting humans. This family had been moving all over Rizal and Quezon province for decades, trying to survive. This was why it took us this long to track them. They don't know about the *Tribunal* and what we do, so we brought them in." Katelin's gentle and matter-of-fact explanation was the perfect tenor to adapt.

"Were they glad about this... move?" Galen asked.

"This family was, as they were almost decimated. They used to number up to thirty, but they are down to eight now. The years of hunting by the venandis took a toll on them," Edrigu said. He had taken out the hand that was in his pocket earlier. A sign that his son-in-law had relaxed.

"*Venandis?*" Galen's eyebrow rose and glanced at Ysobella.

Edrigu nodded and replied, "Venandis are humans that hunt our kind."

"Oh, that makes sense. The humans will organise to fight

back," Galen said, looking proud. "So, what do we call those that hunt the *harravis?*"

Edrigu's smile deepened. Galen's unconscious use of the pronoun "we" revealed his intention and determination to be part of their family. And that reassured every single De Vida in the room.

"That would be the *iztaris*. They are our kind's version of special forces. Our primary mandate is to implement the laws that keep the *Veil of Secrecy* intact. That includes stopping harravirs, rehabilitating them, and eliminating harravises." Edrigu's response was simplified. A wise move, as they still needed caution at this point.

"Papa is the *Chief Iztari* in the country," Ysobella added.

"Chief? How many iztaris are there?"

"There are about thirty to fifty in every city, depending on the size of the territory," Edrigu replied, taking a sip of his wine.

Nita's entry into the living room interrupted their conversation. She carried a wooden tray with a beautiful cloche made of darkened glass. They all turned towards her. The slow steps she took seemed prolonged. The item inside the cloche became the focus.

This was a genuine test of Galen's resolve.

Without being told, Galen seemed to know what it contained. His posture straightened, as if he was bracing himself for a blow.

Nita placed the tray down on the tall cocktail table that was set up in the room for the evening. There was a brief pause that felt like hours, everybody's eyes on Galen. Margaita broke the tension by lifting the cloche and revealed fresh, human liver on a wooden platter. Beside it was a sharp carving knife and fork, and several dessert forks. She handed the cloche to Nita, then took the knife and fork and started carving half-inch slices of the raw liver, blood pouring out of the cut, coating the knife bright red.

Galen was transfixed. The scent of raw flesh and fresh blood did not faze him. His profession prepared him well for this experience. But he was unsure how he would feel when they ate the viscera, so he steeled himself. He did not want to show any adverse reaction; he did not want to offend. This was the test, not the revelation Ysobella made yesterday.

His stomach quivered when Margaita placed the carving knife and fork down on the side of the tray. Seven bloody liver slices lay in its center. Margaita then took one of the dessert forks and speared one slice and brought it into her mouth. She tipped her head back and slid the slice onto her tongue. Galen's stomach clenched tighter as he saw the raw liver disappear into her throat. There was no mess, not a drop of blood on her lips.

Lorenzo followed suit. Then one by one, they took their turn swallowing the liver slice in the same manner. Katelin patted the corner of her lip with a napkin to remove a blood drop. Galen's stomach knotted at each swallow. Bile rose into his throat as he struggled to control his gag reflex. It nauseated him. Cold sweat dampened his brow and trickled down his back. Mercifully, not one of them made eye contact with him.

Except Ysobella.

He knew she could see how he was trying to stop himself from throwing up; and noted the sweat that glistened on his top lip, his cheeks and brow, his white knuckles that held his glass in a death grip. She had not taken her liver slice yet. He knew she wanted to see how he would react to seeing them eat it. Misery lined the stoic facade she displayed. Her distress deepened as his skin turned grey in gradual degrees throughout the whole thing.

When Yuana stepped close to the tray to get her slice and moments later slid it down her throat, he could not hold it. He muttered a quick, "Excuse me," and rushed to the powder room without waiting for a reply from anyone. He closed the door and retched until his throat was raw and he could taste his own bile.

Ysobella watched in helpless anguish as Galen rushed from the room. She could feel everyone's stare — the sympathy, understanding, support, and it made her want to howl in pain. She could not subject Galen to this every time she and Yuana needed to sustain themselves. Tonight, she would not partake to spare him.

Uncomfortable silenced reigned in the room as they tried to ignore the sounds of Galen dry heaving in the nearby comfort room. Every wretched sound was a stab to her heart. Her stomach churned in reaction. By the end, she was swallowing hard to fight off her own nausea.

The powder room door opened, and Galen emerged. His face was pale and damp from splashing water on his face. He looked sheepish and apologetic as he patted himself dry with a handkerchief.

His gaze fell on her. And she could not mask the anguish on her face. Galen's expression changed to dismay. The tears she tried to hold back spilled down her cheeks. Galen rushed to her and pulled her into his arms.

"Shh... Why are you crying, Bel?" He wiped her tears with his thumbs.

She took a deep breath to stem the flow of tears and smiled

at him. "I am okay, just being dramatic." She pulled out of his arms, conscious of the spectacle they made in front of the family. She motioned for Nita to take away the wooden tray where her liver slice lay untouched.

Galen stopped Nita as she was about to pass him by, his questioning frown upon her. "Are you not having your sustenance?" He tipped her chin up to peer into her eyes. She shook her head.

"It's okay. I don't have to." She turned away.

"Hey... Bel, it's okay. Go have your slice," he insisted when she hesitated. "I want you to take your sustenance."

"I do not want you to..."

"It's okay, go take it... I promise I won't look." His teasing was true. She knew he would prefer not to see the act.

Ysobella gave him a slight smile, her heart grateful. "Yes, close your eyes."

Her efforts to tease him back were weak. She passed her fingers over his lids, and he closed them. She turned her back to him, and with quick movement, speared the liver slice and swallowed it.

The whole De Vida clan watched the scene unfold and saw Galen display the depth of his love for Yuana and Ysobella, his determination to belong, his willingness to do whatever it would take to adapt. The tension that gripped all of them for days now eased and faded. Galen was on his way to making history in the De Vida clan.

Ximena's heart squeezed hard; her throat tightened. Her niece was lucky with the man of her choice. Unlike her. Galen had the fortitude. Unlike *Martin*.

"So, are we all ready for dinner? I am starving, I could eat a human," Katelin quipped.

At Galen's startled expression, everybody laughed. Including Galen.

———

Later that night, while they were preparing for bed, Galen remarked to Ysobella, "I guess it is safe to say the old myth that declared garlic and salt can kill aswangs is not true... The garlic mushrooms served earlier were superb."

Ysobella laughed.

"Yes, that was a pure but useful myth. Some of our kind in Aklan encouraged the belief in the human communities. It helped identify the villages who had vigilant venandis among them. The copious amounts of garlic bunches that hung on windowsills and doorways signalled the intensity of the fear in the village. The higher the fear, the more likely it was they have active venandis protecting the village. Our kind learned to stay away from such villages as a matter of self-preservation. So, the belief that we are afraid of garlic became a maxim to the humans."

"And the salt? How did my kind come about the idea that salt is an aswang killer?"

She found Galen's curiosity in the superstitious belief about their kind amusing. His scientific brain had turned it into a study in sociology.

"We avoid salt, because it can slow our ability to heal, but not enough to pose a fatal danger to us. How did the humans find out? We are not sure, but we think maybe in one of the old skirmishes between some unfortunate aswang and humans, someone threw salt on a wounded aswang, and it made the aswang flee. I mean, have you ever experienced putting salt on an open wound? I'd recoil as well."

Galen chuckled. He seemed happier since he had passed the first night of witnessing the most gruesome side of their nature. Sure, it was stomach-turning, but as he had said, as long as he did not watch them do it, he could move past it.

This would work, they could succeed at this.

She felt relief and gratefulness flood her veins as he pulled her closer into his embrace and kissed her. A full night of loving was in order.

Meanwhile, Yuana stared at her ceiling, still wide awake. Her father passed the test with flying colours and convinced the family of his sincerity and loyalty to her mother. They all now believed this would work. She was thrilled for her father and mother.

They did not discuss Roald's situation because everyone focused more on the immersion of her father into their world, and it was not the right moment for such a discussion.

She worried for a while when her father turned grey during the ordeal, and she felt fearful when he threw up. But then, her father proved his mettle and rallied after that.

Now, she wondered if Roald would do as well. Her father was a doctor, used to seeing, smelling, handling raw flesh and blood. Yet the act of eating the raw liver turned his stomach.

Roald had no such medical training. This would be more challenging for him, more gut-wrenching and stomach-turning.

What if he can't handle it?

This would be infinitely more traumatic for him. Maybe sparing him the truth would be kinder, better for him and his psyche.

8

PRELUDE TO THE PAIN

Her ringtone woke Yuana up. She fell asleep at dawn because of exhaustion. Groggy, she groped for her phone. It was Roald.

"Good morning, sleepyhead..." His voice low and concerned.

She neglected to call him the night before as was their normal practice every day for the last two years.

"Good morning, Ro..." she rasped, her lids refusing to open. Her eyeballs felt dry and irritated.

"Are you all right?" Roald's question was sharp. He seemed alarmed.

Perhaps she sounded under the weather. At this hour, normally, she would already be up and about.

"I am good, just overslept," she murmured.

"It's a good thing I did not show up at your door this morning. When you did not call last night, I assumed you might want a late start this morning..."

"Thanks, Ro. You know me so well..."

"Would you like to sleep some more? I can call you later."

She sensed he wanted to probe but stopped himself.

"No, it's fine. My brain is awake now. A shower will perk me up." She stretched her limbs to get her blood flowing. "I can be ready in an hour, or so," she added.

"Yu, there is no urgency to get up. You need not be in the office if you are not up to it. I can come by later when you are ready."

"Okay..." It was easier to agree with him than argue when he adopted the brook-no-argument tone. "I will go to the office later today. I think I can be ready in... a couple of hours," she said, after glancing at the clock. It was past nine in the morning. Her usual work hour began at eight.

"Good. Rest well and I will see you later," Roald said and hung up.

Roald's call brought back the reasons that kept her awake all night. It cleared the cobwebs of sleep from her brain. Perhaps a bath to soothe her nerves would calm her into a decision.

Under the thick spray of warm water, the choice that had been see-sawing in her mind all night came back. There would be considerable pain in either choice.

Which one would leave a less indelible mark on Roald's heart?

Her own pain and the wound it would leave in her soul did not matter. She had accepted this last night. She closed her eyes against the water flowing over her face.

If only it could wash away the obstacle that nature placed between her and Roald.

Two hours later, she was still as torn. Roald would come to pick her up in five minutes. She needed to present a more pleasant front to him. He was much too perceptive. She chose a bright red dress, one flowy and light to mask the turmoil inside. Her outward appearance no longer reflected the sleepless night, concealer hid the dark circles under her eyes.

Her great grandmother sat at her favourite chair in the living room when she came down. She was reading a history book, 'The Age of The Enlightened Despot.' Her Abuela's passion was history. She called it useful gossip. A slight smile on her lips welcomed her as she came down the stairs.

"Good morning, Yu-yu. You had a bit of a lie-in this morning..." her Abuela commented as she bent and planted a kiss on her forehead.

"Yes, 'Ela. Too much excitement last night. She gave her the brightest of show of teeth to mask her disquiet. She was not feeling up to any confession or heart-to-heart conversations at the moment.

"Is Roald coming to pick you up, or are you taking your own car?"

"Roald is picking me up. We will have lunch with Mama and Papa today."

"It's a pity the boy is not our kind... He's a good man..." Her Abuela's words made her wince.

As if on cue, they heard Roald's car pull over. She remained seated on the arm of her Abuela's chair as she waited for Roald to come in.

"Good morning, Señora," Roald greeted Margaita, bending towards her raised hand, and touched his forehead to her knuckles.

"Good morning, Hijo," Margaita responded warmly.

Roald then shifted to her, scrutinising her face. She was sure he was searching for signs of fatigue.

"You look fresh, relaxed, well-rested and glowing." He gave her a satisfied smile and offered his arm to her, "Shall we?"

She linked arms with him. "Sure, let's be off," and with one last peck on her Abuela's cheeks, they left Margaita to her book.

The drive was uneventful. Inwardly, Yuana's brain and heart were engaged in a battle for supremacy. She had called her parents earlier to tell them of her vacillating decision. They advised her to just let things unfold, that they would follow her lead.

There should not be any pressure to reveal anything to Roald today. There was no looming deadline, except her own mental clock. A few more weeks of delay would not make much difference, she told herself often, yet the sense of urgency would not let her be.

Roald could not put a finger on it, but despite Yuana's serene expression, something weighed on her. And this bothered him. It never sat well with him that Yuana withdrew deep into herself, as she would do now and then. In the three years they had been together, no matter how convinced he was of the love between them, that small invisible barrier she erected remained. And one of his goals in life was to break that down.

Perhaps her father would help him. Galen would need *his* help to get to know his daughter better and may be the key to weakening that last blockade that prevented Yuana from giving all of herself to him.

They arrived at Protogenis, a Greek restaurant chosen by Yuana's parents for their lunch. The server ushered them to a secluded private room that overlooked the garden. Cosy, airy and well illuminated, the glass doors, when closed, shut the noise from the main dining area. There were several layers of lace curtain which when drawn provided limited to complete privacy.

Within a few minutes of their arrival, the restaurant manager ushered Ysobella and Galen into the room. The couple held hands and giggled like newlyweds. A sudden jolt of envy hit him. This was the future he wanted with Yuana — an enduring love and burning passion for each other, a veritable heaven on earth.

Galen pressed a kiss on Yuana's cheeks, then shook his hand. Yuana gave her mother a hug, and he bussed Ysobella's cheek. After a few exchanges of pleasantries, they sat down.

Galen ordered a bottle of rosé, a Chateau Miraval, and favourite of both mother and daughter. The weather was warm, and it seemed a perfect wine to start their lunch. They feasted on light salad, pasta, and seafood, the specialty of the restaurant.

Their conversation was light, pleasant, and entertaining. Roald didn't let it show, but he sensed Yuana's disquiet throughout lunch. She became withdrawn as the hours progressed. Sure, she laughed at her father's jokes and took part in the conversation, but there was a not-quite hidden desolation in her.

At one point, he glanced at her by instinct, and the look in her eyes sent a jolt to his gut—she appeared to be memorising his features, like she was planning to say goodbye. It was gone in an instant. He thought he imagined it, but the dread remained.

And this frightened him.

While he enjoyed and valued the time spent with Yuana's parents, he was impatient for it to end. He wanted to uncover what troubled Yuana. It had been growing and creating a divide between them, which grew wider every day. That invisible thin barrier had been thickening.

He thought back to when he first noticed it. It was when he first mentioned marriage. Perhaps she panicked because she did not want to get married yet. He could give her more time.

Don't jump to conclusions, Roald. Maybe the issue was about work, or her parents.

But her parents noticed Yuana's mood as well, as they glanced at her often during lunch, and then exchanged a quick glance between them. There was question and concern in their eyes. And that added to his unrest.

What is bothering her?

The finale of the meal was rich revani and hot Greek coffee. The syrup-soaked dessert paired well with the bitter tang of the dark coffee.

While Galen engaged Roald in a discussion about technologies in the medical field, Ysobella stared at her daughter over the rim of her coffee cup. Yuana had been quiet for most of the meal, her smiles, superficial. The decision had been weighing on her only child.

If only she could take on her burden. But this was a choice only Yuana could make, the consequence she would have to bear. As a mother, she could be there during the storm, to give comfort and help pick up the pieces if she falls apart.

Yuana *looked* serene, relaxed even, but she sat at the edge of her seat, like a cat poised to flee. Galen and she waited for their daughter to make the choice, her timing unknown to them. It was inevitable though, and the sooner the better.

All the signs of Roald's forthcoming proposal were all there. She suspected the only reason Roald had not done so yet was because of the untimely appearance of Galen in their lives. He was being considerate of Yuana. But he would not wait long. And now that Roald had met Galen, she was certain Roald would recruit Galen into the act.

As a mother, she hoped that if Yuana chose to tell Roald, he would rise to the occasion, just like her Galen. After last night, Galen would prevail over anything.

Every one of them had put their trust in someone they loved, and for various reasons, their trust was misplaced, but as far as she could recall, based on what her great grandparents had told her, those instances ended in the eventual Restoration Plan being brought into effect. And it had been shattering to the people involved.

She pondered if every single one of her relatives who opted to reveal themselves to their loved one were as confident about their decision, and as elated as she was over the knowledge that her trust was well-placed.

Then the unwelcome thought intruded in her mind: they must all have felt the same elation, and then the devastation when they realised they made a mistake, and they would need to pay for that mistake with blood on their hands. The blood of their loved ones. She shook the image out of her mind.

Galen would be... was... the first human taken into their circle, and he would remain there. She was sure of that.

But will Roald turn out to be the second?

Or will Yuana be another one in the family who will have to Restore the Order?

Yuana sipped her coffee just to mask her inner turmoil. That was not the best choice of beverage when her nerves were as taut as a drawn bow. Roald's proposal would come anytime now. She could almost hear and read Roald's thoughts every time he looked at her father—he would involve him, take him in as an ally to make her say yes.

Who am I protecting with this decision, really?

My heart?

Or Roald's?

If the Restoration would take place. She would not have the strength to kill him.

Yuana excused herself from her parents to visit the ladies' room. Roald pulled the chair out for her. After she closed the glass door of the private room behind her, he turned to Ysobella and Galen. He had to do something. If Yuana would not tell him, perhaps her parents would. They loved her as much.

"Tita Bella, something is eating at Yuana, and I am concerned about her. Has she mentioned anything to you?" This was not the time to be timid.

Ysobella and Galen were both surprised and exchanged a quick glance. More tension infused him. What bothered Yuana was significant, and her parents both knew what it was.

"Why don't you ask her?" Ysobella said.

The gentleness of her response implied a kind of sympathy that added to the foreboding that crept into his heart. Ysobella then excused herself to follow Yuana to the ladies' room, and Roald could only nod weakly.

There was pity in Galen's gaze when they met his. Yuana's father tried to distract him by asking about his tech business.

He did not want to talk about anything except Yuana's problem, but realised he needed the time to recover his composure. Whatever Yuana would say later would require a calm mind.

As Ysobella expected, Yuana sat at the pristine and comfortable waiting area just inside the ladies' room as she deliberated on the options before her. Her daughter seemed nowhere near to making any choice. Yuana had run out of time, and she wanted to tell her that.

She sat beside her daughter and put her arms around her shoulders. Yuana gave her a dejected glance. There was no need to say anything.

"Roald asked us what was bothering you," she said without preamble.

A spark of life glowed in Yuana's eyes, "He did?"

She nodded.

"Should I tell him, Mama? Or do I do what you did to Papa?"

"My darling, you know I cannot make that decision for you. The only thing that can help you make the right choice is the outcome, and regrettably, outcomes happen in the future, and we have no way of knowing in advance. Either decision will hurt," she replied. "Choose the route that will offer a better chance at a full life for you, for Roald."

Yuana took a deep breath and straightened. She kissed her on the cheek and stood up. Arm and arm they walked back to the private room where the two men waited. Her daughter seemed to have decided on her course.

"Papa, can we go to your hotel suite after this?" Yuana

asked Galen as soon as they entered. Galen and Roald were both on their feet as they came into the room.

Galen's nod was automatic, a question conveyed in the slight narrowing of his eyes. Roald, however, was focused on Yuana's face. The firm determination of an unpleasant decision made etched in the angle of her chin and jaw. That she averted her face seemed to unnerve him. Roald's jaw tightened, but he kept silent.

For now, her daughter had closed herself off from Roald, and the young man did not like it. Roald was determined to break the barrier that her daughter placed between them. The boy did not know what he would face later.

A better chance at a full life.

Yuana's decision was going to be based on that premise. She hoped Roald would see it the same way.

The ride to Galen's hotel was quiet and fraught with tension. Galen offered to drive them all in his car. Galen's driver drove Roald's car back to the hotel.

He and Yuana sat at the back. Not knowing what was torturing Yuana was excruciating. He was certain it involved him and their relationship. He only hoped it was not something he would be powerless to fix. Everything else was fixable.

Yuana held herself distant from him, her spine rigid as she sat. He did not like the emotions the distance roused in him, as if Yuana was severing their connections. He battled the frustration and the hurt that gripped his heart, but he would not let her do that.

Not today. Not ever.

He lifted Yuana's right hand from her lap, his much bigger hands covered hers. She stiffened and tried to pull away, but he tightened his hold, and she relented. Her fingers softened, her palms warmed and melted into his. Her wall crumbled a little, and it pacified the savage beast in his heart for the moment.

Their interlinked fingers gave him hope and bolstered his confidence. He wanted to remind her with his touch that her pain was his to bear. And the distance would not make the bearing easier.

Soon enough, they arrived at Galen's hotel. He released her hand as he descended from the car, but claimed it back when he helped her out. Her hand was clasped in his until they reached Galen's two-bedroom suite. He did not care if her parents witnessed his desperation, his vulnerability to Yuana's power over him.

There was no casual conversation on the way up. The tension was so thick the other guests in the elevator shot nervous glances their way during the minute-long ride.

Galen opened the door to his suite, and they followed him into the dining area. Roald released her hand and pulled Yuana into a chair. She sat down and he sat beside her. He wanted her to feel his presence throughout the wait he was forced to endure. Her parents did the same; Ysobella sat close to Yuana.

Yuana turned to him in a determined move. Yet she did not seem to know how to start. Tears sparkled in her eyes, and it squeezed at his heart. On instinct, he caught her hand and trapped it between his.

"Yuana, just say it. It will be fine, I promise you." That was his hope, anyway.

Her deep breath shook, a tremor in her voice. "Roald, I need to tell you something about me..."

There was a lengthy pause as she struggled with her next words.

Roald felt his heart thump faster in panic, that he had to

lighten the mood. "Don't tell me you were born a man, Yuana," he joked.

"What? No!" Yuana frowned, confused, especially when it elicited a snort of laughter from Galen, cut short by a sharp glare from her mother.

"Sorry..." Roald mumbled. "You are making me nervous, Yuana. Just tell me what it is." His heart hammered against his chest.

"Roald, I want you to believe that I love you very much. And that will not change no matter the outcome." Her voice thickened with emotion; tears welled in her big brown eyes.

Panic sparked in him. A declaration of love at the beginning of a discussion did not bode well.

"I know that, Yuana. I believe that. And I love you as much, so just tell me."

All this was making him more apprehensive and that her parents were in the same room, at the same table, made his misery more acute. He was convinced she would leave him for a cause too big for them to overcome.

The hand he held clenched in tension. "Roald, I... I am not human like you," she sobbed the words.

But it barely registered. He could not believe what he heard.

"What? What do you mean, not human?"

His analytical brain could not compute what she'd just said. He glanced at both of her parents' faces, trying to anchor his mind into something real. Ysobella's face was gentle in sympathy, Galen's was blank.

"I'm a *viscerebus*... an *aswang*. My entire family are..." she whispered. Tears ran down her cheeks.

The word struck terror in his soul, and he did not know why. His confusion doubled, he felt staggered. It was the last thing he would have expected her to say.

"Yuana, I do not understand... why are you saying this?"

His bewilderment numbed his earlier panic. He just wanted her to give him a logical explanation, a statement he could dissect, solve, put a structure to. Something he could do something about.

"Is it because you are not ready to get married? We can wait for as long as you want..." He would supply her with any plausible excuse he could think of. Anything within the realm of acceptable reality.

She shook her head, then bowed. "No, Roald. It is not about that... I want you to know what I am before we even consider marriage." The sobs made it hard for her to speak.

"Yuana, what you are is the woman I love. That is what you are to me. The rest does not matter. There is nothing else we need." He could not express his plea for her to take it all back, or at least logically explain why she called herself an *aswang*.

Yuana stared at him and understood what he wanted her to do. Her demeanour changed as she took a deep breath, her back ramrod straight. Grim determination was etched in every line of her neck and jaw.

"Roald, I am an *aswang*. I wish I can take it back. I wish I can say being an aswang is a euphemism for some medical condition that can be cured. That with the right and enough treatment, I will no longer be one. But that's not the case. I, and my family, are all *aswangs*, and we have been for centuries."

Her voice had firmed, her declaration, calm, but his brain couldn't seem to grasp what she said.

Galen grimaced at Yuana's statement. Ysobella threw Galen another sharp glance, as if able to read his thoughts. And this confused him more.

They knew what Yuana was talking about?

"Yuana, how can you be one? They do not exist. They are

folklore, just one of the fantastical creatures in our mythology..."

The despair in him grew. He was afraid Yuana suffered from a psychosis that required medical attention. But he could deal with her mental illness and support her through it for the rest of their lives.

"We exist, Roald. And I can prove it." Her voice intensified, a tinge of frustration in the heightened pitch. She pulled her hand from his grasp and stood up.

Her father shot to his feet, and he followed suit.

"Mama, Papa, can you leave us?"

"Ah, Yuana... no, I draw the line on you getting naked..." Galen exclaimed, paternal protectiveness rising to the surface.

"Galen, relax... and shut up." Ysobella's gentle admonishment stopped him, a restraining hand on his arm. She tugged at him, but Galen refused to move and intended to stand his ground. Ysobella pulled at him. Galen relented and allowed her to pull him toward their room, an expression of surprise at the hand that led him away.

As the door closed behind them, Yuana turned to him. They were now standing face to face, just inches apart.

"It's all right, Roald. Whatever your decision after I show you, I will accept. I only ask that you keep everything I told you and what you will witness, a secret. You cannot expose us. It is dangerous, and fatal... to us..."

A trembling right palm rested on his cheek. It was an act of love and comfort, to prepare him for what was coming. The gentle action made him more anxious.

"Yuana, you do not have to do this..."

He did not know what he was denying her to do. The terror must have reflected in his eyes because Yuana's hand stilled.

"Roald, I can stop here, and we can forget this conversation ever happened. But our relationship cannot progress. Everything has changed, and there is no going back. Without you accepting this truth, there is no future for us. Without it, you cannot accept me. And this acceptance is crucial to us being together, for you to join me in my world, because I won't be able to survive in yours." Her voice broke, but he could not mistake the finality in her words, the desolation in her posture.

"Yuana..." He did not know what to say. His chest hurt like his ribs were being ripped apart.

"You can walk away now, go home, think it over. Or you can stay, keep an open mind and let me prove to you what I am. The choice is yours," Yuana said in a calm but determined voice. Her decision clear in the firm lift of her chin.

He sank back into his seat, his knees weak, his mind a jumble of tumultuous thoughts. It was so unlike him, as his one great skill was making a quick analysis of any situation, listening to his gut, and making a decision. Those skills failed him today, at the moment when Yuana and their future were at stake.

Yuana decided for him. She pulled him up and out of his chair and led him to the door of the suite. His steps were wooden, but he did not resist. She opened the door, gave him a light but lingering kiss on the lips, and with a gentle push she closed the door on him.

He stood outside, faced with the closed door of Galen's suite. His soul in chaos, but the need to run was overwhelming. The terror was familiar, like a long-forgotten emotion, a monster that used to haunt him, and had come back to life.

It was paralysing.

───────

His ear pressed against the door; Galen tried to listen in on what was happening in his living room. There was no discernible sound from outside. He looked back to confer with Ysobella, who sat on their bed, one elegant leg crossed over the other, watching him.

"I cannot hear a thing," he whispered.

She nodded. "Roald left, Yuana let him go." Her confident assertion confirmed that her keener sense of hearing was able to pick up the sounds in the other room much better than him.

Galen opened the door and found Yuana still standing by the front door, her back rigid, taking deep breaths to calm herself. And as soon as she saw him, she lost control, her face crumpled, and she burst into tears.

He rushed over and enfolded her in his arms, offering comfort to the wonderful brave young woman who had just gone through something he probably wouldn't have the strength to do himself. Seeing her broken made him understand what his Bel must have suffered when she left him, and whatever remnants of anger and resentment he harboured in his heart vanished completely.

Ysobella stood by the bedroom door as she watched them both, heart-warmed by the sight of father and daughter together, but her eyes gleamed with concern and heartbreak for their only child.

With a sigh, she walked closer and embraced Yuana from behind. Yuana became sandwiched between the two adults who would do everything in their power to make things better for her, including taking on her pain if that was possible.

Roald trudged up to his condo unit, consumed by his own thoughts and emotions. He did not know how he got home without running over anyone along the way. His phone rang off the hook, but did not bother to pick it up. He was shell-shocked, like his psyche was detached from his heart and body.

He went to the sidebar in his dining area and poured himself a measure of cognac. The fiery trail of the spirit down his throat defrosted the icy chill that covered his heart and thawed the feeling back into him. And with the thawing, the remembered chaos and pain followed.

How did such an enjoyable lunch turn into this nightmare?

Yuana's claim upended his well-ordered world and shook the foundation of his existence.

Why would Yuana claim to be a mythical creature?

Either she believed it, or it was an alibi to drive him away somehow. As a deterrent, the latter makes little sense to use as an excuse - it was too far-fetched and the least effective one to stop their impending marriage. It was far more plausible she believed herself to be an aswang.

He poured another measure of cognac into the glass, took the bottle with him, then slumped his exhausted frame onto the couch. His thoughts restarted; his brain resumed its usual pace. He was ready to analyse and put order to what happened earlier.

In all that muddle, one thing was clear to him - Yuana thought that being an aswang made it impossible for them to be together. She wanted to protect him. This was the last barrier he needed to shatter. And the only way to do this would be to listen to her, to keep an open mind. And perhaps he would make heads or tails on what caused her mistaken pronouncement.

Then he remembered she emphasised they could only be together if he accepted her and adapted to her world, that it would be impossible to move forward without it. He would give her whatever she needed, listen to her, and adapt to the circumstances until he guided her out of this psychosis that clouded her reality. He would do everything necessary for them to get over this hurdle, because if there was something he would never accept or adapt to, it would be the loss of Yuana.

Yuana would need strong proof to shake her out of her belief. He would let her talk, take notes and get clues, and then he could research about it and find the proof to present to her. She could have a psychosis that remained untreated for years. In the three years they had been together, Yuana had exhibited no telltale behavioural signs or symptoms of any mental issues.

It came out of nowhere. So, maybe, it was buried in her subconscious and his offer of marriage triggered it to the surface.

Dinner would be strenuous tonight. She was not up for the questions, or worse, the concerned glances her family would throw her way throughout dinner. She had cried long and hard earlier, but her tears still hovered under a fragile facade. A word or a look would shatter it.

She would rather stay in her room and curl up in a ball to soothe the ache that bloomed in her insides since Roald left. Today, she learned a heartbreak was not a quick pain like a stab or a bullet shot, but a long, lingering, expanding kind that intensified hour by hour. It was like poison spreading all over her body, and there was no stopping it.

She still held hope that Roald would not stay away too long, that after the initial shock had dissipated, he would call her. But she had to prepare for the outcome that Roald may not come back.

Maybe this was the best outcome. She did not reveal verifiable information that could endanger their kind, but it was alarming enough for Roald to walk away.

This could be the middle ground for them, a less painful option.

That had to be better than the others.

Her father's heartbeat was steady in her ears. His scent, which should be new to her, was familiar. He smelled of juniper berries and moss. Being curled up between her parents gave her a measure of comfort. She could sense her mother's concerned gaze; her pain and exhaustion must be visible to her.

The drive to their house was cheerless and short. As they pulled up in front of the drive, she pushed herself up into a sitting position and uncurled her legs from under her to find her shoes. It would cause alarm if she walked into the house looking like death was upon her. She would need to make herself presentable.

Her mother's gentle hand stayed her fidgety one as she rummaged in her bag for a mirror.

"Would you prefer your dinner sent to your room tonight, Yu?"

Bless her mother's sharp instinct for reading her so well. She shook her head. "I am not hungry, Mama." Food was the furthest from her mind.

"Okay." Her mother nodded.

She took the moment her parents gave her to check her reflection in her hand mirror. She was as wrung out as a used mop. Her emotions raw, her mind in a whirl. Blessedly, her eyes were no longer puffy. She would pass muster.

One more deep breath, and she got out of the car, braced herself for the quick moment that it would take for her to say goodnight to her family and take herself off to her room.

Dinner ended earlier than usual, Katelin noted. Each one of them had masked their concern for the youngest member of the clan when she kissed everyone goodnight. Yuana opted to go to bed early, without dinner, and more worrisome, without sustenance. This was the first time she had turned down that which was vital to their survival. They did not badger her because she needed time to herself and she had about two days before her vital hunger kicked in.

They all guessed that things did not go well between Yuana and Roald. It must not be too bad because there was no forewarning from the three for serious consequences the family would have to face. They hoped they would not need to deploy the Restoration plan. They had not needed to for decades.

Katelin worried about her granddaughter. It would be the worst outcome if Yuana was forced to end Roald's life herself. Her granddaughter possessed a sweet and sensitive soul, and it would destroy her to do so.

She was tempted to ask Ysobella about what happened when Yuana left the dining room, but her mother shot her a warning glance, one that everyone caught. That was a clear non-verbal instruction from her, the Matriarch. They would not discuss the issue in front of Galen. A quick hand signal from her informed them all — the discussion would be for the following day, nine a.m.

And their topic would be the Risk Reduction and Intervention Plan, the *RRIP*. They would not allow Yuana to reach that point of catastrophe. She was far too young to carry the memory, the trauma of taking the life of someone that could very well be the love of her life. It would not be a good way to live the rest of the long life their kind had been blessed, or cursed, by nature to possess.

Edrigu's figure emerged from the adjoining bathroom, his hair damp from the shower. It was a quick one, and she could guess why - her husband wanted to speak to her. He harboured the same thought that niggled with persistence in her brain since Yuana asked to be excused. The thought refused to be banished and stayed in both their heads the whole evening.

His eyes hunted for her on their bed, but shifted to the window where she sat, when he found their bed empty.

"We have something to discuss," he began.

"Yes, I know."

Edrigu stared at her. She was sure that he recognised the seriousness of the topic by whatever grim expression graced her face.

Meanwhile, in another room, Margaita and Lorenzo were discussing the same thing—the De Vida *RRIP*—and the last time they implemented it. It did not end well for Martin, and the emotional toll for their daughter, Ximena, was crushing.

Their eldest daughter had been paying for the consequence of her choice for over fifty years. And there was no sign of Ximena forgiving herself soon.

With heavy hearts, they discussed the merit of setting up the preemptive actions they might have to deploy to protect their great granddaughter. They would hold a big family meeting at home tomorrow.

Without Galen.

Without Yuana.

And not so far away, Roald had been pacing.

He turned over in his mind several possibilities and justification on why Yuana believed she was an aswang. The presence of her parents in the room, their silence while Yuana made the claims, baffled him.

Did they understand what she said?

How can they accept it?

How can they support it? Or even encourage it? They were both doctors.

And he wished he had the mind to ask earlier. None of it made sense. His stomach muscles clenched ever tighter as the evening progressed. He sipped his drink, welcoming the slow burn as it travelled down his throat, trying to shake the sense of disconnect in himself.

The chaos in his mind, his heart and his gut created unbearable tension all over his body. He flexed his shoulders to relieve the tension there, then took a long deep breath to release the pressure that had not left his chest since he quit Galen's condo.

Hours later, he gave up drinking cognac as he dissected his own thoughts; the spirit did not help at all.

His exhausted mind gave way to sleep around dawn, but just as he fell into sleep, an idea murmured deep into his subconscious...

What if Yuana was telling the truth?

That night, a long dormant nightmare that used to plague his childhood came back with a vengeance.

Yuana could not summon the energy to get up. The clock on her wall showed it was almost noon. On normal days, by this time, she would be at her weekly meeting with her team, an activity she considered crucial.

Today, she had no enthusiasm to care about anything, or do anything. Not even to think. She overslept, and yet she was still exhausted. She only wanted to sleep, to get a respite from the pressing weight on her chest, to numb it.

For just a few more hours...

There was a soft knock on the door. Yuana closed her eyes and pretended to sleep. When she did not answer, her mother entered, approached the bed and sat by the edge. Yuana kept her breath steady, even as her mother caressed her hair. She did not want to talk, did not want to be reminded.

She wanted peace, she just wanted Roald.

Her act must have been convincing, because her mother got up after a while and left. She would be back to check up on her again later. That was her mother's nature.

She was certain her mother and the entire family had already been told what happened last night. And they had discussed what to do next. It should worry her, because the next steps would involve the Tribunal.

But she could not muster the motivation to care.

Ysobella retreated from her daughter's room. Her child was suffering, and she felt helpless. Yet she could do nothing about it. Galen had been furious about the situation last night, but the one thing that mellowed his rage was Yuana's action. Their daughter snuggled close to him like a child, and Galen's heart melted. He was grateful to be there to comfort his daughter.

The De Vidas had a meeting earlier about the circumstance with Roald. They did not include Galen in the meeting because her grandparents deemed it too early for him to know the inner workings of their society and the Tribunal.

During their meeting, they decided they would implement the RRIP—their Risk Reduction & Intervention Plan as a proactive move, albeit at a slower pace. But the RRIP's Final

Wave would only be deployed on her go-signal. She had spoken for Roald, on Yuana's behalf. She believed, or hoped, that Roald would come around.

For the moment, at her request, they all agreed to give Roald some time, a chance to prove himself worthy. For Yuana's sake, she wanted to give her daughter a chance at happiness. She just hoped her faith in Roald would prove worth it.

With a sigh, she proceeded downstairs to wait for Galen.

———

Galen arrived just before lunch at the De Vida home. He would meet Ysobella there. He wanted to check on his daughter. Nita opened the door for him, greeted him like a part of the family. He followed her to the living room where everyone congregated.

All of them except Yuana.

It was not a good sign.

After exchanging handshakes with the men and buss on the cheeks with the ladies, he kissed his Bel last on both cheeks and murmured, "How's Yuana?"

Her absence concerned him, but it did not surprise him she was a no-show. Ysobella glanced upstairs.

"Should I go to her?" he asked, uneasy. "I am clueless about this... fatherhood thing."

Ysobella gave him a slight smile. "Perhaps she will come down for lunch, for you."

———

Yuana did not come down for lunch. Nita came back from her room, lunch tray still full, and informed them Yuana was not hungry and would rather sleep. Seven pairs of eyes exchanged worried looks all around. Every single one of them fought the impulse to go up to Yuana's room.

No one did. Lunch had the thick air of false ease. It was a good thing the menu featured light dishes. It was hard to eat anything on an already tight stomach.

He expected the family to discuss Yuana and Roald's situation, but no one brought it up. The grim expressions on the faces of the older men and the disquiet in the women meant something was afoot. He wondered if the board meeting that Ysobella attended earlier was truly about business. It annoyed him they excluded him from the discussion of Yuana's future; he was Yuana's father, after all. Perhaps his new family had not learned how to share yet, and old habits were hard to break.

During coffee and teatime, he excused himself to see Yuana.

He knocked, and when she didn't respond, he opened the door a crack. Her room was dark, her blackout curtains prevented the daylight into her bedroom. His eyesight hunted for his daughter in the room, as he called out her name in a whisper.

He found her in the middle of her bed, curled up like a child. With no response from her, he tiptoed to her bedside and looked down at his daughter. Yuana was deep in a fitful sleep. She was in the middle of a painful dream. A slight frown creased her eyebrows. Tears leaked from the corner of her lids; small sobs escaped her. His paternal heart ached. He wanted to wake her up, but she quieted after a shaky breath, and settled into her slumber.

Yuana tugged at his heartstrings. His only daughter. This young woman who made Ysobella's bitter exile sweet would be his Bel's solace when he left this earth. His daughter, the other half of the sole reason he wanted to extend his life past his prognosis.

He needed to talk to Roald and knock some sense into him. And if that did not work, he would make the boy pay for hurting his baby girl.

The object of Galen's outrage had a terrible night. Roald woke up more anxious than the night before, caused by the nightmares that felt familiar. It filled his dreams with horrific interwoven images of him frozen and helpless as he watched Yuana attack faceless individuals, of him eating raw and bloody human organs — of their newborn child turned into a monster baby attacking a faceless nurse.

One particular portion of his dream bothered him the most, but he could not remember the details. What jolted him awake was the primal scream of a child, a child that might have been him, yet separate. He sat up, sweaty and panting. His heart pounded so hard against his chest he feared he was having a heart attack.

Thoughts of Yuana came to him. He was a heel for not texting her to assure her he was still there, that he would not leave. That he just needed some time to sort himself out.

He must phone her.

Two hours later, his anxiety reached fever pitch. He could not contact Yuana, or she had decided not to pick up his calls. And this disturbed him so. He wanted to go to her, but his emotions were in such a disarray that seeing her might do more damage than good. The state of his emotion was so precarious.

He checked his emails for want of something to do, and when there was nothing that required his immediate attention, he just exited his inbox. He had no motivation. Nothing seemed to matter. His future did not interest him like it used to. It was like his mind and heart anaesthetized him from life. The sense of impending doom had not left him since yesterday, and it was mounting in intensity like a looming deadline.

He was about to dial Yuana's number again when his phone rang; it was the reception.

"Mr Magsino, you have a visitor, Dr Galen Aurelio... Do I send him up?"

Galen is here?

Alarm bells rang in his head.

Is he here because he was mad at him, or did something happen to Yuana? She had not been answering his calls.

"Yes, please send him up."

He opened the door for Galen at the first knock. And judging from the grim frown on his face, he was more angry than worried. Either way, his presence would bring unpleasant news.

Galen pushed past Roald and walked into his living room. He looked like he wanted to throttle him and knock his teeth down his throat. Galen had the right to be protective over Yuana. As her father, he could pummel him to the ground, and he would be justified. But at the moment, Roald did not care.

"Is Yuana all right? She was not answering my calls." His first concern took precedence over Galen's wrath.

The worry in his voice must have taken the edge off Galen's anger, for his mouth twisted in annoyance.

"Humph, serves you right! I would ignore your calls too, if I was her," Galen said, exasperated.

His eyes bore into him, and he must have seen the signs of a sleepless night on his face, as Galen's sigh sounded resigned.

"So, what is your plan, Roald?"

He was not clear what Galen was asking from him. Or why

Galen seemed more interested in his relationship with Yuana, rather than the state of Yuana's mind. Galen appeared to have accepted Yuana's impossible statement that she was an aswang like it was the truth.

"Sir, why does it seem like you are supporting Yuana's statement she is an aswang? Why are you not alarmed that she made those pronouncements? You are a doctor; does this not bother you?"

Galen's brow rose. His mouth opened as if he was about to say something but stopped himself. A long sigh preceded his statement. "The issue between you and my daughter is not a medical one. It's a test of faith in each other."

Galen's cryptic response confused him.

Why was Yuana's father not concerned about her mental health?

"What do you mean? Did she say those things to see if I would stick around? I cannot believe that Yuana would resort to something so petty. It's not like her. And she sounded serious... Was she?"

Galen kept silent; his probing gaze so prolonged it made him uncomfortable. Yuana's father seemed to have seen something inside him that changed his expression.

His sigh was deep, "It is not my thoughts or feelings that matter in this, Roald. It's yours, and more to the point, what you believe." A small, sad smile twisted Galen's lips. "You and Yuana need to finish this. The sooner, the better. If you want your relationship to move forward, there is no other route but that," he said. "Hopefully, your path won't end up diverging."

Roald could only nod.

And the anxiety lodged in his chest grew.

Roald spent the next couple of hours trying to contact Yuana, but to no avail. Her father told him she was resting in her room, but she could not have been sleeping all this time. The growing urgency to speak to her, to reassure her and himself all was well between them was making him frantic. He told himself maybe she just needed some space, some time for herself. Perhaps he needed to give her that much, for now.

He spent another two hours see-sawing between wanting to give Yuana more time and trying to contact her. He had been sending her text messages until he realised the phone recording stated her phone was out of reach. Her phone was off. She would not receive the text messages or the missed call notifications.

Finally, he could not take it anymore. He grabbed his car keys and rushed out of his unit. Securing Yuana was the most important thing. Together, they could triumph over any obstacles. Apart, they would have no chance.

Ten minutes later, his car pulled up in front of the De Vida's driveway. It was half-past nine in the evening, so he was sure the family finished dinner already. He was uncertain what kind of reception to expect from them. The De Vidas would know the discord between him and Yuana. He hoped they would not find it disrespectful for showing up this late.

Nita opened the door for him. While the De Vida's housekeeper displayed slight surprise, her amiable manner toward him did not change. It was an encouraging sign.

"Is Yuana in?" he asked.

She hesitated, but led him to the receiving area, through the anteroom to the main living room. She bid him to wait. When she returned, Katelin was with her.

It was disconcerting to gaze into Katelin's less than cheerful face. But she did not look angry.

"Good evening, Mrs Orzabal, I am here to see Yuana."

"Good evening, Roald. Yuana is in her room. I am not sure if she is up to seeing anyone, including you." Her candid response hurt.

But his feelings did not matter at the moment. "Is she all right? I have been trying to call her the whole afternoon, but she hasn't been picking up my call." He just wanted an assurance that Yuana was fine. If she would not see him, at least her family could reassure him.

"Please come and sit down, Roald," Katelin said. She gestured towards one of the plush seats in the living room.

He complied.

"We are concerned about her. She stayed in her room the whole day, she did not eat, and she refused to talk to anyone... What happened between you and Yuana?"

He had the impression Katelin already knew, and she wanted to hear from him, find out his side of the argument. Her face was emotionless, and she seemed ready to give him a chance.

"I do not mean to be disrespectful, ma'am, but I do not think it is right for me to discuss this with you until Yuana and I have sorted it out." He could only apologise, but he would not betray Yuana's confidence unless she told him it was okay. "And I'm worried about Yuana. Is it possible for me to see her?" he added.

Katelin's blank face softened. She stood up and motioned for him to follow her up the stairs, through a long corridor that overlooked the vast living room. Yuana's room was at the end of the hallway. Every door was heavy, ornate, and antique-looking with distinct carvings. Each door had a unique design, but he had no time to inspect or admire it.

They stopped at her dark hardwood door with carvings of trees and birds. Katelin softly rapped on the door. There was no answer, so Katelin knocked again.

"Yuana, *hija,* Roald is here."

For a moment, he thought Yuana would not respond, that she would ignore his presence. But the door opened a crack, then widened. Yuana emerged from the dark, her eyes swollen, dark circles underneath. They were big and tortured in her pale face. The sight took his breath away. His heart squeezed tighter as he noted her gaunt face. She had lost weight in the two days they were apart.

By instinct, he took a step forward, to take her into his arms, but she stayed him with an outstretched hand. The act of rejection hurt, and he retracted his own hand and rested it on his chest. He rubbed the jolt of pain in his chest away.

In silence, Yuana opened the door wider to let him in. He came in and stopped in the middle of the room. It would have been in total darkness except for the light that spilled through the opened door. She had drawn the heavy blackout curtains closed. Not a single lamp, or a candle was lit, which was strange because Yuana loved being surrounded by lighted candles.

Yuana had a short, murmured conversation with Katelin before her grandmother walked away and left both of them. Then she stood still, surrounded by the light from the hallway. She stared at him, then flicked the light switch on the standing lamp by the side of the door, bathing the room with soft illumination. She closed the door shut and walked towards the end of her bed. Her eyes never left his as she sat down. Her exhausted sigh made his heart ache a bit more.

"Are you ready to listen to my truth?" She sounded resigned.

"Yes, but not until we have taken care of you first. Your father said you haven't eaten in days."

Unable to help himself, he crossed the room and pulled her into his arms. Yuana resisted for a moment, her body rigid. He knew she wanted to keep the emotional wall she built during the past days between them. But he was determined to offer her comfort and make her feel the longing in his soul.

After a while, she yielded and relaxed into his warmth. The tensed muscles of her back eased, her body moulded into his. His own sigh of relief was deep. It was like coming home.

A short eternity passed. Then she pulled away, a tired smile on her face.

"I am okay now. I am ready to talk when you are."

He shook his head. "No. Tonight, you will eat first, then sleep. We will talk tomorrow. I will come back here to continue the unfinished discussion between us." He pushed the tousled hair off her face. Yuana needed care for now. "Understood?" He kissed her forehead to soften the command.

She nodded. "Okay."

As Roald drove back home, he felt better, more reassured about his relationship with Yuana. Yet his apprehension remained stronger than before. He told himself this time he knew what they would talk about. Unlike the other day, when surprise overtook him. Next time he could control his reaction, and the situation.

She had promised to provide proof, and he should look forward to that proof.

So, why do I feel anxious about seeing it?

Its presence would help him determine what mental issues were plaguing Yuana, and the absence of credible proof might help open her eyes.

Never had he perceived the dawning of another day with such trepidation and anxiety.

Meanwhile, Yuana went to bed calmer, and despite having some soup and bread, she did not feel revived. Her resolve to settle the issue in the morning strengthened. Not having to guess the status of their relationship was freeing.

She had the foretaste of life without Roald, and it was an unpleasant experience. And a big part of it was the uncertainty.

Roald's visit tonight lifted some weight off her chest. He proved he would not just leave. But tomorrow, she would know for sure if he would stay and what her future would be.

Roald's logical brain would not accept her words alone. He would need a proof he could not discount. Only shape-shifting would achieve that. The one irrevocable proof she had would also be the most dangerous and damaging.

Still, there was hope. Roald came to her tonight. She would keep that hope in her heart.

For now, she needed her rest. Perhaps a good night's sleep would cure the slight tremor that plagued her body.

The light of the moon provided extra illumination for a small woman. She was tracking the footsteps of the wild boar she was hunting. Her sun-browned skin dry and wrinkled, her curly hair thick on her head. She was an experienced hunter. Her responsibility to her human tribes-people was to provide them with food. This had been her task for the last ninety years. In exchange, they sacrifice their dead and their sick for her needs. One could say it was a fair trade, but she did not like it.

The Tribunal now provided her sustenance. There was no need for her tribes-people to sacrifice anyone to her. They offer her the organs of their dead now and then as a gesture of gratitude.

She shook herself out of her thoughts; she had a boar to capture. Their tribe needed the food as the recent drought devastated their cultivated fields, leaving nothing for them to sell or to eat. She needed to provide for them.

She could smell the wild boar, hear its snorts and the rustling of the leaves as it hunted for something to eat. The boar was big and would need strength and cunning to catch and subdue. *Should I shape-shift?* If she got close enough to the boar, her human form was better equipped to handle the boar than her dog form.

She moved closer to the wild boar, taking care not to alert it to her presence. It had found some tubers and was busy digging it out with its tusk. She crept closer to her prey. At ten yards away, with a burst of speed, she sprinted to it, grabbed its hind legs and swung the boar against the nearest tree, bashing its head. The boar did not stand a chance.

The animal could feed the tribe for two meals; she needed two more to assure three days' worth of food. She was scenting her environment, trying to pick up the odour of any nearby potential prey, when she scented another *Aswang* in the area. Someone she was not familiar with. She had not encountered other aswang in this part of the woods for decades.

This was curious.

She was looking for the aswang by scent when she heard the zing of a travelling bullet a millisecond before it hit her at the back of the head. She was dead before she hit the ground.

From behind a tree, the unfamiliar aswang stepped out to approach the fallen aswang that he shot. He laid the hunting rifle down beside the body. He inspected his prey for a moment, noting she must be a middle-aged, maybe a hundred to a hundred fifty years old. It was hard to tell with these indigenous people.

He took out his hunting knife and with quick, practiced movements, disembowelled his prey. His mouth watered when he got to the heart. This was his favourite organ. He sat by the root of the old tree where she dropped dead and enjoyed his spoils in leisure.

He felt the energy of another aswang course through his veins, and satisfaction suffused him. The risk of the crime was more than worth the reward for this kind of power.

Sometime later, he cut up the remaining organs and placed it in a collapsible ice bag to preserve them. The kidneys would be good for another eleven hours, and the liver another twenty-nine. Then he took out the folding shovel he carried in his back-pack and started digging. He needed to bury her body so no one would find her. And the iztaris would never know there was an active harravis predating in the area.

9

YUANA, THE VISCEREBUS

The day started at half-past nine in the morning for Yuana. She still felt weak, and the tremor in her body had not dissipated. A tight ball of muscles ran up and down her spine. It rested at the small of her back where it shot sharp jolts of pain that jerked her upright. It took several deep breaths to relax her back until the spasm faded.

Her entire body ached, like some sort of malady.

Did I sleep in a bad position last night?

Once the pain disappeared, she continued to dress. She pulled on a light, flowy, and silky summer dress over her head. The dress was appropriate for later. It would be easy to pull off. With her hair tied in a loose bun, she proceeded downstairs to the breakfast room.

She was on her second cup of tea when her great-grandparents came down, their fingers intertwined. It was bittersweet to see their instinctive display of love for each other. It was something she wished for herself and Roald.

"Good morning, 'Ela, 'Elo." She greeted them with a smile.

She knew they worried for her, and she wanted them reassured. They smiled back at the greeting, bent down and gave her a kiss on the cheek.

"Did you sleep well, Yu-yu?" Her 'Elo surveyed her pale face and touched the slight grey circles around her eyes. But he smiled in satisfaction.

Yuana gave her Abuelo a quick nod of confirmation. "Elo, Roald is coming at lunch today, to finish our talk." She wanted them informed. And she needed their help.

They exchanged quick glances and nodded their acknowledgement. She understood they would let her take the lead on this, but their support was unequivocal.

While her great grandparents had omelette and toasts, she continued to have tea to calm her nerves. She had no appetite, and the tremor in her body returned and had intensified. The muscle spasms restarted. The knot at the base of her spine reformed and travelled up her back in a slow roll, tightening the muscles along the way. It had now rested at the base of her skull.

She regulated her breathing in silence, to will it away. Her great grandparents might get alarmed. It seemed her body was unaccustomed to emotional distress; it had no previous practice. This was the first real one she had ever experienced, and it was major.

"Yu, we want you to know that we readied the Risk Reduction and Intervention Plan. We placed the First Wave team of iztaris on alert, but we will not deploy them until your mother gives us the signal."

The information made her heart jump. This was no longer just between herself and Roald and their relationship. The hypothetical danger to Roald's life was now a reality.

She could only nod. "I understand, 'Elo. It is our law, after all. You had no choice. It would cause concern in the Tribunal, your position as Patriarch and Matriarch would be in jeopardy."

"But we are not so tied to the law that we cannot give the youngest of our clan some special privileges. It is within my call as Matriarch to allow your Roald a chance to redeem himself. Take your time if you are not ready for a full revelation today, because the RRIP's deployment would only kick in once you do." Her great grandmother smiled at her encouragingly.

"Thank you, 'Ela. But I am ready to do it today. I do not want to wait. I think my nerves can't take it..."

She grimaced as another spasm hit her. A soft gasp escaped her. She clenched her hand to stop the tremor, a smile pasted on her lips so as not to worry her elders. She regulated her breaths to will the spasms away, but they kept coming in waves, increasing in frequency and intensity.

Her great grandfather stared at her, noting the sweat on her brow, the strain of pain around her mouth. His hand shot out and closed over her clenched palm.

"Yuana, you are having a reflexive transformation episode. You're about to auto-morphose." Her great grandfather's voice was as tense as the hand that covered hers.

Her great grandmother's gaze became alert as it swivelled to her.

"What do you mean, 'Elo?" She tried to calm the tremor in her muscles and stop the spasm that travelled up and down her back. The pain of it robbed her of breath. She was panting within a minute.

"You haven't had sustenance for two days, and your vital hunger is growing. Your bones and muscles are preparing to transfigure, but your crux, your inner control is preventing it, hence the tremors and the spasms. If you don't get sustenance soon, you will be too weak to fight your vital instinct and it will overpower your crux, and you cannot stop the transformation. Our vital instinct will ensure that you hunt, to secure sustenance," her great grandfather explained as he watched her fight off the transfiguration.

Without sustenance, she had a few more hours before she shape-shifted into her animus. She never had to fight off her vital instinct before. She had no experience or practice; her crux was not that strong.

Her great grandmother's conversation over the phone with her Uncle Íñigo floated to her. She asked for help. Her 'Ela walked back to the breakfast room to the sight of her hyperventilating in an effort to stay the spasms and the tremors.

"Yuana, relax... Take long slow breaths in... long slow breaths out. Focus on your breathing, not the spasms or the tremors. Just focus on your own breaths..."

Her 'Ela's voice was as soothing as the warm hands that enveloped her clammy ones. She obeyed, slowed her breathing, and within a few minutes, the spasms subsided, the tremors abated.

"Thank you, 'Ela," she breathed. Wisps of loose hair had stuck on her sweaty neck and face. She was drenched.

"You're welcome, Yu. Íñigo is coming with victus in about an hour. Can you hold on until then?" Her calm voice was reassuring. Her gaze travelled all over her face, and she looked satisfied colour was back on her cheeks.

She nodded. She was glad she would be better soon. It would not do if she shape-shifted into her big cat form in front of Roald without warning.

And worse, what if my vital instinct took over my animus, and I attacked Roald, being the only human in proximity?

"Eat, Yuana, even if you have no appetite. You need protein

in your system to boost your strength," her great grandfather said.

As if on cue, Nita came into the room with some slices of beef, cooked medium and sautéed.

She complied, recognising now she was hungry on both fronts. Her physical hunger was easier to satisfy than her vital hunger. If it would help stave her vital instincts from kicking in, then eat this beef she would, until Uncle Íñigo arrives.

———

Roald also got up early, for a different reason. He spent the morning researching online about the malady that Yuana could suffer from. He discarded a few of the listed symptoms. So far, the closest he found was Clinical Lycanthropy and Renfield Syndrome.

Clinical Lycanthropy might be the best explanation for Yuana's psychosis. Those who suffer from it were convinced they turn into wolves or other animals. If those patients assumed themselves to be werewolves, it was not a stretch for Yuana to believe she was an aswang.

Those diagnosed with the disease sometimes barked or howled like wolves, but as far as he knew Yuana never behaved or exhibited animal behaviour. She had been perfectly and beautifully normal until her pronouncement.

As for the Renfield Syndrome, Yuana had not exhibited an obsession to drink blood or any other behavioural patterns associated with the syndrome. They had been together almost daily for three years, and she had shown no signs of paranoia, let alone the desire to drink blood which seemed to be the primary component of the malady. His stomach turned at the idea. He was glad to strike that one out.

The research, while not conclusive, gave him hope. If it was a medical condition, it just needed treatment. Maybe her condition was rare that she believed herself to be a mythical monster rather than a normal animal. But it did not matter, because if psychiatry sessions could treat Clinical Lycanthropy, then her psychosis was treatable.

It was a relief to hold the results of his extensive research. The pressure on his chest eased to a degree he felt almost the same as before. Thank the tech gods for Google and Reddit. With the relief came the realisation he was famished. He had not eaten a proper meal for what seemed like an eternity, so while he printed his research materials, he made himself breakfast.

After eating, he planned to take a shower and drive over to Yuana's as agreed. He was due there at eleven a.m.

Hours later, his mood was buoyant, even excited, as he jumped into his car, briefcase in tow, to drive himself to the De Vida home.

Since ten a.m., the whole De Vida clan, except Ysobella and Galen who were still on their way, gathered in the living room. They scattered around, each trying to project calm in the tension-filled morning.

Not one of them knew how the day would unfold as Yuana never discussed her plan. And on top of it, she was in danger of involuntary shape-shifting because her vital instinct was triggered. Even now, they watched Yuana calming herself down, trying to keep her crux in control, to delay the shift for as long as possible.

Íñigo had not called yet. The sources he worked on this

morning were not appropriate, so he called all their other branches to see if they could find what Yuana needed - fresh human viscera. The location had to be less than an hour away. They also had to make sure they were not taking away from other aswangs.

Ximena realised they needed a plan just in case Yuana transfigured. Her vital instinct to hunt might override her control.

"Mama, Papa, we need a place for Yuana to rest while we are waiting for Íñigo, just in case she transforms. We need to make sure she is away from Roald and Galen..."

Margaita and Lorenzo both nodded and scrambled into action.

Her great grandfather led her to the entertainment room. It was a spacious room, with twelve well-upholstered maroon leather seats and padded cream walls for better sound quality. This was her favourite. It had a lingering smell of butter popcorn courtesy of the automatic popcorn machine in the corner. There was no obvious movie screen on the wall, instead, it would descend from the ceiling via remote control. Her grandparents commissioned it for watching movies and playing games. It was perfect to keep the noise in and out.

Her great grandmother sat with her to keep her entertained and distracted from the tremor and the spasms. They sat in companionable silence, breathing in and out in unison to keep her focused on her breathing.

The reflexive transformation and all the burning sensations that kept coming in waves all over her took precedence. She had never experienced this before. She never had to go without sustenance and worry about having her vital instinct kick in to the point of desperation. And if Uncle Íñigo did not come soon, she would have firsthand knowledge of the desire that drove their kind to hunt humans.

Already, the tremors were getting harder to quiet, the knotted ball of muscle at the base of her spine more difficult to subdue. Her skin tingled, creating goosebumps, and her stomach muscles twisted into knots. Her transformation was imminent.

Will I shape-shift into my favourite animal, or will my vital instinct decide what form I will turn into?

"It is likely you will turn into the animal you most often shape-shift into," her 'Ela replied.

"Did I say that out aloud?" It startled her. But she was glad to focus on something else.

"Not so loud, but yes, you did." A reassuring smile on her great-grandmother's face.

"Likely? What other animals can I turn into aside from my usual go-to panther?" She knew very little about this impending process.

"It seemed that De Vida women have a partiality for sleek felines. Your grandma Katelin's animus is a leopard." The idea amused her great-grandmother. "So, why a panther? Like your mother?"

"Yeah, well, a panther is sexy, 'Ela. And it is easier to hide in the dark when your coat is black." She was curious now what her great grandmother's spirit animal would be. "So, what is yours, 'Ela? And how about 'Elo's?"

"I shift into a wolf. Your aunt Ximena's animus is also a wolf. Your 'Elo is a bear."

Interesting. "So, what other animals will I transform into?"

"It's hard to tell. Your grandfather used to transform into a fox until he discovered that his true animus was a dire wolf.

Mine had always been a wolf, and it was the same when I auto-morphosed."

"But why do we have two spirit animal forms? Shouldn't we just aim to transform into our animus in the first place?"

"In the olden times, we didn't choose our spirit animal. The adults force an auto-morphosis while the child is young, and the child's first transformation would usually be their animus. Later on, we discovered we can master our transformation skills, and we learned to shift into many other animals. And children learned to choose their form to some extent. Times changed, and soon, our kind trained to transform with the animal form of our choice, rather than what our spirit dictated."

"So, what is the likelihood of my animus being wolf like yours, 'Ela?"

Her Ela shook her head. "Not a chance. You have a natural affinity for feline beings. Your spirit animal was a panther, your animus, if it is not a panther, would most likely be one within the cat family."

"Ah... I like my current animal form. I am used to it. Can I keep it even if I transform into another cat?" She felt regret at having to give up being a panther.

"You can always shift into your old form. But your true animus will be the most natural and powerful form for you. You will have more synergy with its attributes and powers. You will know the difference when it happens."

"I feel foolish. I have been an aswang since birth, trans-formed multiple times. Yet I still have a lot to learn about being one."

"We all do, my dear. The modern times had limited us to the rudimentary layer of our being. We allowed ourselves to ignore and forget our elemental power deep inside. Just like most of our kind transform only into their chosen animal form, very few do in their spirit animal. And majority of our kind would die without knowing and experiencing their animus."

"Well, if there was a silver lining to this excruciating process, it would be the unravelling of my true animus."

Her great-grandmother nodded, smiling.

"Ela, shouldn't I be wearing an impedio?" She recalled the use of the contraption that all of them were required by the Tribunal to have for such a time like this.

Her Abuela shook her head. "If you were alone, or if your companions would not be able to restrain you, then yes, you should be strapped in one. But with all of us here, there is no need for it." The confidence in her voice was enough to reassure her.

Voices from the living room streamed through the door left ajar by her great-grandfather, who went out to join the others. The voices of her mother and father were in the mix. She heard them ask for her and her Aunt Ximena's reply, pointing to where she was.

Her mother and father rushed in and hugged her. Her father's face lined with concern. "How are you, sweetie?" he asked, his gaze scrutinising.

"I'm okay, Papa. I..." she gasped.

A sharp stab of pain from her gut to her chest jolted her out of his embrace, cutting her voice off. The spasm at the base of her spine restarted hard and fast, the force of it bent her over. She clutched her stomach.

It alarmed Galen to see the spasming knot of muscles run up and down his daughter's back while she was bent over with what appeared to be severe stomach pain. He panicked for a split second, not knowing what to do, then his doctor side kicked in. He moved to examine Yuana, but Ysobella held him back. Her eyes were wide with urgency as she pulled him out of the room, closing the door behind them.

"Where are we going? Yuana needs me." He tried to resist Ysobella's pull, but her strength prevented him from going back to the room.

"You need to be away from her as she might shape-shift by reflex." Ysobella kept pulling him farther away from the room.

"Why do I need to stay away from her? I have seen you transform."

"That was different, Galen. Mine was a voluntary transformation. Yuana had taken no sustenance for the past two days, and her vital hunger has surfaced. When it takes over, her vital instinct will force her to hunt, and she might be too weak to control it. When that happens, she will go for the closest human around."

Terror struck his soul. The thought of his daughter attacking a human was too big a shock to take in. He never thought of his Bel, his daughter, or the whole De Vida clan as savage man-eaters. Despite their penchant for human organs, they were as sophisticated as the most affluent people he had met. Being told and almost witnessing a display of this nature of an aswang was jarring.

The front door opened, and an older gentleman walked in. He went straight through to the living room, like he was a part of the family. He had a peppering of grey hairs on his temple, and his smart, casual clothes fit his toned physique. The guy must have been a decade older than him.

"Thank god you're here, and just at the nick of time!" Ximena said as she jumped up from her seat.

She took the familiar ice box from the hands of the stranger. Nobody seemed to have thought of introducing the new arrival to him. All eyes were on the icebox that Ximena had rushed to the kitchen. Galen did not need any explanation of what it contained or what it was for. In this matter, he was in sync with the aswangs in the room.

Katelin hastened to the entertainment room, and the sounds of Yuana's gasp of pain and heavy breathing echoed in the living room.

He shot to his feet; paternal instinct overriding his sense of self-preservation. But Ysobella's grip on his arm prevented him from going to his daughter. Ysobella was strong; the power of her physical capability to restrain him was clear. Another aswang trait that separated them from humans like himself.

The doorbell rang loud and there was a synchronised swivelling of heads towards the main door, all breathing suspended. Roald had arrived.

After a split-second pause, Edrigu sprung from his seat to open the door for Roald.

Roald came into the room carrying a briefcase. He looked nervous and became more uneasy when he saw the entire family gathered. He searched for Yuana among them. Unsure of what to do, he stood just at the edge of the room.

"Is Yuana here, sir?" Roald inquired.

Edrigu nodded and motioned him to a seat but said nothing else. He threw a side glance at Katelin, which she understood. Katelin got up and walked past Roald towards the entertainment room.

Roald remained standing where he was.

Just as Katelin opened the door, the sound of agony rang from the room. And to Roald's ears, it was unmistakable; it was Yuana. The briefcase fell out of his nerveless fingers, and without a thought, he rushed towards the entertainment room. The terror in the sound and fear for her propelled him.

What he witnessed rendered him speechless. Yuana was on all fours in the middle of the room, Margaita on her knees beside her, calming her. Yuana was heaving, her back arched, her spine rippled. A ball of muscles travelled from between her shoulder blades down to her lower back, the movement stark under her silk dress.

Even from a few feet away, he could see the feverish flush that covered her body. The heat wave she generated reached him. Her skin vibrated, it changed colour and texture. Her smooth flesh-toned skin darkened into glossy jet black...

Stunned and shaken, he did not remember being pulled in haste out of the room. He found himself seated on the couch; a glass of dark liquid thrust into his hand by Galen. When he looked back toward the entertainment room, he saw Lorenzo and Edrigu disappear inside the room. The door closed behind them, shutting out the sound.

Vaguely, he looked around. All eyes were upon him, their expressions grim. He felt as dazed as someone who suffered a massive blow to the head; he could not think. Galen's hand steadied the glass, the liquid in it sloshed by the tremor of his hand, spilling some on his fingers.

"Drink, it will help," the older man directed him.

Steadying himself, he took a sip. It was brandy. He was too bewildered to note its quality. The drink spread warmth through his chest. The fiery trail it created along his throat was the only thing that anchored him to reality.

Galen looked at the young man he had liked from the first time they met and felt extreme pity for what he was about to face.

He could recognise a kindred spirit in him, a shared experience. The abrupt manner of Roald's discovery of Yuana's secret shook the boy far more than when he found out about Bel's hidden nature. And this was worrying.

A chorus of sighs of relief broke from everyone's lips when the kitchen door opened and revealed Nita bearing the wooden tray that Galen had nicknamed the organ-bearer. She hastened to the entertainment room.

The moment the door was ajar, a chilling animal sound echoed from the inside. It was something he did not recognise; it sounded like a cross between a human scream, a panther roar, and a bird call.

Yuana may have transformed. He just didn't know what she turned into.

The wooden platter was an answered prayer. For the moment, Yuana quelled her transformation, but it took every ounce of energy in her body to do so. Panting, she looked up, her body covered in sweat despite the air-conditioning in the room. Nita rushed the platter over. An entire heart, sliced in inch-thick portions, fresh and bloody, lay in the middle. Her trembling hand reached over for a slice; her instinct took over.

An overwhelming sense of well-being washed over her as she consumed all of it. It was beyond normal satiation of a physical hunger and thirst. It was an explosion of sensation that suffused her from head to toe. Like water poured over a flame, it extinguished the burning pain in her middle. The sliver of a human heart encapsulated her fundamental need for human organs.

Free of the tremors and the spasms at last, she leaned back in her chair. Her hair was damp, the natural waves more pronounced. Her muscles ached with the strain; her lungs felt raw. The exhaustion fled her body like smoke dissipating in the air and was replaced by an electrifying energy that made her whole body tingle. Its power radiated outward to the top of her head and to the tips of her fingers and toes. The chilly air made her shiver and raised goosebumps in her skin. Nita dropped a warm blanket around her shoulders.

"Thank you, Nita," she said as Nita leaned over to plant a kiss on her forehead.

Nita lifted her bloody fingers and wiped them clean with a warm, wet hand towel. With that done, she took the platter away with her.

Yuana sat still for a moment to temper the energy that coursed through her veins. Movements in the room caught her attention as she noticed her 'Elo and grandfather. Their presence reminded her Roald would be here soon. She must look a fright. She pushed herself off the couch.

Katelin pushed her back to her chair, "Calm down, Yuana. We can handle Roald for you for a while. Take a few more minutes to collect yourself."

There was caution in her grandmother's tone, and that made her frown.

"Meet with him when you are ready, and only when you are ready." Her great-grandmother, in contrast, was the picture of composure and serenity.

She nodded, although they averted one crisis, she would need to deal with the original issue at hand. It was impossible to remain calm.

"Yuana, Roald saw..." her grandfather Edrigu said in a quiet voice.

Her stomach dropped. Her 'Ela and grandmother looked up in surprise.

"What did he see, Lolo?" A sense of foreboding was back.

"He saw enough, Hija," Her grandfather's response was gentle, his gaze apologetic.

"How did he take it?" Her heart ached for Roald. She would have preferred a better way for him to find out.

"He's still outside with your father and mother," her Lolo replied.

The lack of a direct answer was answer enough. Roald did not take it well.

"I didn't think this through, Lolo. I don't know what to do," she admitted, "Any suggestions?"

Edrigu considered the question, "He's a logical sort, very technical. So, appeal to his logic, if he is still willing to listen."

Is Roald still willing to listen?

She was hoping he would be.

There was only one move forward. She could start with finding out what part of the myth Roald knew and believed. Other proof could come later, if needed, to support her explanations about their kind, and how it was to live like them, how similar and dissimilar they were from humans.

Bolstered by a semblance of a plan, she picked herself up and smoothed her skirts down. With her shoulders straight and head held high, she walked towards the living room.

Her elders followed suit.

A gamut of emotions bombarded him when Yuana walked into the living room. She looked pale, but there was a fierce light in her eyes, her expression serious. His heart's elevated heartbeats had not slowed down yet, but it galloped faster at the sight of her.

The earlier images of her on her knees, the spasming muscles running down her back, her vibrating skin, and the howl he heard, all came rushing back. The dread morphed into terror. He wanted to run, but her gaze held him in place.

"How are you?" she asked him and touched his cheek.

He laid his hand over hers in reaction and felt his own icy skin. No doubt because of shock. Her warm fingers anchored him to the present. There was dampness in the roots of her hair, the clamminess of her skin contradicted the heat of her hand. And yet the knot in his chest stayed, and the sensation of being in a nightmare remained.

Her family sat themselves in a half circle on the long sofa, the middle seat empty. She led him to sit across her and her family before she took the vacant seat. This was an explicit statement of both support and instruction from them.

"What do you think you saw, Roald?" Yuana asked without preamble.

His terror grew like a cloud overhead. He did not know how to describe what he witnessed. He was unsure if he imagined it.

"I am not sure, Yuana…" he rasped. Half of him wanted her to reassure him he just imagined it.

"I was transforming, shape-shifting into my animal form. I did not want for you to find out that way," she sighed.

"Your animal form?" he echoed, baffled, his panic rose.

"My hunting form. Our kind shape-shifts into animals so we can hunt for human prey. That's what aswangs did in the old days. We no longer do that." Yuana's voice was calm, even, and dispassionate.

"What does that mean? Being an aswang?" He was desperate to receive lucid information his thinking brain could handle. Something his mind could understand. Anything that made sense to him.

"It means I have to consume human liver, heart or kidney with regularity to survive; that I transform into an animal

234

whenever I want or need to. It means I live thrice as long." Her voice increased in intensity, but not in volume.

"Why are you saying this, Yuana?" He wanted her to retract all of it.

Yuana's eyes flashed. "Because I want you to understand exactly what you will sign for if you choose to be with me. And what you will leave behind."

Roald's heart sank deeper at every statement she made. There was no need for proof. He realised he believed her. The presence of everyone in the room was confirmation. His brain felt like exploding. He cradled his head between his hands, trying to ease the throbbing that had begun earlier, and had now doubled.

Anger sparked in the depths of Yuana's eyes.

"And, Roald, it means our future kids will be *aswangs*. Like me..." Her words sharp. It cut through his heart like a hot knife. "They will eat human organs, transform into predatory animals... They will all be like me."

His head snapped back up. Horror enveloped him. That was too much to take in. He stood up and walked out. A new terror screamed in his head. His legs were too shaky for him to run, but his heart was ready to burst with the enormity of his panic.

Yuana watched Roald walk away. Anger and grief cloaked her soul. If their relationship would end, it was best that he severed it himself.

Seconds later, Roald's car zoomed away. Silence dominated the room. The whole De Vida clan, including her father, didn't know what to say. Tears ran down her face as she tried to keep the devastation in. Her shoulders shook with the effort not to howl.

Roald failed the test.

That night, Galen and Ysobella spent the night at the De Vida mansion. Yuana needed her family now more than ever.

Galen was unaware of the exact plans of the De Vidas, but he suspected they had contingencies for cases like this since it was paramount to their survival as a species to remain hidden. He would give Roald up to forty-eight hours himself to adjust to his new reality, and then he would whip him into shape. He did not want his daughter to end up with the burden of having to kill Roald herself.

If it came to it, he would be more than happy to do it for her.

Beside him, he could sense Ysobella was trying hard to suppress her rage. There was a hardness in the lines of her face. He had never seen her angry, but the set of her jaw showed him how formidable his sweet wife could be.

He touched her clenched fist, and Ysobella let out a deep breath.

"I asked the family to give Roald two chances to redeem himself. He's blown his first chance. For Yuana's sake, I will keep to that arrangement. But *Holy Prometheus*, Galen, I wanted to pluck his heart out and crush it with my bare hands for hurting our daughter..." The fury made her voice tremble.

"If it comes to that, you will have to give me the honour, my love. I'm giving him two days to come to his senses, then I will come after him."

Ysobella stared at him. Tears glistened in their depths, out of anger, frustration, and heartbreak.

As planned, Edrigu sent a message to Dr Sanchez to prepare her team. Lorenzo would meet the iztari teams tomorrow, for their individual task assignments.

He would update Roald's dossier. He would deploy the First Wave team of iztaris.

Hopefully, for the sake of Yuana, their deployment would not go further than the Second Wave.

10

THE FIRST WAVE

Roald didn't realise it was already morning until the doorbell rang. He did not want to answer it. He just wanted to be alone, but the ringing was incessant. It became obvious after ten minutes of the constant peal of the doorbell whoever was on the other side of the door was not going away.

He dragged himself off the couch, still wearing the same clothes he had on yesterday. His limbs were stiff from sitting for so long. He peeked through the peephole — Daniel. He opened the door while trying to recall if they had set an appointment today.

"Dude, what took you so... long... What the heck, Roald? You look terrible!"

Daniel looked him up and down. He was sure that Dan noted the rumpled clothes, the shadow of beard on his face, the dullness in his eyes, the exhaustion. Daniel had never seen him like this, but he did not care.

He returned to his couch and dropped back on it. His head was still pounding, his mind and body drained. He felt heart-heavy and soul-weary. The dissonance in his mind and heart was so great he had no words to describe the anguish he was in.

"Bro, c'mon, talk to me. What is wrong?" Daniel persisted and followed him to the living room.

He saw alarm on Dan's face. But he did not have the energy to respond and converse at the moment. And even if he did, he did not know how or where to even begin. He still could not believe it himself.

His dry, tired eyes hurt. He had not slept since he returned from Yuana's house. He was beyond miserable.

Roald sighed, then he heard Daniel walk to his kitchen and putter about. Soon, the hiss of steaming water and the smell of coffee permeated the room. And something in him thawed. His mouth watered at the fragrance of the brew, but he kept his eyes closed. He did not want to encourage conversation.

"Come on, Roald. I will not leave until you tell me what is wrong," Daniel called over from the kitchen, with the badgering tone that he was familiar with. There was no avoiding Daniel's presence. He roused himself and sat up straight.

With two cups of hot coffee in hand, Daniel approached and placed both cups on the coffee table. His friend sat across him and waited for him to say something.

He reached for the cup that Daniel brought and took a sip. The bitter, toasty flavour and the heat of the coffee cleared the cobwebs from his brain.

Perhaps if he went out with Daniel to whatever appointment they had for the day, it would give him respite from the quagmire of emotions that was twisting him up inside and loosen the knot in his chest and stomach.

"Are we supposed to go somewhere today?" He met Daniel's assessing gaze over the swirling steam of the coffee.

Dan shook his head. "No, we have no plans. I came by to ask for your advice and feedback on the pitch deck I prepared for my Series A."

Daniel fished out a memory stick from his pocket and placed it on Roald's coffee table.

He could only nod. He felt depleted, yet restless; dog-tired, but unable to sleep. The glare of the sun aggravated him and made him nauseous.

"So, are you going to tell me what happened?" Daniel persisted.

"I am not ready yet." He sounded strained and disoriented, even to himself.

"Okay," Daniel relented. "But if you need to talk about it, just give me a holler. Go get some sleep, your face would put a zombie to shame."

He nodded, leaned back, and closed his eyes once more.

Daniel could see the damage to Roald's psyche. He was grief stricken. The misery that enveloped him was severe. He had thought, or rather hoped, Roald and Yuana would tire of each other in due course, that their relationship would cool down, that their breakup would not be this devastating. He did not expect Roald to be this shattered about it.

How long will it take Roald to climb out of it?

He should call Yuana and check how she was doing. She must be as devastated as Roald. But he had a job to do, and that required watching over his friend and preventing further damage to Yuana. And to Roald.

They continued to sip coffee in silence. Daniel understood Roald was not ready and was still in shock— more likely in denial. For now, he would be a sympathetic friend and allow Roald the time to come to terms with what he discovered.

After half an hour of companionable silence, he patted Roald's shoulder in a silent gesture of sympathy and farewell.

He had a preliminary report to write.

Roald could not sleep, no matter how hard he tried. When Daniel left, he had drawn the curtains closed to darken the room, but his thoughts still would not slow down. He laid there for hours, unable to fall asleep.

More than thrice, he considered working. He scanned his email inbox, trying to find a message that would motivate him to do something, but for the life of him, he could not rouse himself to do so. He lost his appetite for food, his work, his life.

He caught sight of the red car-shaped memory stick, a miniature Ferrari, on the coffee table. Maybe reading something colourful like Daniel's pitch deck would help serve as a distraction or even an impetus for him.

He reached for his laptop stored under the coffee table, turned it on, and plugged the memory stick in. He clicked on the only file, and it opened into the elegant visuals of Daniel's company - Domestech's investor's deck.

Ten minutes later, he failed to make headway on the material. His laptop screen had darkened into a snooze because of lack of activity. All he gathered from staring at this deck was that the corporate colours of Domestech were the same shade of burgundy and silver of Daniel's father's company. The words, the graphs, the visuals did not make any impression on him. After another ten minutes, he gave up altogether, and closed the lid of his laptop.

He looked around his unit, and contemplated if drinking some cognac would help today, as it did not offer him any solace yesterday.

An hour later, his second shot remained untouched on the coffee table. He had not slept for over twenty-four hours, and he knew his body needed sleep, but nothing seemed to work. Every kind of distraction he tried had not worked so far. In the past, when he was in a troubled state, all he needed was... Yuana.

The thought of her sent a streak of agony through his heart. He should not think about her. Not today, not yet. If he did, it meant he would have to deal with what happened, what changed, what loomed in their future. And what was driving him to the edge of panic...

To take his mind off Yuana and the impending decision he knew he needed to make, he hit the gym. Working out always engaged his brain, and he figured this was better than drinking.

Edrigu received a message from the First Wave Team. They reported they were all in position; the *Breach* was in place, but not yet triggered, and that Roald was just about to go over the edge, his reaction a little more pronounced than projected. The revelation had hit Roald hard.

Edrigu replied and gave his instruction to his team. Roald's actions could bode well, or be disastrous for them, a first in half a century for their clan.

Yuana did not lock herself in her room this time, but spent it walking around in a daze in the garden or sat in solitude at the library. She seemed disinterested in doing anything at all.

Tomorrow, Ysobella and Galen would take Yuana to their

estate in Mindoro, at the foot of Mount Halcon. She needed to get away, to be closer to fresh air and the sun, and to give herself the space to run around in her animus to vent.

Nita left early for Villa Bizitza to prepare the house and the household team for Ysobella's family. The trip served two purposes: to distract his granddaughter and to keep Galen away from their activities on implementing the RRIP. Galen need not know the details of their operation. He was still under observation and not integrated into the family yet.

Two weeks on, Roald came back from the now usual three-hour gym session. His six-foot frame more toned than it had ever been in all his life. But the gruelling workouts that allowed him to escape for the past days lost its diversionary value. He needed to find an alternative or a supplement to it.

He sat down to have a tall drink of lemonade, replacing the lost liquids the backbreaking work-out squeezed out of him. It was moments like this, when he did not have a task that required his focus that the forced restraint he placed on himself crumbled under the avalanche of emotions.

For the past sixteen days, he was like a zombie. He filled the days with physical activities, meetings that never held his interest, and nights going out with Daniel. He refused to deal with the core of his unease, was postponing the inevitable, because something about it scared him. But he kept telling himself he just needed more time to figure out why he felt so disordered.

He missed Yuana, and the need to hear her voice was getting stronger every day. It all contributed to his disquiet. But he had no business calling her until he sorted out his views and feelings about her... nature. He needed to deal with the panic whenever he thought of her being an aswang. He did not want to lose Yuana, but he was uncertain how, or if he could even get past it.

His sleep, when it came, was troubled by recurring night-mares. He was not eating well, his appetite shot. And his mother worried about him. She called every day since he and Yuana failed to show up to the opening of his mother's new shop. She knew something was wrong, but he could not open up to her.

How would one tell their mother that her future daughter-in-law was an aswang?

Ten days ago, she'd showed up unannounced to his condo, took one look at him and guessed in an instant what was wrong. She worried most about his lack of appetite and his inability to sleep. He blamed the nightmares, but instead of being molli-fied, she worried even more.

Her mother booked appointments for him with a psychia-trist, but he kept cancelling on her. Her mother persisted, and for some reason, the doctor kept allowing the reschedule.

Now, he was bone tired, his emotions and mind stretched taut, and he had developed a permanent chest ache. Their company doctor found nothing wrong with him physically, so it had to be psychological.

Maybe it was time to obey his mother's and take Daniel's advice. He needed professional help.

Yuana fared little better.

She accomplished her days on autopilot. Her mind, in one hand, was full of imaginings of Roald coming around, accepting her like her father did with her mother. And in another, preparing herself for the future without Roald.

She knew her despondency, her lack of energy and interest in anything directly resulted from her depressed state. Her family insisted that she focus on her well-being, and not to worry about anything else. It gave her permission not to bother with anything else but herself.

Her parents were enjoying themselves, at least. But their concern for her marred their joy. So, she spent time out in the woods to give her parents opportunities to be alone, and not watch her mope around the house.

The decision to get away and go to the Villa had been a good thing. Nature soothed her disquiet. She spent hours walking in the forest that bordered their land and running long distances at night in her panther form. Her lone treks into the woods worried her father. Not even a display of her strength compared to humans appeased him. It took her mother's instruction to take two of their aswang household staff to shadow her, to convince her father to let her go out.

The mountain had been hers alone during her outings. It was easy to avoid the human hikers. She could smell and hear them some distance away.

But the setting sun always reminded her the respite was temporary, and there were people expecting her and a reality waiting for her back home.

As she looked out into the vast expanse of their land from her bedroom verandah, across the lush undulating green at the base of Mount Halcon, she felt a measure of peace. It reminded her of her youth and the days when she had no cares but her childhood curiosity. The enormous and ancient trees beckoned to her, as if they sensed she needed healing. And while in their midst, time had no influence.

With her hair drying in the natural air, the hem of her purple wrap dress stirred in the breeze, the whisperings of nature called to her. The sun sank behind the mountain peak. It would be dark soon.

Then a familiar, soft whirring sound blew in with the wind. It came over the horizon. The sound grew louder. She knew what it was before she saw the familiar Dynali H3 helicopter the family owned. It was flying in from their Calapan branch, carrying the sustenance for the household.

With the helicopter's arrival, her parents would expect her to come down to the living room soon. To join them in the cocktail hour that they had taken a habit to before dinner. Maybe a glass of G&T would stimulate her soul for a few hours.

Ysobella got off a phone call with her father, who informed her of the First Wave team's action so far. They had deployed an iztari in Roald's condominium tower, another in his gym. Two others were tailing him in shifts.

Roald had been suffering as much, if not more, as Yuana. And he had been drowning his pain in physical activities, mental challenges, and a lot of trivial pursuits. It softened her anger against Roald. It gave her hope for her daughter.

The sound of the approaching Dynali helicopter broke her reverie. Their sustenance was here. She turned to see Galen dressed in smart casual clothes, looking elegant and ready for dinner as he came out of the adjoining bathroom. They would have cocktails first, as was their custom. As part of the compromise with him, the cocktail hour afforded her and Yuana the ideal occasion to consume their victus out of Galen's sight in consideration for his stomach.

"So, what did your father say?" Galen asked as they descended the stairs to the living room.

"Not much. Just updating me of what was happening at work." She shrugged.

She felt uneasy not telling him everything, but her parents requested she not to divulge the iztari operations until it was necessary.

Yuana sat on the couch, her expression pensive, as she contemplated the cinnamon stick, orange peel and basil leaf garnish on her clear drink. Gone was the lifeless expression that graced her face over the past few days. This was an improvement.

She glanced at Galen and noticed a similar approving glint in his eyes. They agreed. This version of Yuana was better. They both pasted a pleasant expression on their faces; presenting a cheerful facade to their daughter helped reduce her anxiety.

"How was your walk in the woods, my sweet?" Galen asked and kissed his daughter's cheek.

"I went to the beach today." Yuana smiled, there was a twinkle in her eyes. She seemed more upbeat, not so melancholy.

"Oh. Did anything interesting happened?" she asked.

"Yes, I met some of our kind from the Lantuyan tribe. It surprised me to find out that our aswang kin live in open and cooperative existence within the human Mangyan community. Does our Tribunal know?" Yuana's gaze focused on her, keen interest in its depths.

She nodded. "Oh yes, the Tribunal knows. It was your 'Ela's grandmother who secured the permission from the Supreme Tribunal two centuries ago."

"Oh..." Father and daughter's remark came in unison.

"Their relationship with the tribe's people is unique. While it deviated from the Veil of Secrecy law, the SVT granted them an exception. The reason behind it was their tribal practices, which remained unchanged to this day. The tribe considers the aswang among them as divine. In return, the aswangs use their skills to provide food for their tribes-people. It is a symbiotic relationship. And if one or two ever thought of claiming there were aswangs in their tribe, the modern humans would never believe it. They will dismiss it as a folktale."

"Isn't that ironic, mama, that an unsophisticated tribe has more freedom than us, the civilised kin?" Yuana's mouth turned up in a slight curl.

"That is fascinating," Galen said, one eyebrow arched in keen interest. "How big is this tribe? And do they know about us?"

She nodded. "The Lantuyan aswangs is a small group, just seven of them. Our company employs them to do a thorough search of the island for other aswangs. One of their covers is as guides for hikers during the limited hiking season in Mount Halcon. Some of them work the grounds of Villa Bizitza together with some human Mangyans. We need a few to cover the property, as it is twenty-hectares."

Galen's eyes widened. "Oh. So, all of them work for companies owned by your kind?"

"Well, a few of them work with the city hall of Calapan, where a small community of lowland aswangs live and work with the GJDV branch in Calapan. Part of their benefits, just like all aswang employees of the company, is the daily ration of sustenance. The Tribunal provides for every one of our kind," she replied.

"Your Tribunal certainly functions better than any human governments that I know of," Galen said.

"It's a matter of survival. We have no choice, Papa," Yuana said with a tinge of bitterness.

One hundred forty-nine kilometres away, Roald stared at the photo of the psychiatrist his mother had chosen for him on his phone. He had done some research on her and found her credentials top notch. He had checked the top in her field of study and his search kept leading him to Dr Emme Sanchez. She was the preeminent expert in this field of psychiatry.

The vice in his heart loosened. If he would spill his guts and Yuana's secret to a stranger, at least it would be to a medical professional. She would have the skills and experience to help him. And any information he divulged, the doctor-patient confidentiality would protect both Yuana and him.

Dr Sanchez would think him crazy for giving credence to Yuana's claim, but he was not concerned about being believed, he did not need the validation. What he wanted were some answers to the questions in his head and what steps he could take to find relief from his inner torment.

For now, he would take a shower and meet Daniel at the bar across the street. His hours of avoiding his own thoughts would end tomorrow, so he might as well take advantage of the remaining hours. Hopefully, tomorrow he, and by extension, his mother, would find satisfaction from the session.

Dr Emme Sanchez felt a certain sense of grim satisfaction as she put the phone down. It was apparent their RRIP, deployed for the second time in her lifetime, worked as predicted. The subject had called her to confirm their appointment set for tomorrow at lunch. The Breach was flawless, as expected.

She typed the message: *the yarn is on the spindle,* and sent it to the First Wave team to trigger the next step in the plan. She opened the file waiting in her laptop - Roald Magsino's dossier. The more she knew about him before their session tomorrow, the better.

Roald Magsino's case would not be a repeat of the last time. She would not have another De Vida suffer from her mistake. Death would be a better alternative for this young man should he fail the test.

The first one, decades ago, a man who did not deserve what he got, ended up with a fate worse than death. She contributed to the horrific fate of imprisoning his mind into a never-ending nightmare. Both she and Ximena were still paying for what they did to him fifty years on.

This was the most personal case she has ever had to do as a psychiatrist since then. She would do better for this one.

Maybe Roald Magsino was to be her penance, her atonement.

Daniel arrived half an hour early at the bar where he and Roald agreed to meet. He ordered a whisky while he waited. He had just met with the First Wave team. They discussed each other's updates. The software he deployed on Roald's laptop channelled him to the office of Dr Sanchez, as they meant for him to do.

He felt a deep sense of guilt for introducing Roald to Yuana three years ago. If he had not, his friends would not be in this predicament. He should have recognised Roald was smitten the first time he saw Yuana. His friend's firm resistance to diversion and discouragement was a dead giveaway.

Roald would have met Yuana that day, anyway. Roald would have found a way.

Despite Roald's firm interest then, he also never thought it would turn serious. Yuana always put a barrier between herself and the men she dated, and understandably, too. And Roald was the quintessential perpetual bachelor. He assumed Yuana and Roald would end up as friends, like how most of Yuana's flings ended up being.

He remembered the teenage pact he made with Yuana when they first became friends as teenagers; he could be her perpetual boyfriend shield to protect her from falling in love. It seemed like a marvellous idea in the first few months until Yuana released him from the pact because it hampered both their dating lives.

Perhaps they should have taken the pact more seriously, and they would not face this now.

Maybe it was providential because it positioned him to help Roald get out of this as unscathed as possible. At least, with his mind or his life intact.

It was to Roald's credit he never mentioned to him Yuana admitted to being an aswang. He had kept the information to himself, even if he was having a hard time accepting it. Roald had kept Yuana's secret for weeks now. There was no doubt in his mind Roald believed Yuana, even if he was still in denial. And tomorrow, they would find out from his session with Dr Sanchez to what extent that belief was, and if Roald could keep it a secret for the rest of his life.

He was halfway through his whiskey when Roald showed up. Tonight, he had a job to do, and he had better do it well if he would ensure that Roald lives and remains sane.

Roald pulled up the bar chair next to Daniel and ordered a

OZ MARI G.

cognac. A brief exchange of small talk passed between them as Roald waited for the bartender to pour his drink. The man was still busy making cocktails for another customer.

"Dan, how long have you known Yuana?" Roald asked out of the blue as he received his drink from the bartender.

Oh, fuck! He hoped Roald would pass this test.

"I've known her awhile. We met in Oslo during a holiday. She was fifteen, I was eighteen. Then we became close in Melbourne. I used to live there, and she was studying there. So, about thirteen years... why?" He kept a casual tone.

Roald did not answer, his focus was on the glass in his hand as he swirled the contents.

"How come you never dated her, Dan?"

Roald's eyes were now on him, watching his reaction. He was sure Roald was trying to find out if he knew about Yuana's nature.

He smiled. "Oh, we did, briefly, when I first met her. We dated for a few months, but we ended up as dear friends, and that is what we remained to be." He felt a twinge of remembrance in his heart at the memory.

It was true, and he was sure that if they had continued dating, perhaps he would have fallen for Yuana as Roald had. He would have been a better individual for someone like Yuana. Being an Erdia, there would be no need for the soul-destroying revelation as he was aware Yuana was an aswang. And he was already part of their world.

What stopped him was not wanting to have aswang kids. He did not want them to have the same rootless existence that every aswang had to endure, the constant move to avoid making long-term friendships that left social footprints, the recurring predicament every female aswangs would go through when they fell in love with humans. He wanted normal kids, and a mate he could live with, grow old with, die with.

Roald had no readable expression on his face, so he could not quite guess what he was thinking. There was no response from Roald, instead he was back to contemplating his glass. He took a sip, and then said, "I took your advice, Dan. I will see the psychiatrist that my mom found for me tomorrow."

The change of topic made his heart skip a beat.

"Really? That is good..." He injected surprise in his voice.

Roald nodded.

"So, what happened between you and Yuana, bro? You seemed really broken up about it. Did you guys part ways?" He was reluctant to push the issue, but he had a job to do.

"No! We are still together." Roald's quick denial spoke volumes.

He heaved a brief sigh of relief. "So, what is wrong? What went so wrong that you need a psychiatrist to put you to rights?" he persisted, trying to prompt Roald into telling him what he already knew. He could see the internal battle Roald was going through, wanting to open up, yet resisting to. Perhaps out of pride, self-preservation, or hopefully, out of love for Yuana.

"Yuana told me she is an... *aswang*..." Roald said, unable to look at him.

"What? An... *aswang*?" He feigned emphatic surprise. "Do you believe it?" he asked, injecting incredulity in his voice, and felt guilty for the pretense.

"That is why I need to see a psychiatrist," Roald said.

Roald's inability to answer a direct question confirmed his assumption that Roald believed Yuana's declaration, but it terrified him to look deep into himself.

"Is the psychiatric visit for her state of mind, or yours?"

"I do not know, bro." Roald's reply came after a deep sigh and a big swallow of the cognac.

He patted Roald's shoulder in encouragement. He was

certain that pressing Roald further about it would make Roald suspicious over his undue interest in the subject.

"Okay, bro, if there is anything I can do to help... I can do research for you, if you want." He was hoping for Roald's demand to keep the information secret between them.

"Bro, let's keep this secret just between us, please. I want to protect Yuana," Roald said, his voice low and quiet.

"Of course." The relief was beyond words. Roald was unaware that he just upped his own chances to live with that request.

Roald might never know that Daniel was bound to the same *Veil*, and that he had never been so glad to make such a promise in his life.

By ten thirty the following morning, Edrigu, Lorenzo and Margaita were ready at the conference table. Their focus was on the small secondary screen where they were watching Daniel test their access to the cameras set up at the Session Room Three in the clinic of Dr Sanchez. Daniel was broadcasting online from the Technology Department of the iztari office across town. Mateo Santino, one of their senior iztaris and Daniel's father was also present.

Two minutes later, the wide primary screen flickered to life and reflected a clear transmission of the digital cameras installed and camouflaged in Dr Sanchez's office.

The whole technical set up included a powerful microphone and noise cancelling sound system. They could listen to every conversation in Dr Sanchez's office.

Satisfied and ready to begin, Edrigu rang Dr Sanchez to tell her they were live. She raised a thumb to the digital camera located across her seat. It was one of the six installed in the rectangular room. They disguised this camera as a power indicator by the light switch.

With everything ready, they all sat down to wait for Roald's arrival for his appointment.

Roald arrived ten minutes early. Dr Sanchez saw it on the screen of her laptop. She saw him approach the receptionist. The receptionist had instructions to take Roald to Session Room 3 as soon as he arrived. It was a room reserved for aswang treatments and all aswang related cases only. The sole room connected to the iztari office.

Dr Sanchez rose from her seat when the door opened. It was her receptionist.

"Doctora, Mr Magsino is here," Sara said, then stepped aside to allow Roald to come in.

"Thank you, Sara. Good morning, Mr Magsino."

She noted the signs of sleeplessness and exhaustion on his face. He was a handsome young man, tall and confident. He was fit and healthy, apart from the slight dark circles and the dull sheen in his eyes. Pain underlined the mild smile. The boy was in emotional distress.

"Good morning, Doctor Sanchez. Thank you for seeing me despite the many cancellations. I assure you; my mother did her best to make me go." Roald shook her offered hand.

"You are welcome, Roald. And do not worry about it. Your behaviour was normal. Men resist shrink visits more than women. I am glad you came anyway, as this will be valuable for the medical journal I am writing."

She smiled and bid him to take a seat on the plump beige leather couch. Roald sat on the edge, his posture rigid.

"Can I offer you a drink? Or some light sandwiches, perhaps?"

He looked like he needed food. He declined the sandwiches but accepted the chamomile tea.

After the secretary placed the tea set and a platter of finger sandwiches on the coffee table between them, Dr Sanchez poured them both a cup. Roald regarded her with curiosity and a tinge of suspicion.

"Am I what you expected?" she asked with a smile.

"I'm sorry. I did not mean to stare. You look... younger in person." Roald's answering smile was apologetic. He sat deeper into his seat, his back still ramrod straight.

"I would thank you for the compliment if my looks were my doing. I inherited it from my parents. So, good genes count a lot."

Roald relaxed, and he slid further into the couch. They sat in silence for a few minutes. She picked up a slice of finger sandwich and took a bite. She was not hungry, but she wanted Roald to eat. And as she expected, he took one as well. She let him eat a couple more before she set her cup down on the table.

She turned on the digital recorder to begin her patient consent spiel. Roald set his own cup down.

"Before we start, I want you to know I always record all my sessions because I need to review it multiple times later, so I can do proper diagnosis. This recording shall be confidential and will only be between you and me. But in extreme cases, where I will need outside assistance, I will only share it, with extreme discretion, with the relevant third parties. These instances are, first, if I believe there is an imminent and violent threat towards yourself or others; second, if there is a need to facilitate client care that will involve other providers and sharing information is necessary for your treatment... Do you agree to this?"

She paused and waited for him to accede.

His agreement was a salve to her conscience as she would share this with people who would be in imminent danger if he revealed to others what he knew, and lethal violence may come his way if he did.

He nodded. "Yes."

Her words seemed to have met his approval. The tensed line in his mouth relaxed. He liked the idea of anonymity. That boded well for him.

"All right, shall we begin?"

After a long deep breath, he nodded. She nodded with encouragement and set the digital recorder down on the table between them.

"So, tell me what is on your mind, Mr Magsino?"

Roald began with what he must have thought to be the safest door to open - his observation that his girlfriend of two years seemed like she was withholding something from him. He recounted the days prior to the revelation. His tone was almost dispassionate as he focused on the facts. Roald seemed to avoid any mention of how he felt about it.

With gentle leading questions, she pried the details of the day of the revelation. He related it like a story he saw in a movie or read in a book. His words were careful and minimal.

When he reached the day of the revelation, he hesitated and looked torn between continuing and stopping.

"She made a claim... a revelation..." Roald paused.

"What was her claim? What kind of revelation?" she asked.

Roald had never mentioned Yuana's name. It was a good sign. He was protective of her. His love was still strong.

"She said... she was an *aswang*..." Roald's jaw tightened at the mention of the word, and fear flashed in his eyes.

"Okay. And how do you feel about it?"

"It could not be true... I think she was just misguided. Or perhaps she suffered from a form of clinical lycanthropy..."

She had no trouble reading between the lines of Roald's statements, the unconscious peppering of justification, rationalisations, and hidden entreaties for help.

"I am worried, Doctor Sanchez. It affected my sleep... my girlfriend could not be..."

It was very significant Roald had not asked her yet if there was a treatment for Yuana's malady. Roald was not conscious of his tacit admission that he believed Yuana. The session was about his own fear. But she had yet to determine whether he was appealing for help to overcome it so he could adapt to Yuana's nature, or to move on from them.

Her most crucial task was to find out if his mental state could withstand the terror of the truth. Only then the second question could be asked - whether his love would overcome his deep-seated fear of aswangs. His trauma ran deep. It was at the level of a phobia. All the signs were there.

And that was not good.

Across the distance, just like Dr Sanchez, the First Wave team were focused on the session. They were all looking for signs in Roald's behaviour that would confirm he would be a danger to their existence. The sessions would guide them on what methods to take to neutralise any threat he might present to their kind. The result would be the same, like all the others before him - he would pose no harm to them, either by nature or by their design.

For the De Vidas and the iztaris watching this exchange on their screens, it was notable that Roald never once mentioned Yuana's name to Dr Sanchez. He referred to her as his girlfriend. Despite being in a safe environment, Roald was still protective. If he continued to do this in the succeeding sessions with Dr Sanchez, this may just turn out well for Roald.

To Margaita, it was also clear Roald's anxiety sprung from a deep trauma. It was more than just a boyhood fear from horror stories told by the adults when he was young. She flicked open the printed dossier of Roald, checked the data that detailed his background, his family and childhood.

This required a closer look.

An hour later, Dr Sanchez wrapped up the session by posing a question to Roald.

What was it about the revelation that bothered him the most?

Roald winced when he heard this, like bumping a wounded knee at the corner of a table by accident. But he left Dr Sanchez's clinic feeling easier. This was an improvement from the grim existence he had been living with for the past week that felt like an eternity. The session gave him the sense that a light at the end of the tunnel would soon become visible to him. Perhaps in a few more sessions onward.

Their next session would be three days later, at three p.m. He declined the eleven a.m. time slot, an automatic reaction to keeping his lunch hour free - for Yuana.

His own instinctive thought startled him into admitting to himself he was missing Yuana. Badly.

Perhaps a call would not hurt. She was still his girlfriend, after all.

Roald stared at his mobile phone, trying to think of what to say to Yuana when she picked up. Maybe he should text first. She might be in a meeting or something.

He was re-reading his text for the umpteenth time, but the words seemed inadequate. It read impersonal, not to mention presumptuous, since he had not texted or called her for days.

So, how will I know it's the right time to call her without sending the text?

He called Yuana's office. Her secretary, Sochi, answered the phone.

"Hi, Sochi, is Yuana free to talk to me?" he asked. His heart hammered like a drum, he was certain it was audible to Sochi.

"Hey, Roald. She's not here. She's on leave for over a week now, didn't she tell you?" Sochi's surprise rang clear through the line.

"Hmm... no, I was on leave myself. Would you have any idea when she will be back?" Not knowing Yuana's location made his heart drop into his gut.

"It was an indefinite leave, so I do not know when she will return. But she's with her parents." Sochi's voice was controlled and speculating.

"Thank you, Sochi. I will just call her mobile." His stomach tightened; dread burned it like acid.

Yuana had told him about how her mother left her father without a word twenty-eight years ago. And that Yuana might do the same to him was something his entire body raged against.

It took him a few minutes to calm his panic down before he dialled her number. Again, and again. For hours. She was not picking up. Finally, an automated message echoed from the line: her phone was out of reach.

Fear settled inside him, leaden and cold. He pushed the possibility that Yuana left him out of his mind. He had those three years together with her that he could bank on. He refused to believe that Yuana would cut him out of her mind, her heart, her life with such drastic ease. Time spent together may provide him some leeway, but time would also erode his advantage fast.

He needed to sort himself as soon as possible. This development brought back the question that Dr Sanchez put forward earlier.

What was it that bothered me so much about Yuana's revelation?

***

Her dark blue shoes made staccato beats on the tiled hallway floor of the psych ward. Its steady rhythm belied the beating of her heart. She always had mixed feelings when she visited this part of the hospital. A mixture of longing, regret, and massive guilt.

And yet she would come twice a week, like clockwork.

What compelled her to walk this way, without fail, was patient seven in the special wing of the ward. As she neared his room, she took a fortifying breath to shore up her heart against the familiar surge of the emotions that would assail her once she saw him.

For fifty years, this had been her routine, a twice-weekly dose of emotional pain and restitution. It was a heavy price; one she continued to pay and would keep on paying.

Like her usual practice, she viewed him through the small glass panel in his door for a few minutes. As expected, he was busy painting. It was the only thing that occupied his time, his only focus in the fifty years in that room.

She watched him wield his brush like a maestro, fluid and effortless, his enormous talent clear. His tortured soul showed in the colours, the strokes, the technique applied in his paintings. The trauma that ruined his mind communicated to the world through his art. The paintings were all dark, grim, horrifying, yet compelling. He painted with only one theme —*Aswangs*. With one ruling emotion—horror.

The effects of the treatment he got for not keeping the *Veil of Secrecy* intact, the mixture of mind-altering drugs and trauma had broken his mind beyond repair. For half a century, she asked herself whether death was a kinder fate. Her cowardice to end his life brought him to this state, a breathing shell of the man she loved.

She punched the key code on the door pad and the lock snapped open. She entered as quietly as she could. Not that it mattered because he never seemed to notice anything outside his line of vision. She approached him and stood beside the easel. He stopped painting and looked at her.

"Hello, Martin," she breathed. His blank eyes looked back at her. No sign of recognition, no emotion. And that was the most painful of all. Those eyes used to gaze at her with such passion, deep love, and adoration.

She looked down at the painting that had occupied him for the last month. This one took longer than the others. He used to finish a painting every three weeks. By the look of it, this one still had a long way to go. It appeared to be in its early stage, just big splodges of black, grey, red, and other melancholy colours.

She collected all his work, the payment for each one she deposited in an account in his name. She had hoped to give the account to him when he got better, so he would have the funds to support his art. He had a small fortune to his name. But he had not gotten better. The money lay untouched in his bank account for half a century.

He looked every bit his age of eighty-five, deep lines etched on his gaunt face, this man, who owned her heart and soul. His time was running out, and she could almost feel grateful for that. She wanted him to achieve the peace of mind that her kind had stolen from him. Taken from him because of her.

She sighed and turned to leave, and was halfway to the door when she heard him whisper, "Mena..."

She looked back in surprise, her breathing held. But he was still painting. Then she saw it from a distance and realised he was painting... her.

11

FULL CONTACT

They watched the sun set in the horizon, the colours of the surrounding sky changing from bright yellow to deep orange. There was a certain quiet power at this time of the day. For an aswang, it was symbolic of their own physical change.

Yuana glanced at her parents. Both were holding a wine glass, poised for a sip. Her father's free hand rested on her mother's. The way they looked at each other displayed an enduring love she envied and coveted. Their displays of affection were now a common sight to her. It was bittersweet to witness since this could have been hers and Roald's ending.

While the uncertainty of their situation hurt, she could not find it in her to blame Roald. What she was expecting him to accept was difficult. This was the longest time since they met, they had no contact. It was hard to bear, but she had no choice. This trip was both a prelude to her future and a chance to clear her mind.

Can I survive the life my mother lived when she left father years ago?

Her mother had her then, a daughter to take care of, a motivation to live for. She did not have that. Only her family and her work. The tramway would separate her from her family, and her work would not be enough. She knew that now. Her soul needed a higher purpose to get her through the rest of her long life.

As the sun disappeared behind the mountain peak and daylight bled into night, their only illumination were the dimmed lights from the living room, making the millions of stars overhead visible. The stars seemed to twinkle in harmony with the cricket song and night bird calls. And she felt, once again, the pull of her nature, her spirit's need to unite with the land. To run in the woods and experience the night in all its mysteries.

Her mother had the same impulse glittering in her eyes, but the warmth of her father's hand rooted her. And for her mother's sake, she stood there beside her parents, in her human form.

"Bel, is there a difference in how aswangs perceive the night?" Her father's question came out of the blue.

They both glanced at him. Her father seemed attuned to her mother's thoughts. She threw Yuana a questioning gaze and she understood her mother's intent.

Her father's question was a testament that he had taken another step to acceptance, the further integration of his life into their world. Seeing their display of humanity in daylight and very human settings was one thing, to be with an aswang in the middle of the night, in darkness and within their hunting ground was another.

"Do you want to come with us into the woods, Galen? We can show you..." Her mother's invitation had the flavour of a dare.

He smiled at Ysobella; the dare was accepted.

"Yes, I would love to." He relished the adventure. To know all the facets of the non-human side of his wife and daughter in their natural habitat was essential to his adaptation to their world.

They grinned at him and stood up in unison. He followed them down the stairs by the side of the verandah and out into the vast expanse of the garden. The thick, dewy grass cushioned their shoes, dampening them. They walked further into the woods that bordered the foot of Mount Halcon. The growth of the trees thickened as they walked deeper. The forest floor was damp, and it muffled the sound of his steps.

Only his, as the two ladies were light on their feet.

The canopy above added another layer of darkness, muting the glow of the full moon, but his eyesight had already adjusted so he could still see Ysobella to his right and Yuana to his left. They both took a hand. He paused as they did.

The women inhaled slow and deep, as if taking on the entire forest into their lungs. He copied them, his eyes closed on instinct, and the muscles in his body loosened. He noticed the sounds of rustling as a small animal moved among a patch of dry, dead leaves and broken branches on the forest floor, the chirping of crickets, the mournful call of an unknown bird and the whistling of the wind as it travelled through the leaves in the trees above them.

It was mysterious. It was magical. And supernatural.

He opened his eyes, and the trees seemed to glitter around him. Thousands of fireflies darted all around them. He turned to Ysobella. She was watching him. Her dark eyes were gleaming, so black that it was almost alarming. Her irises were dilated to absorb more light, enabling night vision.

"How far can you see in this darkness?" he whispered, unwilling to break the spell that lingered in the air.

"About two hundred yards," she whispered back. "There is

a mouse deer over there..." She pointed to the trees in front of her. He squinted to see, but failed, so he just took her word for it.

"And a tamaraw with her young bull just to your left, Papa," Yuana added, as she pointed to the gap between the trees across from her. They both followed her direction. His vision could not penetrate past the wall of darkness. Ysobella squinted.

"I cannot see it, Yuana." He felt somewhat silly about his human inadequacy.

"And I can barely make it out," Ysobella said, a little amazed. "You have a much better vision than me... Must be the age difference."

Yuana looked surprised.

They walked deeper into the woods; hands still linked. At one point, Yuana paused and turned to her right. "Let's go to the river, Mama."

Ysobella nodded. She angled her head, trying to pick up the sound of the river.

"This way, Ma. I can hear the water." It seemed Yuana's hearing was also keener than her mother's. Never mind his.

They followed Yuana's lead, and about two hundred fifty meters on Ysobella paused. "I can hear the water now."

Ysobella glanced at him. He shook his head; he could hear nothing. They walked on, and another three hundred meters on, he picked up the sound of the rushing water hitting rocks and soil.

"Aha! I can hear the water."

That made both mother and daughter chuckle. They continued on.

They stopped at the edge of the river, the sound of the rushing water louder now, the scent of vegetation in the surrounding areas more intense. Yuana closed her eyes and sniffed at the air. She seemed focused on picking up the distinct smells, her lips notching up into a knowing smile as she identified the scents. As if she was cataloguing them all in her head. It was fascinating to watch. Her mother was doing the same thing.

He was going to copy what they were doing, when Yuana angled her head to the right, a slight frown on her face. Her nose must have picked up something peculiar. Yuana glanced at her mother, waiting for her to react.

A second later, Ysobella's brows knitted. Her lids snapped opened, mother and daughter's gaze locked.

"I smell a man, mama. I do not recognise him," she murmured. Her mother nodded.

"He's not one of our staff..." Ysobella confirmed. The two women faced toward the source of the mysterious odiferous man.

Minutes later, a tall figure emerged from the trees bordering the other side of the river. He was wearing a dark shirt and jeans, his raven hair long. He was barefoot and walked in a fluid motion. The stranger had a rugged, almost wild aura about him, like a hunter. His almond-shaped eyes assessed them with interest. He looked Japanese.

The man stopped by the edge of the river and gave a friendly wave. He seemed to regard them with the same curiosity as they did him. It must have looked odd to encounter three people, dressed in clothes more suited in a city, out in the middle of the woods in the dead of the night.

"Good evening..." Galen waived at the stranger, surprised that another soul, apart from them, was out there.

"Good evening." His accent confirmed he was Japanese. He looked to be middle-aged.

"He might be Mr Nakahara. The Japanese straggler who went into hiding at the end of the war. The one our family was collaborating with in this area," Ysobella informed them in a sotto voice.

"Are you Mr Nakahara?" Ysobella asked. And the older man nodded and smiled.

"I am Ysobella, this is my daughter, Yuana, and Galen, my husband." Her introduction of him, an acknowledgement of what they were to each other, made his heart swell.

Mr Nakahara walked a short distance back and signalled his intention to jump across the narrower channel. He landed with a soft thump on their side of the river.

It astounded Galen. The gap was too wide for any normal human to jump across, and the height the other gentleman achieved was also impossibly high. He realised this Japanese gentleman was an aswang. He never thought about there being foreign aswangs.

Mr Nakahara drew near and held out his hand to shake theirs. Galen would have bowed to him, but Mr Nakahara seemed to have adopted western ways. After the exchange of more pleasantries, Ysobella asked the same question that was playing in Galen's head.

"What brought you out tonight, Nakahara-san?" Ysobella asked excitedly. The story of Mr Nakahara fascinated her.

He felt a slight twinge of jealousy. There was something self-assured and wise about this older man. Nakahara was attractive. His demeanour and aura, elemental.

"Exercise, I often run around in these woods at night," he replied. He was looking at Yuana with profound interest.

"In your human or animal form?" Ysobella asked.

"I enjoy testing my senses and skills in both forms. It is good to keep them sharp," he replied in Japanese-accented English, his gaze still fixed on their daughter. Ysobella and Yuana noticed Nakahara's interest. It was not strange or creepy, just very concentrated, and it intrigued both women.

"How long have you lived in the area, Mr Nakahara?" Yuana asked.

This elder gentleman piqued his daughter's interest. She was establishing rapport with the Japanese gentleman, a skill her daughter was good at. Nakahara's gaze was fierce and speculative. He seemed as keen on establishing rapport with her.

"Since 1942. The war ended, and I stayed," Nakahara replied, shrugging.

"Why? Didn't you want to go home to your family?" Yuana's eyebrows quirked.

"My family died in Nagasaki when the Americans dropped the atomic bomb. No reason to return." A quick, nonchalant response.

Since World War Two?

"Oh... And you've always stayed here? In Mindoro?" Yuana was as surprised as he with Nakahara's response.

He wondered how old this man was. He looked mid-fifties, but given that he was an aswang, he could be over a hundred.

"Yes, here in Mount Halcon. This is my home. I love it here. The Mangyan aswangs are friendly. They helped sustain me after the war. When there was fighting, it was not a problem, but with the war finished, no more source. And I did not want to kill innocent people. So, they come and share their sustenance with me..." Nakahara said with a grin.

His Ysobella appeared touched by his story, and proud of what their Mangyan kind did for a stranger who, by all intents and purposes, was an enemy.

"I read somewhere... Didn't they send a search party here, looking for you?" Galen asked. He remembered seeing the article years ago.

Mr Nakahara's smile was mischievous.

"They did. They spent a week looking for me. I was watching them the entire time, and I stole some of their supplies. Especially the nori... I miss nori." The man chuckled at his recalled memories.

"How did you evade them?" he asked.

"I transformed into a dog, as a pet of one of their Mangyan guides..." he replied. His eyes glittered with mirth.

Feeling more comfortable with him, they sat down on the nearby trunk of a fallen tree. Mr Nakahara remained standing but was back to staring at Yuana again. Unable to quell her own curiosity, Yuana asked him pointblank.

"Mr Nakahara, why do you look at me with such intensity?"

"Forgive me, but I can sense a similar spirit in you..." He bowed to her in apology.

"What kind of spirit?" she asked.

"In time, Ms Yuana, you will know." A mysterious smile spread across his lips. "Have you discovered your animus yet?" Nakahara asked after a brief silence.

That gave them all pause.

"No, not yet," Yuana replied.

"You should find out, it will reveal your true self, and maybe the path of your soul," he said. And with that, Nakahara walked away. He glanced back at them with a brief wave of farewell before disappearing into the woods.

Her brows knitted in bewilderment. Yuana turned to her mother, a questioning look on her face. Her mother just shrugged, as if it was not important that day.

"So, Yuana, what do you transform into?" He was interested as he did not get to witness it that day.

"I can show you, Papa..." Yuana teased.

"No... no... I don't want to see you naked. Just tell me," he blurted, alarmed at the thought. That made Yuana chuckle.

"There is no need, Papa. Just close your eyes. It takes less than a minute. But I have to remove my clothes prior to transformation. It is impractical to be running around as a predator wearing a dress, shoes, or jewellery."

"It is also easier to get dressed after, when it is all in one place, quicker if you do not have to hunt for a missing shoe," Ysobella said, dryly. It made him laugh.

For Kazu Nakahara, meeting the young lady brought him excitement and anticipation of what was about to unfold once she discovered herself. It may take her a while, as she remained unaware. Maybe he could help facilitate her *emergence*. She would need plenty of time to learn about herself and her powers.

The young lady would be in for a monumental surprise. The key thing was that she had no choice. Her animus was unfurling from her core. Hopefully, she would embrace it and fulfil her full potential.

It was crucial to the big shift that was about to come.

Meanwhile, in Manila, Katelin was busy with her immediate task - searching the record system of their Local Tribunal. She was looking for any reported incidents of accidental human exposure or aswang attacks in Santo Tomas, Batangas between the period of 1989-1999. Roald was born and spent his childhood there. Her mother was sure Roald had a close encounter with an aswang when he was young, and Dr Sanchez concurred in her first assessment.

Nothing showed up in Santo Tomas, so she expanded her search and added the places where Roald's parents have roots. And that included the province of Laguna and Quezon. She got lucky when two events caught her attention. One was in Pagsanjan, Laguna in 1993, and another in Mataas na Kahoy, Batangas in 1994.

Katelin focused on the Pagsanjan event first. It detailed a gruesome Restoration of Order Campaign that involved three of their best iztaris, Benjamín Carrión, Troy Villegas, and Felix Coronadal. The ROOC was against a group of harravirs who had been terrorising the area for months. The report said the team got into a violent clash with a notorious band of harravirs led by Major Felipe Ona, a retired scout ranger, and an excellent tactician. Apart from the Major, the harravirs were an uneducated poor family of four, loyal to their leader, and had been serving him when he was still a soldier. Major Ona kept them in his employ when he retired.

Their band started their illicit hunting three years after Major Ona retired. The attacks appeared indiscriminate until a pattern emerged. Every full moon, they would kill a pregnant woman. It meant one of the harravirs had Visceral Metastasis, a lethal form of cancerous growth that affected aswangs. The only known treatment to halt the growth of the disease was the amniotic fluid of a foetus. Whoever it was, he must have attacked and ingested the viscera of an infected aswang. This meant the afflicted aswang was likely a harravis and more dangerous. Major Ona turned out to be the afflicted harravis, and had been one for years, but his symptoms did not show until twenty years later.

The iztaris had a hard time tracking and apprehending them. They used an unwitting pregnant woman as bait. They watched over her for weeks until Major Ona's group went after her. Their faulty intelligence pointed to a group of three harravirs based on the statements of the witnesses in the previous attacks. It was Major Ona's strategy to expose only three to the actual hunt to fool the iztaris into sending a small group, thus improving their odds of winning should the Iztaris catch up with them. In reality, there were five of them, so they outnumbered the iztari force from the very beginning.

The last encounter was a bloodbath. Felix Coronadal died when the harravirs ambushed him. They tore him to pieces and ate his liver, heart, and kidneys. It was pure luck that Ben Carrion and Troy Villegas heard the ambush over their walkie-talkies, and with another stroke of luck they found the mangled remains of Coronadal before they encountered the group. When they saw the body, they knew that the raw viscera of their fallen buddy powered the harravirs. They now faced a group of harravises, a much stronger and faster adversary.

Carrion and Villegas outmanoeuvred the group by setting traps and waiting through the night until they caught two. The strategy turned out to be their saving grace, because after the second harravis got caught in the wolf pit, he called for help to his companions and revealed their number.

By dawn, they were in a death match with Major Ona and the remaining two. The fight took over an hour and well into the daylight; the area rang with the sounds of bolo striking bolo, metal cleaving flesh. They could not use guns because of their proximity to the village. Gun shots would have brought the humans into the skirmish area to investigate. The other two harravises were strong but had no combat training. The iztaris dispatched them with relative ease. But it took both of them to defeat Major Ona. He was a skilled bolo fighter, and the aswang viscera powered him. In the end, the coordinated attack and complementary skills of both iztaris prevailed.

The incident was the first in over a hundred years where a ROOC ended up with all aswangs killed. The harravirs could not be rehabilitated, they were almost feral and had been brain-washed by Major Ona. With the number of humans and aswangs Major Ona's group killed, they had permission from the Punong-Ama for complete elimination of the targets.

The Sanitation Team burned the bodies afterwards. The Social Sanitation strategy implemented in this case was to let nature run its course. They were sure that convincing the actual victims the attack didn't happen would not work and instead worsen the situation.

They created a story that a small group of wild boars attacked the villagers, and the military came and hunted the sound down and circulated it in the neighbouring towns. Soon enough, the incidents were reduced to folktales and rumours.

This event was notable as it influenced the change in their standard procedure when deploying iztaris during ROOC operations against harravirs and harravises.

Tomorrow, Katelin would call on both gentlemen and interview them. One of the attacks by Major Ona's band may have been the event that traumatised Roald. Perhaps iztari Carrion and Villegas could shed light on minor instances that did not make it to the report.

Ysobella, Galen and Yuana came back to the villa at two a.m., still pumped with adrenalin. Galen had asked them to show him what it was like to be an aswang, and the closest way was to show him what they could do. It turned into a demonstration of strength, skill, and speed—a hunting exhibition in her human form rather than her animal hunting form.

It was thrilling to listen to the sound of a potential prey, to pick up its musty smell that gave away its location. Yuana's prey was a wild boar, foraging on the forest floor. With her heart beating hard in her chest, she tried to recall everything her grandfather taught her when she was young. She crept up closer, sprinted at full speed, grabbed the animal by the hind legs and bashed it against the trunk of the nearest tree.

Her lack of experience showed. The boar was stunned, but it struggled and fought her. She did not want to bash its head against the tree again and ended up twisting its neck. She had never killed any animal that way; it took her a while before she succeeded. The boar's tusk slashed her arm during their tussle, but she did not feel the pain. Her first hunt since childhood, and the beat of the blood in her veins, was primal.

Her father took the boar from her. He regarded her with a mixture of paternal pride and awe.

"Oh, the boar gored you?" Her mother inspected the long gash on her arm.

She shrugged. "It's shallow. It will heal in a few minutes."

They took the wild boar home. Her father wanted roast boar for dinner the following day. He had told Yam-Ay, the lady in charge of the household, that she was to preserve a tooth as he wanted to make it into a pendant, a memento of his daughter's hunting prowess. It made her smile. Her heart warmed by her father's adoration as she washed her wound and the boar's blood from her hands over the kitchen sink.

The hunt, while exhilarating, stirred something inside her. And the sensation had not left her since. It was a certain disquiet, a restlessness of the soul.

That night, despite the physicality of the evening's activities, one thought kept her awake. Discover her animus. What Mr Nakahara said to her about herself earlier had piqued her interest.

———

Roald endured a similarly sleepless night. His bed sheets in a messy heap behind him as he paced in his bedroom. He had done push-ups to tire himself to sleep. All it did was give him tight shoulder muscles. He had been dialling Yuana's number all day and night, but her phone line remained out of reach.

He even gave in and called Daniel. It would serve no purpose to hide his concern.

"Dan, Yuana is out of reach. Do you know where she is?"

"Sorry, bro. I don't..." Daniel's low voice was understanding.

His chest tightened. "Do you know anyone who can tell me where she is?"

Daniel's sigh was deep. "Have you tried calling her home?" Dan sounded like he doubted the efficacy of his own suggestion.

"I have not... I am not sure if her family would help me." Stating the obvious tasted bitter in his mouth.

"I will see what I can do, bro, but I cannot promise anything."

He nodded, even if Daniel could not see it, for his own benefit.

All kinds of scenarios ran through his head after he hung up of Yuana hurt somewhere, of her finding somebody else who would accept her fully. The battle between heart and mind raged inside him: the need to ensure he did not lose Yuana, the fear that he already had, the instinct to reach out to her, and his apprehension that he would not overcome this. It was driving him crazy.

Would I have pursued her so single-mindedly if I had known then what I know now?

Memories of when he first met her flashed back in his mind. The jolt of electricity that struck his heart when she came onto the stage was as fresh to him as if it happened yesterday. She was beautiful in her navy-blue flowy dress, but he had met a fair number of beautiful women before.

Physical attributes were not reason enough for his attraction. What set Yuana apart were her eyes. The sparks of energy, passion, playfulness, and suppressed power were clear in that one side glance she threw in his direction as she passed by him. It was an unseeing gaze, not directed to him, and yet it captivated him.

He had wheedled Daniel for an introduction. Half of the guys in the room were in a literal queue to shake her hand as she came down from the stage after the panel. He was certain he would make a better impression on her consciousness if a common friend introduced him to her.

He was so determined to succeed then, would not leave without meeting her. It cost him a Sonos One speaker three days later, a payment to Daniel for giving him Yuana's mobile phone number.

Would I have pursued that introduction had I known?

Daniel warned him then she was only interested in casual dating. He now understood why. The twinge in his gut intensified. His desperation to make certain Yuana was still his, rose like acid from his stomach. He could overcome anything for as long as he and Yuana remained together. He could not envision his future without her or bear the thought of not having her in his life.

So, why am I having a hard time accepting Yuana's nature? What am I scared about?

Sleep, when it finally came to him was disturbed, full of disjointed images of Yuana, a dark moonless night, the treehouse of his childhood, a flash of light, and a monstrous figure bent over a prone woman covered in blood.

His own scream of terror woke him up. Sweat poured down his back, his heart hammered out of his chest. The images were so vivid he still felt like the child he was in the nightmare. The tears on his wet face were real. The terror had left him shaking.

He recognised the treehouse. His father built it for him in their holiday home. But he did not recognise the face of the woman lying in a pool of blood, nor the man crouched over her. His hands and face bloody, a terrible rage reflected in his eyes. The nightmare felt familiar, like he had dreamt of it before.

Had my subconscious fused an old dream with my current concern about Yuana and merged them?

He got dressed in a daze. The question Dr Sanchez asked him to think about was now an incessant echo in his head.

What was it about Yuana's revelation that bothered me?

He could not answer it.

Do I believe Yuana?

A thud of realisation hit him in the chest. He did, one hundred per cent. And he feared what that meant.

He sat on the edge of his bed and picked up the business card of Dr Sanchez lying on his bedside table. Hopefully she could spare him a few minutes today.

Katelin, Margaita, and Lorenzo sat in the secret briefing room as they waited for the rest of the group to arrive. Edrigu arrived five minutes later. The screen connected to the private covered parking lot located across the street flickered to life.

They watched Ramon, the loyal and long-time driver of Lorenzo and Margaita, escort a group of people to the car repair shop beside the parking lot. He steered them down the stairs to the underground pathway that connected to the briefing room disguised as a granny flat attached to the principal house.

General Mateo Santino led the group, followed by his son Daniel, *Iztaris* Ben Carrion and Troy Villegas. Security cameras all the way to the primary room covered the group's progress through the hidden hallway. Within seconds, they emerged from the utility room of the granny flat into the living room where they all sat.

Daniel looked around the room. His interest captured as he noted all the well-concealed security equipment that peppered the cosy surrounding.

"Gentlemen, now that we are all here, let us move to the meeting room."

Lorenzo got up and proceeded to what appeared to be the bedroom. The group followed him. The door opened instead to a sound-proofed room, equipped with a wide screen and computer system, and a conference table that seats eight.

"So, what do you have?" Lorenzo sat on Margaita's right after he pulled a chair for his wife. The meeting had started. Everyone sat down, laptops got turned on and files opened. Mateo took the floor.

"Punong-Ina, Punong-Ama." He nodded at Margaita and Lorenzo, as a greeting and a sign of respect, then continued on. "We deployed five people, one leased a condo unit on the same floor as Mr Magsino's, all listening devices planted in his unit now. The second one acts as the subject's social shadow for his day activities, and a third one for his evening activities. For his workplace, Daniel will cover it. The fourth and fifth iztaris will shadow his parents. We had bugged their home as well."

"Is there anything we need to worry about?" Margaita asked, a slight frown on her face.

"Nothing yet, Punong-Ina. But we expected this given the depth of the relationship between Mr Magsino and your great-granddaughter, plus the level of emotional maturity of the subject. We predict he would be very reluctant to share this information to his social circle for fear of derision, not just for himself, but for your granddaughter too," Mateo replied.

This was welcome news for the family. For the sake of

Yuana, they did not want him harmed. Not unless it became necessary.

"Okay. How about the issues I mentioned earlier?" Katelin asked. She addressed Iztari Carrion and Villegas.

"As far as we had gathered, Mrs Orzabal, the witnesses had no connection to Mr Magsino or his family," Ben Carrion replied. "They were all residents of Barrio Balanac as we keep an extensive record of all those witnesses. We have kept close track of them and their families over the years. As far as we know, they have not crossed paths with the family of Mr Magsino."

"It's a pity that we do not have the same extensive records on Roald." Katelin sighed.

"What are we looking for, Mrs Orzabal?" General Santino asked.

"We are certain Mr Magsino had a traumatic experience with an aswang when he was young, that perhaps he had seen an aswang attack during his early childhood," Edrigu explained.

"There was no reported incident in his place of birth, Santo Tomas, Batangas, that coincided with the timeline," said Katelin. "So, I searched in the nearby environs. And the only thing worth noting seemed to be the Pagsanjan incident in 1993 and the Mataas na Kahoy incident in 1994. The Mataas na Kahoy incident did not seem to be the right event as it was a simple extraction of a pregnant single mother aswang and her child."

"Ah, I remember that case. I led it," Mateo quipped. There was a slight grimace in his expression.

Daniel threw his father a sideways glance of surprise.

"Can you tell us more about that event, as the reports provided little detail?" Katelin asked.

"Nothing much to tell. A tip reached the office about a near attack of a pregnant aswang in Mataas na Kahoy. By coincidence, I was in Lipa City for a three-week holiday with my late wife's family. They assigned the case to me as the lead since I was already there. It took about a week to trace her. We found her by accident. There was a reported tiyanak attack that evening in Balete. We thought those were two different incidents, but the tiyanak turned out to be the lady's three-year-old son. The lady was about seven months pregnant. She was suicidal and intended to starve herself and her son to death. She caged herself and her son in the rented house where they lived. But the child ripped through his cage and attacked the neighbour." Mateo's description was dispassionate and dismissive.

"Wow! The report never detailed that," Katelin uttered.

"Carlo Quizon, the second lead, was bad at reports," Mateo said.

The location seemed to have triggered something in Daniel's recollection; he sat up straight, an urgent look on his face.

"There must be something to this, Dad. If I am not mistaken, Roald's family has a rest house in Lipa. I remember they had a company budget meeting in that house, because he invited our gang to follow and join them for a weekend swimming party. I cannot remember why I could not join them, but the place could be in Mataas na Kahoy," Daniel said, a lilt of excitement in his voice.

"Why don't you ask him so we can confirm?" his dad suggested.

Daniel did. He dialled Roald's number, who answered within two rings.

"Hey, bro, what are you up to this morning?" Daniel asked in a pleasant tone, his phone on speaker.

"Hey, D! I'm just about to get to the car, I'm on my way to my doctor," Roald replied.

This was a surprise to all, as they knew that Roald's next appointment with Dr Sanchez was the following day.

"You feeling okay, bro?" Daniel asked, a frown on his brow.

"I'm okay, bro, just another session with the shrink." Roald's reply was nonchalant, oblivious to the crowd listening to their conversation.

"Okay. Hey, bro, don't you have a rest house in Batangas?" Daniel kept his tone as casual as possible.

"Yes, in Mataas na Kahoy, why do you ask?" Roald asked.

"Well, I was thinking of places where my team and I can do the mid-year budget, and I remembered you did yours two years ago at your place... Can I borrow it? If it is okay with you."

"Oh sure, when? We may need to have it cleaned and prepared. We have not been back there for over a year."

"I will let you know; we are still planning it. Thanks in advance, bro."

"You're welcome," Roald replied, and he hung up.

Silence ruled for a split second as the call ended. Daniel looked at the group, waiting for reaction.

"Okay, let us look into that rest house. It may lead to something," Edrigu said and glanced at Mateo, whose face was grim. Mateo nodded.

A message came from Dr Sanchez. Edrigu turned on the system in Session Room 3. Minutes later, they had live audio and video access to the session and saw Roald enter the door. Dr Sanchez stood up to greet him. Roald sat on the couch, Dr Sanchez in her usual seat.

"Thank you for seeing me today, Doctora. I know you're busy and I really appreciate you made time for me at such brief notice." Roald's voice was pleasant.

"It's my pleasure, Roald. It is additional research material for my medical journal." Dr Sanchez's smile was gentle.

After tea was served, and short pleasantries exchanged, Dr Sanchez bid Roald to relax, and said, "So, tell me what's on your mind." Her calm facade was admirable being that the group eavesdropping on their conversation were all tensed.

"Your last question had been on my mind since I left our last session... on what bothered me most about my girlfriend's revelation..." Roald paused. "I think I fear it, about her being an aswang, and I do not know why..."

"Are you scared she will hurt you?"

Roald paused, then shook his head. "No, not that. I'm not scared of her."

"You said you feared something. What was that something?" Dr Sanchez prompted him.

"I had a bad dream last night. That question was the last thing on my mind before I fell asleep... The certainty that I fear aswangs, what she is, came to me when I woke up. What exactly I am scared about, I do not know, except the fear was there."

"Tell me about your dream..." Dr Sanchez asked.

"It's a mix of images... but it was the emotion that came during and afterward that stayed with me. It felt familiar... and recurring. I was a child in my dream, and I saw a woman lying on the ground, blood pooled all around her, and a man crouched over her, his hands and face bloody..." Roald's terror was clear in the tremor in his speech.

"Did you recognise anything in those images? Places, the woman, the man?"

"The place — I'm certain I was on my tree house, the one my dad built for me when I was young. It used to be my favourite playhouse when I was a child," Roald's brows knitted as he scoured his memories.

"How about the man and the woman?"

"No, I do not think I know them. I may have, but just do not remember, but it felt like they were strangers to me."

"So, in your dream, the event happened at your place?"

Roald shook his head. "No, the bloody scene was outdoors. It happened in the garden of the house next door. My treehouse sat atop an ancient mango tree beside the perimeter wall. It was made of wood and glass and offered three views. It overlooked the lake, our garden, and the front lawn of the neighbour's house."

Dr Sanchez nodded and jotted down notes as Roald talked.

"You said the woman was lying on the ground, bloody... was she dead?" she pressed. At the nod of Roald's head, she continued, "And the man, what was he doing?"

There was a long silence from Roald, his eyes closed, as he tried to dredge up details from the nightmare. Sweat beaded his upper lip, his face in a grimace of terror as the images came back to him.

"It looked like he was... eating her, and he looked savage." Roald's response was a hoarse whisper.

"What time of the day did it happen?" Dr Sanchez asked, her interest keen.

"Night, it was night." His reply came quick.

"Was there a moon that night?"

"No, it was dark, but I remember a flash of light, and the man looked up at that flash, and that's how I saw his face." Roald's shiver was visible, even on the screen.

Dr Sanchez stared at Roald. "What do you think he was?"

They all waited for Roald's answer with bated breath, but he kept silent.

"Could it be you assumed him to be an aswang, because he looked like he was eating her?" Dr Sanchez said, her suggestion gentle.

Roald stared back at her. His indecision clear. Then he sighed, "Yes, it's possible. I am sure my nanny at that age used aswang stories to scare me into behaving, to make me eat my greens, or abide by my bedtime schedule."

"Do you think the event in your nightmare actually happened?" Dr Sanchez asked gently.

"I am not sure. Maybe I need to speak to my parents. If it happened when I was young, I must have talked about it then."

"Yes, that is a good idea. It may just be an irrational fear borne from an unusual event that got melded into the scary stories your nanny or any of your elders were telling you then," Dr Sanchez said. Her demeanour was composed and non-judgmental. Roald's shoulders relaxed. "Will you keep me updated on that?"

Roald nodded.

"Do you believe your girlfriend is an aswang?" she asked.

This was a crucial question, and his answer would determine the course of action she and the rest of the people listening in on the conversation would take.

"Yes... I think I do... Or at least I think I did." Roald's quiet rasp was tortured. The verbal admission seemed to have unlocked something in him. His shoulders straightened.

"Doc, do you think my girlfriend is an aswang?" Roald asked, his gaze focused on Dr Sanchez. It appeared that he needed some validation, a professional opinion.

Her smile was enigmatic. "I cannot make that assessment, Roald, as she is not my patient. You are. I would have to speak to her myself to make any diagnosis. She could very well believe herself to be one, and that is a different kind of neurosis," she replied.

"I thought the same at first, Doc, until I saw..." Roald stopped in mid-sentence.

"What did you see?" she prompted.

They had briefed Dr Sanchez of the event. The good doctor was fishing for Roald's genuine thoughts about what he saw. It would determine how convinced Roald was, and if there was a space for them to plant reasonable doubt.

"I saw her changing... her colour, her skin texture. I felt her temperature, the heat haze from her skin..." Roald's voice was wondering, the tremor audible.

"What did she change into?"

"I did not see beyond that. They pulled me away."

"What was your state of mind that day, the previous night, or a few days before? Were you well rested? Were you eating well?" Dr Sanchez asked.

"No, after the first discussion about it, I was not sleeping well, barely ate," he admitted.

"So, it is safe to say your anxiety level was high, right?" He nodded. "There is a possibility you misinterpreted what you saw?"

"It is a possibility, Doc, but right now, I am sure of what I saw." Roald's insistence was emphatic.

"Okay. We will take it as it is." She nodded, her expression placid and placating. "What do you plan to do with that knowledge? With your relationship with her? What is next for the both of you?"

"I am working to get our relationship past my fear," Roald replied, sounding less certain of the outcome.

"Have you spoken to her since the revelation?"

Roald grimaced. "I haven't had the luck. Her phone has been out of reach for days now. I also want to be completely sure of my mind, my heart. If I am to convince her we have a future together, I need to know how I can deal with this."

To his hidden listeners, the statement was a welcome relief.

The session ended with Dr Sanchez giving Roald permission to call her anytime if he had any more concern about his fear of aswangs. They had established that he had some trauma about aswangs, and it was affecting his perception of his girlfriend's nature. The following day's session was cancelled. Instead, they would have an on-call consultation from then on.

Roald left the clinic with a more relaxed countenance. The frown on his face eased, and his steps were more purposeful. He told the doctor that his next stop was to find out where his girlfriend was so he could get to her.

They knew he would come to the De Vida house.

The session yielded many investigative points for the team. The most obvious one was for them to go back to Mataas na Kahoy to find the house the Magsinos owned, find out if the episode Roald detailed in the session happened, and if it was an aswang-related one.

With all the tasks assigned, Lorenzo dismissed the group. They had achieved excellent progress in this case, and judging by how Roald behaved in the sessions, the future for him and Yuana was looking up.

The team left the briefing room in batches suffused with enthusiasm.

Everyone except Mateo.

He was going back to Mataas na Kahoy tomorrow. And it filled him with foreboding. The memories of his last visit to the area were best forgotten and left undisturbed. But he would not defy a direct order from the Patriarch. So, he would go with Edrigu in the morning. He had a feeling he knew its exact location.

He hoped it was not the one beside the lake house he rented for a few weeks in 1994. His past and the family secret he kept from Daniel for twenty-five years had caught up with him.

With a heavy heart, Mateo bid the De Vidas goodbye. Daniel followed him, unaware that his life would soon be upended.

Roald slowed his car down at the corner street to allow half a dozen vehicles to cross. He could see the main gate of the De Vida compound from where he was, a mixture of trepidation and anticipation in his veins.

A familiar dark blue BMW pulled out from the car repair shop across from the De Vida compound — it was Daniel's. That was odd. Daniel's house and office were nowhere near the area.

Two minutes later, he pulled into the driveway of the De Vidas. Nita showed him to the living room where Katelin and Edrigu De Vida waited to meet him.

"Good afternoon, sir, Ma'am." He recognised nervousness in his own voice.

Edrigu had a spark of satisfaction in his eyes. He must have found consolation in his discomfort.

"Good afternoon, Hijo," Katelin replied with a gentle smile.

He appeared miserable and tired, but her reception emboldened Roald, so he took a deep breath and ploughed into the purpose of his visit. "Ma'am, I am here to ask for help. I need to find Yuana."

His directness made Katelin blink, and she threw a glance at her husband.

"Why do you want to find Yuana?" Edrigu's quiet question told him clearly that they would protect Yuana to all ends.

"Sir, I want to make things right with her, and I cannot do that if I cannot locate her and talk to her." He would not discuss what was in his heart with anyone but Yuana.

Edrigu looked at him for a long time until he felt uncomfortable, but he refused to look away. He wanted Yuana's grandfather to see his determination and the sincere desire to fix matters with their granddaughter.

Finally, Edrigu spoke, "Villa Bizitza, Baco, Oriental Mindoro."

He was dumbstruck for a split second but understood Edrigu was giving him permission to try his luck with Yuana.

"Thank you, Sir." He grabbed Edrigu's hand and shook it with uncharacteristic vigour.

"Good luck," Katelin said, her face serious.

After a quick farewell to the couple, he rushed back to his car.

He had a travel plan to make.

12

THE APEX

Despite not finding sleep till dawn, Yuana woke up full of energy. The last thoughts before she fell asleep remained foremost in her mind. It was a nagging inner voice to discover her animus.

Roald still pervaded her consciousness, but her preoccupation to find out this hidden facet of her nature diverted her from her heartache. A new door was before her, one that could lead to a different path, an option that was never on the table before.

Her parents were at the ground floor verandah, enjoying a bottle of rosé, probably a Graci Etna Rosato, her mother's recent favourite. Her mother laughed at whatever funny story her father regaled her. It was the happiest she had ever seen her. Her father's eyes sparkled with joy, passion, and satisfaction; his own lips deepened with a smile.

As usual, seeing them this happy evoked a mixed feeling in her; gladness to see her parents contented, and envy her own relationship did not pan out the same way, no matter how similar their situation was. Some people were luckier than most.

She stood by the stairs for a while, unwilling to break the happy circle, when they noticed her and beckoned her over.

"There you are, my sweet. Come and join us. The rosé is chilled to perfection." Her father waved her over.

She walked closer, gave them both a hug and sat down. She poured herself a glass of the rosé. There was slight tension in the air, like suppressed energy poised to explode. Both her parents looked excited. Her mother was beaming, but there was a nervousness in her gaze.

"So, what is it, Ma? Pa?" she asked.

A twitch appeared at the corner of her father's mouth, and it widened into a grin. His excitement was that of a boy on Christmas morning who discovered he got everything he wished for.

"I proposed to your mother... and she said yes!"

"You did?... She did?... Oh my god!" she squealed, jumping up to hug her mother.

Her own heart overflowed with happiness for them. Perhaps the adage was true, that for every end, there was a fresh beginning, and that genuine joy was born out of genuine pain. Her parents found their joy and a new beginning after twenty-eight years of pain. They were ecstatic. Her family was now whole, and that was enough for the moment.

"When is the wedding?"

"We haven't discussed the details yet, but I want to get married on the tenth of May. It was the day he first proposed. I want to pretend there was no time wasted between us..." Her mother's face glowed.

"May tenth it is..." her father murmured. He picked up her mother's hands and dropped a kiss on her palms. Heat rose to her cheeks. She felt like an intruder in their circle.

"We can tell the family when we return. I will plan the wedding, Mama. It will be fun."

It was something to be excited about, and she was glad. She could set aside her concern for her own relationship. Her parents' happiness was a balm to her sore heart. "Let me raise a toast to the most beautiful parents a girl could ever wish for..." Her glass raised.

"To the family I have always wanted and now have..." her father said.

"To a love that was lost and now found..." her mother's voice cracked.

Their glasses met and clinked. It was an emotional but heartfelt toast. Silence followed as all three of them dealt with the feelings the moment created.

"It was not really lost, was it, Bel? We just got... misplaced, you and I," her father said. His tender gaze turned to her mother.

"Yes, you are right..." Tears pooled in her mother's eyes.

Yuana swallowed the lump of emotion that formed in her throat, constricting her heart as she witnessed the enormity of her parents' love for each other.

"Shall we toast to that then... To misplaced loves that found their way back..." she said, wanting to lighten the mood.

They raised their glasses in agreement.

The bottle of rosé was consumed in a series of toasts until the air cleared and became easy and cheerful again.

"Have you heard from Roald, Yuana?" Her father's gentle question came out of the blue.

"Not yet, Papa. But then, I have not turned on my phone since we came here," she replied.

"Why not? Do you not want to talk to him anymore?"

"I do. Yet I am afraid to turn it on and only to find out he has not tried to contact me at all," she admitted.

"I doubt that very much," Galen scoffed. "I have seen the boy's torment. It would surprise me if Roald was not beside himself looking for you."

"We have been here for over a week, Pa, why hasn't he showed up here yet?" The underlying bitterness seeped in her tone.

"He doesn't know where we are, Yuana. Our office did not, as well, and even if they did, our SOP would not allow them to divulge that. And the family will not tell him unless they believed it would be the best thing to do," her mother said.

As if on cue, the phone rang. It was Edrigu calling. After a brief exchange, Ysobella looked at her with a smug smile on her face.

"Your grandfather just called to inform us he just gave Roald the address to the villa, that he might show up anytime."

Hope filled her heart, and it lifted her spirits.

"There you go, Yuana. I told you so..." her father said confidently, but she heard the sigh of relief under his breath.

"I am glad he is coming here. Then I would not have to go through the inconvenience of flying to Manila to beat him within an inch of his life," his father said in a sotto voice to her mother.

She smiled.

———

The news put Yuana in anticipation the whole afternoon, and after a few hours, left her overwhelmed. Her mind kept playing scenes of reconciliation and rejection one after the other. It was like being on an emotional rollercoaster. Finally, she could not take it anymore. She went for a run in the woods.

An hour into her sprint deep in the forest, the afternoon sun had already descended low on the horizon. It gave the surroundings an auburn gleam. The breeze blew through the trees and cooled the sweat-dampened fabric of her shirt. She proceeded to the riverbank where they met Mr Nakahara the night before. The persistent thought about her animus led her there. It did not surprise her to find the gentleman seated on the same fallen tree trunk, meditating.

She watched him for a while, noting the lightening at the hair on his temples. There was a rugged yet serene air about him, like a well-worn pair of jeans. He exuded mystery and wisdom, no doubt brought about by his war experience and years of living in the mountains. He could be the same age as her grandfather, but he looked more hardened and battle-tested. His sun-browned skin made him appear younger, as well.

She approached him with care, not wanting to disturb him. She planned to sit by the bank until he was done, but he spoke, his eyes still closed. "Good afternoon, Ms Yuana."

She came closer and sat down beside him on the fallen trunk. "Pleasant afternoon, Mr Nakahara," she said.

He opened his eyes and stared at her, a slight smile on his face. "You are here to find out about your true nature, yes?"

She nodded. "How? I do not want to starve myself just to induce an auto-morphosis. I almost had one of those. It was not a pleasant experience. And I have no plans to repeat it."

"Reflexive transformation may be the usual way, but not the most ideal, or the only way," he said.

That was intriguing. "What other ways are there?"

"Meditation is one, but that takes a long time to master, and I sense you are impatient." His focused gaze was knowing.

"Yes, I want to know now. Is there a faster, less painful and easier way to discover my animus?"

"Faster? Maybe. But it is not easier, and it requires considerable effort to achieve. Are you willing to do whatever it takes to *emerge*?" Challenge glittered in the depths of his dark eyes.

Her heart thundered in her ears. "Is it worth the effort to find out? Most of our kind lived until their end without knowing their true animus and still had a full life."

He smiled. "Most of us do not have the potential that you have. When you emerge, you will discover more than your spirit animal."

"Will you teach me?"

He nodded.

"I can teach you now... Are you ready?"

Am I? She took a deep breath. "Yes, I am. How do we begin?"

"You need to increase your heartbeat to a degree that you can hear it, then you transform with no form in mind. You just let it happen."

Nakahara's soft instruction crawled into her heart like a mist on a moonlit night.

"Transform with no form in mind? How can I do that?" Nakahara's method was counter-intuitive to what she was taught.

"You focus on your heartbeat, not on your form," he said. "That is why raising your heartbeat is crucial."

"Raising my heartbeat? How? Like through... running?"

"Yes, running hard. Very hard. Until you can feel your blood pounding in your ears.

She thought of where and how long she would have to run to achieve the feat. She ran for over an hour earlier and she did not achieve that, so she needed to run faster and harder.

"Okay, I can do that."

With a glance of goodbye to Nakahara, she ran at full speed away from the river and toward the foot of the mountain where she planned to run uphill until she achieved the required audible-heartbeat state.

And run she did.

Air whizzed past her hair and face as she zigzagged around the trees in her path. She jumped over fallen trees, boulders, and low branches; her sight focused on the inclined ground ahead. Her legs burned, but she quickened her pace still.

In her peripheral vision, she saw wild animals, ground and tree dwelling alike, scamper away from her path. Still, she kept the punishing pace and speed, knowing that if she slowed down, she would have to start again.

She was not sure how long and how far she had covered, but she pushed herself to run longer. Farther and faster, even as her lungs felt scored by the effort to breathe and bring oxygen to her muscles. She sprinted until she could not, anymore.

Until her heartbeat drowned out the sounds of her surroundings.

She stopped and looked around, her senses on high alert. She was on a small hilltop; the sun had set, and the horizon was darkening. Behind her, she could see Villa Bizitza from a distance. With that as the last picture in her mind, she pulled her yoga pants off, her shoes and her top. She closed her eyes to begin her transformation, her focus on her heart beating loud in her ears and strong in her veins.

The familiar tingling started at the base of her spine and spread all over her body until it reached her fingertips. Her core generated heat, expanding outward, enveloping her from head to toe. She focused her mind on her heartbeat until she became a passive observer of what was happening in her body. She waited for her spine to bend her to all fours, but the familiar sensation started on her shoulder blades instead. Her bones stretched out, growing outwards. She opened her eyes when her skin vibrated, saw the start of the transformation from her human form to whatever animal she would turn into.

In the waning light, it surprised her to see that her skin had turned from her normal flesh tone into a familiar yet unfamiliar midnight dark sheen, and into a texture that she had never seen before. In the countless past transformations, shiny black fur had covered her body.

This time, the black fur transformed into something else; small, downy, glossy feathers of dark blue-black, or dark violet. She flexed her hands and saw the long and thick talons that replaced her nails. Her hands did not transform into paws. And she was still upright.

The stretching pressure on her shoulder blades turned into a familiar spasm that halted into a jolt. She looked back and saw a black arch over her shoulders and head. She reached back to touch it, unable to believe her own conclusion.

Wings! I have grown a pair of wings!

She flexed her shoulder blades, and the wings moved like an extra pair of arms. Enthralled, she unfurled both wings and tested the range of motion that she could make. She expanded them wide and flexed to test their strength.

An imposing figure hovered over her, startling her. The figure landed with a soft thud nearby. She took an involuntary defensive step backward, ready to fight, until she recognised him.

It was Mr Nakahara, in his animus form, winged like she was.

His wings, however, were bat-like. Dark, glossy fur covered his humanoid form. It was hard to tell in this low light what exact colour it was, but it looked black. His features were unmistakable despite the now dark colour of his skin. He had claw-like hands with dark talons like hers. She did not feel threatened by him, although he looked intimidating.

He walked closer to her. His eyes glowed. "Ah... Your animus is avian..."

She was too overwhelmed to respond to him. Her wings flexed and spread wide, caught a strong breeze, and lifted her a few meters up into the air. She staggered back onto her feet and folded her wings back.

"Do not use your wings yet, Ms Yuana. You need to learn how to fly first..."

His smile was full of satisfaction. He walked a slow circle around her as he inspected her full form. He stopped in front of her, a friendly, almost paternal, expression on his face.

"Why did I transform into this? It is unlike anything I have seen, or known..."

Her own form mystified her. She did not just turn into a bird, which was unusual enough as their kind could only transform into land-based animals, she turned into what looked like an avian humanoid. And judging from the form that Mr Nakahara had taken, his animus was a... bat-man.

"Ms Yuana, you and I, we are an *Apex*..."

"An Apex? I'm an *Apex*?" she breathed, still unbelieving.

Mr Nakahara remained quiet.

"But... That's not... possible... I can't be?"

"You need no other proof than your current form. Winged-creature transformation is impossible to achieve for any normal aswangs. Only Apexes, the super shape-shifters, can achieve this."

She nodded, her brain still in a scramble. She knew what an Apex was. Their history talked about previous Apexes in past centuries. They were very rare, and only one in every two hundred years would emerge in their midst of the two hundred fifty million strong aswangs.

No one in her family knew of any that ever existed in their lifetime. To be one was mindboggling.

Why me?

Apart from being a De Vida, she had no exemplary achievements of her own, no notable physical or intellectual contributions to their kind. She did not deserve to be an Apex or suited to be one. She realised with a jolt that Mr Nakahara being an Apex meant there are now two in their lifetime. And that was even more rare.

"How come no one knew you are an Apex?"

"I choose not to let anyone know. I do not want the responsibility." His response was guarded. But she understood.

"What responsibility? What are we supposed to do as Apexes?"

"You will know soon enough, when you expose yourself..."

"Why reveal yourself to me?"

"I believe you and I have a destiny to fulfil. So, we have to work together. But at the very least, I want to help you achieve your potential. It is up to you. But once you are ready, I offer my assistance to train you... in due time..."

Her mind buzzed with confusion and questions. It elated her in a way that she now knew what her animus was, but she was uncertain how she felt about being an Apex. Everything that happened was so unprecedented in her existence as a human and an aswang.

"So, what is next for me, Mr Nakahara?" she asked, needing guidance.

He took her hand in his.

"You rest, you think, you test your wings, then you decide," he said, the friendly smile back on his face.

She sighed and nodded.

"Damn, does that mean I need to walk back? I cannot fly yet, and I think I am too tired to run," she muttered to herself.

Mr Nakahara grinned.

"I will fly you back," he said. "But only this one time..." His eyes twinkled.

She grinned and picked up her yoga pants to put them on. Her taloned feet distracted her. She felt taller, similar to being in high heels, only this time, the height was because of her bird claw feet on perpetual tiptoe.

Not bad.

She picked up her top and pulled it over the feather-covered mound of her breast. The back of the shirt bunched over her shoulders where her wings sprouted from her shoulder blades. On instinct, her wings shrunk into her back, and she returned to her human form. She pushed her bare feet into her shoes and turned to find Mr Nakahara with his back to her as he took in the view and waited.

"All done," she said.

He held out his hand and scooped her into his arms. Then his powerful bat-like wings opened, and lifted them into the air. The flight was not as smooth as she assumed it would be. The beating of his wings created an up and down motion as they cut through the wind to generate the lift. He flew close to the tree-tops to avoid being spotted. Old habits for survival die hard. This was what she could expect, she supposed, when she learned to fly on her own.

The flight did not take long, and soon, Mr Nakahara landed at the edge of the forest.

"Thank you, Mr Nakahara. How can I get in touch with you?"

"You're welcome. If you need me, you can find me by the river. I would know when you are there."

"Okay... So, I shall say goodnight..."

"Ms Yuana, please do not tell anyone about me. I have hidden my nature for decades for a reason," Mr Nakahara said gravely.

Her nod was solemn. "Don't worry, Mr Nakahara. It is not my secret to tell. I will tell no one."

"Call me Kazu. We will work together closely. Nakahara is a long name to say, Kazu is shorter." He smiled.

"And call me Yuana. Thank you again, Kazu."

And with that, she turned to walk the rest of the way to the villa. From behind, she heard the *thwack-thwack* sound his large wings created as he flew away.

As she neared the compound, she saw two of the Mangyan aswangs that were tasked to follow her every time she left the house. They looked relieved when they saw her approach. She had forgotten about their usual habit of tailing her. No doubt they lost her in the woods and were anxious.

"I am sorry, Kuyas, did I worry you?"

"It worried us, Miss. You ran so fast. We cannot keep up," they said, almost in unison.

"Sorry, I forgot you were following me, I did not mean to," she said. "We can keep it a secret, if that would make you feel better... I will not tell Yam-Ay," she teased.

Their eyes widened, and they both nodded, vigorously.

"Okay then, I shall go inside now. See you tomorrow." She walked straight to the kitchen. She was hungry and in need of food and sustenance.

Her parents were in the living room, looking all cuddly and affectionate with each other when she came in.

"Kids, kids, stop that... You're being a terrible role model for me," she said in mock disgust.

They both turned around with an identical shamefaced expression.

"How was your run, Yuana? You were gone awhile," her mother said.

"It was good, Mama. Can we eat first? I am starving and what I need to tell you and Papa requires sustenance."

Their eyebrows rose.

"Is it serious?" her mother asked.

"It may be. I can't believe it myself still." She was already halfway up the stairs on her way to the room.

"Okay, I will have the food and the sustenance prepared. Are you showering first?" her mother called after her.

She was ravenous but preferred to eat feeling fresh. Her shower was quick. She dressed and combed her wet hair back; she would not bother with a blow drier. Food was first in her order of business.

Her father was in her parents' room when she came down to the kitchen, the victus ready for both her mother and herself to wolf down. It had become a practice in their household to ensure her father would not see them eating raw viscera in consideration for his stomach. With their aswang needs met, they went to the dining room to wait for him, but he was already there, picking at the appetiser. He was as famished as she.

Dinner atmosphere was light and quick, with all of them starved. Her confession would wait until dessert. For complete privacy, she requested for it to be served in the entertainment room. Five minutes later, the dessert trolley was wheeled and stationed in one corner of the sound-proofed entertainment room. They sat down with slices of the dark purple ube cheese-cake, lava cake and hot beverage in hand. Her parents looked at her with anticipation.

"Mama, I know what my animus is, I have transformed into it earlier..." She was uncertain how to break the information to her parents.

"Oh, so what was it?" Ysobella asked, puzzled at the impor-tance she placed on finding her spirit animal.

"It's a raven..." she replied, as she watched her mother's expression.

"A raven? How can your animus be a raven?" As expected, Ysobella was baffled.

"Why can't she have a bird as her animus? Can you not transform into any kind of animal you want?" asked her father.

"She cannot be a raven because we can only shape-shift into land-based animals. It is impossible for us to transform into any winged creature, unless you're an..." The meaning of what she said dawned on her mother. "*Apex...*" Her head whipped back toward Yuana, unable to say anything, her expression incredulous.

"What's an Apex?" Galen asked, intrigued. His eyes darted between them.

"A super shapeshifter, Papa. One that can transform into a winged animal," she replied for her mother, who was still speechless in shock.

"And I gather it is extremely rare?" One eyebrow quirked; his gaze focused on her mother's dumbstruck expression.

"Yes. One in every two hundred years," Ysobella said in a throaty voice.

"Wow!" Her father swivelled in her direction.

"You are an *Apex...*" Ysobella said in wondering, still unable to believe what she heard.

She nodded. "Yes, Mama, I turn into a raven... I think."

"You think? You are not sure?" her father asked.

"Well, it could be a crow, I can't tell the difference." She shrugged.

"Can you show us?" Ysobella requested in a whisper.

Yuana understood why her mother wanted to see for herself. She needed to validate what her brain could not process-the fact her daughter was an Apex.

She stood up. There was no need to undress for this as she had chosen a dress with a low back. With enough room for her wings to sprout out without constraints. She expected she would have to show them.

Galen forgot to worry about seeing his daughter naked. He was as caught up in it as Ysobella. The transformation, while he had seen it before, was still mesmerising. However, the heat haze surrounding Yuana, her vibrating skin, the change of her colour from human tone to dark bluish sheen was something else.

Wings grew out from behind her and loomed bigger over her shoulders and past her head. The stark contrast between her skin now covered in small dark and glossy fan-shaped contour feathers, and the light-coloured dress was dramatic. The dainty, flowy dress was incongruent with the black-red talons her fingernails turned into.

Her hair had transformed into an aerodynamic crest of semi and filo plume feathers that fanned around her face. It gave her a majestic and intimidating look. It reminded him of a monkey-eating eagle, and it looked like the feathers could flatten close to her scalp when in flight.

The skin on her face was the only thing that kept its human colouring and texture, but on her eyebrows grew a pair of bristle feathers. It made her appear as if she had very long eyelashes. Even her eyes turned black, like raven's eyes, with no visible iris. The effect was menacing and spellbinding. Yuana looked formidable in her avian humanoid form.

Her father's mouth hung open.

"Oh, *holy Prometheus!*" Ysobella breathed out her amazement.

She approached Yuana, touched the soft, downy, feather-covered arm and then her face, as if contrasting her new reality with the old one.

"How do I look, Mama?" Yuana asked, her voice soft and vulnerable, yet proud.

"You look magnificent, Yuana," Ysobella replied, sounding proud and overawed. "You are an *Apex*... The first one in our recorded history for over two hundred years..."

Galen felt an answering pride and something grand inside his heart.

Yuana inspected herself in the bright light. The blue-black sheen of her feathers, the dark red talons on her hands and the jet-black ones on her feet fascinated her.

He handed her his cell phone. "Take a picture of yourself," he urged.

With the camera open, she did. She saw her face for the first time in her raven humanoid form. Her eye area had an iridescent, dark feather growth that made her look like she was wearing glittery goth make up.

It surprised Galen when her flesh-coloured face changed to match the rest of her body.

"Wow! You can do that?" He could not help but exclaim.

Yuana shrugged one shoulder. "So, it seems. It could be useful for a full camouflage."

"True..."

He took the phone from her and moved back to take a full body shot, then handed it to her to view the photo. Yuana's mouth dropped open.

"*Holy Aquila!* I look terrifying..." she breathed.

"Yuana, do you understand what being an Apex entails?" Ysobella asked. It interrupted Yuana's preoccupation with her own form.

"No, mama. Except for its rarity, I know very little about being an Apex. I mean, what is the purpose of being one apart from the ability to transfigure into a winged creature?"

"Let us ask your great grandmother, she might provide us insight on this. In the meantime, what do you want to do?"

"I need time to process this. Let us not tell anyone yet, Ma, Pa? I need to think."

"Okay, take your time. Let's find out everything we can about it before we let our world know of your existence..." Ysobella said.

And he could not agree more.

Yuana turned back into her human form. The process was as quick as a blink.

It must have been the loss of the wings, but in his eyes, Yuana looked deflated. Things just became more complicated for his daughter. She now had to deal with the appearance of her father in her life, with the uncertainty of her relationship with Roald, her Apex capabilities, and what it meant to her as an aswang.

His daughter's plate was overflowing, and there was nothing he could do to help.

And for the first time in the longest time, another first in a day full of it, he was glad the dessert tonight had the chocolatey kind.

Roald was busy with the arrangements for his trip to Villa Bizitza, Baco, Oriental Mindoro. There were no available flights to Calapan the following day, so he would take the bus, the ferry, and hire a car in Calapan City to drive to Yuana's holiday home at the foot of Mount Halcon.

He did not want to wait another day.

In his head, he rehearsed what he would say to convince her not to give up on them if she had not ended their relationship yet or give them another chance if she did. Either way, he would not go home without Yuana back in his life. No other outcome would be acceptable. With determination, he went to bed early; he wanted to be at Yuana's house before dinner time.

Roald was on the road by seven a.m. He wanted to make sure he had plenty of time for the eleven-a.m. ferry to Calapan City. The knot in his heart, a constant reminder of what was at stake. His head played scenarios of how he would win Yuana back. He pushed any thoughts of failure away. He would not consider the possibility of losing her.

The long, quiet journey provided him with plenty of thinking time. Memories of their time together surfaced like buoys: echoes of the days when he wooed Yuana, how much effort it took for him to get close to her, to make her open up — how he had to learn to be a friend to her first. He thought those were the most torturous moments of his life as he watched other men flirt with her while he acted as her wingman.

How wrong he was then. That could not have compared to what he was going through now.

More images floated into his consciousness; eight months since they first met, he had launched a stringent campaign to win her heart. Multiple times during the courtship she tried to discourage him, but that had the opposite effect. There were many moments in those months he almost gave up and accepted that he would never win her, but those glimpses of pain and longing in her eyes when she thought he wasn't looking kept him going.

He could understand now why she was so guarded then, why she did not want to gamble her heart away. And it was the same reason she tried very hard to keep him at a distance, why she tried every trick in her book to put a wall between them, to keep herself apart from him, because she was protecting both of their hearts.

And she was doing it again. But like before, he would not

let her succeed. They could not protect their hearts from each other anymore. It was too late.

Another car was driving along the Star Toll, with Mateo and Edrigu on board. As their destination drew closer, Mateo's gut tightened at every kilometre covered, in direct contrast to his loosening grasp on the closely held secret that he had kept for over twenty-five years. He was still hoping this incident had nothing to do with his past, that it was unrelated.

That it was just a bitter coincidence.

An hour and a half of driving in complete silence, they turned right into the entrance to Mataas na Kahoy. They slowed down at the junction to allow a truck loaded with rebars to turn the corner when Edrigu saw a police officer walking down the street. He rolled down the window on his side of the car to ask about the Magsino home. Daniel had told them it was in Barangay Manggahan but did not know its exact location.

The instruction given by the police officer was not very clear except that it was a grey house at the end of the street with an enormous mango tree and a glass treehouse on it. It was the crucial confirmation that it was the house they were looking for. The police officer offered to have them assisted, but Mateo declined it, much to Edrigu's surprise.

"It's okay, officer, I know where it is." Bleakness enveloped his heart now. It dashed the hope he was holding onto. With grim determination, he drove to the house of his nightmare. Sure and true.

He knew that his precise knowledge of the house's location was not lost on Edrigu. As a friend, Edrigu would give him the space to stew in his own thoughts and allow him the silence that he needed.

Five minutes later, they stopped in front of the Magsino's house. A concrete six-foot high wall and a dark blue metal gate enclosed it. They parked in front, and both got out. The house was empty and locked up. They did not have the key, but that was not a problem for them. They glanced around to make sure no one was in the vicinity. With that assured, they both vaulted over the wall with ease.

"I will take the inside of the house, you do the outside," Edrigu said.

He replied with a quick nod and walked towards the front lawn where the tree house was.

Mateo paused by the foot of the incline as he looked up at the structure. This kid's play area was no traditional tree house, its unique use of wood and glass a direct give away that a prominent architect designed it.

The strategic placement of the glass windows he suspected was for the adults to see what young Roald and his playmates were doing inside. The main house was elevated and must have provided an unobstructed view of the interior of the treehouse.

He walked the wooden board incline that wrapped around the base of the tree and lead to the doorway. He took in the interior of the beautiful playhouse. The room was square; the floor was hardwood. Play mats must have protected it at some point.

As Roald had described it, three walls of the room were almost floor to ceiling plexiglass. Hard wood panes about an inch thick and two inches wide framed and bisected the glass, giving it a French window design. It acted as both decoration and support. The treehouse looked like a square gazebo perched on a tree. The only wooden wall had a furniture set against it. It looked like a low child's bed, judging from the shape under the white sheet that covered it.

By the foot of the bed, there was a low table with shelves built under it. Above the table, and fixed on the wall, was an empty built-in bookshelf. He could picture it full of children's books and toys. The two parallel glass walls— one faced the main house, and the other faced the neighbouring property.

He moved closer to the dusty plexiglass wall that looked out at the front lawn of the neighbouring house. The sinking feeling that had pervaded his being since they left Manila had settled low in his stomach. He felt numb as certainty had severed the last thread of denial that he did not know he still harboured.

He was the man Roald saw that night, and the boyhood memory that haunted his nightmares was true. The grief of that night rushed back. His jaw ached with the effort to control himself from howling. The deep breaths that he took did not help. When the release came it made his shoulders shake.

He took another deep breath to collect himself and straightened his back. There was still work to be done.

"What happened that night, Mateo?" Edrigu's quiet voice startled him. He did not hear him approach.

"It did not begin or end that night. And that one night cannot explain everything." The weight of his misery was a bitter taste in his mouth.

"Explain, then. I will listen," Edrigu said, his voice low.

"Remember the 1987 battle with the Moros, the one headed by Lt. Colonel Enrico?" At Edrigu's nod, he continued. "Do you also remember why the Tribunal executed him?"

"Yes, I was not part of the judging panel then, but I remember it well. It was for abuse of power for forcing his aswang soldiers to commit harravis practices," Edrigu replied.

He nodded.

"Both Major Ona and I were part of his battalion. He forced us to go harravis to save our lives and our troops. For most of us, it was a onetime thing we had to do to survive. But Lt. Colonel Enrico wanted to continue the practice and turn all his aswang soldiers into full harravises, so I blew the whistle on him. I thought that was the end until Major Ona started his active hunting party in Pagsanjan in 1993. After he was killed, they autopsied his body, and confirmed he had Visceral Metastasis. He had been hunting pregnant women to stay the progress of the disease. He used the hunting party as a cover for his own need to secure amniotic fluid. I would have ignored his Visceral Metastasis diagnosis if I did not recall Lt. Colonel Enrico's autopsy also revealed he had the same disease." His voice broke, unable to continue.

"You have *Visceral Metastasis*?" Edrigu prompted, shocked.

"Yes, I had myself checked, and the results came back positive. They gave me two years to live. It devastated me. My wife was pregnant with our baby girl, and Daniel was just five years old, so the next thing I did was to prepare to die and ensure the future of my family. There was no way I would kill women and babies regularly just to prolong my life."

His distaste for the act was still fresh.

"But my wife decided otherwise. That night, we had dinner outdoors by the garden. Daniel was in bed by then. She brought up again her earlier suggestion to sacrifice our unborn child for my cure. I would not have it. She told me her doctor diagnosed her with cardiomyopathy, and giving birth to our baby might kill her, so I needed to survive for Daniel. Still, I said no. I wanted a second opinion for her because she needed to live for both our kids. But she gave me no choice."

The ball of pain that he thought he had got rid of resurfaced with a force of a tsunami, threatening to obliterate his control.

"Her last words to me were *'Do not waste my sacrifice, promise me you will survive'*... right before she shot herself in the head."

He closed his eyes at the avalanche of buried emotions and the vivid images of having to open her up and eat his own child's viscera. It was beyond description. It made his stomach turn. Bile burned his throat, and he swallowed hard to push his nausea back.

"And you had to do as she asked," Edrigu said. His grim expression and taut jaw conveyed that he understood the torment Mateo went through, the devastating loss of his wife, and having to kill and consume his own child.

"Yes. I found out from her doctor after her burial that she did not have cardiomyopathy..." He forced himself to breathe out the fury he was feeling. "She made me eat my daughter, Edrigu."

The anger at the act she forced him to commit under this pretext was still raw in his heart. He realised he was still angry at his late wife, and had not forgiven her for what she did to him and to their family.

"She decided long before that night, Mateo. She planned it. Did she suffer from depression during her conception of Daniel?"

The question gave him pause.

"Yes." He looked back at Espie's pregnancy with Daniel and remembered that she suffered from postnatal depression months after Daniel was born.

"That may have been the trigger, why she did what she did... Does Daniel know?" Edrigu asked.

"No." He sighed. "I told myself that I will tell him when we are both ready, when the right time comes. But I have never found the right time to do so. I guess I have never been ready. I am not sure how I will tell Daniel, without destroying the image of his mother and father in his mind."

Edrigu sighed. "If there was a way to keep the truth from Daniel, I would not be averse to helping you do that, but this might not be possible, given the circumstances."

"I know... Perhaps it is time."

"You would have to tell him, Mateo, the sooner the better, before he finds out during the briefings. You owe that much to him," Edrigu said.

"I know." The rhythmic tip-tapping of a small branch against a glass wall sounded like a countdown to a deadline.

He would prolong the time, if he could, but he had no choice.

13

THE FORK IN THE ROAD

Y uana spent the first few hours of the morning examining her animus from front to back, head to toe. In the natural sunlight, her feathers were more dark blue-violet than black. The contour feathers that covered her body had an iridescent quality to it. The violet hue in the feathers gave off some dark red, green and gold at certain angles.

She loved her Apex form, her wings in particular. It was a superhero fantasy come true. She discovered her wings were flexible; she had wrapped them around herself like a blanket and used them like an extra pair of arms. They were so big that when stretched, the wing tip touched the high ceiling.

It was a pity that once she learned how to fly, she would have to limit her flight to remote locations and moonless nights.

She had tested the talons on her feet earlier and grasped items with them like birds of prey do. To test the grip strength, she played tug of war between her hand and feet talons and discovered that her feet talons were as strong as her hands.

Last night, she researched as much as she could find about ravens, crows, eagles and hawks. In daylight, she did not look like a raven as she had first thought. She was a combination of various bird species.

Would I inherit birdlike powers apart from flight?

Maybe I should research about Apexes.

She picked up her bathrobe and threw it over her shoulder. Her human form was back by the time she tied the robe tie around her waist. She sat down on her reading couch and logged into their viscerebus archive.

Her research about Apexes yielded fascinating, but superficial information. Past Apexes transformed into a chiropteran form, like Mr Nakahara. Her avian form was rarer. There had only been a single recorded avian Apex, and he turned into something similar to a snowy owl. It made sense as he emerged from the Alps. Perhaps her colour had to do with being able to blend into her surroundings.

She was only the second avian Apex in history.

In their recent past, the Apex had served as a figurehead, someone the aswangkind rallied behind, like a unifying royalty, during some momentous change in their society. Those previous Apexes were not required to rule, as the Tribunal still did that. There was nothing that showed what else the Apexes were good for. It seemed they were just figureheads.

Like a modern monarch?

She was not sure if she wanted that role - all the trappings of authority, but without real responsibility or accountability.

Hmm... perhaps there were some documents in the Vivliocultatum that could provide more information. Her great grandmother may be able to secure access to the Viv from the Supreme Tribunal.

An entry in the system caught her attention: *The Dawn of the Dual Apex.*

What?

She clicked on the link. It opened to an article about the

written works of Aiden O'Cuinn, an Apex who lived during the medieval times. He was the chieftain of their clan and known as a poet. He had written ballads and poems and recorded much of the momentous events in his life. Just before he died, he wrote an unfinished ballad called *The Rise of the Viscerebus*. And there, he predicted the coming of the two Apexes.

It read:

When the era of the Two Apexes born in the same lifetime dawns, it will be the beginning of the cataclysm. The first will emerge at the same moment the seed of the great crisis is sowed. The second will rise to signal its turning point. Two have to become one to overcome, for as long as they remain separate, the enemy prevails.

The text said the first Apex was a forewarning of a great crisis. And the second one would signal the turning point of the crisis. The first pointed to Kazu Nakahara, and the second, to her as they were the first two Apexes ever to exist in the same lifetime. The rest of the words seemed to suggest they would need to fight some enemy.

She was not a warrior. No training for it, either physically or mentally. She was unsure if she could handle the responsibility of leading all the aswangs in the world. Kazu may have a point in keeping his identity a secret.

After reading that, she was leaning towards anonymity herself.

It was during brunch when a call came through from Calapan. The iztari team who tailed Roald informed them he had boarded the eleven a.m. ferry from Batangas Port to Calapan City. They expected him to arrive in Calapan by one thirty. He had booked a car from a local travel agency, so Roald should get to Villa Bizitza by around three in the afternoon.

Ysobella instructed Yam-Ay to prepare the guest room. She had a feeling Roald would not be going back to Manila tonight. Knowing his determination, he would not give up on Yuana easily.

It was unnecessary to inform Yuana about the call or she would twist herself into knots. She would know soon enough. Plus, it would be more romantic if there was an element of surprise.

Daniel arrived home midafternoon, much earlier than usual. It was rare for his father to ask him to dine at home on a Friday evening. Friday and Saturday nights are prime time for people his age. But he could not say no. He sensed it was important to his father. His voice had sounded flat, a sign that something was bothering him.

His father was in the living room, slumped on the sofa, scotch in hand, his mother's photo album set in front of him. And this alarmed him even more. His father would only drink scotch one day a year - the death anniversary of his mother and his unborn baby sister. And that would not be due for another five months.

Instinct prompted him to sit with his father. Maybe it was time to share the burden of whatever drove his father to drink himself into a stupor once a year.

Daniel poured himself a measure of the scotch. His father looked at him with tired, red-rimmed eyes. He looked defeated. This was distressing because even in those annual drunken days of the past years, he was in pain but never this beaten, like a general who lost a war.

They continued to drink in silence for a while, both unwilling to break the mood, waiting for the other to speak. Finally, his father put his glass down, rubbed his eyes, and sat up straight from his earlier slump, like a soldier deciding to fight one last battle despite the odds.

"Daniel, have I done well as your father?"

The question astonished him; he did not know what prompted his father to ask it.

"You did very well, dad, more than I could ever hope for." They had a relaxed father and son relationship, more like buddies.

His father's pupils darkened and glittered with intensity; his jaw clenched tight. "I need to tell you something that I wish with all my heart I could spare you from. All I ask is that you do not judge me too harshly." His voice was rough, like the scotch had scorched his vocal chords.

Daniel felt a kick to his heart.

His father sat back on the sofa, the glass of scotch cradled in his hands, his profile to him. He could see his throat forcing down whatever emotion he wanted to control. Seeing his father this distressed made him nervous.

"In 1987, when I was still a Captain, I was part of an anti-insurgency campaign in the mountains of Lanao against Moro rebels. Someone tipped them off, and they ambushed us, killing half of our troops. They trapped us in an unfamiliar terrain and surrounded us. It was a very dangerous situation, their number double than ours, and they knew the area well. To survive, our commanding officer, Lt. Colonel Enrico, an aswang, commanded a group of us to turn harravis to save ourselves and the troops. We consumed the viscera of our fallen aswang comrade to get out of there. And we succeeded. It saved us, including the human troops," his father said in a flat tone.

Mateo inhaled, then took a swig of the scotch. Daniel sat

still as he waited for his father to continue. There was no doubt the story was very important.

His father cleared his throat. "When we got back to civilization, our Commanding Officer wanted to turn us fully into harravises, to make it part of our Standard Operating Procedure as a battalion. My fellow officers and I disagreed, so I turned in my CO to the Tribunal. They found him guilty, and he was executed. I thought that was the end of that. Twenty years later, that one incident came back to haunt me..." he broke off. Fury reddened his face.

"What happened, Dad?" he asked, a sense of foreboding in the air.

"Do you recall the Pagsanjan 1993 incident and the head perpetrator, Major Ona?" Mateo asked instead, the quiet question ominous.

Daniel nodded.

"He was one of the company leaders under Lt. Colonel Enrico and was part of our battalion in the fateful 1987 clash. After they killed him in the Pagsanjan campaign, his autopsy confirmed he had Visceral Metastasis. My former CO's autopsy revealed he had the same disease. It was too much of a coincidence, so I had myself tested..." His father's voice quavered.

"And?"

"And it was positive." His father's grim reply was like a lead ball in his chest.

"You have *VM*?" His heart sank.

"No... I no longer have it. I was cured," Mateo replied. His voice cracked.

"How? I thought it was an incurable disease."

"It is, but there is one cure... the viscera of a foetus, specifically one with the closest DNA to the afflicted."

There was pain and panic reflected in the depths of his

father's eyes. A chill invaded Daniel's body. "What does that mean?"

"Your pregnant mother shot herself in the head to force me to..." his voice broke, "so I can be cured..." Mateo swallowed a few times to force the lump of emotions down.

The silence was uncomfortable as the cloud of confusion cleared. Daniel's chest tightened to the point of bursting as the truth sank into his comprehension.

"You... ate... my...?" He reeled back.

The image of his father eating his baby sister was repulsive. He jerked away and rushed to the guest comfort room, his stomach heaving. All those gory and horrendous stories about aswangs as told by every human adult in his childhood, stories he considered a joke, became a horrifying reality.

Waves of excruciating sensation enveloped his body, varying degrees of disgust found its way out of his gut and radiated all over his skin as he heaved over the toilet bowl. He could not comprehend where his pain was coming from, his heart, his head, his soul.

His stomach emptied; he had no strength to get up from the floor. The stark proof of his father's nature hit home for the first time in his life. He grew up knowing this; it did not matter to him, or so he thought. This information made him see the non-human part of the only parent he had, the man who had the most influence in what he was now. And he realised he had not accepted his father's aswang side, that he avoided the core of that truth all his life.

This was why he never allowed himself to fall in love with aswang women, not what he kept telling himself about wanting to spare his future children, but because it repulsed him. And this sickened him, to come face-to-face with his own intolerance. And yet, even knowing his own failing, the fact remained that it revolted him.

Part of him wished he had never learned the truth, or that he could just forget. But this was his father waiting outside, not some stranger he had no love for. He could not just walk away from this. They both needed to live with this truth. He pushed himself up and trudged back out to the living room where his father waited for him.

"What now, Daniel?" his father asked, not looking at him, his head bowed.

"I do not know, dad..." He slumped beside him on the sofa.

He could no longer look at his father and see just that—his father—now, he was an aswang who ate his baby sister. Images of his father opening his mother up came bubbling up from inside him. He closed his eyes tight to will it away.

"I understand..." Mateo said. He sounded disheartened and resigned, as if he expected this, but was unprepared for it. He recognised the pain that accompanied the feeling of rejection that his reaction generated. His father's grim expression, the lines of misery around his mouth and eyes, told him he had broken his dad's heart. And his own chest quivered with the same agony.

He shot to his feet and walked out, unable to process the emotions and thoughts that churned in his guts and heart in front of his father. He felt a thundering of rage directed at anything and everything: at his father, the aswangkind and their nature, at himself, and at the situation that had placed him in an impossible position.

Hours later, Daniel was nursing his sixth glass of vodka and getting increasingly frustrated because the mind-numbing state he had been expecting since the fourth glass had so far eluded him. Tonight, his mind remained intractably sober and active.

Why tell me now?

He was contemplating the bottom of the glass through the transparent spirit, when he realised the connection — Roald.

Oh, holy fuck!

It was his father who traumatised Roald when he was young. Roald saw his father's heinous act from his treehouse.

Damn!

Another sin to feel guilty about.

Another load on my already over-burdened conscience.

He sighed and chugged the drink in one swallow and grimaced at the spicy burn of the liquid down his throat, then poured himself another one.

Anyone in his position deserved to numb the pain and confusion with alcohol for a few hours.

Roald, with steadfastness, kept his thoughts positive throughout the one hour and a half ferry ride by going through all the photos of Yuana and himself together on his phone. There were very few photos of her, he realised. He never noticed before, never needed them, because she was his, then.

He groped for the small ring box in his pocket and pulled it out. The cushion cut, eight carat emerald that would be the centrepiece for Yuana's engagement ring was exquisite. She had a unique taste in jewellery and a traditional engagement ring design would not suit her. He wanted this one, and their eventual wedding ring to be a collaborative effort.

The ring was a non-issue in their conflict, though. The chief obstacle remained - whether he could live with her aswang side and her world. He could not answer it with a clear yes, but he knew in his heart that he had accepted what she was. And he would dedicate his life to finding a way to reach the point where everything about her otherness no longer bothered him.

This idea occupied his thoughts during the three-hour drive to his destination.

Roald slowed down and paused by the gate of Villa Bizitza. His pulse raced. Now that Yuana was close by, all the days he missed her hit him like a ton of bricks. This woman who could both be infuriating and adorable in two seconds flat, be fire and ice in a smile or a word, the softness to his hardness, and strength to his weakness. Even now, she was the only person who could ever present him with a dilemma impossible for his brain to decide on, so he allowed his heart to do it for him.

He rang the bell at the gate and waited. Thereafter, a small person opened the walk-in gate.

"Yes, Sir?" the dark-skinned man inquired. He looked like a Mangyan.

"I am here to see Ms Yuana Orzabal," he said with a confidence that he did not have.

"Okay, sir. Ms Orzabal is waiting for you," the man said.

"Yuana?" he asked, startled. A jolt of optimism speared through his heart.

"No, sir, Ms Bella," the man clarified, instantly deflating the hope that ballooned in him.

The man moved to open the gate, leaving Roald with no choice but to go back to his car and drive it inside the compound.

A vast, well-manicured lawn flanked the drive on both sides. There was a profusion of ornamental bushes and flowering plants that made the gardens appear like an explosion of colours. Huge, ancient trees stood like well-spaced sentinels that surrounded the house and shielded it from outside view. The drive curved to reveal the circular driveway, similar to their house in Manila. The building was about two hundred meters from the gate, made of wood and distinct granite accents.

It surprised him to see the same man who opened the gate for him was at the front of the house, waiting to open the door for him. The man bid him to follow and brought him to the living room, where Ysobella and Galen were waiting for him by the couch.

Yuana was nowhere in sight.

"Good afternoon, *Tita, Tito.*"

He felt awkward and vulnerable. Yuana's parents could very well send him home before he could see her.

"Good afternoon, Roald. What brought you here?" Galen asked.

There was no animosity in Galen's greeting. It boded well for him and his cause.

"I am here to make it right with Yuana. Can I see her?" His breath held; his heart pounded.

Ysobella and Galen exchanged a glance. Ysobella's expression was serious, Galen's was impish. Ysobella turned to him with an impassive face. "Give the car key to Yam-Ay, she can have your bag brought up to the guest room."

She directed his gaze to a small, dark-skinned woman who appeared silently and unnoticed beside him, startling him. He fished the key from his pocket and handed it over to the woman, who bustled past him toward the front door where his car was parked.

"Yuana is in the morning room," Galen said, "hmm... that way." He pointed to a hallway to his right.

"Thank you, Tito, Tita." He nodded his thanks to both and walked towards the morning room, where Yuana was.

To make right what he ruined, to reclaim what he lost.

The morning room was bright and cosy with its country-style decoration. The breeze that blew through the French window ruffled the lavender-coloured curtains and stirred the cinnamon and vanilla flavoured air. Beyond was a verandah with white outdoor wicker tables and chairs. They were empty.

He moved closer to the window to find Yuana when he noticed the coffee cup on the corner table, and an open book lying face down on the seat. It was a Roald Dahl Collections book, one that he gave her on her birthday.

He moved to the verandah to seek Yuana and found her standing on the steps that led down to the lawn. Her hands tucked into her pockets; her gaze fixed on the mountain range ahead. He stood there for a while, thinking how to approach her, when she stiffened and whirled around.

For a moment, they were both frozen in time, their eyes locked on each other, their breath held.

"Roald," she breathed out his name.

And that was the impetus that jerked him back to the present and propelled him to her. He hauled her into his arms and buried his nose in her fragrant hair. He missed her with every fibre of his being, from the top of his head to the tips of his toes, all his senses clamoured for her. The need to kiss her warred with his need to keep her in his arms. He would not risk looking into her face or he would not be able to stop himself from claiming her lips. He had no right after the way they parted last time.

"I missed you," he murmured in her hair, his arms locked around her, unwilling to let her go.

"I missed you too," she breathed.

Her scent shot straight to his heart. He allowed himself the luxury of being wrapped by her presence, the warmth of her body.

She rested in his embrace a few moments more, then pushed herself out of his arms. He was reluctant to let her go. She walked back up to her seat, set her book aside, and sat down. He followed her lead and sat across from her. His gaze never left her.

Her sigh implied a multitude of emotions. "Why are you here, Roald?"

"I want to make everything right between us, Yu. I want us back." He wanted to say more, but words would not come.

"Which 'us' do you want back, Roald? Our old 'us' is gone." The sadness in her voice squeezed on his heart.

"No. Our 'us' never went away, Yuana. Circumstance may have changed, and time may have come between us for a short while, but you and I remain the same—we are one," he insisted.

He had to stop himself from reaching over to her clenched hand. But the invisible barrier created by the past few days was almost tangible and thickening by the second.

"Did you take my *aswang* nature in consideration when you refer to 'us'?"

Her gaze was sharp and intent but he glimpsed the spark of hope and wariness in its depths. An answering hope bloomed in his chest.

"Yes, I did... carefully, torturously, and I am resolved to accept everything that comes with it." He heard the intensity in his own voice.

"Everything?" she asked. Her eyes glittered. "What do you see in our future together, Roald?" She challenged him to lay down his expectations.

"Us, together, facing whatever comes. Adjusting to each other, to the circumstances, but always committed to handling whatever life will throw against us."

He did not have a clear picture of what their future would be like, or how hard it would be for him, but he did not care. He just knew how life would feel without her.

Focused on him, she got up and walked to him, sat on his lap and laid her head on his chest. She drew out a deep sigh.

Tension left her rigid spine, her warmth melted into him like a tired child needing a cuddle.

He responded by instinct. His arms wrapped around her, and he rocked her in a soothing rhythm. The movement was for him as much as for her. Peace settled in his soul, knowing she had not severed their connection, that she had not given up on him, and she had banked on the love between them as he did.

Tears of relief and gratitude pricked behind his closed lids. He squeezed them shut to keep it in. He felt an enormous gratitude to the universe.

"Did it really take less than a month for you to accept me and my nature?" She sounded disbelieving.

"No. It took just less than a month for me to accept I cannot live a joyful life without you in it. I can work on the rest for as long as you and I are together."

Yuana smiled. She seemed satisfied by his response.

"What's next? How do we proceed from this?" she asked.

He understood what she meant, as they could not ignore his struggle about her nature, but he was resolute in taking his time to find the cure for her. She was half human. There might be a way to separate her from her... otherness.

"We can go on as usual, let us not dwell too much on our differences. Let us just focus on where we are similar, our goals, our core values. I will try my very best to adjust to the situation."

Yuana frowned and became thoughtful. "We could stretch the status quo until you have adapted to my world. We could apply the same arrangements we have in place for my father..." She brightened at her own suggestion.

"Oh... You have a special arrangement for your father? What is it?"

"Nothing drastic. We avoid doing some of our... practices in front of him." She shrugged. "How can I make it easy for you? What can I do?"

He smiled and kissed her forehead. "Be patient with me. Help me understand the things I do not."

"Okay." The brief reply encapsulated her intention to do everything in her power to help him succeed.

"And Yuana... please promise me..." he said. His hands cupped her face and made it impossible for her to look away. "... you will never leave like that again..."

She nodded, her eyes teared up, and she swallowed as if her throat was too thick with emotion.

"I cannot fix what we broke between us if you leave. Promise me..." he repeated.

"I promise," she whispered.

His gaze became focused on her lips, his thumb rubbed her lower lip, a prelude to a kiss, his way of asking permission, of giving her the time to say no. A tremulous breath was her response, and that was all he needed. He closed the distance between them and touched his lips to hers and shared an evocative, deep sealing kiss that spoke of penance and forgiveness, of passion and love, of vows of commitment asked for and given.

The kiss was both familiar and new. Their future flavoured it, certain and uncertain. And it tasted of Yuana.

He lifted his head, looked lovingly at her face, smoothed her hair back. His hand came to rest at the back of her head.

"You have my heart, Roald Magsino," her voice cracked. A beaming smile spread sweetly on her face.

He felt an answering jolt of joy in his heart. "And you have mine, Yuana Orzabal, and everything else that you might need. You only have to ask."

EPILOGUE

Edrigu reached home, soul tired. Roald should have reached Villa Bizitza by now, and he felt optimistic that all would be well between him and his granddaughter. Regardless of the outcome, the team would shadow him for the next few weeks until they were convinced he posed no threat to their safety. The bugs in his premises would remain until they were fully satisfied that it was safe.

A tinge of worry surfaced in his mind as he remembered Mateo. He wondered if his friend was able to speak to his son, Daniel.

How did Daniel react to the revelation?

Kazu flew overhead toward the Villa Bizitza compound, high enough not to be visible to anyone on the ground who might look up by coincidence. He circled the house a few times. Yuana must join him, so he could fulfil what he vowed to do.

Just a few more months and his destiny would unfold.

Their training had been continuous. They had to be better than the *Iztaris*. The go-signal was given yesterday, and their plan set in motion. With grim satisfaction and a small amount of regret, came the acknowledgement that the *Tribunal* was unprepared for what was coming to their doorstep.

The fate of the viscerebuskind is about to change.

TO BE CONTINUED

Dawn of the Dual Apex – The Second Chronicle

WORLD OF THE VISCEREBUS
GLOSSARY OF TERMS

These are the Viscerebus terms mentioned in the novel.

Animus (Heart or Instinct Animal) or Spirit Animal — the true animal form of a Viscerebus. All Viscerebus have one, although not all would discover theirs. An Auto-morphosis, or reflexive transformation, usually reveals to a Viscerebus their Animus. Some Viscerebus transform into one animal all their lives and discover that their Animus was a different form.

In some Viscerebus families, it was part of their tradition to deny sustenance to the child of twelve to force an Auto-morphosis. This is usually done under the supervision of the adults. The practice lost favour over the centuries because it often resulted in injury to the child and usually the said child would elect to transform into the animal form they habitually turn into, thus defeating the object of discovering their Animus.

Now, the term is used erroneously by modern Viscerebus to refer to their animal form, whether it is their true Spirit Animal or just their hunting form. (*See Auto-morphosis. See Spirit*

Animal, Reflexive Transformation – World of the Viscerebus Almanac).

Apex – A super shapeshifter. A very rare Viscerebus that can transform into a winged animal, either in chiropteran (bats) or avian (birds) form. They can transform fully, or partially. Other special Apex skills manifested by previous ones are echolocation and sound blasting, magnetic field manipulation. Apexes can also turn on their brain's theta waves and read other people's brainwaves or influence it.

It is said that the full skill set of an Apex has not been fully revealed yet because new skills keep getting discovered by each successive Apex, and each would depend on the core strength of the individual. (*See Apex Shapeshifting – World of the Viscerebus Almanac*)

Aquila—the other name for the giant eagle named Aetos Kaukasios, one of the two primary mythical gods to the Viscerebus, the other is Prometheus. The Viscerebuskind attribute the beginning of their race to the two gods. According to the legend, Zeus sent Aetos to devour the liver of Prometheus every night as his eternal punishment for giving fire to humans and for tricking Zeus to choose a less valuable sacrificial offering from humans. The Viscerebus' need to eat viscera is attributed to the saliva of Aetos that contaminated the liver of Prometheus, which was used by the latter to create the Viscerebus.

Aetos was the offspring of two other Titans, Typhon and Echidna, the father and mother of mythical monsters in Greek

Mythology. (*See Prometheus. See Origin – World of the Viscerebus Almanac*).

Aswangs – The Filipino term for Viscerebus. Of all the countries in the world, the existence of Viscerebus is the most entrenched in the Philippine culture for two reasons:

First, the Filipinos launched the most aggressive campaign against the Viscerebus. Their Venandis were the most experienced. The Venandi practice, which started as a family endeavour, became traditionally and habitually passed on to the next generation. There are still active, albeit lesser number of Venandis operating in the country.

The superstitious nature of the Filipinos allowed them to believe that Aswangs still existed, albeit in exaggerated and erroneous form. Many books have been written, and movies made featuring Aswangs as evil creatures, usually depicted as the minions of the devil.

Like every culture, the existence of the Viscerebus has been relegated into myth and lore, and the term Aswang is used as a blanket term for almost every man-eating and blood sucking ghoul in the country.

Second, the local tribes in the country were also the first to accept the Viscerebus into their midst and established a collaborative and symbiotic relationship. Native Viscerebus in the Philippines were the only one sanctioned by the Tribunal to work openly with the human tribal members. Their Veil-binding applies only to humans that were not part of the tribe. (*See Venandi*)

Auto-morphosis – also known as *Reflexive Transformation* is the involuntary shapeshifting into the animal spirit of a Viscerebus. The vital instinct to hunt and secure *Victus* or *sustenance* triggers this transformation. The vital instinct is triggered when a Viscerebus fails to consume human viscera for over three days.

It is possible to induce an Auto-morphosis through practice and meditation. Some Viscerebus do this to discover their *Animus*. (*See Animus, Victus, Crux, Reflexive Transformation, See Shape-shifting – World of the Viscerebus Almanac*)

Crux—is a subconscious inner control of a Visccrebus to stop or start shape shifting. A Vis can call forth their Crux into consciousness to prevent a reflexive transformation. A Crux is strengthened with practice or meditation. This is similar to human willpower. (*See Auto-morphosis, Reflexive Transformation, See Shape-shifting – World of the Viscerebus Almanac*).

Emergence – the term used when Apexes discover their authentic form, also known as Animus. The Apex can induce emergence by forcing an Auto-morphosis or reflexive transformation. Part of the traditional Auto-morphic rituals include the excited wish of a child to "emerge as an Apex" which normally results as disappointment as Apexes, or super shapeshifters, are extremely rare. (*See Animus, Apex. Auto-Morphosis. See history of Apexes – World of the Viscerebus Almanac*).

Erdia—an Erdia is a half-blood, born from a Male Viscerebus and a Female human. Erdias are very human in their nature except they would be slightly stronger, faster and live longer than their human counterpart. They may inherit some enhancement on their senses. They don't inherit the shapeshifting and need for human viscera.

Most Erdias who use their enhanced strength and speed become athletes. Erdias who inherit a superior sense of taste and scent usually become renowned chefs, perfume makers and other professions that maximise their abilities.

The knowledge of the Erdias about the Viscerebuskind would depend on whether the Viscerebus father tells his offspring. If the Erdia was told, they would be bound to the Veil of Secrecy just like their Viscerebus parent, and they become part of the Viscerebus world.

A significant number of Erdias are unaware of the Viscerebus world because the Viscerebus father abandon them from infancy. These Erdias, being non-Veil-bound, are treated as human. They live normal human lives, unaware of the existence of the Viscerebus. (*See Eremite. See Mejordia, Veil of Secrecy – World of the Viscerebus Almanac*).

Gentem—(nation in Latin)–the current country of residence, or the immediate, previous country of residence of a *transitting or tramwaying* Viscerebus. A Viscerebus can have between six to ten Gentems in their lifetime. This is not to be confused with **Patriam**, which is the country of birth of a Viscerebus. (*See Patriam – World of the Viscerebus Almanac*)

Harravir—also known in the Philippines as ***Tiktiks***. They are Viscerebus who hunt humans for the *Victus*. They mostly exist only in rural, uncivilised and remote areas. Harravirs are the same as the modern Viscerebus, except they have not adopted the modern way of surviving without killing humans. In most circumstances, this was because they have not heard of the existence of the *Tribunal*.

Most modern Viscerebus sustain themselves without needing to kill humans because the Tribunal provides the *Victus* required by every Viscerebus. The practice of Harravir-ring is a capital crime in the Viscerebus world and may be punishable by death.

To prevent the commission of the crime, in very rare circumstances, a Viscerebus can use a temporary alternative using pork or beef organs. But this is not advisable and should only be used in emergencies. Consumption of animal organs can make a Viscerebus sick.

A captured Harravir may be rehabilitated, educated and integrated into the Viscerebus communities, but if this is not possible, they are executed by the Iztaris.

Harravirs are the prime enemies of the Venandis, which are humans who actively hunt Viscerebus victimising human villages and communities. (*See Tiktik, Venandis. See Maniniktik – World of the Viscerebus in Almanac*)

Harravis—also known in the Philippines as ***Wakwaks***; are Viscerebus that hunts other Viscerebus for their viscera. The Harravis' fundamental goal is to consume Viscerebus organs, as it is far more potent than a human's.

Viscerebus' viscera make the Harravis stronger and faster

than a normal Viscerebus, and they remain so for as much as sixty to ninety days.

Harravis practice can also be addictive as it raises the dopamine level in a Viscerebus. And like drug use, regular and sustained Harravissing habit drives the Harravis to hunt more often and at shorter intervals.

There are perils in this practice as consumption of the viscera of another Viscerebus enables the transmission of Harravis diseases. Most notable and deadliest is the Visceral Metastasis.

A Harravis power or diseases is transmittable to another Viscerebus through sex within the first forty-eight hours of infection. Harravissing is a capital crime in the Viscerebus world and is punishable by death. (*See Visceral Metastasis, Wakwak*).

Impedio – a leather vest and chain contraption meant to restrain a Viscerebus from attacking humans during a reflexive transformation. And when appropriate, a muzzle is part of the set. It is strapped tightly to the body of the Vis, the chains attached to it are to be attached to a strong foundation like a wall or a huge tree. Every Vis is required to own one, and carry it with them if they travel to remote places, especially if they travel for more than three days.

The modern Impedio has a Tracking Device that is automatically triggered when the Distress Transmitter is turned on. The Distress Transmitter can be activated manually, or automatically by the change of the heartbeat in a Vis during complete transformation.

The transmitter sends signals to the nearest Iztari office,

indicating that someone is in need of human viscera. The Iztaris are then deployed to rescue the unfortunate being.

It is considered illegal to activate a Distress Transmitter as a joke or a prank. The punishment consists of a huge fine, and a demerit point on their record. (*See Auto-Morphosis, See Demerit System -World of the Viscerebus Almanac*)

Iturrian—the source. The term used for the pregnant woman who provides, voluntarily or involuntarily, the foetus growing in their belly as a treatment for Visceral Metastasis. The receiver, or the VM-inflicted Viscerebus who takes the treatment, is called the *Ontzian,* or the vessel. The act is called the *Messis,* or the harvest. All three terms are spoken in a hushed voice as the Tribunal do not sanction the practice. (*See Ontzian and Messis*)

Iztari—the law enforcement of the Supreme Viscerebus Tribunal. They are embedded in the human armed forces, police and security community as a way of hiding in plain sight, acquiring military training and gaining knowledge on the human military and police system.

The Iztaris' main mandate is to implement strict adherence to the Veil of Secrecy. They are deployed to either a) hunt Harravirs or Harravis, b) implement the Veil procedures, c) defend humans or other Viscerebus from Harravirs and Harravises, d) Find other Viscerebus communities.

The Iztari system is unique, as there are no ranks among the Iztaris. However, there is a Team Head appointed when a team is deployed. The only figure of authority is the Chief

Iztari. Iztari office employs both Viscerebus and Erdias with the right skills. The Erdias are office bound and do analyst and research tasks rather than fieldwork.

Only the Viscerebus may go on field because of the inherent danger of dealing with a vicious Harravir and Harravis. Iztaris are well-trained and well-equipped for combat. The Iztari office uses the latest technologies that the human and the Viscerebus kind can offer. Ten percent of the Viscerebus population are Iztaris. (*See SVT – World of the Viscerebus Almanac*).

Messis—the harvest. Originally, this refers to the harvesting of the human viscera, or *Victus*. But the use of the term has lost favour because humans ask for explanation when they overhear it. The term now refers to the illicit act of securing amniotic fluid from a six-month-old foetus within the womb of the mother, also referred to as the *Iturrian*, the source. The amniotic fluid is the only treatment that stays the progression of Visceral Metastasis in the body of an infected Viscerebus, also referred to as the *Ontzian*, or the vessel.

Messis, as a practice originated from the traditional Harravir acts where an infected Viscerebus hunt for pregnant human females. At the implementation of the Veil of Secrecy, the practice became illegal. It evolved into using abortion clinics to secure the treatment for the infected.

The practice remains hidden. The Tribunal tolerates it but does not openly endorse it. (*See Ontzian and Iturrian, Visceral Metastasis*)

Ontzian—the vessel. The name used to refer to the VM-infected Viscerebus receiving treatment by sucking the amniotic fluid of a six-month-old foetus from the mother's womb. (*See Messis and Iturrian*).

Prometheus—A Greek Titan and the god of creative fire and the creator of men. He was the son of Titan Iapetus and the Oceanids, Clymene. His siblings are Atlas, Epimetheus, Menoetius. He is known for his intelligence, as the author of human arts and sciences, and a champion of humankind. His name meant "Forethought".

According to the Viscerebus legends, while he created humans out of clay, Prometheus made the first Viscerebus couple from his own liver, the soil and rocks of the Caucasus mountain where he was bound and tortured.

With his DNA, the Viscerebus inherited godlike traits of super strength, speed, senses, healing abilities and long life. Prometheus also imbued them with the ability to shapeshift so they can hide themselves from Zeus.

It was said that he created them out of his need for companions to distract himself from the pain of having his liver eaten every day by Aetos, and the loneliness during the regrowing of the organ every night.

During the day, the first Viscerebus were in their animal form, a feline and a canine, but they transform into their human form at night to keep Prometheus company. This is also why cats and dogs were regarded as the closest companions to humans. (*See Apex, Aquila. See Origin story – World of the Viscerebus Almanac*)

Reflexive Transfiguration – also referred to as *Auto-morphosis*, the involuntary transformation or shape-shifting into the animal spirit of a Viscerebus. The vital instinct to hunt and secure sustenance triggers this transformation. This instinct, in turn, gets triggered when a Viscerebus failed to consume sustenance, weakening the Crux, the subconscious and internal control of a Viscerebus to retain their human form. Once weakened, a Viscerebus' human form becomes unstable. Once sustenance is consumed, Crux control is regained, and the Viscerebus can shift back to their human form with ease.

It is possible to induce a Reflexive Transformation through practice and meditation. (*See Auto-morphosis, Impedio. See Shapeshifting – World of the Viscerebus Almanac*)

Spirit Animal – or Anima Mea (Soul), also called *Animus* (Heart or instinct)—is the true animal form of a Viscerebus. They are usually revealed during an Auto-morphosis or Reflexive Transformation. All Viscerebi have one, although not all Viscerebi can discover theirs. For example, a Viscerebus can transform into a leopard all his/her life and discover that his/her Animus is different. (*See Animus, Auto-morphosis*).

Supreme Viscerebus Tribunal – or the SVT. This is the primary ruling body of the Viscerebus. It is composed of previous and current Matriarch and Patriarchs from different Gentems all over the world. SVT functions as both as the main legislative and judicial body of the Viscerebi. The execution of the laws, however, is the responsibility of each Gentem's Tribunal. Members of the body meet bi-annual, where laws proposed by members are discussed and voted on. The main mandate of the Tribunal is to oversee the compliance of every Gentem in the upholding of the Veil of Secrecy. The SVT is the ultimate rule of law for the Viscerebi. (*See Veil of Secrecy. See 5000BCE Constitution, Implementing Rules and Regulations – World of the Viscerebus Almanac*).

Sustenance– or *Victus*. The blanket term used by Viscerebus to refer to human viscera that they take regularly. This is crucial to stabilising the human form of a Viscerebus. This is the term used by modern Viscerebus, as the term does not invite unnecessary questions and explanations. (*See Victus, Crux, Auto-morphosis. See Reflexive Transformation, Vital hunger*).

Tiktik – is the Philippine term for ***Harravirs,*** which are Viscerebi who hunt humans to survive, (also referred to as Human-Hunting Viscerebi), they mostly exist only in rural, uncivilised and remote areas. They are the same as the modern Viscerebi, except they have not adopted the modern way of surviving without killing humans. Most modern Viscerebi sustained themselves without needing to kill humans. The practice of Harravirring is considered a crime in the Viscerebus world. (*See Harravir*)

Tiyanak – a Philippine Mythological name for a monster that adopts the form of a human baby. According to legends, it lures a human to pick it up by crying piteously, but it transforms into a blood-thirsty monster once a human picks it up. Humans usually encounter them in remote areas like the woods. In reality, they are a baby Viscerebi, or a ***Tzikiavis,*** who had reflexively transformed due to hunger.

A baby Viscerebus cannot achieve full transformation because of immaturity and inexperience, and they end up looking like a baby-sized, fanged and clawed monster. Humans who were attacked by a hungry baby Viscerebus assumed Tiyanaks differed from a Viscerebi. The legend was created thereafter. (*See Tzikiavis – World of the Viscerebus Almanac*).

Transit—also known as *tramway*. The program of relocating a Viscerebus and his/her family to maintain the Veil of Secrecy. A Viscerebus can be under a Life Transit, a mandatory, scheduled relocation every thirty years; or a Forcible Transit, unscheduled relocation because of the Viscerebus' violation of the Veil. A Forcible Transit is equivalent to an exile in human government.

A tramwaying Viscerebus is required to cut contact with any of their *non-Veil-bound* human or Erdia friends, relatives and connections. But they can keep contact with other Viscerebus and Veil-bound Erdias friends, relatives and connections.

A Transitting Viscerebus may keep his or her old name and profession or may take on a new one. The new tramway location must be in a different country or continent. A Transitting Viscerebus can return to their *Patriam* or previous *Gentem* after 100 years to ensure that any human they had a relationship with before are already dead. Visits to the Patriam and previous Gentems are permitted on brief holidays and only once every ten years. Veil of Secrecy restrictions apply. (*See Gentem, Veil of Secrecy. See Patriam, Transit Program – World of the Viscerebus Almanac*)

Veil of Secrecy—the inviolable law of the Tribunal to keep the existence of Viscerebus a secret from non-Viscerebus. The Law makes exceptions to a) Human spouse; b) Human kids. However, the exceptions apply only if the above people prove themselves loyal to the Viscerebuskind and to the Veil.

The strict adherence to the Veil guides every interaction of a Viscerebus with humans and non-Veil-bound Erdias. The violation or breaking of the Veil would entail severe punishment that could result in the death of the human or the non-Veil-bound Erdia, and the violator is expected to execute the punishment. (*See SVT, or Supreme Viscerebus Tribunal. See 5000BCE Constitution – World of the Viscerebus Almanac*).

Venandis – are Human Viscerebus-Hunters, also referred to as **Maniniktik** (or those who hunt Tiktiks or Harravirs) whose primary aim is to eradicate the Viscerebi as a means of defence and survival. Over the centuries, Venandis have died out because of the effectiveness of the Tribunal's campaign to have the humans believe the Viscerebus are just figures of lore and myths.

However, there are still some small pockets of Venandis in the world who work in secret. These are usually a small family of Venandis who kept the belief by passing on the training from parents to children. (*See Types of Aswang hunters – World of the Viscerebus Almanac*)

Victus – colloquially called as *Sustenance*. This is the blanket term for human viscera, heart, liver and kidney, that a Viscerebus must consume regularly to keep their Vital Hunger at bay and prevent involuntary transformation to their animal form.

This term had become less popular than its colloquial counterpart as humans who overheard ask question what it means. The Tribunal encourages the use of the term *Sustenance* in a public setting to avoid the questions. (*See Sustenance, Crux, Auto-morphosis, Reflexive Transformation, Vital Hunger*)

Visceral Metastasis—the cancer that can only be transmitted to another Viscerebus at certain conditions. The disease attacks the viscera and the blood vessels. A Viscerebus can contract the disease when they consume an infected Viscerebus viscera.

The disease can be transmitted to a woman if the infected male has sex with a female Viscerebus within forty-eight hours of initial infection. And if that woman was pregnant at the time of the intercourse, the disease will also infect the foetus in utero. Past the forty-eight hours, the disease is no longer transmittable. An infected woman, however, will transmit it to all her offspring.

However, if a Viscerebus is born with the disease, their VM

is transmittable every time they have intercourse with another Viscerebus.

The disease cannot be passed on to humans or Erdias.

The disease can take at least 10 years before it manifests the symptoms. And it can take as much as thirty years to some. The symptoms are like a human kidney, liver, heart disease and leukaemia. Once diagnosed, the primary treatment to stay the progression of the disease is the amniotic fluid of a six-month-old human foetus.

The only cure is consuming the viscera of a foetus that is a close blood and DNA relation to the infected. This means siblings or child of the infected. This cure is highly confidential and requires prescription/endorsement of a Viscerebus doctor and sanctioned by the SVT's Matriarch and Patriarch. It also requires the complete agreement from the donor, which is either the siblings, parents, or the mother of the child.

Most of those infected will never have themselves checked by the Viscerebus doctor, because it is tantamount to a confession that one has a Harravis habit or was infected by a loved one. Harravissing is a capital crime and punishable by death.

Apart from natural causes, the leading cause of death for a Viscerebus is the disease. And because of the Veil of Secrecy which inhibits the availability of the treatment, Visceral Metastasis is considered a death sentence. (*See Iturrian, Ontzian and Messis*).

Viscerebus/Viscerebi (pl.)—or Viscera-eaters, colloquially known as *Vis*. They are a different species of human. They live two to three times longer than a human, are stronger, faster, and have quick healing abilities.

Physically, they look exactly like humans, but they can

shapeshift into a land-based predator. The Viscerebus need to eat human viscera and stabilise their human form. To normal humans, they are monstrous man-eaters.

Viscerebi are known by many names in many cultures. And the descriptions vary because of the dilution of the truth engineered by the Tribunal to bury the existence of the Viscerebus under myth and lore. The common thread among these lores is the shapeshifting and the viscera-eating.

Most modern human societies have completely ignored the lore, but the belief persists in some pockets of rural communities all over the world. This is especially true in Asian countries, particularly the Philippines, where stories about Aswangs, the local name for Viscerebus, are still told. (*See Aswang*)

Vital Hunger—the term used to refer to the need to consume *Victus,* or *sustenance.* The sensation is similar to physical hunger, but it pertains to the need of a Viscerebus to secure sustenance to keep their Crux strong and prevent an Auto-morphosis. This manifests if the Vis has neglected to consume sustenance for at least three days. This triggers the *vital instinct* to hunt, which triggers the Auto-morphosis, or reflexive transformation.

The symptoms are usually a loss of energy and physical weakening of the Viscerebus. Some Vis develop physical hunger like symptoms, like shaking and trembling. Vital hunger itself is not painful, but the accompanying pain comes from the battle between the body's Crux and the vital instinct. (*See Auto-morphosis, Crux, Reflexive Transformation, Vital Instinct*)

Vital Instinct—the basic survival instinct of a Viscerebus drives the need to consume *Victus,* or human liver, heart or kidney. This is interchangeable to the term Vital Hunger. This surfaces when a Viscerebus fails to partake of human viscera for over three days. At this point, there is a battle between the Vital Instinct and the Crux of the individual.

The stronger the Crux, the longer the Viscerebus can control the transformation. However, inevitably, the Vital Instinct wins, thus forcing an Auto-morphosis, or the reflexive transformation into the Viscerebus' Animus. Once the Vital hunger is quenched, it restores the Crux control of the Viscerebus. (*See Crux, Auto-morphosis, Reflexive Transformation*).

Vivlioccultatum—the hidden archive and library. This is a massive structure that contains the original works, written history, books, manuscripts, arts of the Viscerebuskind made by the masters and notable members of the race.

Works are collected for its preservation and in compliance with the tenets of the Veil of Secrecy. The Vivliocultatum was established in 202AD. The Tribunal mandated the owners of works that can prove the existence of the Viscerebuskind to surrender them and forbids the replication of those materials. Those works were taken and stored in the Vivliocultatum.

In several, but rare instances, original owners were allowed to make a replica of their material for their own collection. However, they can replicate only works that can pass off as an artistic expression of myths or legends. Replication of such works require the highest permission from the Commission of Art in SVT.

The Vivliocultatum also became the repository and archive center of all the records of the local and the Supreme Tribunal.

The location of **The Viv**, as it was colloquially called, remains a secret. But one thing is sure, it is located underground. Every year, the SVT organises an exclusive exhibit for their kind to view selected works in various notable museums in the world under the guise of cultural artifacts. (*See SVT, or Supreme Viscerebus Tribunal, See 5000BCE Constitution – World of the Viscerebus Almanac*).

Wakwaks – the Philippine name for **Harravis,** is a Viscerebus that hunts other Viscerebus for sustenance. The latter's fundamental goal is to consume Viscerebus organs as it is far more potent than a human's. One Viscerebus liver can sustain a Viscerebus for 3 months. The consumption of a Viscerebus viscera makes the Harravis stronger and faster than a normal Viscerebus, and they remain so for forty-eight hours. The practice of Harravissing is considered a capital crime in the Viscerebus world and is punishable by death. (*See Harravis*)

Note: *All novels in the World of the Viscerebus series contain a glossary of terms used in the book. The full glossary of terms and other information can be found in the* WORLD OF THE VISCEREBUS ALMANAC.

Dear Reader,

It is my ultimate goal to be the best storyteller I can be, and to share compelling and exciting tales that entertain, inform, and stimulate the mind. I built the World of the Viscerebus as richly as I could. And aside from the main books, the first of which is this book, there are other published companion novels in the series. These are BEASTS OF PREY, THE KEEPER. Plus, the upcoming Second Chronicle, **Dawn of the Dual Apex**, and the Third Chronicle, **InEquilibrium**.

So, to improve on this fantasy world, your feedback would be very valuable to me. If you can please leave a review of my book either via this link or through the email listed below, I would appreciate it very much.

Thank you.
Oz Mari G.

A SNEAK PEEK

THE Keeper

She was a young Erdia, a half-human, half-Viscerebus who longed for a life of simple freedom. She left her privileged but secret life to go after what she wanted — to make friends and live openly as a human. He was a young Iztari, a Vis warrior with something to prove, a goal to achieve, and a path to follow. He was tasked to bring her safely back to her family.

Along the way, it became a choice between her choice, his goals, and the love they did not ask for. Theirs was a tale of love and a supreme sacrifice only beings like them are capable of. A love that could transcend space and time.

BEASTS of Prey

In the hidden world of the Viscerebus, two brothers inherited a tainted name, a deadly disease, and a beastly nature.

One brother vowed to rebuild their fortune and restore the glory of their name, the other followed their father's heinous path. A half-blood woman came into their lives, unaware of her bloodline, and a dark past that threatened well-laid plans.

To be with her, the Veil of Secrecy that binds every one of their kind must be broken and sacrifices must be made. Then the deadly disease kicked in and the countdown to death began. It became a choice between honour or family, the life with the woman he cherished or her blood that carried their salvation.

ABOUT THE AUTHOR

 She was born in a province known for butterfly knives, strong coffee, and feisty people, where one grandfather nurtured her with stories of myths while another took her trekking. By the age of three, she had acquired an incurable reading habit. She collected fairy tales and developed an affinity for herbs, spices and trees. As an adult, she became an entrepreneur and a proud sales professional. Finally, she stopped dilly-dallying and answered her calling.

To learn more about Oz Mari Grandlund and discover more Next Chapter authors, visit our website at www.nextchapter.pub.

Rise Of The Viscerebus
ISBN: 978-4-82418-955-4

Published by
Next Chapter
2-5-6 SANNO
SANNO BRIDGE
143-0023 Ota-Ku, Tokyo
+818035793528

22nd December 2023